S0-AVC-201

PRAISE FOR "WHAT I HID FROM YOU"

"What a book! Nail-biting tension on every page, alongside a poignant portrayal of a mother, wife, daughter and a woman juggling it all. Highly recommend!"
—*Lauren North*

"An addictively tense read." —*Lesley Kara*

"An absorbing tale of secrets and lies with a delicious sting in the tail." —*Caroline England*

"What I Hid From You is Heleen Kist at her absolute best. Beautifully written, with relatable, real characters that shine in a psychological thriller packing real human punch. Brilliant and distinctive." —*Rob Parker*"

"I was overcome by a creeping sense of dread as dentist Radha digs herself into a deeper and deeper hole... All the more terrifying for being completely plausible."
—*Alison Belsham*

"An addictive amalgam of secrets and lies."
—*Gordon Brown*

"Kist's brilliance lies in her ability to weave together tiny specific details of imaginary lives to create a compelling human drama." —*Sarah Moorhead*

"A real old-fashioned pacy thriller, with realistic characters, an unusual premise that's superbly executed, and tension that builds and builds." —*Louise Beech*

"Thoroughly enjoyed this consuming tale about a woman ravaged by mounting pressure - professionally & personally - who finds herself in the grips of an addiction that drags her into dark & dangerous places."
—*Deborah Masson*

"Heleen Kist really gets her teeth into a domestic psychological thriller with probably the first dentist protagonist in the genre. A rich read from which you will find it tough to extract yourself." —*Douglas Skelton*

"As moving as it is suspenseful, What I Hid From You is proof that Heleen Kist is at the top of her game."
—*Awais Khan*

"A hard-hitting insight into just how quickly a life can implode, and just how far people will go to protect what's theirs." —*Robert Scragg*

"With a unique set-up and a convincing family dynamic at the centre of the story, I found myself very much invested in Radha's journey as the tension cranked up and the book reached its climax." —*Alan Gorevan*

"I was hooked from the first by this beautifully written, highly original thriller. A must-read!" —*A.A. Chaudhuri*

Also by the author

IN SERVITUDE
STAY MAD, SWEETHEART

WHAT I HID FROM YOU

HELEEN KIST

First published in Great Britain in 2022 by Pollok Glen Publishing.

Copyright © Heleen Kist, 2022

The moral right of Heleen Kist to be identified as the author of this work has been asserted in accordance with the Copyright, Designs and Patens Act 1988.

All rights reserved. No part of this publication may be reproduced, stored in a retrieval system, or transmitted in any form or by any means, electronic, mechanical, photocopying, recording, or otherwise, without the prior permission of the copyright holder and/or the publisher.

A CIP catalogue record for this book is available from the British Library.

Paperback ISBN: 978-1-9164486-4-3

eBook ISBN: 978-1-9164486-5-0

Audiobook ISBN: 978-1-9164486-6-7

This book is a work of fiction. Names, characters, places and incidents are either a product of the author's imagination or are used fictitiously. Any resemblance to actual people living or dead, events or locales is entirely coincidental.

Cover by Jelena Gajic @coverbookdesigns

POLLOK GLEN
PUBLISHING

To my mansized boy

CHAPTER ONE

'*Your future is in your hands,*' they'd say at school. Never was this more a lie than now.

I stood weighing the thin, blue-and-white envelope in my palm. Light.

Was that good?

I wouldn't normally open post in between patients. It was hard enough to stick to time. But Pauline, the practice receptionist, had thrust it into my hands with a knowing look the second I exited my surgery.

There were letters and there were *letters*. Unlike handwritten ones to be savoured at home – the odd thank you for surprisingly painless treatment, or bills and financial statements to be disregarded until the end of the week, this one demanded my immediate attention. This one I'd dreaded for months, fuelling an anxiety that pushed me to do things I never thought I would.

I leaned against the wall, cooling my face against its imperturbable sterility. My fingers trembled as I flipped the envelope over and pulled out the single sheet.

Three stacked words filled the top quarter of the page, the font bolded, as though their importance needed further underscoring – it didn't.

General
Dental
Council

Three words that put any dentist immediately ill at ease – whether they'd done something wrong or not. And I was about to find out if I had: if the old woman's death was my fault. If everything I'd worked for, everything I ever wanted, was about to be ripped from me. So much of my identity, ever since I donned my brother's oversized school shirt and poked at my teddy bear's mouth with Kirby grips. Ever since I'd proudly sported a home-crafted nametag, should anyone be in any doubt that I was Radha, the dentist.

My breathing constricted. My eyes flashed down, past my name, past the reminder of what the case was about – as if I'd forget – and straight to the last sentence.

The Council has determined that your fitness to practise has not been impaired.

I sank into a squat, the cotton folds of my stiff uniform digging into the back of my knees. I dropped my head into my lap. I'd been cleared. Tears pooled in my eyes as a huge sob escaped my lips.

It was over.

A soft cough made me look up. Pauline pointed at her watch and winced. 'Radha, I'm sorry but ... Are you all right?'

I nodded, sniffed, and heaved myself up. 'I'm fine. I'll be right there.'

As I strode back to my surgery, my husband Arjun stepped out of his.

'Whoah! Be careful, Babe,' he said, grabbing me by the elbow to prevent a collision. He flashed his perfect teeth. Teeth that attracted people from far and wide to get their cosmetic work done at our practice; a smile that made me fall for him all those years ago at uni. He frowned. 'What's wrong?'

'Not wrong.' I shook my head and smiled. 'The opposite of wrong. The GDC ...' I waved the letter in front of his eyes. 'It wasn't my fault.'

'Oh, Radha, that's fantastic. You see? I told you it would all be OK.' He held my face and rubbed away remnant tears with his thumbs. His warm touch soothed my nerves like a soft blanket. 'Never a doubt in my mind,' he said. A strand of hair escaped my plait. He curled it over his finger before gently tucking it behind my ear. 'Trust you to think it could ever be your *fault* the woman had an episode. You big worrywart.' He stroked my back, then sent me on my way with a pat on the bum. 'Better hurry. We don't want to lose any patients.'

I stiffened. A chill ran over me.

He grimaced. 'Sorry. Poor choice of words.'

'It's OK,' I heard myself say. But it wasn't. *I* wasn't. Even though I'd been found not guilty, I knew that throughout this whole ordeal, my innocence had been lost. I hadn't been able to save the woman, my first patient to die. And with my frantic search for peace, free from her – ubiquitous her – free from the council's intimidation, free from the distressing memories her death resurfaced, I was failing to save myself.

I returned to my surgery at the back of the clinic, still shaken, unsure whether to laugh or cry. An awkwardness in my movements, like I was relearning how to function after an oppressive shroud had been lifted, giving my limbs forgotten free rein again. I reached for the tap to wash my hands, my slowed arm not quite doing what I wanted.

It reminded me of Manesh's wayward extremities, and a warm sense of kinship crept over me. My gawky fifteen-year-old had shot up like a bean sprout in the last year, all arms and legs. A bruised skull from where his spatial awareness was still to catch up with his height. I savoured the memory of his bright, round face of years ago. Despite the now chiselled chin and darkened upper lip, he was still my little boy. And, oh, his laughter: a heavenly high-pitched giggle. It had fallen an octave as his body stretched. My smile faltered. His shoulders were now so tall and wide my arm wouldn't reach around them anymore for a squeeze ... even if he'd let me.

The buzzer sounded. I jumped. A new patient would be approaching. I looked at the clock on the wall. Crap, twenty minutes behind.

Cheryl, the dental nurse, walked in carrying a tray of gleaming instruments. 'I swear that steriliser makes more noise every day,' she said.

I sighed. 'Please let us not need to replace that too.'

'It's starting to sound like the Tardis,' she chuckled and hummed the *Dr Who* theme tune.

I frowned. Not a day went by without a TV reference. I often wondered how she kept track of the Islands and Jungles, Voices and Dates she jabbered on about. But this wasn't funny. Since Dad passed the clinic to Arjun and me nearly three years ago, I was engaged in a constant, exhausting balancing act.

Cheryl dawdled across the room. Why was she so unbearably slow?

'Put the tray down, Cheryl, quickly.'

A flicker of alarm crossed her young, heavily contoured face, but she did as she was told. It wasn't the first time a snipe of mine caught her off guard – a temper I didn't use to have. A tetchiness that had steadily crept up on me these last few months, alongside irrational flares of panic and sudden surges of irrepressible anxiousness. I breathed out in a slow, steady stream, mentally blowing the flush from my cheeks.

Cheryl settled wordlessly on the stool at the computer on the window-side of the room, her dip-dyed hair facing away from me, no doubt planning her later moans to Pauline. I needed to tread carefully: dental nurses were flighty. Arjun would kill me if we needed to train up a new member of staff again and I didn't have an ounce of energy left.

The patient popped her head around the open door. 'Hello.'

Both Cheryl and I greeted her with the enthusiasm to which a customer was entitled, mouths pulled valiantly into wide smiles. Patients were nervous enough about dental work as it was; they didn't need to know what went on behind the scenes.

The woman took off her cardigan, placed it across her lap, and settled into the chair.

'How have things been?' I asked, while I gathered my protective equipment. With a register of twenty-five hundred patients, many of whom we only saw once a year, it was hard to remember who was who. I took a little peek at Cheryl's screen. Twenty-five years old. A name that didn't ring much of a bell. That was usually good news.

'I'm fine, yeah,' she said.

'Just a check-up, then?' I rolled my stool to her side and reclined her gently.

She grinned, her discomfort seeping through. 'Uh-huh. I hope so.'

'Scooch down a bit,' I said, adjusting the lamp. 'That's great.' I put on my protective glasses and pulled the mask over my mouth. Years of practice had rendered me immune to patients' bad breath, but I was still self-conscious about mine. I wriggled my fingers inside the gloves. 'Open wide.'

The patient looked up at the ceiling, at the world map that could enthral even the least curious about capitals and rivers – anything to distract them from what was going on in their mouths, while they sat immobile; helpless.

I ran the compressed air over her teeth to remove the saliva bubbles that often obscured decay. When I reached the rear, she flinched. I pecked the explorer around her lower left jaw, angling the rounded mirror to search for a suspicious spot. Everything looked fine. Probably just sensitive. I changed to a finer probe and scraped around the gumline, the sound of metal on enamel triggering a new wave of saliva.

Her eyes darted from the map to me, apprehensive. Her pupils were like pinholes. Around them, concentric rings of light, reflected in her dark-blue irises. They formed a tunnel that pulled me in. Those eyes ... transforming ...

The room shrunk and darkened.

I stared into pinhole pupils ... but not hers ... the wetness washed over red-veined eyeballs ... slithering into the deep wrinkles ... the smooth, flawless complexion of the young patient morphing into the crepe-like, powdered skin of an old woman.

I was confronted again with her look of terror as I'd pulled back her sallow cheek and inserted the needle. My voice, an echo. 'It's all right. Relax. This may hurt, but only for a second.'

Her deep intake of breath.

The spasming of the hand on her lap. The other reaching for me, hooked fingers grabbing my tunic.

That gurgle. That gurgle emerging from the depths of her. Chilling.

'Mrs Douglas? What's wrong?'

Eyes wide open, still.

Skin pale.

Panic.

Nurse.

No breath. A pulse.

Her legs in the air, reclined head flopped to the side. Her beige slip sliding down.

My hand guiding a quaking, desperate needle into the narrow blue vein visible through translucent skin.

Quick.

Her improbable lifelessness.

My mouth on her dry lips.

Pumping. I was sweating. So much sweat.

Her exposed chest, brown moles, yellowed lace bra. The beeps of the defibrillator. Piercing.

Her open eyes.

Not a blink.

Not a breath.

Nothing.

'Agh.' The high-pitched squeal hurled me back into the present. A crimson trickle snaked its way down my young patient's gum.

I heard Cheryl swivel round. My temples throbbed. Shit.

'There's a little blood,' I said. 'I'll let you rinse that out.' I handed her the tiny paper cup. 'How often do you floss?'

She wiped her mouth with the back of her hand. 'Probably not as frequently as I should?'

A drum was beating inside. I tried to steady myself by leaving the water to run in the small, round sink, watching her blue spittle swirl away like a hypnotic wheel.

'I think we're done anyway,' I said, relieved no treatment was needed.

'We are?' she said.

'Yes. We're all good. Only, mind your flossing.'

I clenched my jaws. *Go*, I thought. *Please go.*

'OK, thanks.' She briefly turned to Cheryl. I followed her gaze. The nurse smiled politely. The patient swung her legs off the chair.

She carried her cardigan with her. I gave her a ten-second head start.

'What happened there, Radha?' Cheryl asked.

'Not now.'

The toilet was only around the corner. I was sure to make it.

A bubble of air caught in my throat, having escaped from the balloon inflating inside my chest. Bigger and bigger. Painful pressure.

In an attempt to ground myself, I rushed down the corridor, letting my hand trail along the wall, feeling every rough speckle on the paint – rough and coarse like the old woman's skin.

I locked the door behind me and clung onto the cool ceramic sink. I ran my wrists under cold water. Counted to ten. Once more. My heart thudded at a boxer's tempo; my pulse echoed in jittering eyelids.

I tried to draw in oxygen through shallow breaths – too deep and my lungs would burn. My head swirled. I worried I would faint.

Who'd find me?

What would they think?

They couldn't know.

Nobody could.

The fear of them – anyone – knowing about my panic attacks swamped me like a crashing wave. I cooled my forehead on the mirror, my steamy breath dampening my already clammy cheeks. The moist, warm air mingled with the overpowering smell of air freshener and made my stomach turn.

Inside my head, I screamed. No amount of deep breathing could help me now.

The blister pack crinkled as I fiddled inside the pocket of my pale green uniform top. I'd hoped to do without, as I did every time. But the pull was too strong. I looked down at the crumpled square of metal and plastic in my hand. Last one. I placed the blue pill on my tongue and held my mouth under the running tap, gulping, thirsty for the promised relief, the rapturous feeling of being enveloped by a fluffy cloud of tranquillity. Swallowed into whiteness. Glorious oblivion.

CHAPTER TWO

Gunbir

The ochre velvet curtain hung half drawn across the bedroom window, obscuring the already limited winter sun. Gunbir rummaged through his wardrobe to find matching socks. The five he held in his hand were all the same length but different shades of brown.

Gunbir hadn't bought his own socks in decades and wondered whether they'd begun as distinct pairs or whether they'd suffered such varied hardships, such widely diverging cycles of wash and wear, that their vibrancy had faded unevenly – like with people. He chuckled. What had he become? It was the kind of observation only old people made. Either way, he deemed the hues compatible enough and picked two socks at random, throwing a third, with a noticeable hole, into the corner of the room, where it landed on a multi-coloured mound of fabric.

This morning's porridge rolled like a stone in his stomach as he sat on the bed. He preferred his wife Meena's apple bread rolls for breakfast, but this was a necessary, stodgy concession driven by his doctor-imposed diet. He was looking forward to his next meal: lunch at the clinic, like every day.

His belt dug into his middle and the wool of his brown suit tensed across his thighs as he lifted his feet to slip the socks on. Gunbir's temples grew warm and he waited a moment for his breathing to recover. He rubbed his toes along the rug and noticed two of them felt numb. He'd ask his daughter Radha to examine them.

He pushed himself up and picked his jacket off the bedside table. He checked the half of him he could see in the full-length mirror, his legs obscured by stacks of boxes. He knotted his tie; it was important to look professional, even in retirement.

Gunbir came down the stairs, maintaining his balance with the mahogany banister, while navigating the narrow band of carpet that remained jumble-free. At the bottom, he removed a small comb from his chest pocket and ran it over his bushy, greying moustache.

'Darling? Any idea where my glasses are?' he shouted. He entered the study and ran his hands over the alpine-like range of cluttered tables, side tables and bookshelves. He found his dark-rimmed specs next to one of his two monitors. 'Never mind. They're here on my desk.' He smiled. 'Yes, I know. Always the first place you'd tell me to look.' He imagined Meena in the other room, hands on sturdy hips, shaking her head at her daft husband.

He stepped into the hallway, dust dancing in the air as he progressed along the patterned red silk rug towards the kitchen. He opened the fridge and picked a vial of insulin. 'Can't forget this, can I?' he said. Although it wouldn't matter all that much if he did: Radha had convinced him to keep an emergency dose at the clinic. He tucked the medication inside his black leather diabetic kit, which he'd chosen because it resembled the leather on a lawyer's portfolio – another noble profession. He patted it and tucked the case in his outer pocket. It was the one thing he could always trust himself to find.

His keys took another few minutes to locate and then came the tricky part: shoes. He sat on the third step of the stairs and leaned forward. The lip of his overly sturdy shoe was difficult to prise open, and he slipped his foot in as gently as he could, letting it be swallowed up by the pink specialist foam. Once he'd safely stowed his other foot, he pulled himself up using the handrail. He looked down at the clunky footwear. These diabetic shoes really spoiled his look.

With one hand clasping the handle of the front door, he did a last check of his pockets – keys, wallet, medication – and looked at the clock.

'I'd better go, my dear. Time to keep an eye on things.'

CHAPTER THREE

I cringed as Pauline shouted from reception. 'Radha? Could you man the desk for a few minutes while I make a private call in the break room? The next patient is a no-show.'

I reluctantly made my way to the front. I knew we had been lucky to find her when our practice manager disappeared on maternity leave three months back, but she was neither as experienced nor professional. Nor as friendly, if I was honest.

Outside, the sky was classic Glasgow grey. The road was empty bar a passing learner driver. The testing centre was nearby; last-minute lessons frequently took this quiet, residential route. The city council recently installed new speed bumps and you'd see the branded signs atop the little cars bobbing up and down beyond the stone front wall that enclosed the practice's small, pebbled yard.

Four of the five seats lining the waiting room wall were occupied by patients, but the middle seat was empty, exemplifying the social gulf between the two groups. A young mum in Adidas lounge wear, with a large blond bun on her head and gold hoop earrings, fidgeted with her phone. Next to her a small boy hunched so far over his tablet I thought he'd fall off the chair. She didn't register my presence. Unlike the other two: men in suits who looked up eagerly from their phones as I came in, only to go back to their screens when they realised I wasn't my husband; their frowns failing to hide the irritation that, as private patients, their time wasn't more valued.

A more comfortable seat by the wide window facing the road, was, as always, occupied by magazines. I'd long stopped fighting Dad's ruse to reserve his spot; they could stay there forever, for all I cared. There was enough other reading material on the coffee table, usually brought in by Cheryl who cunningly claimed the cover price from petty cash, despite their well-read state.

When I leaned over the desk and reached into the drawer, the mum looked up. 'I'll be with you in a few minutes,' I said, for once delighted I might be able to see someone early. Saying nothing, she flipped back to her colourful screen. In my most casual manner, I pulled out the prescription pad and selected the correct stamp. As the stamping mechanism reached its satisfying clunk, a dark shape appeared in front of the frosted glass entrance door. I tore the page off the pad, quickly slipped it into the back pocket of my uniform and returned the items to the drawer.

Dad threw open the door and surveyed the waiting area like a priest might do his flock. I forced a smile. 'Hello, Dad.'

He came towards me and placed both hands on the desk. 'Where's Pauline?'

'She's in the back.'

'Really.' Had it been a question, I might have answered, but I swallowed the judgement and busied myself with paperwork instead.

'Are you ready for the Section 22 check on the nineteenth?' he asked.

I looked at today's date on the open calendar on the monitor. Blast, that was only three weeks away. I was becoming forgetful. Only a few months ago it would've been ludicrous to think I could forget the Health Board's most important clinic inspection – our first since taking over the practice from Dad. A flutter grew inside my chest. I breathed deeply to quash it. The prospect of failing was frightening enough without having to worry about facing my father afterwards.

'I'm on top of it,' I said, wiping a moist palm against my thigh.

Pauline arrived from the rear, her makeup refreshed even though it was only mid-morning. 'Hello, Dr Khanna,' she said cheerfully, rushing to remove the magazines from Dad's chair.

Inwardly, I rolled my eyes. Pauline insisted on calling him 'Doctor' even though I told her on day one it wasn't normally used for dentists. But she'd gauged that it made my dad's chest just that little wider and decided to do it as a sign of respect. A respect she clearly didn't see the need to bestow on Arjun and me. Not that I minded: our generation of practitioners liked to keep things more informal to put patients at ease. But I was certain her fawning played no small part in Dad always hanging about.

Dad beamed. 'Good morning. Isn't it windy out today?' He smoothed his black hair, present only on the sides of his head, to mark his point.

'It sure looks it,' Pauline replied.

I snaked my way out from behind the desk to give Pauline her spot back. Dad leaned in and whispered, 'You know, you shouldn't deal with everything by yourself, Radha.'

Tension crept over my shoulders. I had enough on my plate without him watching, interfering; without being constantly alerted to my failings in running the clinic. When would he let go? I nodded. 'I know.'

'Anyway,' he said, 'I'll need you to look at my feet later.'

A flash of concern crossed his eyes. We both knew the risks: diabetic feet were prone to reduced blood circulation, leading to areas of numbness. Left unchecked, the smallest cut could give rise to virulent infections and ultimately, amputation.

I lowered my hackles. 'OK. I'll fit you in after this one.'

Pauline invited the mother and child to follow me to the surgery. I walked down the corridor, wondering how far from ready we were for the Health Board's inspection, trying to remember all that was involved, worried whether we had enough time to prepare, cursing myself for dropping the ball. So caught up in my rising panic was I, that I nearly banged into the doorframe.

The patients stopped in their tracks behind me. I peeled the shock off their faces with a friendly 'oops'.

The boy's check-up went without a hitch. A slight squirm at the start, but once I told him that Hadrosaurs had the most teeth and Tyrannosaurus Rex's teeth were the longest, he was putty in my hands.

Cheryl recorded the codes I recited as I inspected his mouth.

He got to gargle and spit twice, for fun, even though there was nothing to rinse. Manesh used to love that, and I imagined him again, grinning, a drop of blue liquid leaving the corner of his mouth, his legs squiggling in excitement.

The patient had been a good brusher and I told him so, making sure to also give his young mum a thumbs up. It made a nice change from the shameful Scottish statistics on childhood decay.

'So, which sticker would you like?' I asked him. He took his time perusing the two sheets. I spotted Cheryl handing his mum slightly more toothbrushes and trial packs of Colgate than she was meant to, but the gratitude on the woman's face as she tucked them into her handbag reminded me of all my privilege. Despite how it sometimes felt. The boy settled on a purple circle with *Superstar* in gold letters surrounding a flying molar.

'Good choice,' I said.

I reminded the mum to talk to Pauline about the next appointment and hunched down to meet the boy's eye line.

'You keep brushing especially well, OK? And be a good boy for your mum.'

He nodded and took his mother's hand. I watched ruefully as she ruffled his hair, like I used to do with Manesh. She didn't know the hurt she had in store, when those little displays of affection tying mother to son, those small, instinctive loving gestures you take for granted, would be rejected, replaced by scowls and shrugs, or worse – by nothing at all. A cold shoulder that froze your heart.

'Thank you,' she said.

'My pleasure.'

I watched them walk away and was expecting the buzzer priming us for the next one, when I felt the mobile phone in my pocket vibrate. My heart leapt: there were only a few numbers programmed to override the 'do not disturb' setting. Cheryl stepped outside with the used equipment. I checked the screen. It was school.

What could it be?

Did I miss a meeting?

Was it a sports day?

Was he hurt?

'Hello?'

'Mrs Bakshi? It's Mr Haas, the vice-principal at Lochiel Academy. I'm afraid Manesh has been involved in an altercation. I need you to come pick him up. Please ask for me when you reach reception.'

My head was spinning. Manesh? A fight? That made no sense. But a lot of his behaviour made no sense lately. Should I tell Arjun? No, we couldn't both leave the clinic. Hell, *I* couldn't really leave the clinic. What would I tell the patients? Dad would probably tut me out the door.

I leaned my hip against the grey, speckled worktop and rubbed my temples, not sure how much more I could take. My pulse pounded in my ears.

I fished the stamped prescription sheet from my back pocket and found a pen. Just a few more ... just to help me over this stressful patch ... I wrote it out in the young mum's name – the first patient that came to mind. Dithering on what would be an acceptable number, I ended up writing: *3 x 10 mg Diazepam.* It wasn't a lot, but it was more Valium than I should be getting – which was zero. And a prescription I should never write for myself.

But what choice did I have? Go to the doctor and what? Get diagnosed with anxiety? Have that on my file and be obliged to notify the GDC? They'd be on me like a flash. Perhaps one could normally get away with a little medical help without them clamping down, but they'd only just finished their investigation. No, it was too risky. I had to stay out of their sights.

A hot flush rose up my chest as I remembered the patient I accidentally made bleed, earlier. I shook my head. That was a one-off. Could've happened to anyone. In fact, every dentist would've faced a little slip like that at some point.

No, I couldn't afford to get embroiled with the GDC again. Not this soon after the case. They'd never trust me to practise – ever. I shuddered. Could they re-open the case if they knew? Would they see things differently, through a new lens? Believe I'd been professionally impaired even before the incident?

My mind jumped back to the old woman, the moment her eyes froze in fear and her pulse dropped so quickly ... so quickly that nothing I did, nothing I tried in the blur of those bewildering minutes, brought her back. I remembered my brain sparking diagnoses like an uncontrolled machine gun. Stroke? Seizure?

Yes, seizure – she spasmed.

No, stroke – look at her tongue. Bring her head up!

Shit, shit. No, wait.

The fear; she was afraid. She'd said so. Never had a cavity in all her seventy-seven years. That's it! The fear; she fainted. Vasovagal syncope. Quick!

Head up, not down. Recline. Legs up.

Oh God.

Oxygen. It should be oxygen.

Am I too late?

I was left panting as the distressing tailspin of her death faded from my mind. Would she have lived if I'd realised sooner what was wrong with her? Was it my fault? The GDC didn't think so, according to their verdict: a severe syncope was a rare occurrence, often misdiagnosed as an epileptic seizure. It took the autopsy to tell the difference; so it was reasonable to have been unsure.

I knew they believed that now, after reading their letter; not then, as she perished in front of me; not all these agonising months, with me on the precipice.

The sensation of falling hit me again and brought back the image of her lying, afterwards, arms dangling from my chair, pale, bruised, stripped of her garments and her dignity. Motionless. I reheard my scream, a petrifying, primal sound lodged forever at the back of my consciousness; the loud clatter of tools as Cheryl stepped back. I felt Arjun's strong hands pulling me up, the warm tears on my cheeks, the hard, hard, hard thumping in my chest. I'd struggled for air, gulped, nearly choked on the glass of water someone – Pauline? – handed me.

She was the one who called 999 and sent the other patients home. As people milled around me, took care of the body, shouted, carried, cursed, I lay on the floor sweating, heart palpitating, dry-tongued and head spinning. Cheryl prattled on. I needed her to stop. Make her stop!

Someone in green – Arjun? The paramedic? – handed me a pill from out of nowhere. Round, blue. And I felt better. Calmed. Absolved.

A feeling I would yearn for again. And again.

I snapped back to the present. I shook my head, thinking how stupid I'd been to take only one day off to recover, not wanting to disappoint customers who had been waiting for weeks already, not wanting to burden Arjun, not wanting to appear deficient to Dad. 'Old people die,' he'd said, encouraging me to shake it off.

'You need to get back on the horse,' Arjun had concurred.

How naïve to think I could. But how was I to anticipate how badly affected I'd be? That only struck me on my first day back, when with every open mouth, every set of concentric rings of light reflected in patients' eyes, I surged back to *that* moment: the haunting gurgle that kicked my pulse into high gear, made sweat spring from my temples, and brought a shake to my hand. After a morning of escaping the surgery for air, I remembered what was in one of the drawers: an unused anti-anxiety prescription left behind by a patient who'd been braver than expected. And I reached for relief. It was only one pill ... well, two in total by then.

Thankfully, the flashbacks reduced in frequency in the three months between then and now. But their intensity remained overpowering, turning me inside out, viciously unearthing my repressed pain, besieging me with new visions; memories I'd smothered in order to cope.

And every day the dread had grown. The constant, humming dread for the investigation, the interrogations – for the sword to fall. What would the GDC find? What did Cheryl say? Why did it take so long? It wouldn't take so long if it was clear cut. There had to be a problem. The uncertainty crippled me more than any guilt for the woman. Having replayed my actions over and over in my head – to the point where I could make sense of the fog – I wanted to believe I'd acted quickly enough; done all I could. But had I?

Had I?

Those questions pecked at me incessantly, implanting permanent recrimination under my skin. And I longed for release, blessed liberation from being swung between one angst-ridden episode and the next, from perpetually worrying that the next patient would also die.

Having experienced what the medication could do, I ached for more. The only way to get pills three, four and five had been to write a fake script. If there was another way, I would've taken it. But I couldn't find one.

I recalled the itchy burning on my chest as I signed the prescription pad that first time, the side of my hand avoiding the wet, smudged, black ink from where I'd pressed the stamp down, shaking. It had been the most forbidden thing I'd ever done. Me, the model child, model student, model professional.

That night, I'd lain awake, imagining black-clad men crashing through the doors to strong-arm me away. Nothing happened.

I grew braver.

The next script came easier; so did the following. And week after week, my illicit drug-taking went as unnoticed as the distress it cured. And was it really so wrong? A doctor would've given me a prescription if I'd asked. I was saving valuable time, appointments best reserved for people who were genuinely ill. And I wasn't taking much. Not really. Though admittedly, I'd lost count.

I would stop soon, truly I would. I was getting better every day. And maybe now, now that the GDC was done, I could relax. After all, I hardly needed it anymore; tried not to take any at work, only to sleep. But then sometimes ... like today ...

Sometimes the tiniest thing could trigger me. And I would be lost.

I looked at my handwriting on the sheet. It was only three pills again. I'd make them last. I'd have to, because I couldn't do this for very much longer. I'd almost – almost – been caught. The NHS, in its all-knowing national-health-service efficiency, had sent a warning I might be overprescribing controlled substances. So I'd changed tack.

After a final check to ensure I'd used Arjun's official stamp instead of mine, and a quick prayer asking for forgiveness, I carefully, yet by now fluently, forged my husband's signature.

CHAPTER FOUR

The big advantage of living and working in the leafy suburb of Pollokshields is that everything is within walking distance. It was a handy quadrangle of home, clinic, school and the small train station, itself only minutes from Glasgow city centre. I left Pauline with hushed instructions, and grabbing my grey winter coat, headed for the school.

I pulled the fur-rimmed hood tightly around my face as the wind whipped tears into my eyes the moment I exited the practice.

My steps quickened and heart rate rose as my worry grew along the two corners and three street lengths to my destination. I imagined finding my boy bleeding, strangled, black-eyed, groin-kicked. What the hell did 'altercation' mean? By the time I approached the sprawling campus of Lochiel Academy, I was out of breath and convinced I'd have to carry him home.

I crossed the car park leading to the main entrance of the yellow-bricked modern structure and pressed the intercom. The kids all had the access code, but despite being the ones to pay for it, the parents weren't as welcome. The blue, metal-rimmed glass doors buzzed almost instantly, as if there wasn't a second to waste. I collided into the left door handle I'd instinctively pushed. I tried the right handle, then left again, pulling, pushing, every bloody permutation, until finally one door gave way to the main hall.

The middle-aged receptionist took an aeon to come from the back office towards the glass partition. 'Good afternoon,' she said – when 'hello' would've been quicker.

'Radha Bakshi. Manesh's mum. Mr Haas called?'

'One moment.' She put her glasses on, the attached metal chain looping along her cheeks like a bulldog's jowls. She licked her finger and flipped through a paper directory. Paper! I shifted my weight from foot to foot. She dialled. 'Mrs Bakshi is here,' she said into the phone. And to me: 'Make yourself comfortable over there.'

I smiled politely but with no intention of going 'there': the airless glass holding pen with its impossibly low foam seats. Showcasing rows of matching books and a multitude of photos of school highlights, it served to impress new visitors, and to remind parents being called to the office of what their children stood to lose.

Two long corridors sprang from the hall in opposite directions. Their bright lemon linoleum flooring guided pupils to their classrooms, like a yellow brick road to enlightenment.

Which side would they arrive from?

My heart jumped when I saw two bodies appear in the distance: Mr Haas's frame, purposeful, with Manesh shuffling a few steps behind, his head stooped. I knew to stay put and fiddled with the zip of my coat during their interminable approach.

'Mrs Bakshi, thank you for coming,' Mr Haas said, extending his hand for a shake.

Manesh's dark fringe hung in front of his eyes. He chewed the inside of his cheek. A quick visual scan revealed him to be injury-free.

'What's going on?' I asked.

'I'm afraid we have to suspend Manesh for the two remaining days this week. He got into a fight with another pupil who sustained some bruising.' Mr Haas pointed, wincing, at his own upper arm, as though he'd been the injured one.

My mind whirred. Suspended! Nobody in my family – nobody I knew – had ever been suspended. Suspended happened to other people.

I took a breath, smiled at Mr Haas. 'And you're quite sure Manesh was to blame, because he's—'

'We're quite sure, Mrs Bakshi. There were a number of witnesses.'

'Manesh?' I asked, cocking my head, trying to catch his eye under that flop of hair.

He shrugged.

'Well, I'll take him home, but I will want to see the report when it's completed,' I said, shaking Mr Haas's hand again. I'd been involved in the parent association and endured the gossip from the other mums long enough to know there was always a report. But short of appealing to your data protection rights, it was nigh on impossible to get your hands on them.

Mr Haas pursed his lips; turned to Manesh. 'Remember, you still need to hand in your history assignment on Friday, even if you're off, because it counts towards your Nat 5 preliminary exam.'

Manesh followed me outside, his orange schoolbag thrown over his shoulder, his hands buried in the pockets of his unbuttoned blue blazer.

I turned to face him. 'What the hell happened?'

A distinctive green SUV drove into the car park and slowed by our side. It was the last thing I needed. 'Smile, quick,' I said.

Heather lowered her window. 'Radha! Hey. Great to see ya,' she said, her accent and expressions never letting us forget that she was from the US of A and therefore like an exotic bird in parochial Glasgow. Her husband came here to work for some global company that did something with energy, and Heather had demonstrated, through her sharp elbows and taking control of the school's parent association, that their daughter Emerald's wellbeing and success was her primary preoccupation. She narrowed her eyes, taking in Manesh's slumped demeanour. 'Doctor's appointment? Bit early to be leaving class.'

'Yes,' I said, and out of nowhere, 'allergies.' I cursed myself. If there was ever a topic school mums could talk about at length, it was allergies. I'd never hear the end of it. 'Sorry, Heather. We have to go.'

'Sure thing,' she said with a wide smile of straight white teeth we both knew hadn't always been that way.

I grabbed Manesh by the arm and pulled him along. 'So? What's the story?'

'It's nothing, Mum.'

'You got suspended!'

'They overreacted,' he said, shaking my hand off him and accelerating his pace.

'Who did you fight with?'

'It doesn't matter.'

'It does to me,' I shouted. 'I made Pauline cancel patients to come pick you up. And this is going on your record!'

I hobbled beside him, my legs no match for the length of his, as we swerved around the corner of the local tennis club into Sutherglen Drive. Our pale sandstone semi-detached house stood a short distance away, the old broken aerial on the roof a constant reminder of how there was always something needing our attention; one more thing to take care of. Much as I was tempted to tie the boy to a chair for a thorough interrogation, I'd have to leave him there and go back to work.

'Manesh ... Manesh. We're not done here.' I reached for him again and just missed the strap of his bag.

'Mum, leave it. You don't need to know *everything*.' He skipped across the road and sprinted to the house without even a backward glance.

I walked on, trying to stem a virulent mess of emotions: relief that he wasn't hurt, shock at his suspension, anger at his behaviour, and an immense longing for the little boy who wanted nothing more than to spend time with me, who would climb onto my lap at every occasion and sit, thumb in mouth, little chubby fingers twirling a strand of my hair against his cheek.

My boy.

I suppressed a sob and pulled the hood of my coat down, willing the cold wind to carry me back in time. To when he still loved me and everything was all right. To before my mother's fall three years ago ... before the old lady, the anxiety ... before I fell apart.

The pharmacy on the corner of busy Nithsdale Road rose into view. Its clean ivory frontage and green cross sign conveyed professionalism among the row of mismatched façades on the neighbouring shops and cafés, ground-floor dwellers of the Victorian tenement buildings.

I'd already messed up my appointments; another few minutes wouldn't matter.

Double-parked cars obstructed the view of oncoming traffic and I leaned into the road for a better look. I heard 'Watch out!' and pulled back, alarmed, as an unexpected cyclist whooshed past so close that the fur on my hood pointed in his direction.

I'd always hated this intersection, where four streets came together at odd angles. I looked up at the grimy windows of the top-floor flat Arjun and I had rented as our first home. I wondered who was in there now. Another young couple? Someone who didn't clean, clearly. Did they have the sofa in the same place because of the awkward corner? Did they struggle, like we had, to make a proper meal in the supremely small galley kitchen? It seemed incredible how far Arjun and I had come in only four hundred yards.

The pharmacy's automated door opened on approach. I ignored the two aisles of over-the-counter medication, hygiene products and assorted gold-ribboned gift packs way too early for Christmas, and headed straight to the counter at the back. The young pharmacy assistant, with thickly drawn eyebrows and a broad Glasgow accent, was explaining to a pale-faced woman how to fill in the back of the orange prescription slip.

To the left of the sales desk was a high partition that separated the shop from the dispensing area. I spotted the top of Tamasi-aunty's head moving back and forth like a duck in a shooting arcade. There was no stopping that woman.

When it was my turn, I pulled the script from my back pocket and unfolded it. The girl said, 'Hello again,' and took the script to the rear. I hoped Tamasi would be too busy to notice me.

A DPD deliveryman, in a red and black windbreaker, came in and joined me at the desk. The girl greeted him, lifted up a large blue plastic tray filled with boxes and placed it on the right side of the counter. He scanned the parcels, each beep confirming a successful entry into the system. My eyes flicked to Tamasi's cubicle as I waited.

'Hold on, Owen, there's one more,' the girl said. 'But it's too heavy for me. Can you come to the side?' Her coy smile looked to invite a different kind of pick-up. Having gone through my share of excitable dental nurses, I learned this generation thought it was perfectly OK to flirt at work. I suspected her boss would have none of it, if she knew.

As if summoned, Tamasi appeared from around the corner and frowned disapprovingly at the events unfolding before her. I'd heard her complain to my father how much she hated the fact that profit margins were so tight that she was forced to take on additional services. *Five years of university for what?* she'd apparently scoffed. *To be nothing more than a common post office worker.*

The girl pushed the deliveryman from behind the counter. He deftly balanced an impressive number of parcels under his arms and made his way out of the door, stepping sideways to fit. The girl then turned to the row of medication on the back wall, making a passing semblance of usefulness.

'Good afternoon, Radha,' Tamasi said. 'Wondered if it was you again.' She held four white paper bags with stickers on them in her hand and arranged three next to the cash register.

'Good afternoon, Aunty.' I didn't like the way she was looking at me: her eyebrows knitted together and her chin jutting forward, accentuating her extensive, decidedly unfeminine sideburns. Two white hairs sprung like accusing fingers from the mole on her cheek.

I swallowed a hard lump at the back of my throat. 'I see you have some Christmas stock in,' I said, my tone as light as air.

She humphed. 'Damned distributors, thinking we all want to be a big everything-seller like Boots.'

Her small green cap slipped back, and she readjusted the hairgrips meant to hold it in place against her low hairline, while keeping her eyes on me.

'Yes, it's all about extra services nowadays, isn't it? Give the customer what they want, not what they need.' I said, hoping to bring her on side. 'That's why I'm picking up patients' prescriptions more often.'

'Are you saying they don't need this?' she asked, holding up my pills.

I swore I thought she'd hear my heart; it was pounding like a jackhammer. 'No, I mean, of course they need those. I only meant, you know, they used to pick up their own prescriptions – before.'

'Hmm. People looking for easy solutions. In my day you went to the dentist and learned to grin and bear it.

No anti-anxiety medication. You were lucky if you got an anaesthetic.'

'Times have changed,' I said, taking the package from her with a small shrug.

She leaned over the counter and clasped her hands together. A look of maternal concern softened her face. 'I thought maybe your patients had been impacted by what happened with Mrs Douglas. Had somehow heard,' she said gently. I swallowed. We'd hardly told anyone but Tamasi always kept a beady eye on the GDC website for cases of professional misconduct. Part of the job, she'd explained once. 'But now it's Arjun's patients that seem to be needing medication too.' She sucked her tongue. 'I suppose it's just what's expected by everyone.'

A draft hit the back of my head from the open door. Tamasi straightened up and waved at the newcomer. 'Good afternoon, Mrs Farooqi,' she said.

I saw the short woman advance, leaning on her walking stick.

'Hello, Mrs Farooqi,' I added, delighted at the interruption. She took a second to recognise me and smiled, her black headscarf framing the deep wrinkles around her twinkling eyes. She mumbled something; usually had her English-speaking husband with her.

'Goodbye,' I said, and walked ever too briskly to the door, victorious.

This time.

CHAPTER FIVE

Gunbir

Gunbir stood in front of the window, hands clasped behind his back. His front drive needed weeding. Thin, serrated leaves sprung from the stone chips; black shadows in the yellow street lighting. He rocked back and forth on his feet to stimulate circulation. He'd been waiting all evening for this. When he called Radha to reconfirm Manesh would come round, she'd said maybe tonight wasn't the best time. Something happened at school. But Gunbir reminded her that postponing homework was akin to not doing it, and she relented.

Manesh passed the stone pillars bookending the thick hedge that ran around the entire property. The boy had taken a stretch of late, but with his shoulders hunched and his head bent low, he might as well have shrunk. What could be wrong?

'Hello Manesh, come in.' Gunbir watched him drop his backpack on the floor and take off his shoes. The smell was most unpleasant and stirred a memory of his own son, an unruly boy who was thankfully settled with a nice wife in London. He wondered when he'd see their kids again. At least Manesh was nearby; he so enjoyed his company.

'I'm told I need to tell you my life story for homework?'

'Yes, it's for my history assignment,' Manesh said. 'I need to write an essay about immigration.'

'Good, good. Go get us some water and join me in the lounge.'

Gunbir sat in his favourite brown armchair. He still got a small thrill whenever he pressed the recline button and his legs shot up. He did it only partially this evening, as facing your guest feet first wasn't proper decorum.

Manesh returned with two glasses, and a notebook tucked under his arm. 'Is the world running out of tinned tomatoes?' he said, grinning. 'I saw them standing by the pantry.'

'They were on sale.'

'Great. But I really don't think you need four whole crates, Grandad.'

Gunbir flinched a little at 'Grandad'. His preferred 'Nana' had proved to be too confusing for the Brits; the women at pre-school always expecting his wife. Meena got to keep her traditional grandmother name of 'Nani', while he conformed, as – in a way – had always been expected of him.

Manesh put the glasses on the floor while he made room for them on the side table, shoving the stacks of newspapers aside. He sank into the large, brown corduroy sofa, tucking the gold-threaded maroon cushion behind his back.

He placed his notebook on his lap. 'So basically, I need you to tell me about how you came here and what it was like to be new to this country.'

Gunbir exhaled loudly. 'Where to begin?'

'Your life in Uganda?'

'Very well.' Gunbir took a sip of water, its crispness at odds with the hazy dribble that came out of the tap in his youth. 'I lived in Entebbe with my father and mother, who were both born there. Like many Indians, their parents had moved to Uganda, and other British colonies, to help build the railways, banks, commerce and education. You have to picture a very backward and impoverished country in those days. And for a long time after.' Manesh scribbled away. 'My parents met at school and instantly became inseparable.' Gunbir gave a rueful smile. 'We rented a nice enough house, sitting within an enclave that was predominantly Indian, most from Gujarat originally, though some, like us, from the Punjab. As you can imagine, we didn't mix often with the surrounding Pakistanis – the partition of 1947 still too raw. But I had plenty of Black African friends. We played football in the streets, in the sun.'

Manesh shook his pen. Looked around. Found another and nodded at Gunbir to continue.

'When Idi Amin came to power things changed. He was a horrible dictator. He resented our people, particularly the bankers, business managers and shopkeepers who'd built a comfortable middle class. He accused them of keeping the Black population in poverty deliberately. Within a year, he expelled many tens of thousands of us. Just like that. He wanted to "give Uganda back to ethnic Ugandans."'

'Sounds a bit like Brexit,' Manesh said. 'Some of the kids in my class with European parents felt very targeted.'

'Yes, I can imagine.'

'What year was that, Grandad?'

'1972. I was only nineteen. This was the only home I'd ever known. I didn't understand: this was our country; we never harmed anyone, yet we were accused of disloyalty and corruption.' Gunbir rested his eyes for a moment. 'I was in my first year studying dentistry.'

'I thought you'd been a brick layer?'

'I'll come to that.'

Manesh dropped his pen and stretched his fingers. He pulled the phone from his back pocket. 'I think I'll record this, if you don't mind.'

Gunbir didn't mind at all, quietly pleased his tale would be conserved for posterity, in his own words. You never knew how long you had left. Gunbir leaned forward. 'We were told to go, but my father was made to stay.'

Manesh's eyes grew big as saucers. 'What?'

'He was a schoolteacher. He was valuable.' Gunbir paused. He didn't want to tell Manesh about the nights he spent listening to his parents' whispers through the wall, the hushed arguments, the weeping. He pressed his lips together and took a deep breath. 'We were citizens of the United Kingdom and Colonies as it used to be called. The British didn't want us at first, but none of the overseas territories would have us, so the specially created Ugandan Resettlement Board put us on planes. Hundreds of flights to Stansted.'

'Why Stansted?'

'We weren't told.' Gunbir pressed the recline button; he was growing tired. A sliver of bulb shone directly in his eyes from underneath the lampshade.

'Did people smoke on the plane? Manesh asked. 'I hear that used to be allowed.'

'Everyone smoked back then,' Gunbir said, remembering the pungent mix of body odour and tobacco as he protected his mother from being trampled in the throng. The overwhelming brouhaha. Hundreds of people pushing, vying for early seats to get away from the escalating commotion outside the airport. Aggressive soldiers ordering people around at gunpoint. Spitting on them. Laughing. Taunting. Smoking.

He remembered his arms being lame from encircling his mother with the heavy-duty suitcases they bought specially. They'd left so much behind. His father ... lost in the crowd before they'd reached this far.

Then as they approached the steps of the gleaming silver aircraft, he'd appeared on the tarmac as if by magic. The magic, Gunbir learned later, involved a soldier who'd been his pupil, and a wad of cash. His father had placed his hands on Gunbir's shoulders and beamed a large smile, seemingly intent on keeping his family's spirits high. The effort that must have taken. 'Here, take this,' he'd said, and handed Gunbir a fist-sized wooden elephant figurine. One ear was damaged, smaller and pointier than the other. It looked filed into shape. 'It's you. See?' he said, rubbing the sharp edge of the altered ear with a thumb. 'Half African, half Indian. And as the only male elephant now, it is your job to take care of your herd.' His father nodded solemnly at Gunbir's mother, who stood forcing a smile, moisture coating her eyes. 'Do me proud,' he said as he'd grabbed him into a hug that squished his insides.

Gunbir hadn't wanted to let go of the embrace, but it was his mother's turn. Her tears soaked his father's khaki shirt as she melted into him. He'd watched as his father caressed her head through her scarf and swayed, shushing gently. They didn't know then it was the last time they'd see each other.

'Grandad?'

When Gunbir opened his eyes, Manesh was standing next to the armchair. 'Yes. Ahem.'

Manesh chuckled. 'Did you fall asleep? You said something about an elephant.'

'Oh that. Never mind.' Gunbir looked across the room to where the sculpture sat on top of the TV. His heart sank. He'd not done his protection job very well, had he?

Over another glass of water, Gunbir talked Manesh through how they then caught a train to Leicester, having been told there was large Asian community there that was kind to the Ugandans. They were lucky to get housing. The influx had become too big, and soon Leicester City Council was actively recommending people stay away. Whether it was a shortage of resources or plain racism wasn't clear. They didn't need telling twice that they weren't wanted, but they were stuck.

November in England had come as a shock, and their basement room in the over-stretched house of a shopkeeper's family, was draughty. Determined not to rely on charity, Gunbir learned to lay bricks. University would have to wait. Two months later, a letter came from his father instructing them to go further north to Scotland, where the family of a missionary who'd come to his school would take them in.

'And that's when your mum died of pneumonia, isn't it?' Manesh asked.

'Indeed,' Gunbir said with a sigh. 'She was already ill when we moved up, but the harsh winter weather made it worse.'

'That's so sad,' Manesh said, eyes downcast.

'Losing your mother is one of life's greatest heartbreaks.'

Manesh nodded; Gunbir saw a way in. 'How's your mother?'

'She's fine.' Manesh swiped the screen on his phone.

'Is she? She seems concerned about you. Do you want to tell me about today?'

Manesh shrugged. 'There's not a lot to tell. A friend was doing stupid things. I tried to stop him.'

'Does she know this?'

He shrugged again.

'She'll keep worrying. You'll see. We all worry about our children. It can't be helped.'

'I know. But it's fine.'

Gunbir frowned and raised his index finger. 'Be kind to your mother. She loves you.'

'Uh-huh.' Manesh checked his phone and said, 'I've got to go soon. But before I do, can you tell me about meeting Nani in Glasgow?'

Gunbir smiled. Such a sweet boy. A credit to his mum.

CHAPTER SIX

Later that evening, Arjun wore his blue velvet suit with rounded collar, over a silvery-grey cotton shirt I'd quickly ironed. It had been lying on the bed and he'd intended to do it, but I knew he'd like a long, hot shower to get rid of the clinic smell, so I took care of it. A thank you would've been nice, but he seemed strangely put out.

I watched him check himself out in the tall mirror beside our wardrobes, the scent of his cologne filling the room. He'd always been a nice-looking man, if a little on the short side, but with his increasing dedication to cycling these last few years, he'd become quite buff. His jawline was well defined for his forty-four years and the weather-beaten creases on his forehead gave him a sophisticated air.

I looked down at my boobs – which had felt sore all day – past the roll of fat around my middle squished in half by the elastic of my pants, and down to the thick stumps that used to be my ankles. What curse of nature made men age better than women?

'I'm looking forward to tonight,' he said. 'All the guys are coming.'

'Sadly, all the guys bring with them all the wives.'

He laughed. 'They're not that bad.'

Easy enough for him to say; he wasn't the one who'd have to spend the evening with them at the school gala.

'No patch on you.' He winked. He looked me up and down as if I was still the woman he hadn't been able to keep his hands off. I stirred inside; could think of considerably nicer things to do than going to a school event.

'What are you wearing?' he asked. I thought it was meant as an indication that the clock was ticking rather than actual interest, but when I replied, 'the navy dress,' his smile lost its lustre.

'No sari?'

'Not this time,' I said, reaching into the wardrobe. 'I'm tired of getting all that attention.'

'Attention is good for business,' he said, not for the first time. Ever since he became trained in cosmetic procedures, he'd encouraged me to discretely drop Botox and fillers into the conversation at social occasions. I always felt awkward doing it, but I had to admit the money was a great help in paying down the loan we took out to extend and refurbish our clinic.

I slipped my dress off the hanger, undid the long zip and stepped inside, the soft lining caressing my thighs. I drew my hair to the side and twisted my back to Arjun. Seventeen years of marriage communicated more than verbal instructions ever could: he zipped me up.

'What did Manesh say?' I asked while pulling tights over my legs. When I returned home after work, I'd been met by a locked door. I disagreed with Arjun's plan to take Manesh's dinner to his room – how was that not rewarding bad behaviour? – but it had given father and son an opportunity to talk.

'Look, I understand you're upset,' he said, knotting his shoelaces. 'I'm angry he got suspended too. It was a shock. But you shouldn't worry so much. Sometimes boys need to let off steam. Besides, he claims he's not the bad kid in this scenario.'

'What's that supposed to mean?'

'I don't know. He wouldn't say. Just that he was doing the right thing.'

I sat at my vanity table and brushed my hair. 'He's like a caveman. Never speaks. Just holes himself up inside his room.'

Arjun stood behind me, stroking my shoulders, and laughed. 'That's normal, Babe. I used to lie in my dark, stinky room for hours listening to grunge music. Drove my parents mad. Don't worry.' He kissed the top of my head, missing the flash of hurt in my eyes caused by his dismissal. 'He's a good student. He's great at hockey. Give him some slack.'

I'd lost count of the number of times Arjun told me not to worry. He meant well, of course, and always listened if I asked him to. He offered solutions – endless solutions – but it was never as simple as he made it out to be. He didn't understand. And I couldn't explain the thrumming disquiet that lived within, the rumbling malady that consumed me more and more often. It was almost as if I enjoyed fretting, he'd said one day, frustrated at my batting away his advice again. Over the years, I grew to receive his playful 'worrywart' less as a term of endearment that bound us, and more as an accusation.

I sighed and separated my hair into three smoothed parts. As I crossed one part over another, Arjun placed his hand on mine and locked eyes with me in the mirror. 'Leave it loose. It's nice.'

Having not given in to the sari, I felt I owed him this. I rummaged through the little drawer of the vanity unit and found a butterfly hairclip to at least keep the hair out of my face.

Arjun was by the door when I stood up. 'By the way, I'm going on a long ride with the guys on Saturday. You don't mind, do you?'

I did, of course. Didn't want to be all alone in a quiet house. But who was I to deny him his pleasure? He worked hard and the cycling made him happy.

'Yes, no problem,' I said, following him onto the landing.

We walked past Manesh's room. I rapped on the door and shouted, 'We're off. Remember, Grandad's expecting you.'

No response.

Downstairs, Arjun put on his big coat. It may only be three hundred metres, but the November heavens had opened with a vengeance. 'Hold on,' I said, picking at a strand of lint on his shoulder, plus a few more imaginary strands, stalling. I didn't want to go; didn't want to submit myself to the scrutiny of other parents. We were meant to be this perfect, good- looking, successful couple, with the perfect son. Where would they find fault today? They certainly always tried.

My insides churned. I rubbed my thumb over my orange clutch bag that contained more than the usual lipstick and twenty-pound notes for the fundraiser: I'd wrapped a pill inside an old taxi receipt, in case of emergency. My mouth felt dry. Should I take it now? It would make things hugely more tolerable ...

I shook my head and cursed myself for being weak. What was wrong with me?

Surely I was able to survive a damn party.

CHAPTER SEVEN

The Hilton hotel in the city centre was a regular venue for charity fundraisers, corporate Christmas parties and other large gatherings. I lost count of the number of events I'd attended there. The pale stone high-rise looked pinkish in the daytime, but now, in the dark, it wasn't much more than a tall, dark rectangular shape, speckled with alternating lit windows. We'd made the mistake of going on foot once, having taken the train into Central, but the hotel's designers clearly only counted on guests with chauffeurs, for whom they'd installed an elevated, sweeping drive directly off the main road, without a pavement. To access the building safely on foot, however, one had to cut through a back alley where the hotel bins were located.

Arjun held the taxi door open and offered his hand as I stepped out of the car. A rounded Art Deco-style awning crowned the entrance. Long dresses flapped in the wind as guests sprinted inside, frantic hands keeping the expensive blow-dries in place.

Piano music and a giant floral arrangement greeted us on entry. To the left was a small bar. A group of five men in tartan trousers laughed loudly around a high table. I recognised two. The women sat on the pink velour seats, holding small fishbowls of berry-topped alcohol. Pre-drink drinks, I supposed, bemused.

Arjun pulled at my hand. 'Over here.'

We walked the carpeted corridor to the ballroom. The tables were decorated with bouquets of blue and gold balloons: the school colours. One Billy Joel song merged into another in the background. I thought it an odd, dated, American choice. A waiter came to us with a tray of champagne. 'No thank you,' I said, and we made our way to the girl with the orange juice. I looked around the different clusters of people, wondering who I'd be dragged to first.

It wasn't hard to spot where Heather would be. A dozen women hovered near the front of the stage on which she'd no doubt later give a spontaneous-sounding, but in reality, well-rehearsed speech. Fair enough; she did most of the organising. Probably explained the music.

'I'll see you at the table,' Arjun said, and walked towards his healthy-looking dad-friends, some in kilts to show off their cyclist calves.

'Are you ready for this?' a voice whispered by my side. It was Claire, one of the mums who lived in our street. She wasn't one for the mommy brigade either, keeping to herself and friends from her choir. But soon a group of three heavily sequined women advanced towards us like a walking disco ball.

'Radha, you look AMAZING,' Lucy said. 'Your hair is so lustrous.' She reached and stroked it. I flinched. 'Hello, Claire,' she continued, cooler. 'Have you met Kathryn yet? Her daughter joined S1 this year.'

'No,' I said, holding out my hand.

She shook it and asked, 'Rada? Like the theatre school?'

'But with an H,' Claire said, no doubt meaning to help. 'R-a-d-a-h?'

'No, after the D,' I said. 'Never mind. It's fine. Most people call me "Manesh's mum" anyway.'

'Well, that's not surprising,' said the woman I only knew as 'Esther's mum'. 'Manesh is a real star, isn't he?' She elbowed the new mum. 'Radha and Arjun have a successful dental practice. He's bound to become a dentist too, no?'

'He's more into history and drama.' I smiled meekly, conscious this didn't fit her stereotype.

She flashed a quick smile and looked away. A young waitress approached with a tray of mixed drinks. I took water; the orange juice had been bland, with limp bits of who-knows-what passing for pulp. The others helped themselves to what Kathryn complained was 'merely' prosecco.

'Boy, do I need this after the day I've had,' Claire said.

'Tell me about it.' The last woman, Lucy, raised her flute to her lips. 'I'm not sure how much longer I can be a taxi for my kids.'

Esther's mum leaned in and whispered, 'I heard the police came to school today.' She paused, no doubt relishing its effect on the others, who also leaned in. 'They came to warn about drug dealers around school. One of the S6s got approached to buy pills.'

Kathryn, clutched her necklace, perhaps regretting her choice of school. 'You're kidding?'

'I'm not. I'm told we're to get a letter.'

The group fell quiet for a moment. 'Jeezo, can you imagine your kid getting into that?' Lucy said. She turned to me. 'You're a doctor, Radha – sort of. How quickly could someone get addicted to drugs?'

I felt four pairs of eyes burning into me, a tingling at the back of my neck. Did they know? No, they couldn't. I composed myself. 'It all depends. It's not something I have a lot experience with. Though I did once have a patient boast to me he was the biggest drug dealer in Glasgow.'

Kathryn gasped. 'Did you treat him?'

'Of course. The NHS doesn't discriminate,' I said. Esther's mum scrunched her nose. 'That was at my old clinic in Giffnock,' I reassured her. 'Before we took over this one in Pollokshields, near home. Anything could've happened to that man since.'

A loud guffaw rose from Arjun's group. At least *someone* was having fun. The waitress returned, this time with a large wooden plank covered in assorted canapés, napkins, and a highball glass positioned perilously on one side. I skipped the smoked salmon because it had capers on it, and reached for the mini sausage roll.

'Be careful. That's got pork in it,' Kathryn said.

It took me a second to realise she was speaking to me. 'I'm aware of that,' I said. She looked puzzled. The other mums went quiet. Then it hit me. 'Oh, you think I'm Muslim.'

Kathryn rubbed the rim of her glass and mumbled, 'I'm sorry.' She faced me again. 'You weren't drinking, and you live in Pollokshields ...'

'That's OK,' I said. 'It's a fair assumption. Loads of Muslims in Pollokshields. But not us.'

Kathryn buried her nose in her drink.

I smiled sweetly in the face of palpable tension. 'Anyway, I'm not drinking because I don't like the taste of alcohol – not for lack of trying.'

They laughed. All seemed well. Then Heather appeared with a small posse in tow.

'Hello, ladies. Are we having fun?' she asked.

After we'd all commented on how lovely the evening was so far, and the quality of the decor, she took me in her sights and asked, 'Are you still helping at the uniform sale, Radha? Just making sure.'

One meeting. I missed one meeting a year ago and she wouldn't let me forget it. 'Of course.'

'Good. How's Manesh now?' she asked, solemnly. She at least had the good grace not to mention the allergies.

'He's fine,' I said. 'How's Emerald?'

'She's fabulous. We got her the cutest haircut. It totally suits her. Want to see?' Buoyed by the others nodding, she fished her phone from her clutch and swiped through a series of posed shots, Heather's duck face occasionally joining her daughter's. 'Isn't she great?'

I breathed deeply. However much I was tempted to smash the phone to the ground, I needed to keep Heather on side. She wielded a lot of power at school; influence that I suspected could extend to the selection of head boy and girl next year. My heart began to beat faster. What if Manesh's suspension has ruined his chances?

'How do you stay slim like that, Heather?' Lucy patted her small, but noticeable tummy. 'I've tried everything.'

The always-sensible Claire shrugged. 'Not much point. We're merely reaching that age.'

'Oh God. Tell me about it,' Esther's mum said, stretching her forehead upwards with her fingers to make the wrinkles disappear.

'For me, it's here,' Kathryn pointed at her crow's feet.

This was my cue. I didn't have long: behind them, people were breaking up and making their way to the tables. I hoped the warm flush rising along my chest wasn't visible. 'You know, Arjun does Botox and fillers in the evenings.'

'Does he?' Kathryn asked, more than a little interested.

'So I'm told,' Heather winked comically.

Kathryn giggled. 'Is it expensive?'

Before I opened my mouth, Lucy jumped in. 'Not sure it's worth it. We all end up looking like our mothers in the end.'

'Too true!' shrieked Esther's mum.

I clamped my teeth together, rattled by the veiled rebuke. My whole body felt warm. I exhaled slowly, waving my hand towards me with little reward in the unventilated room.

'Excuse me,' I said, and left.

Long live polyester, I thought as I sat on the toilet, my scrunched-up dress at no risk of creases. I dabbed at my nose with the back of my hand. As I reached to pull at the ragged tip of paper sticking out of the tiny hole in one of those annoying modern dispensers, I heard new voices enter the room, seemingly mid-sentence.

'... and then she said the boy fell to the ground and blacked out for like a full ten seconds.'

'Boys will be boys, eh?' the other said.

The doors to the stalls clanged shut. 'Well, I think it's a bit more than that!'

I could never understand people who kept talking on the loo. I fell back as I succeeded in wrenching some paper free.

'Sounds like a typical case of bad parenting,' one of them said.

'I'm told it might have been Manesh. Heather saw him leaving around lunch time.'

As I bunched the paper in my hand, I froze.

'Really? That's surprising. Then again, what do you expect when you put such pressure on a boy? He's bound to pop.'

The toilets flushing mingled with the rush in my ears. My hands shook on my lap. I felt dizzy.

The subject changed to lipstick. I exhaled silently; lifted my feet off the ground to go unnoticed. The sound of hand-dryers filled the room. Then quiet. Nothing but my internal scream as I sensed panic rising.

I dared to flush, unlocked my cubicle and walked to the sink. I flipped on the cold water and held my wrists under it. I counted to ten. And again. And backwards. But I struggled to control my breathing; too fast. My heart banged in my chest as my lungs swelled painfully. I shook the water from my arms. Opened my clutch bag. It was still there, wrapped up. Thank God.

I swallowed the blue pill, tears building in my eyes. This wasn't me.

The room swirled. My hair moved in the mirror, but I was sure I hadn't. My face morphed into my mother's; her biting disapproval etched in the thick lines of a frown. Her stern voice, in my head: *'Weakness is for other people.'* As I clung onto the marble with both hands, the face grew pale, her eyes wide open, her lips hung slack – like I found her in the garden.

CHAPTER EIGHT

Why hadn't my surgery's buzzer sounded yet? It had been a long day already – Fridays always were – but I knew there was one more appointment. Must be late. In reception, Pauline tidied the desk and locked the drawer, no doubt relishing the idea of an early escape into the weekend. I stretched my neck both ways and yawned, not for the first time that day. I could've done with a rest myself. I'd suffered through two hellish nights with minimal sleep since the party, the women's accusations of bad parenting screeching through my head at all hours.

Did I push Manesh too much? He seemed keen to go back to school again on Monday, bored at home by himself. Surely that was a good sign?

'Any word?' I asked.

'No.' Pauline lifted her tote onto her lap and tucked her mobile inside.

'Let's give them another ten minutes,' I said. Her eyes flashed to the clock and she put the bag back down. 'In the meantime, it would be useful if you could go over the Health and Safety folders and make sure all the procedures have been updated.' Her shoulders slumped. I couldn't blame her; the bureaucracy was mind-numbing.

'Do you only need the dates changed on them?' she asked.

'Yes, that. But you'll also need to cross reference each of them with the dates the requirements may have changed.'

'Where would I find that?'

I squeezed my fists and sighed. We were paying her too much for this level of micro-management. But we didn't have a choice: maternity cover was expensive no matter who you got. 'You know what?' I said, 'Why don't you begin by making a note of the dates and I'll do the rest.' I slid open the top part of the cabinet and pulled out two of the seven colour-coded ring binders. 'These should be straightforward.'

The door opened. A woman came in. Pauline checked the monitor; I glanced at the clock on the wall. Nine minutes. Like it or not, we were up.

'Please check in with Pauline and I will see you at the back,' I said to the late arrival.

I crossed Arjun on the way to my surgery. He'd have a few more patients yet, as evening appointments suited the private ones better.

'The steriliser is making horrible sounds again, Arjun.'

He groaned. His usual response to bad news.

'Would you have a look at it please?' I asked.

'Yes, later.'

'It's always later,' I grumbled.

He arched an eyebrow. 'It doesn't *have* to be right now, Radha.' His firm stare unnerved me. I slunk forward. No, maybe it didn't need doing now-now, but then again how could we know? What if it broke? What would we do then? We'd have no tools.

Imagine having to reschedule all the patients because of a stupid piece of machinery! My chest tightened. I stood still and lay both hands flat on my uniform top, breathing deeply, pressing down. I felt the tears push against my eyes. Why couldn't I stop panicking? My mind was always running away with itself.

I craved a pill. It would take the edge off. Get me through the rest of the day.

No.

I sensed the patient behind me and walked into my surgery.

'She's here,' I said to Cheryl.

'Oh good.' She positioned the tray of new equipment by the chair and took her place at the computer.

The moment I put the light on the woman, I could tell she was unwell: flakes of skin on the rim of red, crusty nostrils, dark bags under her eyes, a feverish sheen on her forehead. I wasted no time in putting my face mask and gloves on.

'Please open,' I said.

The examination yielded little wrong beyond slightly receding gums that I suspected came from brushing too hard rather than poor oral hygiene. As I completed my checks, a trickle of snot snaked along the edge of her nostril onto her upper lip. I took my hand out of her mouth, intending to grab a tissue for her, but she merely sniffed it back up. Suddenly, she bolted upright, coughing and sputtering. I jumped back and accidentally flung the tray off its stand with my elbow. Cheryl turned on her stool. Instruments clattered to the ground.

The patient wheezed and fanned herself, a sure sign she wasn't breathing.

I froze. A rush of nerves coursed through me.

Don't die. Please don't die.

I watched – in what felt like slow motion – Cheryl spring up and give her a hard slap on the back.

I heard a sharp intake of breath.

Another cough. Another breath.

She was fine.

I reached for the tissues, willing my hand to stop trembling.

'Goodness, that was quite a cough,' I said, my tone as light as I could make it. 'Here you go.'

Cheryl gathered the tools from the floor, sneaking peeks up at me with an almost imperceptible frown. I put on a brave face while I quivered inside. 'Well done, Cheryl. That slap was precisely what was needed. Good to see the training pay off.'

The woman composed herself. 'Sorry.'

As she began leaning forward, I patted my hands on my lap and got up. 'No worries. We were done.'

She sat up again. 'Oh. Is everything fine?'

'Yes,' I said. 'It all looks fine, though you might want to invest in a softer toothbrush.'

I opened the door and stood by it, about as clear a message as I could give for her to go. As she passed, I said, 'Get well soon.' I followed her out the room and made a beeline for the toilet.

I ran two paper towels under the cold tap and dabbed them against my fiery forehead and the taut back of my neck. I rested my head against the door. Shit. How could I go on like this? But if I went for help, it would mean having my fitness to practise under the microscope again – the thought of which terrified me. Months of scrutiny, uncertainty, my livelihood in the hands of a faceless committee with no incentive to keep me practising. Yet I had everything to lose.

I shook my hair out. This would pass, I was certain of it. No point in making a big deal about it. I just hoped Cheryl would stay on side. Maybe if I gave her an extra day off ...

Still feeling shaky, I pinched the blister pack from the small pocket in my tunic. Last one, again. How did that happen? I got three on Wednesday. I shrugged. One a day wasn't that bad in the grand scheme, was it? Hundreds of dentists were raging alcoholics. This was nothing. Other mothers drank like fish. 'Gin o'clock' was a perfectly acceptable expression. Reaching for the glass the minute they got home from school pick-up.

In comparison, this was peanuts. This was fine – even if self-prescribing was a big no-no. I was being careful. Nobody would find out.

And it *would* pass. I was sure of it.

I took the pill from the package and rolled it between my fingers before placing it on my tongue. I held my mouth under the tap. The cool water slid down my throat with a wave of relief.

When I entered the break room to fetch my stuff, Cheryl was putting on her coat. 'Any plans for the weekend?' I asked.

'Me and my girlfriend are going to see Cage the Elephant at the O2 tomorrow.'

I knew the O2 Academy was a small concert hall on Eglinton Street, south of the city centre. I'd often seen queues of young people standing outside. I had no idea who or what 'Cage the Elephant' was, but I was delighted she didn't bring up the big one in the room. 'Have fun.'

'I will. And you ... take care of yourself,' she said, her caterpillar-like eyebrow twitching slightly as she spoke.

After she left, I held my ear against the door to Arjun's surgery. He was chatting away. Probably wrapping up. Better be quick.

Pauline had tidied the waiting area before she left. The recessed halogen spots gave the room an eerie sci-fi feel, set against the pitch black of outside and occasional headlights shining by like shooting stars.

The drawer was locked, rightly. I fished for the keys in the blue pencil pot, crud slipping under my nail. The staple remover pricked my finger.

The stamps had been shoved to the back of the drawer and I pulled them both out to check the colour of their plastic tops. I punched Arjun's stamp onto the prescription pad.

I heard female laughter behind me. Placed everything back.

Arjun's voice: 'Tell George he might want to eat some extra bananas. We wouldn't want another one of his cramps to slow us down this weekend.'

Half-sitting on the desk, I greeted them with 'Hi' as they came out of the corridor.

'Hi, Radha,' said the school mum I'd roped into the clinic a few months ago. Her blonde highlights reflected the overhead lights as she scooped her hair over her scarf to leave. Her smile creased the skin around her eyes, something she'd be paying us to correct, though it would take a few days for the cosmetic injections to take effect. 'I'll be off then,' she said.

'Thank you,' Arjun waved. 'Hey,' he said to me, bumping his shoulder against mine. 'How are you? I'm shattered.'

'Me too.'

He flicked casually through the post, then stopped. 'Oh, what now?'

I snatched a glance at the envelope. The Health Board. About the inspection? That didn't make sense; those were normally addressed to me. He raced his finger underneath the lip of the light-brown envelope, in a move that always made me fear a paper cut.

'What the hell?' He ran his hand through his hair, frowning. 'This must be a mistake.'

My nerves stood on edge. 'What is it?'

He handed me the paper. 'They're accusing me of overprescribing anti-anxiety medication. Idiots. I practically never do that.'

I took the letter and scanned it as if I were reading. I didn't actually need to: its content was etched in my brain from when I'd received that same caution only two months ago. What a fright that had been! But why did this come so quickly? I hadn't written nearly as many on Arjun's pad yet. Heat rose in my cheeks. My warning must have put a flag on the practice ... My pulse thumped at the back of my skull, waves of nausea stirring inside.

Arjun was shaking his head, angrily scribbling something on a Post-It. 'I'm going to have to call them. It's bad enough having them breathe down your neck all the time, without them screwing up. It's no sodding wonder hordes of dentists are stressed out of their minds.'

'You're right,' I said, trying to stop my voice from trembling. 'It must be a system error.'

'Unless ...' His hand rested on Pauline's chair. 'Show me the letter again,' he waved. I handed it over. 'Yes,' he said.

'The period is the last quarter ... since Pauline's been here. You don't think ...?'

A flush of anxiety streaked up my chest. My breathing faltered. What had I done? He couldn't start accusing her – she was innocent. And what if we pissed her off? What if she left? I'd be stuck having to do everything again. I bit my lip and exhaled slowly. 'I can't imagine her doing that, sweetheart. Would she be that stupid?' The suspicion on his face faded a little. 'And I wouldn't bother getting in touch with the NHS,' I added. 'It's only a warning, right? If you're not prescribing, this will go away by itself.' I took the letter off him and placed it demonstratively inside a folder.

'Hmm,' Arjun said, that damned eyebrow raised again. He looked up at the ceiling, searching. 'But just in case, we should switch your dad's old CCTV on again. Don't you think? We could do it now, for when she comes in on Monday.'

Inside, I counted to ten. And again – slowly, wringing the colour from my hands. If we put the CCTV on in the reception area, then I'd have to be careful ... No. What was I thinking? I couldn't use his pad anymore anyway. Not after the letter. Nor mine. I focused on a spot on the desk to calm myself. There was really only one answer: I would have to stop. I mean, how hard could that be? I'd never needed them before I started. This was only ever meant to be temporary. Tears pressed behind my eyes. But my pills ... without them, I ...

'Radha? What do you think?'

I turned towards him. I blinked three times to not be confronted too clearly with his trusting face. 'I guess ruling her out would do you no harm.' I smiled meekly, quite unsure of the harm it could do me.

CHAPTER NINE

Gunbir

Gunbir cleared a space on his desk by pushing aside the clutter, some of which fell in a semi-circle around his feet. It didn't bother him that the mess in his study was closing in on him; he still vaguely knew where everything was.

He sat on his wooden chair, comfortably sunken into his orthopaedic cushion, ready for his task. He grabbed a spare piece of card as a base and positioned the plastic template for his *rangoli*. He squirted PVA glue inside the different shapes and spread it out with his fingertips, hoping the glue would be strong enough to hold the rice, so the floral decorations could remain intact until Diwali, the festival of lights.

A sheet of paper hung precariously off a stack of books, a scattering of pink rice holding it in place. He'd deposited the green rice grains on the saucer of his dirty teacup and the yellow rice in a mound by his elbow.

The computer monitor formed a comforting, live background to his efforts, displaying four squares of black-and-white CCTV – one for each side of the house. Nothing ever happened, bar the occasional squirrel. He merely watched out of habit. There were two further dark squares, unused for years.

He pinched the tweezers. White, sticky goo seeped from his fingers into its metal grooves. One by one he arranged grains of rice in the correct hole of the mould. It would take hours to complete the designs, but he didn't have much else to do. Others used rice powder instead of grains for rangoli, but he liked challenging his dexterity. These old dentist hands were still good for something.

As he looked up to release the strain from his neck, the two spare squares came to life with new video feeds. Startled by the sudden movement, Gunbir knocked over the yellow rice, which sprinkled to the ground. He leaned into the new streaming images and rubbed his chin, a cluster of spiky hairs evidence of a sloppy shave that morning.

'Meena, look,' he shouted towards the hall. 'The clinic is back online.'

The reception's camera was angled so that you could see the entrance, the five seats along the wall and the desk – though only from the back. There was nobody seated there but after only a minute or so, he caught Arjun and Radha leaving. Why had they switched the CCTV back on? He hoped it didn't mean trouble.

A sense of apprehension trickled through him. He remembered the morning, years ago, when he arrived at the clinic and found the wide front window defaced by a giant splash of green paint. It took hours to wash off. Patients and people had walked by, all curious, telling him to call the police. But how could he? He'd been at the perpetrators' mercy after the incident: a momentary lapse of judgement that had changed everything.

The young thugs had taunted him and Meena with his guilt; the paint merely one of many vile acts of vandalism to endure. He'd refused to give in to their extortion, figuring there was no guarantee their harassment would stop. And he'd paid the price.

Gunbir hated being so vulnerable and had ordered CCTV to be installed at the clinic and at home. It wasn't to catch the punks in the act – how would he explain to the police why he'd been targeted? But he hoped the CCTV stickers and flashing lights might deter further attacks. Little did he realise then how far they'd go. His shoulders slumped.

Why hadn't he just done what they asked? Not a day went by without regret, without the constant gnawing feeling he'd failed.

He traced his fingers over the contours of the darkened clinic on his screen. Arjun insisted on getting rid of the CCTV when they took over the business: his cosmetic clients valued their privacy. And what was the point? They didn't have any cash or drugs on the premises. Of course, Gunbir never told anyone about all the trouble. He'd casually blamed the odd act of vandalism on the dangers of living in Glasgow. He also never disclosed there was another camera in the main surgery – now Radha's. Connected to the reception system, it had just come back to life too.

Gunbir looked at the new feed in the lower left corner of the screen, the light-coloured leather of Radha's chair visible in the moonlight. He sighed. That camera could've exonerated Radha in an instant, spared her a load of stress over these last few months. It could have proven that Radha did nothing wrong and had followed all procedures to help save the old woman's life.

He remembered Radha coming to him the evening of the patient's death, shaken, telling him what happened. His heart swelled when she asked him for help: he was needed.

They walked through the sequence of events step by step. He tried to calm her, reassure her that she would be fine. Old people died, that's all. But she tormented herself with the idea that she'd caused it, gotten things wrong, hadn't done enough. Imagine if he'd been able to pull out a video! How happy and relieved she would have been, jumping into his arms again like when she was small. Hot breath on his neck.

He shook his head at the fantasy. He knew damn well they would never have been able to use that footage: you weren't allowed to have a camera there. Perhaps he should disable it. He wouldn't want them to get into trouble if it were ever discovered.

Outside, fat raindrops clung onto the windowpane, rippling in the wind. His apple tree's dark, bare branches swayed. Gunbir shrugged. There was no hurry. Did he even still have keys?

The yellow rice on the carpet caught his eye. He bent over but struggled to reach, hampered by his swollen stomach. He groaned. Might as well fetch a new lot.

He shuffled into the corridor, stooped under the baggage of memories as he paused in front of his dear Meena's portrait; her fortieth birthday gift. She'd asked to be painted in the same style as the portrait of Krishna they bought on their honeymoon, and to hang next to him. Later, she'd tease Gunbir about keeping him on his toes – what with Krishna being the god of love and tenderness and all.

Gunbir locked his hands together underneath his chin and gazed up at her. Her dark eyes smiled back. Her long hair fell into a single curl on the smooth skin of her bare shoulder, a few strands of grey reflecting the light from the window. Her skin was radiant against her favourite purple sari.

'Forgive me, my darling,' he said. He kissed his finger and pressed it onto her lips. 'I miss you so much.'

He walked to the kitchen and caught his reflection in the glazed door to the hall. *'Hathi.'* His mother's sweet whisper whooshed through his mind. A lump formed in his throat. This old, fat man wasn't who he was meant to be; why his mother had given him that nickname. He was Elephant because he was tasked to protect his herd. His lip trembled. How he'd failed.

Not once, but twice.

There could never be a third time.

CHAPTER TEN

After work, Arjun locked the door to the clinic and put his hand on the small of my back, only the faintest pressure making its way through my padded coat. I slipped my plait inside the collar and pulled my hood up. As soon as we reached the pavement, I buried my hands in my pockets and angled my head down to prevent the wind blowing my ears free.

It was rare for us to walk home together. I did the early shift, to accommodate NHS patients whose jobs may be at risk if they took too much time off. In contrast, Arjun's daytime patients were privileged housewives striving to keep their appearance fresh and their husband's gaze on them. Or part-timers, whose jobs were probably little more than a pleasant complement to the household budget – to be invested in large dollops of 'me time'. This clientele seemed to float in and out of the clinic like clouds of puffy blow-dries, needing rounded cheeks and plumped up lips to match.

The true dentistry began again around 5 p.m., when the time-poor professionals pitched up to finally address long-endured pain or to veneer over the chips and squinty gaps they were convinced cost them their latest business deal.

After we passed the first corner in silence, Arjun pulled out his phone.

'Tom, hi. Still up for tomorrow?' he asked cheerfully, his earlier concern about the NHS letter so easily forgotten; an effortless practice of the 'don't worry' mantra he consistently preached. 'All right. Seven-thirty it is. I'll bring some snacks,' Arjun said, and looked at me with questioning eyes.

I nodded.

He said goodbye.

'Will the weather be OK for the bike ride?' I asked.

He tucked his mobile back in his pocket. 'Sure, it will. It's only wind. We've been wet before.' He breathed in deeply, as if energising himself with fresh air. We were both born and raised in Scotland, yet I couldn't help but feel his genes acclimatised better to the northern weather. I wouldn't be surprised if one day, I found him taking a freezing dip in the pond at Maxwell Park. A picture of ruddy health. 'I don't suppose you could make us some *vada*, could you?' he asked. 'The guys loved them last time.'

'Sure.' Conscious of the cyclists' fitness drive, I'd looked up a recipe for baking rather than frying the O-shaped lentil treats. They still came out deliciously crispy and it turned out I preferred them that way – even if they came served with a pang of guilt for abandoning my mother's method. The rich smell on opening the oven was worth freezing my fingers kneading ice cubes into the dough.

It was one of the dishes I'd agreed to make for Diwali at Shalini-aunty's house the next week – which reminded me

I needed to sort out a lift for Dad if nobody else offered. I smiled, remembering his confidence when he told me he was making rangoli himself. He was exceedingly messy but had challenged my incredulous look: how hard could it be to control rice grains with his nimble dentist's hands?

Arjun and I walked into Sutherglen Drive, our steps in sync. Twigs blown from the trees during last night's storm littered the pavement. The new speed bumps' white painted triangles glowed like minacious warnings under the streetlights. After years of residents complaining about 'boy racers' in black Mercedes sedans endangering pedestrians, the council had finally acted, but only after a fifteen-year-old girl's joy ride along the road had resulted in her crashing into three parked vehicles and being found upside down.

She survived, thankfully. What a stupid girl. Where were the parents?

I sighed. That was unfair. It's not like I knew for certain where Manesh was all the time – even right now. But I was comforted by the notion that at least my son had his head properly screwed on. God knows what other teenagers got up to.

Our neighbour's car swerved into his drive. He stepped out as we reached his gate. 'Evening,' Arjun shouted in passing. 'Hi,' he replied. 'Windy, huh?' I heard the jangle of his keys as I tapped in the code to open our black iron gates.

The brightly lit alarm box blinked from the dark sandstone front of our house. I checked my watch: nearly 6 p.m. Where was Manesh? He was meant to be home, his last day of suspension.

'I'm going into the garage to pump up my tyres,' Arjun said, leaving me to wrestle with our glass-panelled front door whose wooden frame expanded when it rained a lot. I turned the key and shoved the door with my shoulder. Once inside, I flicked on the lanterns along the drive to guide my boy home.

As I progressed to switch on the porch and hall lights, I tripped over a pair of running shoes. Green. Big. I could no longer tell who they belonged to, but I could hazard a guess. I picked them up and arranged them on the shoe rack in the cloakroom. I hung up my coat.

The door to the toilet stood open and light from the garage streamed through the frosted window. I noticed the hand towel lying on the floor. What was it with towels and floors? When I stuffed it back into its silver ring, I spotted a small skid mark in the toilet bowl, a smidge above the water line. Again? I grabbed the brush and went to work cleaning, the scent of pine fooling no one. I flushed and made my way to the next toilet, off the utility room. Might as well squeeze it in, while I was at it.

I didn't have a routine like some of my friends, if you didn't count the big clean at weekends. There was such a wash-list to do that I picked opportunities here and there to stay on top of things. Arjun and Manesh helped with the dishes, but I was the one who left work early twice a week, meaning I had more time for the domestic things. And Manesh was sitting his Nat 5 exams this year; he needed to study.

Where was he?

I rinsed my gloves in the sink. Footsteps by the front door interrupted the ambient silence. A slow, confident stride. Could be either of them. I wiped my hands on my trousers and went to check. I needed to get the post from the box anyway.

Manesh stood in the hall, in school uniform.

'Where have you been?' I asked.

'Special assembly,' he said. He dropped his hockey bag on the floor in the corner and draped his blazer over the newel post – mere steps from the cloak room. 'I got a call to say I needed to come too. Which was just as well, as my hockey kit was still there and the first eleven have a game tomorrow.'

'They're letting you play?'

'Yeah, it's a cup game.'

I snorted. Manesh was one of their strongest players. It was clearly fine to curtail his education with suspension, but God forbid their sporting results were affected.

He unzipped a letter from the side pocket of his bag. 'Here, they handed these out at the assembly.'

I followed him into the kitchen, reading. The rumours were true: drug dealers did approach the kids near school. The letter was short on detail, as usual, and seemed to merely ask parents to instruct their children to report any suspicious activity.

Manesh spread peanut butter on a slice of bread and wolfed it down. He was very hungry lately, perpetually leaving jam-covered knives on the worktop and snack bar wrappers inches from the bin. Could that be a sign? I remembered other students talking about getting the munchies when high on weed at uni. What if he was one of the ... My pulse quickened, but I caught myself. I brought my hand from the cold worktop to my temple. I breathed deeply, annoyed I could be set off into a spiral of anxious thoughts so quickly.

It wasn't him. It couldn't be him.

'What do you know about this?' I asked, the letter in my hand.

He shrugged. 'Only what it says there.' He opened the fridge and gobbled up a handful of cherry tomatoes, testing my restraint by leaving only one in the plastic punnet.

'Please tell me you're not doing drugs,' I said, grabbing him by the arm to stop him from reaching for more food. It was nearly dinner time.

He stepped back and let the door swing shut. 'What? No.' It was a convincing indignant face; yet I saw something: a tiny flicker in his eye that made my stomach jump. Or was I worrying over nothing again?

'Are you sure?'

Manesh laughed. 'Of course I'm sure, Mum. And if I were doing drugs, do you really think I'd tell you?'

I smiled and tried to laugh along. 'Fair enough.'

He shook his head at my foolishness, something he'd taken to doing with increasing frequency. Silly Mum.

To think I started out as Hero Mum, Mum the All-Knowing, a Please-Don't-Go-Yet Mum ...

'One more story, Mummy.' I could still hear his tiny, pleading voice; feel his squishy but deceptively strong limbs wrapped around my arm like a koala, keeping me put. 'I've read it twice already,' I'd have to say. But he seduced me with those innocent dark eyes, their endless eyelashes. 'Pleeease.' And he'd stare at me in wonder as I read about wizards and warlocks, drinking me in as if I were *everything*.

I sighed. 'Mummy' became 'Mum', the firm clinging-on became loose cuddles, then just a kiss, and eventually a nudge nose-to-nose as I pressed the duvet across his chest. I remembered holding the Avengers fabric in my hand, his dark hair fanned across the pillow. 'This isn't my last tuck-in, is it?' I'd asked.

He furrowed his brow. 'What do you mean?'

'You're twelve now. I know one day you won't want to be tucked in anymore. And that's OK. But I'd hate to miss the last time, to look back and wonder where it went. I feel ... I feel we should mark it somehow. Make it memorable. So, will you let me know when it's the last time?'

He placed his hand on my cheek, smiling. 'I will. But I don't think it's soon.'

'That's great, baby. Promise? In fact, I may need two weeks' notice, just to get used to the idea.'

He laughed, his eyes glistening in the glow of his bedside lamp. 'Maybe *one* week.'

I got no notice, in the end, nor that final night-night, which I gauged had come and gone somewhere around his first cup match, aged fourteen.

What I would give now to win even a snippet of those blissful moments. But here we were: I was Silly Mum. Which seemed to have been the natural progression from Embarrassing Mum: the one where I had to drop him around the corner so his friends wouldn't see me, where I got banished from the hockey field for being 'too supportive' and should absolutely not greet his mates too enthusiastically when they came round.

I watched him walk towards the stairs with a self-assured strut. Yes, he'd grown out of being embarrassed last year. Nothing I did fazed him.

My heart sank as I realised perhaps nothing I did even mattered anymore.

I fetched the *atta* flour from the pantry and shook it into a glass bowl. Years of near-daily practice making chapatis ensured I could eye the right amount for tonight and Dad's lunch tomorrow. Two spoonfuls of water to start kneading, then a bit more and a slug of oil. I massaged and shaped until I was left with a ball of soft, elastic dough.

The rain beat down on the window again, dark clouds obscuring the moon. Damn November. It felt like the gloom would never stop.

As I left the griddle on the hob to warm, I went to wash my hands, beginning the dreary task of prising dough from the edge of my cuticles with my short nails. The doorbell rang. I listened out for movement. Nothing. 'Me again, then,' I grumbled and stopped the tap. I quickly wiped some of the pale stickiness onto the freshly laundered tea towel that would have to head straight back onto the never-ending pile.

Passing the study, I heard the *pling-plong* of muted electric guitar strings. No wonder Arjun hadn't heard: he'd have his head phones on. I couldn't complain; the alternative was listening to the amplified sound of him emulating Nirvana.

From the porch, I could only make out a halo of streetlight around a very large, dark shape. Unease crept over me. Who was it? I opened the gate with the remote. As the shape ambled up our drive, I saw it was a woman laden with four fat bin bags, two in each hand.

A sudden realisation.

Crap.

I forgot.

'Hi,' I said, all smiles, waving her inside. 'Come in, quick. It's cold'

She plonked the bags in my entrance, wet drips pooling on my tiles. She wiped her hands on her Canada Goose coat and shook the hood off her head. It was that mum I met at the party. Trust Heather to take advantage of the new girl to run errands. Carol? Kate? I searched my memory but came no further than a K-sound.

'Thank you very much,' I said. 'I presume this is the uniform sale stock?'

'Uh-huh.' She rubbed her hands together and blew on them. She stamped her red, knee-high boots on the floor, presumably to revive circulation to frozen toes. 'You weren't at the meeting. Heather asked me to pop by.' She peeked past me into the house, curious – as we all were. The houses in Pollokshields were attractive Victorian properties, some detached, others, like ours, semi-detached. All expensive; all with different tastes. I followed her gaze to the gold-rimmed mirror in the entrance hall.

'I look a state,' she said, zhuzhing her immaculate hairdo, her makeup flawless despite the wind and the late hour.

'Hardly,' I chuckled. 'Look at me!'

And she did. She eyed me up and down.

In my mind, my stomach distended, my thighs grew to twice their size and the dried chapati dough protruded from my fingernails like witches' claws.

'I can't wait to get home and put my comfy clothes on,' she said, with a smile bouncing between kindness and condescension.

'Well, I'm sorry I made you come here. I honestly appreciate it.' I stepped forward, crowding her towards the door. 'I'll take care of attaching the price labels this weekend.'

'Hold on,' she said, rummaging through her small, leather shoulder bag.

'I really must go. I'm cooking.' I said, my hand on the door handle.

She sniffed. With a hint of offence, she handed me a ball of twine. 'For the labels, Heather said to leave them long.'

'Right. Thanks.'

I waited a polite distance as she walked down the drive. She pivoted and pointed at the garage. 'There's water gushing from your gutter into the neighbour's garden,' she shouted.

'Thanks. Wouldn't want to upset the neighbours, eh?' I shouted back before slamming the door shut. I shook my head. The nerve. As if anyone could possibly care about getting WATER on their LAWN – in Scotland!

The steely smell of hot griddle met me as I re-entered the kitchen. I flicked some water onto the surface. It hissed and transformed to steam instantly. With the base of my hand, I flattened clumps of dough into circles, the rhythmic movement normally cathartic but failing to relieve my irritation. Not helped by Manesh's trumpet blasting from upstairs. After a quick roll, I flung the first two chapatis onto the heat. The dough dried; its prior smoothness pockmarked with bubbles. Unlike my mother, whose calloused fingers seemed fire retardant, I used tongs to flip them over. After all, my hands were my livelihood. I balled a cotton cloth and pressed onto the dough, making it puff up.

As I put the cloth down, my phone pinged. I moaned. Where had I left it? I searched and found it on the console table in the hall. I read the message, while returning to the kitchen.

This is EDS HEATING. Your boiler service is due. Please call us for an appointment.

I exhaled a lungful of air. When I breathed in again, I smelled burning. Crap. I picked the chapatis off the griddle, charred flakes dropping off. No choice but to bin them.

Hot tears pooled in my eyes. It was all too much for one person.

My misty eye wandered through the glazed door to the messy rack of sports equipment in the utility room. Manesh's hockey, his schoolwork, his music. They were all important. And I couldn't begrudge Arjun his hobbies. He worked hard. And how could I gripe about him staying healthy? He kept nagging me about exercising, with middle age creeping up on us. But how in the hell was I meant to fit it in?

Not with all this.

Tension spread across my shoulders. I pressed my lips together, closed my eyes and blew out slowly. Counted to ten. But when I inhaled it was as if a valve had opened and the air kept coming in, blowing up my lungs like a big balloon. A bubble caught in my throat, thumping along with my pulse. I sank to the ground, held my head between my legs.

I tried to press my chest down.

Hoping the balloon would pop.

Fearing the balloon would pop – because then what? Would it hurt?

A pill would take care of this. If I could only take a pill ...

But there was no longer a way to get them.

Fat tears streaked down my cheeks. I longed for my mum. Pictured her smile. Felt her hands run over my hair. Heard her voice: *'Shush now. Shush.'*

CHAPTER ELEVEN

Sunday evening, sitting on the sofa, I flipped back three pages in my novel. Why were the characters jumping off the bridge again? The seat felt hard. It was usually a lovely spot, where I caught the sun through the bay window; but what few beams of light succeeded in piercing through the blanket of cloud outside were landing on me with a limp flicker.

My stomach felt bloated. I shifted my weight and held the book firmly, tried to focus on the words but it was no use: they were forgotten as soon as I'd scanned them. I sighed. Maybe this one wasn't meant for me. I put it back onto the pile of other abandoned reads – stories I used to devour.

The tumble dryer beeped at the back of the house. I rubbed my hands on my knees and got up. Best to fold when warm.

In the utility room, the washing machine rumbled and sloshed. Last load, thank goodness. It had been on non-stop for two days since that mum came round, four bags of used uniforms needing to be rid of other children's muck before changing homes. And now our own lot as well.

I opened the dryer, hints of lavender escaping. A large, green towel lay on top. I held it to my chest, its warmth penetrating my winter-weary body. A quick fold and onto the knotted octopus of tights. Its static crackled and licked the hairs on my arms as I pulled it apart. I dumped the remaining load into the white plastic basket. Manesh could take care of that later.

But he was upstairs revising; his prelims were soon. I wavered for an instant then grabbed the large items and folded them into three piles. Once the basket was down to a bedding of grey and black socks it would be a nightmare to pair up, I decided to leave it to him after all. It was hardly a big ask.

The washing machine displayed seventeen more minutes to go before the clothes would need to be transported to the next machine. A fleeting pang of guilt hit me. The dryer was an environmental no-no. I knew it was bad, but I strove to make up for it in different ways: never filling the kettle fully, bringing the heating down at night, and the perpetual switching off of lights around the house. I remembered my mother hanging the laundry outside and having to keep a constant eye out for rain; then re-hanging it all inside when the heavens opened. Who could be bothered with that?

Mum hadn't worked. Had more time. Liked housework more than I did. Loved taking care of us: husband, son, daughter. I smiled at a memory of her fussing over my school skirts. They needed to be exactly the right length, and she changed the hem with her sewing machine every few months. While my brother got away with crooked ties and the odd shirt flap sticking out of his trousers, her daughter was expected to be the model student. More than anything she wanted me to enjoy a good education

– something she didn't get. I would not be a dependent woman. I would forge my own future, have it all.

Yet here I was – here we all were, all the working mums – not finding a way to have it all without *doing* it all. We got the rough end of the deal. And it was draining.

I filled the watering can and spent the next few minutes scuttling around, feeding the six large plants that occupied various corners of the house; I always marvelled at how I'd kept them alive for this long.

It was the washing machine's turn to beep, and I carried the cold, damp load to the dryer for a final spin. My eyes were drawn to the jumble of socks beckoning, screaming for order.

Fine.

I'd pair them. But I drew the line at pulling them inside out! I shook my head. It was ridiculous, I knew that; yet for whatever reason, I deemed it important that they be balled with the same mindlessness as that with which the men had flung them away. That would teach them.

Placing the balls atop the mounds of folded clothes was like reverse Jenga. Just when I thought I was done, the top half of Manesh's tower teetered and slipped to the ground. I roared, 'Manesh! Come here.'

I heard his footsteps down the stairs and into the kitchen. 'What?'

'In here. How many times have I told you to take your clothes to your room?'

As he came to join me, he said, 'I was going to do it. I told you.'

'Yes, but when. WHEN? Look at this,' I said gesturing to the sea of fabric on the floor.

His eyes stayed on me, however. 'Mum ...' he said, horror sprayed across his face.

'What?' I snapped.

'You're ... you're bleeding.' He pointed at my middle.

I lowered my head and saw the crotch of my light-grey leggings was splashed with red. 'Oh. Sorry,' I said as I covered myself up with a tea towel. My sudden blush felt incandescent. 'Can you ... take care of this please?' I asked as I sprinted away.

Upstairs, I locked the bathroom door behind me. I pulled at the smudged leggings and my soaked pants, sat on the toilet and inched them down, careful not to streak my legs. I wiped as best I could, toilet paper shredding against the dried smears on my inner thighs.

No wonder I was so irritable. I flicked the fine dust from my hands while making mental calculations. Was it even the right time? Who knew anymore? My period was all over the place since turning forty-three.

Poor Manesh. What an awful thing to see.

I carried my clothes over to the sink, opened the cold tap and pumped a dollop of hand soap on my underwear. I squeezed and rubbed, the freshest blood dissipating easily. Stained water climbed over the leggings as they plugged the hole, a pink, suffocating beast that stirred my memory. I heaved; a dizzy spell forced me to clutch the porcelain rim.

It was the same. I'd been here before. Ten years ago.

A whooshing sound filled my ears and I shivered as my mind transported me back to that night. The night a gush between my legs had woken me, sharp pains in my rounded belly. I remembered my hands at the sink, inside the swirling pink pool. Rinsing my pyjamas, rinsing and rinsing. The metallic smell of blood.

My knuckles raw.

Arjun in the background phoning the ambulance, pleading; concern etched across his face. Me scrubbing and rinsing until the water ran clear. Because it was all I could do to cope. Erase the child that would never be, that would be ripped from me in hospital. The one I'd held onto the longest. A girl who haunted my dreams, still.

I sat hunched next to the bathtub, arm slung over its side, forehead resting on my wrist. My breathing finally slowed. My hair fell like curtains around my face, enveloping me in a cocoon from which I didn't want to emerge. I shook with a hiccoughed sob and heard a high-pitched giggle. A snippet of my would-be girl. An echo of my dreams.

Sadness stirred inside. I was alone in my grief. I couldn't tell Arjun I fantasised about our daughter because he too, had been distraught for a long time. It would only hurt him. I couldn't tell him that I felt her, heard her.

There, a voice.

But wait – actual words.

What?

I sniffed and wiped my nose with the back of my hand. Listened out for more. Manesh's words rose up. His baritone laugh.

As I crossed the landing to my bedroom, I caught a fragment of conversation. There was definitely a girl. A real one. I threw some clothes on and went downstairs, patting my under-eye with the tips of my fingers to reduce any puffiness.

Manesh was in the hallway, leaning against the door frame to the living room, smiling at a young woman I could see only from behind. She wore a fitted green jumpsuit. He straightened as he saw me, a pained expression on his face. 'You OK, Mum?'

'Yes, all good,' I replied, mustering a smile. The girl turned around. Her straight auburn hair was held back with a red bandanna, the ends of the knot springing up like bunny ears. A round face. Cute. The odd spot near her nose. Her eyes grew wide as she smiled. Her metal braces jazzed up her slightly pale complexion.

'Hello,' I said, extending an arm.

'Hello, Mrs Bakshi. I'm Beth.' She curtsied ever so slightly when she shook my hand. I looked over her shoulder and raised an eyebrow at Manesh.

'Drama rehearsal ended early. I told Beth she could stay here until her train was due,' he said.

'No problem. Would you like to stay for dinner?' They exchanged nervous glances. I pretended not to notice. I'd already embarrassed my son enough for one day.

'That's kind of you, but I'll be expected at home,' Beth said, scrunching her nose in apology.

'Of course.' I clasped my hands together. 'Well, maybe next time.' Manesh rolled his eyes. I'd probably veered into uncool territory again.

He placed his hand on her shoulder and nudged her towards the front door. 'Here, let me take you to the station.'

She gave a little wave. 'Goodbye, Mrs Bakshi.'

Good manners.

I headed to the fridge to prep for the cauliflower curry and wondered if she was his girlfriend. He'd brought friends who were girls into the house before, but there was something in his awkwardness and the way his hand slipped down her arm on the way out ...

My heart constricted. He had so little time for me as it was. What would happen now?

I put the pan on high heat on the hob. I scattered fenugreek and coriander seeds, saw them jump and waited for their aromas to be released. Scents of my childhood. I added the other spices and a little extra cumin – Manesh liked cumin. As the grated garlic and ginger softened, I cut the onions for the bhajis.

My knife sliced effortlessly through the bulbs; my chopping skills refined by years of home-cooked meals. Family meals. Tears welled in my eyes. I knew it was the onions but letting one watery drop slide down my cheek triggered an avalanche of sorrow. I wasn't ready to lose my boy.

The front door slammed and Manesh's footsteps approached.

I shook my head, ran my tongue over my teeth and breathed out. Pull it together. These violent mood swings were wearing me down, but I had nothing to calm them.

'Smells nice,' he said as he joined me.

'Thanks.' I beamed my best smile.

He cocked his head and frowned. 'Mum, are you OK?'

'Yes, darling. It's the stupid onions.'

'You sure? You've been a bit weird lately.'

I pulled my apron over my head and set it aside, with a bright nothing-wrong-with-me laugh, while inside I teetered on the edge. But he couldn't know. *A parent's emotional wellbeing is not the child's job*, I'd read early on. I lived by that motto and I wasn't about to change course.

All I needed was to make it through – just a little while longer. I'd soon get a handle on this; I was sure of it. A flush crept up my chest, trepidation building that I wouldn't be able to handle this alone. Not yet. Not without the pills. But I didn't have any.

My eye drifted to the cork board, to Friday's warning letter from school.

Could this be the answer?

CHAPTER TWELVE

'Here, take these,' Arjun said, stretching to grab his thin, black running gloves from the top of the radiator by the front door the next morning. 'You'll need them.'

I put them on, my fingers loose in the warm fabric, and readjusted the collar on my rain jacket, ready to go. My head pounded, eager for fresh air after another restlessness night, jittery from withdrawal. Something I hoped to fix today.

'Oh, and this.' He handed me a head torch.

'It's not that dark anymore,' I argued and batted it away. He looked through the glazed front door at the dawn peering over the trees. 'True. You'll be safe.'

My stomach tightened. Would I?

He squeezed both my shoulders. 'I'm proud of you, going for a jog before work like this.'

'Thank you,' I said, and fastened the laces on my trainers.

'A great thing to do on a Monday morning – fresh start to the week – you'll see.'

I smiled, hoping he wouldn't notice the pricked conscience scalding my cheeks. I hardly ever lied to him.

My keys were on the console table. There was a small pocket at the back of my leggings to store them in. Arjun picked them up. 'Wait. I almost forgot.' He fetched his cycle pouch and unzipped a slit at the side. 'I got you something while up North on the ride.' I could only see it was a metal thing, and he attached it to my keys. 'Here.'

I examined my gift: a key chain in the shape of a little waterfall, the word Scotland scrawled in blue underneath. Why he insisted on always bringing home tat from his trips was a mystery. Fridge magnets, bookmarks, you name it. It was sweet, but also a stupid waste of money. 'Thank you.'

He pecked my cheek, then gave me a gentle push. 'On you go.'

I veered right at the bottom of our drive and did some actual running to keep up the pretence. By the time I reached the tennis courts, I was out of breath and slowed to walking. My nostrils burned from the cold air.

A few uniformed children were making their way to school from Pollokshields West train station. I walked past them, keeping my head down. Not that I needed to. They were so engrossed in their phones I could've worn a clown suit and they wouldn't have noticed me.

As I reached the school grounds, my jaws were hurting from clenching them. What the hell was I doing? I stretched my neck sideways. I skimmed the side fence towards the alley that formed a shortcut to the other side of campus. Every step heightened my anxiety, swirls of nausea inside, despite the increasing realisation the drug dealers couldn't possibly be stupid enough to revisit the same place. Then again, did they even know the police were involved? I watched a throng of children descend from the south side, an unbroken row of fresh faces in light and dark blue blazers. No one there who didn't belong.

Except for me.

I shook my head and turned back, part of me disappointed and the other part relieved. I had no idea how to even initiate a transaction had they been there. *Hi, do you happen to sell diazepam?* What did they even call these pills? It was bound to have a street name; they were hardly pharmacists. They'd probably know it as Valium. Most people did.

It was too soon to go home. Arjun would still be there and while he'd be delighted I went out at all, I knew this wouldn't count as a *proper* run. I turned to do a lap of Maxwell Park. My cheeks felt slapped by the wind and the flimsy gloves did nothing to prevent my fingers from seizing up. If my walk didn't count as exercise, jumping around to avoid the puddles certainly should: I could feel my heart rate rise.

Three teenage boys exited the park just as I reached it, talking animatedly, bumping shoulders, their hands in their pockets. Stepping through the thick bushes that surrounded the park, it struck me this would be where I would have moved my illicit trade: plenty of footfall, plenty of foliage and dark corners for cover. Had someone at the party not mentioned a few kids having their phones stolen here?

I scanned the pond area, the reeds thin and browned, the ducks seemingly unperturbed by winter. Not here. Too open.

Further ahead, I looked into the dark, elm-lined path. Nobody. Maybe the playground at the other end? Isn't that where they're always telling kids to be vigilant? My stomach sank. What had I become? A middle-class professional woman scouring the streets for drugs. And despite it being Glasgow, not even finding them.

I needed to stop, but the mere thought of having to do without my pills for any longer got my pulse racing. It was the expectation that was the worst, the fear, knowing that anxiety could hit at any moment.

My breathing became laboured. It felt like the bushes were closing in on me, spiky holly leaves intent on wounding. Dark clouds circling, swooping down to swallow me up. I ran to the nearest open space, raised my arms and jumped up to reduce the growing pressure in my lungs.

A woman in a dark green duffel coat threw a ball. Her white Yorkie sprinted after it onto the wet grass, slowed only by the occasional paw stuck in the mud. She looked my way and waved. 'Radha! Hey.'

I snapped my arms to my side and was left with no choice but to approach. 'Good morning, Heather.'

'I didn't know you were a runner,' she said, eyeing my outfit.

'Only a beginner.'

'Good for you. Great to keep the pounds off,' she said.

Her Yorkie yapped. We looked over. Two larger dogs were circling it and while the big ones were wagging tails and taking turns sniffing butts, I wasn't convinced the Yorkie was enjoying the attention. It ran to Heather and she hunched over to take the ball from its mouth, stood up and threw it again, launching the dogs into a race her pup couldn't possibly win.

The two women who came with the hounds joined us, looking sporty and glamorous. As they greeted Heather with air kisses and me with curious looks, I felt a strange kinship with that defeated doggie.

'Anyone seen Natalie lately?' one asked. A name I recognised, at least.

The other unfamiliar one tutted. 'No, I think she's given up on our joint walks.'

'In her defence, she does need to come from Cambuslang,' Heather said.

'Yeah, but she's dropping the girls off at school anyway.'

I began jogging in place, hoping this would lead to permission to leave, but they seemed too engrossed in the judging for a polite departure.

'She should've never bought that puppy. She's been WhatsApping me all the time moaning how hard it is with everything else she's got on. Four kids, she's got! Someone needs to take that poor, unloved animal off her hands.'

'I'll go now,' I said, and trotted off, fully aware it would be me under the microscope the second I turned my back.

While I treated my morning patients, my mind kept wandering to the neighbourhood around school. With the alley possibly under surveillance, where would the dealers go? Move to the pedestrian bridge by the train station? Or was that too public?

Would they have given up? Surely not. There were hundreds of kids at the school. Ripe for the picking, if you were to believe the other mums' stories: thirteen-year-olds posing with cans of that new alcoholic teeth-ruining atrocity on Instagram; 'empties' where the parent's alcohol cupboards were completely raided; a bag with coke found in someone's garden after a particularly wild party.

No, they wouldn't give up so easily. These kids had money. Easy prey.

I tried to put myself into the head of criminals. Use my brains, unlike my stupidity earlier, wandering around on a whim as though I would stumble upon what I needed. Something kept drawing me back to the park. I mentally zoomed in and out of its different parts: the pond, the flower beds, the playground, the lanes. But the only place that made sense was the patio at the back of the Burgh Hall.

I thought of the sandstone mansion that was donated by a Mr Maxwell in Victorian days to benefit the community. I'd been to Pilates there, one of a slew of fitness, arts and dance classes in the evenings. With its stunning arched entrance, turrets and sweeping driveway, it was a popular location for weddings. The sound of bagpipes travelled all the way to my house most Saturdays.

I often passed smokers huddled at the back of the property, the smell of tobacco wafting up my nose. They sheltered between the red bricks of the hall and a row of rhododendron bushes that exploded into a magnificent display of pink and purple flowers in spring. It was a small, secluded area with access from the side of the building as well as the meeting of two paths in the park. Easy in, easy out.

It was worth one more shot.

Self-prescribing was no longer an option.

Nor was confessing to a doctor. No, I couldn't entertain anything that could expose me to the GDC. I couldn't cope with that, not again. They'd caused my unravelling, through the uncertainty, the letters ... The waiting had been like a dripping tap, an incessant reminder that I failed the old woman, that I could be stopped from practising at any moment. Their actions a persistent, insidious amplification of the trauma I already suffered. Was it any wonder I needed a little help?

My mind returned to the present. 'All done,' I said to the young man whose filling I'd finished replacing. I pressed the button to bring the chair back up. He mumbled a thank you through numbed lips and left.

I took my gloves off and threw them in the bin.

Pauline walked in. 'Your three-fifteen has cancelled.'

My heart jumped. Here was my chance. Because having thought about it, criminals were unlikely to be morning people, were they? It was *after* school they would strike. I checked my watch. Would I have enough time? 'Great. I'm going on a small errand, real quick.'

'Don't be late,' Pauline said, as I raced out the door.

I hit the corner of Maxwell Park five minutes before the school bell would ring. I followed the Burgh Hall's drive to the path that led past its side wall into the park. The patio would soon be on my right. I hesitated, then chose to walk straight ahead to first catch a glimpse of whoever might be there. I gasped. Three men. I coughed lightly to mask the gasp.

They didn't even look up. Maybe a woman like me was of no interest: neither target nor threat. I followed the path that went round the large, stone-edged flower beds. It would lead me past them again. This time I would stop.

As I pretended to inspect the sad clumps of turned soil that awaited the council's planting of spring bulbs, I monitored the men – boys? – from the corner of my eye. Three youths in almost identical kit: grey and black puffer jackets, skinny joggers, high-soled trainers that looked expensive and were too white to be truly meant for walking. Two Asians, one white, all three sporting an unhealthy pallor. Two smoking, one drinking from a can of Irn Bru, all three with the stooped shoulders of men with time to waste.

A dark-haired boy in a blue blazer and school tie entered the park from the other corner. He glanced sideways a few times and sped up, making an unambiguous beeline for my guys. For a second, his height and gait reminded me of Manesh. My scalp prickled. Could it be? But his hair was longer. And his bag was blue, not orange. And my boy wouldn't ... he said so. I swallowed a lump in my throat, the fear that the words of a fifteen-year-old were perhaps no longer to be trusted. Here was this kid; I bet his mother thought she had nothing to worry about too. I bet his mother didn't skulk in the bushes. What was I doing?

I tried to recognise him, but he appeared older. A year six maybe?

I circled the flower bed, nonchalantly picking at some dead leaves in the dirt, my eyes firmly set on the boy. He was approaching the others. My maternal instincts screamed at me to jump in and drag the stupid kid away by his ear, but I needed to see how it was done: a deal. I needed to confirm I was in the right place. My pulse raced. I'd be next.

The boy was nearly there. I saw movement behind the shady trio. A dark shape neared along the side of the building. It was a woman, in a black uniform, with a large walkie-talkie on her shoulder next to a white logo. My knees wobbled. I gripped the wrought iron frame of the bench that shielded my side. I wanted to shout, *'Run!'*

The boy spotted the policewoman in the nick of time. He kept walking, eyes confidently ahead, and took the first path away from where he'd been headed. I sat down and swivelled to see what would happen next, my knuckles white from squeezing the metal. If I stayed still, nobody would notice me.

The policewoman seemed to know precisely where to go. She swooped in on the patio. Two of the guys ran off. She grabbed the third by the hood of his jacket. He struggled briefly, trying to shed his coat, but he was zipped in. Would she search his pockets? Take him with her?

I watched her gesticulate, grab his phone. She wrote something on her pad. Her voice carried some way towards me, but I couldn't make out any words. She wagged her finger. Then let him go. Just like that. Maybe she needed a bigger fish to catch?

She observed him as he ran deeper into the park, away towards St Andrew's Drive. Her eyes rested on me for a while. I froze. Hot sweat sprung from my temples as I felt her assess me.

Irrelevant, she must've thought as she moved on.

Yet, had she arrived five minutes later ...

CHAPTER THIRTEEN

After work, I dropped by Dad's. Even though he warned me he wouldn't be in for his lunch that day, his absence at the clinic unnerved me.

I opened the door onto an explosion of cardboard, brown curled shavings of what seemed to have been a large roll.

I stepped inside. 'Dad? Hello?'

He appeared in the doorway of his study, colour on his cheeks, his movement free. I breathed out.

'Hello, my dear,' he said. 'This is a nice surprise.' He pushed some of the cardboard away and pulled at my hand, a glimmer in his eye. 'Come see.'

I followed, manoeuvring my way around the assorted types of clutter. I pursed my lips. It was getting worse. It wasn't only boxes anymore; it was anything and everything. Nothing that came into this house seemed to ever leave again – though previous visits had reassured me that he at least seemed to have food waste under control. The minute I caught one fly in this house, I would overrule his frequent objections to getting a cleaner in. Eccentricity was one thing, filth was another.

Mum would've been horrified. She'd kept the house pristine, always ready for visitors. A real social hub, there was always an aunty or two dropping by, feeding or being fed; irreverent cackles and judgemental tongue sucks accentuating the never-ending chatter, their men mumbling as they played cards. I slid my hand along the wall, feeling echoes of my mum's laughter within, as if the house didn't want to let her go. Like we didn't.

I stepped past a dusty pile of her old books, orange and blue spines hinting at covers with exotic sunsets. Dad began the clear-out shortly after Mum's fall, carefully packing her shoes into boxes, her underwear, her jumpers and tops; but when he reached her bright, bejewelled saris, he couldn't finish. The boxes never made it out of the bedroom. I'd peeked once, her distinctive smell escaping with every raised cardboard flap, enveloping me once more. She was so small, yet her hugs took in all of you. I shivered. I hadn't been any more capable of dealing with her things than he was, then. And I still dreaded it just as much.

My brother came to mind. How he complained on his last stay – at my place, not even sleeping here – about the state of the house. But it was easy for him: he was in London. The celebrated son making it big as an engineer in the capital, immune to any sense of duty. Whereas I cooked; I measured blood pressure; I washed; I inspected feet. And I worried – that alone was an unholy burden. I told him, my blood boiling, that if the chaos troubled him so, he was welcome to take care of it. He'd said no more. And did nothing.

I moved an empty vase from its dangerous position on an overfull bookshelf, the greenish residue at its base too dried-on to cause alarm.

'What do you think?' Dad asked as we entered his study, pride in his voice.

Where to look? There was stuff all over. I frowned. Was that pink rice scattered all over his desk?

'About what?' I asked.

'Here,' he motioned to the ground, to where lay a large, bumpy rug – covering up all manner of sins. Its thick woollen tufts depicted a large elephant painted in a red, blue and gold Indian motif.

'Where did you get it?' I asked, biting my tongue to not ask *why*. It was enormous. Garish, frankly. How did he even drag it in here?

He stood with both hands on his stomach, gazing wistfully at the rug, his slippers licked by its fringe. 'After Manesh came and I told him about the expulsion from Uganda, I have to admit I got a bit nostalgic.' He scratched his chin. 'I began searching on the Internet. Nothing specific. A bit of browsing. You know, anchors to my past. To your grandparents.' He patted his belly. 'And then I found this. A bargain.' He laughed. 'Clearly a mistake, made in China or somewhere. But to me, it's perfect.'

I glanced over the surface of the rug for snags or flaws – something that might mark it as defective. It seemed fine, the colours flashy but consistent, the wool loops of equal length, the edges neat. As for the picture: a typical elephant decorated for the Hindu festival of Holi. 'Why a mistake?'

Dad knelt and used his finger to contour the elephant's long, rounded left ear. He looked up at me and beamed. His wide smile took twenty years off his face. 'It's an *African* elephant.'

'Ah.' I felt my heart melt, my hand pressed flat on my chest. The statuette on the TV had always meant a lot to him, the gift from his father with the filed ear to reflect his unique heritage. We were encouraged to stroke it as children, while we listened to his stories of playing barefoot with twigs on dusty roads, chasing wonky bicycles and fetching water at the pump. Back when I could easily have told you which ear shape was which: Asian or African. I helped Dad up and wrapped my arm around his shoulders. I gave him a squeeze and a kiss on the cheek. 'It's beautiful.'

'Help me put it down properly, Radha.'

'Sure.'

It was easier said than done. It was a good three metres long and weighed a ton. We flipped one side over to pull mixed bits of junk from underneath. He cast them aside without a second thought. Once we'd arranged the beast into position and straightened its long fringe, I placed my fists on my sides and surveyed the room. Had anything else new arrived? The hoarding of old possessions was bad enough; the last thing we needed was him surfing the web for more stuff.

His computer monitor on the desk showed the BBC News website, not shopping. We were safe – for now. And thank goodness the monitor for the CCTV was off. What a strange obsession that had been. I remembered how all of a sudden, he'd mounted cameras here at the house and even one in the clinic. Mum told me he spent hours and hours watching the black and white squares, day and night. I'd wondered if it was a paranoia that came with age. When Mum died, he was unreasonably convinced someone had pushed her over in the garden; but there was nothing to see on screen.

Observing him so pleased with his new purchase, it was hard to imagine how angry he'd been when challenged over Mum. No matter how I or Shalini reasoned with him that she had only tripped and fallen over that night, fatally hitting her head on the stone steps, he wouldn't have it. Someone had shoved her; someone was to blame. And even though he wouldn't say who or why, he was adamant in his belief that person would be back. That bit, in particular, was absurd.

I'd casually assessed him for the signs of early Alzheimer's but he passed my tests, his only oddity this annoying infatuation with the CCTV. With him being retired, there was nothing to stop him rewinding past recordings and staying glued to the live feeds on those damned screens.

I shrugged. Ultimately, it was up to him to decide how to spend his days. It just didn't seem very healthy. I looked past his monitors through the window into the garden, dark clouds so low they seemed to be perched atop the outer hedge. The green ceramic window boxes had been emptied at some point, but never replanted. The raised vegetable box further up was overgrown with twisted weeds that appropriated the tipi-like frame intended for growing beans.

A sadness washed over me. I remembered Mum standing at the hob, gently stirring my favourite runner bean curry. I could still conjure the aroma of the mustard seeds and garam masala. In my mind, I heard the music again, the clatter of Mum's trusted wooden-soled sandals against the tiled floor as she added food to a festive table already overflowing with goodness. The animated conversations as guests helped themselves and lemonade flowed.

She slipped outside. It was only when I smelled burning and saw smoke rising from her pan that I realised she'd not come back.

I turned off the gas and opened the door. I nearly stepped on her head lying on the top step, surrounded by a pool of blood. Her body accordioned down the stairs, her legs at awkward angles, her hands holding two courgettes from the vegetable plot. My scream had made time stop.

The memory hit be like a brick. I grabbed the back of Dad's chair and doubled over, a sharp pain in my chest.

She'd lain there for at least fifteen minutes and we didn't notice. Had partied on, never giving her a second thought. I'd never forget it, and I'd never forgive myself. Beckoned by my howls, the others had rushed to us. I checked her injuries, her pulse. It was too late. Someone fainted. There was a ruckus inside. While the ambulance was called, our friends formed a wall to prevent Dad from seeing her in this state. I cradled Mum, a red stain growing up my shirt sleeve. I stroked her hair – as she used to stroke mine. 'Shush, now.'

As I stood in the middle of the room, her image popped into my head again: unmoving, lips hung slack. Her eyes wide, set on me. Dulled, without recognition. The outdoor spotlight shone on her skin, bleaching her dark wrinkles ... to white ... no longer hers ... morphing into the crepe-like, powdered skin of the old woman's face in the clinic. Lifeless. That gurgle. That haunting, demonic gurgle.

I sprung upright and gasped.

'Radha, are you all right?' Dad asked from across the room.

A sense of despair rose in me. It took a second to find my bearings, through this anxious jumble of past and present.

'Radha?' He held my upper arm. His warm touch grounded me. I breathed deeply, counted to ten. I couldn't lose it, not here. Couldn't lose it at all. I had no pills left to keep me from falling apart.

I clenched my fists, sniffed and ran my tongue over my teeth. Smiled.

'It's nothing. I'm fine,' I said. A small tremble remained in my thighs.

'Are you sure?'

'Don't worry.' I nodded. 'It's silly.' I couldn't tell him. No point dredging up his pain too.

'Is it Manesh?' he asked.

'What? No. Why?'

He threw his hands in the air. 'Mothers always worry.' A sly grin spread across his face. 'He told me he had a girlfriend.'

My tension loosened. 'Did he? What else did he tell you?'

'Not a lot. Her name, Beth. They do drama together. Have you met her?'

I shook my head. 'Only briefly.'

'Must be strange,' he said, narrowing his eyes.

My stomach stirred. This man never missed a thing. 'It is a bit. Something else to get used to, I guess.'

He picked up an oak-framed photo of him and Mum from his desk. 'I wish my mother could've met yours.' He sighed, then surprised me by laughing. He jutted his chin towards his new rug. 'They would've both hated that ...'

I giggled. A welcome release.

He admired his vibrant elephant again. 'You really can find anything online.'

And it struck me: yes, yes you could.

CHAPTER FOURTEEN

After dinner, Arjun sat in the study, headphones plugged into the amp, nodding along to notes that must've sounded good, but were nothing more than annoying plucks of the metal strings to the outside. I pointed at my bag, at my ears and to upstairs and he nodded more vigorously, seeming to understand my message that I couldn't possibly work at the computer there while he was jamming.

I climbed the spiral staircase to the small attic room at the back of the house. This was Manesh's domain. I didn't tend to go in – only for the occasional hoover and whenever we ran out of teaspoons; Manesh having developed an irritating habit of eating yoghurts when doing his homework and leaving the empty pots lying around.

His trumpet rested against the wall, the brass bell facing down inside the velvet-lined case. Odd. I thought he'd gone to band practice. Must be drama tonight, then. I couldn't keep track anymore and he never got around to hanging his S4 itinerary on the cork board in the kitchen like I'd asked.

The main thing was that he wasn't here.

I wondered when he'd practised last. My mother had been on me like a hawk, ensuring I played my cello every day, commenting and correcting, even though she'd never learned music herself. All part of the plan to get me into university. As soon as I passed my grade eight, I was free to give up. The certificate was in the bag, the music discarded like an out-of-date tin. I'd been thrilled not have to do scales anymore or have to lug the huge instrument around even if, over the years, I'd occasionally missed it: the fluid glide of the bow over the fine strings, the deep notes and vibrations rising from between my legs.

I reached over to arrange the trumpet the right side down, fitting it neatly into the case's instrument-shaped hole. Manesh seemed to enjoy his music more than I ever did. Started young. Was more gifted. I pictured his excited face stepping out of school, the outsized case slung over his shoulder. He and his close friend Arthur *pom-pom-pomming* the notes to the Star Wars piece they were learning, as we all walked over to the house for an after-school snack.

Where was Arthur? I tried to think of the last time I'd seen him. Months? It struck me it had been ages since I shared a coffee with his mum too. No time like the present. I grabbed my phone from the back pocket of my jeans and sent her a text. Who knew when she'd answer? She wasn't hugely reliable: leaving you hanging for days, often cancelling on you. I scrolled through the other names in my contact list. How many mums had made promises about getting together? I was sometimes as guilty as they were, and I'd given up. Everyone was so busy; it could take an age to arrange even a quick drink.

I felt a sting of regret. I thought of the small groups of women in hijabs I often saw speed-walking past the house towards the park, chatting away; their arms swaying like synchronised metronomes. They probably met at a fixed time every day yet never ran out of things to say. Would they talk about their problems? I sighed, remembering what I'd come up to the attic for – not the kind problem you could talk to your friends about.

The computer whirred into action at the push of a button. I floated the mouse over the circle containing Manesh's picture. Temptation struck. I could log onto his profile and see what he was up to. I pulled my finger back. Did I even want to know?

He was fifteen and, unlike two years ago when we were aghast to discover he'd spent twenty-eight hours in one week watching complete nonsense on YouTube, he hadn't given us cause to breach his privacy. Besides, he quickly learned to clear his browsing history at every opportunity, so there was probably nothing to see. I made a mental note to do the same.

I logged on as guest, navigated to Google and stared at the search box in the middle of the screen. Where to begin? I typed, buy diazepam online. I stopped an instant before pressing *Enter*. I didn't understand much about technology; but I vaguely knew that all computers could be identified with a type of address made up of numbers. What if they could trace this? Whoever 'they' may be. Best to be safe. I changed the query to: browse internet anonymously.

There was a big square at the top of the results page that showed an image of how to select an incognito page. I followed the instructions and re-typed my original query.

The first results were those of big-brand pharmacies. Not even worth trying; they'd need a prescription. I scrolled further down, past results that would lead you to explanatory pages from the NHS or the FDA, and towards the second and third page of results with web pages I'd never heard of, with headlines of order diazepam today.

I marvelled at how many there were. This was a controlled substance!

I clicked through a few. They looked legitimate, and it was quickly clear by going through the steps to purchase that they insisted on a prescription. But the next one didn't. I felt a quiver in my chest. Could it be this easy? I'd heard other mums talking about getting period-delaying medication directly through online pharmacies, not wanting to face the judgement of their GP. You could get prescription birth control from Superdrug online. I reckoned anything was possible, though remained sceptical.

I pressed to buy a pack of ten, then hesitated. If it was this simple, but Boots wouldn't let you, how would I know if they were fake? They could be placebos or any old noxious powder. Then again, benzodiazepines weren't expensive; why not sell the real deal? I let out a deep breath. Was it worth the risk? A ball of anxiety clumped in my stomach. If I didn't get my pills this way, then how?

I moved to the bottom of the screen to see if there was any information about the company, where they were based. The copyright notice showed a date range of two years. I went back through several other search results checking what appeared to be an indicator of how long the websites had been around.

One site stood out as being slick and professional. Nice blue and black text. Pretty pictures. No big, shouty red letters or exclamation marks. I checked their copyright: seven years. I figured if they hadn't gone out of business yet, losing all their customers for selling crap – or killing them – they must be doing something right.

It displayed photos of two doctors on staff and offered a prescription-writing service. What I needed. I read through the instructions. All you needed to do was fill in a questionnaire. They even used DPD as a courier. Surely DPD wouldn't partner with any old company? I rubbed my cheeks with both hands.

Was this real?

It looked real.

The prices looked all right too. The other, more amateur sites priced their drugs way too low to be trustworthy. Maybe there was some sort of loophole that these doctors had found?

I'd almost convinced myself but I didn't want to get excited just yet. Needed to be careful. I copied the name of the first doctor and opened a new window. I went to the General Medical Council's website and pasted his name into the register. There were no photos, but he was there, operating out of Oxfordshire. An easing wave washed over me. I could do this. All I'd need to do is concoct a name and a good enough story, have it shipped elsewhere, and they'd never work out it was me. There was only one more thing I'd need.

Footsteps sounded behind me, climbing up the stairs. My heart saltoed. I quickly fished a folder out of my bag and clicked the icon for Word. A blank page sprang up. I looked behind me. The top of Arjun's head rose into view. I set about typing. Copying a random sheet of paper from the folder.

'Hey,' he said. 'How are you getting on? You've been up here a while.'

I turned and smiled. Sighed demonstratively. 'Got a lot to do.'

He walked towards me. Heat rose up my neck. There was only a paragraph of writing on the screen. He began massaging me and I squirmed as he kneaded the painful knots.

'What's this?' he asked, resting his chin on the top of my head, running his hand through my hair.

My eyes darted to what I'd been copying. I'd picked up something without looking. What could I say? I pressed my eyes shut and winced as I lied, 'One of the health and safety files was corrupted, and we needed to make some changes. So I've been re-typing policies.' I opened one eye, waiting for a response. Nothing. Opened the other eye. Relaxed my face. Turned to him. My insides trembled, still. 'This is number four.'

He flipped the pages of the big pile with his thumb. 'Oh man, that sounds mind-numbing. Shall I take over?'

I smiled. 'That's kind. But I'm almost done anyway.' His eyebrows knitted together. 'It's dull,' I added. 'Didn't you say there was football you wanted to watch?'

'Fine. I'll leave you to it. See you downstairs.' He gave my shoulders a quick, final squeeze and left.

I doubled over. As my head hung between my knees, my pulse banged like a battered bongo.

Oh my God. That was close.

At least now I had a plan.

CHAPTER FIFTEEN

The next day, I led my root canal patient back to the reception area and handed him over to Pauline to make a new appointment. Dad was sitting in his chair, scribbling in a sudoku book. I went to stand by his side. After a few seconds, I pointed at a blank square. 'That's a six,' I said.

He lifted his head, stared at me firmly. 'I don't need your help.'

I raised my hands up. 'Sor-ree.'

He muttered something ending in 'not an invalid.'

The outgoing patient said goodbye at the door in that begrudging manner I got all too often: men who found I hadn't done a half-bad job for a woman, an Asian one at that.

As it was lunchtime, there would be a bit of a lull before the following one would arrive. I walked over to Pauline and rolled my eyes. 'Dad's in a mood today.'

'Oh? I didn't notice,' she said. 'Maybe it's his blood sugar.'

Two piles of envelopes lay on her desk alongside a few parcels with dental impressions that should go to the lab.

She opened the drawer and fished out a book of postage stamps. She rummaged in the drawer some more and sighed. 'We've run out.'

'Is that the outgoing post?' I asked. It could be my chance. I'd realised, the night before, I needed to get one more thing, if I was to properly cover my tracks when buying the pills. If I was going to do this, I was going to be smart about it. I'd been beating off the headaches and the heart palpitations of withdrawal – that much I coped with. But I yearned to climb off the damned knife's edge I balanced on every day, avoiding extremes, to find an even keel.

I was feeling lighter already, confident there was a way forward.

'I'm going to go in a little while,' she said, sticking the stamps neatly on the top right corner of the envelopes until there were no more.

I slid the whole stack towards me. 'Tell you what. I'll take all this to the post office if you give Dad his lunch.'

Pauline's eyes darted to the front window. It was speckled with fat drops of rain. A brown leaf clung onto the glass, one edge shaking in the wind. 'It's a deal.'

'I'll get my coat,' I said.

Dad didn't notice me leaving, immersed in the number games he insisted kept his brain young.

My hood was blown off my head as I turned into Shields Road. Cold air burrowed inside my collar, causing shivers down my arms. Would November ever end? I adjusted the elastic string to tighten the hood, and endured the wet fur tickling my face as I walked down the steep hill towards Albert Drive.

I normally enjoyed looking up, admiring the ornate, Victorian stonework atop the terraced houses, but I kept my head down, rain still somehow managing to hit me on the chin. I clasped the plastic bag containing the post with both hands.

Up ahead, wrapped-up bodies exited Pollokshields Parish Church; the clock on its pointy, stone spire a cue I didn't have long. I walked past its tall stained-glass windows; their colours dull in this weather. I remembered the Bible stories' vibrant shades of red and yellow casting a dancing light inside, as I'd sat through at least four weddings of friends from high school. Pretty building; drab affairs. At least the evening dos were fun, and I thought of all the times I'd been thrown around to near collapse at the ceilidhs in nearby Sherbrook Castle Hotel. It was where Arjun and I held our wedding too.

My heart warmed as I remembered the joyful chaos of the Scottish reels interspersed with the hilarity of our white friends attempting Indian dances; following our families' leads in shaking their hips and moving their arms to the sky, all the while trying to not slip on the flower petals scattered across the floor.

As I reached the next corner, I veered right into the heart of 'Pollokstan', as unkinder Glasgwegians called it, because of the many shops catering to the local ethnic community. The red and white post office sign up ahead hung alongside those of Pakistani grocers, halal butchers, jewellers bulging with gold chains, and beauty parlours offering intricate henna designs. It was the best place to buy herbs and mangoes, if you could tolerate the judgemental looks from old bearded shopkeepers who preferred to see women veiled.

The glass door to my friend Bela's convenience store was covered in notices; a mix of community events, reminders to apply for benefits and Home Office announcements.

When I walked in, there were two short queues in front of the desk – one for the grocery side and one for the post office. Bela zipped from one side to the other serving her customers, seemingly in an order they deemed acceptable; with just enough polite smiles and chit-chat to avoid grumbles as she stopped to write things down a lot.

I stepped behind a man wearing a white lace skull cap, with not one but two jumbo packs of toilet paper in his arms. I knew this winter's norovirus had hit the Muslim school hard and hoped his family were OK. By the time it was my turn, I was the only one left and I was running out of time. 'Hi, Bela,' I emptied my bag onto the counter.

Her long black hair hung limp around her face, its last two inches frizzy with split ends. The blusher on her cheeks was probably her usual colour but looked stark against the grey hues of her face. I'd never seen her look this bad, and I'd known her nearly all my life.

'Fancy seeing you here,' she said, her smile livening up the dark bags under her eyes. 'Is Pauline not in?'

'She is. But I haven't seen you in a while, so I offered to come. I need ten twelve-packs of second class, please. And to send these off.'

Bela placed the first parcel on the scales. 'Second class too?'

'Yes,' I answered, unsure when I should bring up what I'd come for. 'How've you been?'

She gestured towards the shop. 'It never stops.'

'I know. I'm sorry.' I spotted a load of unopened Walkers crisp boxes still needing to be shelved. Bela and her husband shared the running of the store, and had extended their hours to an exhausting 7 a.m. to 11 p.m. when their twins went to expensive universities down south, having missed out on the increasingly limited free spaces for local kids at the Scottish institutions. Balancing long hours with caring for another adolescent daughter, Bela no longer had time for our coffees and shopping trips. I couldn't blame her, but I missed her. I missed having my friend to confide in, to take the pressure off. Looking around, I knew I couldn't unload on her when she had so much going on. It wouldn't be fair. And would she even understand?

She weighed the third parcel. We were nearing the end of the transaction.

'I also need a prepaid credit card,' I said, my cheeks feeling aflame.

'Oh yeah?' she said, with an amused tone. 'In my experience, the only people who buy prepaid credit cards are up to no good.' She chuckled. Winked. 'Got yourself a lover?'

I forced a laugh out of my dry throat. 'Ha-ha. No. Manesh is going on a school trip and I'd like him to have this for emergencies.'

'Where's he going?'

I pursed my lips while I thought of a plausible but unverifiable story, nerves prickling at the back of my neck. How many more would I need to lie to?

'Up North somewhere. Some Duke of Edinburgh excursion thing. I'm not sure.'

'Good for him. How much?' She held the cellophane-wrapped Mastercard packet up.

'Fifty pounds should be enough.'

'Enough for some smokes and two bottles of Buckfast,' she joked. Our eyes met and this time my laughter was real. That was the Bela I knew, my mischievous-minded, but when push came to shove, completely innocent childhood friend. Our own camping trips had been joyous fiascos of blown-away canvas, burned sausages and sloshy wellies.

I wished I could reach over the counter to hold her, for everything to be bright and simple again – for both of us. Perhaps I should tell her the truth? Maybe over a coffee? What would she think?

I couldn't risk it.

She busied herself at the till. I slid my card in the PIN device.

'You don't want to put that on a credit card,' she warned.

'Why not?'

'It gets counted as a cash advance and they charge interest immediately.' She nodded towards my purse. 'Debit card is OK.'

'Oh.' I took out the bank card and shook my head. 'When did all this get so complicated?'

She exhaled loudly. 'Tell me about it. I'm losing the will to live here. We got this new software system imposed on us by Royal Mail five months ago and I'm still coming to grips with it. The numbers just don't add up sometimes. I've complained but I'm getting sent around in circles.' She picked up a lined A4 notebook with rows of hand-written entries. 'In the meantime, I'm keeping a paper record of every transaction.' She handed me my charged-up credit card, looked up at the white circular clock on the wall and noted my purchase down, in great detail.

The CCTV camera blinked at me from the corner of the shop. A sense of dread surfaced inside.

I shrugged it away. I was being paranoid. People were allowed to buy prepaid credit cards. What could it possibly matter?

I was being paranoid.

'Dinner in five minutes,' I shouted from the kitchen.

Manesh ran down the stairs and joined me, still in his hockey kit from earlier, his fringe sticking upright with dried sweat, like a startled cockatoo. I resisted the temptation to smooth it down. Who knew when he'd last showered? When passing his room, I was either met by a wall of deodorant or the nauseating aroma of old shoe.

He set the table, one place mat at the head and two at each side, the remaining long stretch of dark wood leaving the whole space awkwardly imbalanced. My heart sank as I imagined once again the two-facing-two configuration we might have had. Two growing mouths to feed; two sets of school-day stories to enjoy; two bunches of cuddles. But it wasn't to be.

Arjun sat down at the top. Anyone would think this was some statement about patriarchal rights but in reality, we tended to sit wherever and had only settled into this habit when Manesh's legs grew so long that Arjun complained about having no room. He sniffed. 'Smells good.'

I brought the lamb and sag aloo over. As we plated up, Arjun asked Manesh, 'How are things with Maths?'

'Fine,' he answered. He tore a bit off his naan and scooped the lamb into his mouth. He looked at me with an appreciative nod. I smiled. I'd cooked his favourite specially; it was rare for us to all eat together.

'Was there not some university challenge the teacher wanted you to take part in?' I asked.

'Yes, I handed that in,' Manesh replied, his mouth half-full. 'We'll get the results before the Christmas break.'

'Good,' Arjun said.

We chewed in silence for a while. Then Manesh said, out of nowhere, 'Mum, could we have tacos some day?'

'Tacos? Where did that come from?'

He pricked his fork into the meat. 'I ate some at Beth's house. They're ace.'

My hands dropped to the table, a dizzying tousle of questions running through my mind. Beth's house? When did that happen? Was it that serious? Should I meet her mother?

'I love Mexican too,' Arjun said, clearly oblivious to the enormity of his son's admission. A flash of irritation hit me. How could this man have such a lack of awareness? I watched him tear into his spinach, his strong cheeks moving, merry eyes on his food.

I'd loved his easy-going style, how it balanced my fretfulness. I marvelled at his ability to answer 'nothing' – and mean it – whenever I asked him what he was thinking. Not that I did that very often anymore. What was the point? His reply was always 'nothing', which over time I increasingly interpreted as a general lack of interest; a chosen inability to see what was right in front of his nose.

I pressed my lips together. How could he always seem perfectly happy? Then again, my head would also be considerably emptier – calmer – if I didn't take care of him, Manesh, the clinic, the schoolwork, the recycling, Dad, the mums, you name it. Finding time for bloody leg waxing.

'So?' Manesh asked, his expectant eyes on me.

'Tacos. Right,' I said. I breathed in and gave him a big smile. 'Sure. And maybe Beth would like to try some of my cooking?'

Arjun laughed and nudged Manesh with his elbow. 'You might want to think twice about that, buddy. Trust me. You don't want your Mum cosying up to your girlfriend.'

'That's not fair,' I said.

'I know,' Arjun replied with a playful grin. He tugged gently at my plaited hair. 'I'm only teasing.'

I took my napkin off my lap and folded it beside my plate. The others finished eating while I fumed inside. Was I overreacting? Maybe. It was hard to tell. The blitzes of anger came fast lately. I wondered if it was hormones: the dreaded M word – menopause. And if it was, then what lay ahead? Fatigue, hair loss, cancer? My pulse pounded in my temples. I clasped the solid rim of the table with both hands and exhaled slowly. One ... two ... three.

The men cleared the dishes around me, the subject swiftly changed to the football game about to kick off. Thank goodness; I'd be able to go upstairs unnoticed. My scalp tingled. I let go of the table, feeling a satisfying anticipation that I would shortly have help to find myself on an even keel again. I needed a little more time than I'd thought to get back to being *me*. But I wouldn't buy much, honestly. Just enough.

'Where does this go?' Arjun asked, holding up the large metal grater.

'I'll get it,' I said, and returned it to its cabinet.

The dishwasher stood open. Someone had again put the breakfast bowls where the small plates belonged, taking up more space than they should. And the cutlery was pointing in all directions! I huffed as I rearranged the machine to fit in the items left on the worktop. I banged the door shut with my hip. I washed my hands, visualising my frazzled emotions being pulled down the drain with the water. I dried myself. Yes, nothing more than a little bit of assistance was all I needed.

Soon, the sports commentators' banter sounded from the living room. Arjun came back and fetched a beer from the fridge. As he poured the bottle into a pint glass, he squeezed his eyes and asked. 'Are you OK, Babe? You seem a bit off.'

'Yes. Fine. But please could you put the spoons into the dishwasher the right way up?'

'Sorry.' He lifted his glass as if toasting. 'I promise I'll do better.' He took a sip and turned.

I checked from their doorway if the game had begun, and climbed to the attic. I felt my back pocket for the thin rectangle I'd kept on me all afternoon.

Within seconds of switching on the computer, I opened an incognito window and typed in the online pharmacy's web address. I swithered between getting a pack of ten or twenty – astounded twenty was even on sale. But they were only five-milligram tablets. Hardly anything if taken infrequently, in the grand scheme. I clicked through. A long form popped onto the screen. I'd perused all the questions the night before, so was ready to fill it in.

At the bottom of the page, a red-rimmed section with a DPD logo gave you the option of home delivery or consignment at a local DPD partner shop. I'd already worked out there was no point sending it home; we were never there. And if I sent it to the clinic, Pauline would wonder why I'd used my maiden name. Plus, who knew what kind of markings the box would have that might give away its content? I remembered Tamasi's assistant flirting with the DPD man, and selected the pharmacy. That silly girl wouldn't care less.

First name: Radha. This needed to be my real name as the girl would have heard Tamasi call me by it.

Last name: Khanna. My maiden name. I wasn't stupid. Even though the site looked legit, with a real doctor behind it, I couldn't shake the itching feeling that if it looked too good to be true, it probably was.

And on I went, with a new Gmail address I'd set up that morning on my phone and a fake mobile number – I'd already seen I could opt out of text messages.

There were 800 characters available to list your symptoms, for the medics to review the purchase. Hurrah for my medical degree: I wrote a story that would tease a prescription out of the most tight-fisted of practitioners.

General anxiety, restlessness, exam stress (I'd selected a birthdate that made me twenty-four).

I figured that I should tick Yes to whether I'd been given these pills before – doctors wanted to rule out allergies – but specified it was a while ago. I didn't want them to suspect addiction. Because I wasn't *addicted*.

I looked at the friendly photo of Dr Jones in his white coat as I typed, increasingly confident I'd get what I wanted. The small grey writing underneath suggested approval could be obtained very quickly, at most within twenty-four hours. I felt my whole body relax in expectance of the soothing shroud that would soon envelop me. I'd been lucky to have kept attacks at bay these last few days, hiding in the toilet, cooling myself with icy water or my face pressed against the floor tiles. But things had been relatively calm – I couldn't foresee what was around the corner;

when a patient's fearful stare might topple me back into a nosedive.

I checked my entries for spelling mistakes and pressed Submit.

A green rectangle stretched across the screen. Your order has been approved. Please proceed to payment! I read it twice, stunned. So fast. No way a human looked at that. I chewed my lips. The exclamation mark at the end tugged at my nerves. But as I scrolled to the credit card section, with its official Visa, Mastercard and PayPal logos, I figured I'd come this far and reminded myself they could do a lot with technology nowadays. Robo-doctors were a thing.

I tapped my fingers against my lips. And even if they were crooks, I reasoned with myself, they must surely be a better class of criminal than the pushers in the park. They went through all the trouble of setting up a slick operation – one that had been around seven years. Almost fully convinced I wasn't making a terrible mistake, I entered the credit card information and clicked the mouse one final time. Yes, if they put this amount of money and effort into their snazzy website, and were getting decent prices, why wouldn't they ship genuine product?

CHAPTER SIXTEEN

A small boy lay in my dental chair, his father on a stool in the corner. A few rays of elusive morning sun shone through the window, warming my back. As I recited the status of the kid's teeth to Cheryl to input into the computer, I noticed she was wearing purple socks underneath the mandatory light blue cotton trousers. I made a mental note to talk to her about it later. There was nothing I could do about the alarming growth in tattoos on her arm for fear of breaching employment laws, but I was allowed to insist on her wearing the appropriate uniform – one that sadly couldn't be long-sleeved because of hygiene.

When I was done, Cheryl gave the boy a sticker. He beamed as his dad high-fived him. No sooner were they out the door than the buzzer told me the next one was on the way. I hadn't slept well, and my timekeeping had deteriorated progressively since I'd come in. I calculated that, by now, people were having to wait forty minutes past their appointed time. I'd have to skip lunch again. And do better after; I needed to get to the pharmacy by five. The DPD delivery notification had come!

I quickly binned my gloves and washed my hands in the small sink. Cheryl fetched a new tray of equipment.

She returned, frowning. 'Radha, I don't mean to be a pain, but when are we going to get the steriliser fixed? It makes such a frightening noise that every time I open it, I worry it's going to explode,' she said.

'Sorry. I'll get on it.' I'd forgotten to ask Dad the price of a steriliser. I bet it was a lot, a financial strain we weren't in a good place to afford. I cursed the loan, the renovations we undertook. Could we have spent less? Maybe. The idea had been to invest in a glitzier practice to attract more cosmetic clients, who in turn would bring in more money. It was working so far, but only just. I looked at the wide, double-glazed windows, the intricate cornicing, the glimmering worktop. When it was all completed, after many months, Arjun had lifted me off the ground and twirled me around. It had been a hard slog, but we had our very own practice, the first one where we'd get to work together. Finally.

I remembered the heartache when Arjun left for a post in Hamilton straight after dental school, leaving me in Dundee for another year. Then the great number of interviews I attended in and around Glasgow, the dentists all wondering why my father didn't just hire me. I offered my prepared excuse that Dad's practice only had one surgery, but the opportunity to extend the property had always been there.

I thought of my father sitting outside, in the reception area, reading his book on a makeshift throne, staking his territory even still. I'd wondered more than once whether he genuinely wanted me to earn my stripes in the real world first – make a lion out of a lamb, he'd called it – or whether I'd merely been unwanted, not good enough for the Khanna practice.

I picked a new box of latex gloves from the cupboard and threw the old one in the mixed recycling. I wondered how many pairs I went through over the years; how many times my fingers wriggled into their slots, professionally devoid of jewellery or varnish.

Some interviewers had dared to ask how quickly I planned to have children – that was before I figured out to remove my engagement ring. Nobody wanted to train up someone who'd then disappear for months, if not a year. It wasn't until I met a lovely woman with five kids of her own, that I was hired. Manesh came only two years later but I rewarded her with hard work and loyalty. It was a stroke of luck when she retired at the same time Dad offered us the clinic. I hated letting anybody down.

My phone pinged on the worktop. It was a new ping: one I set up to alert me to emails to the new address. I raced over and saw the email header flash onto the screen.

Your DPD order has been delivered.

My stomach fluttered.

The new patient walked in. I ushered them to the chair and skipped the small talk. I had somewhere to be.

With only ten minutes to spare before closing time, I jogged to the pharmacy. The girl was tidying up a shelf of sinus medication. I looked around, hoping Tamasi continued to uphold the tradition of joint grocery shopping on

Wednesdays with Shalini, even after Mum died. It seemed she did: her raised cubicle was dark.

'I'm here for a parcel,' I said, waving my phone. 'DPD.'

'Wait a second, please.' The girl aligned two more boxes of nasal spray before walking to the counter. She grabbed the thick, black barcode reader and scanned my phone. It beeped. She hardly looked at me. 'Name?'

'Khanna.'

She nodded, put the device down and stepped towards a large blue plastic box. 'Do you know what size it is?' she asked, sighing.

'Not very big,' I said. I was tempted to clarify it would be like the medicine boxes they gave out but chose safer ground. 'Like a brick, at most.'

She lifted a few large parcels out of the box and searched. My chest tightened. Was it not there?

'Aha,' she said, and scanned a bright-orange package before offering it to me. I turned it over in my hands. They'd not put any obvious markings on it identifying the sender, but why the showy colour?

The girl shifted her weight. 'Anything wrong?'

'No, no. Thanks. It's all good,' I said.

In fact, things were more than good.

I walked along the tenements of Glencairn Drive, their low boundary walls flanked at every entrance by what could only be described as stone erections. I needed to go back to the clinic; I left so quickly, there were still cabinets to lock.

I peeled off the wide sticky tape from one side of the parcel. I pushed my thumb inside and pulled open the flap. White miniature balls of stuffing spilled onto the pavement. I flipped the box sideways to stem the flow, and looked around to make sure nobody saw me make a mess. It struck me how well-packaged it was. It bode well. From the top, I started pulling out a smaller box between my thumb and forefinger, high enough to see the blue cursive lettering and braille dots. My heart swelled. I grinned. This was totally the real deal.

Twenty pills. Just like that.

I nearly skipped. I still couldn't believe I got away with it.

CHAPTER SEVENTEEN

Moments later, I felt a presence behind me. Footsteps. More than two people. Accelerating. Near.

Annoyed, I stepped aside to let whoever chose to crowd me on this very wide pavement pass. But rather than pass, one young man slipped in front, facing me. Another stopped at my side. They moved on me like prey and before I knew it, I was hemmed in between them and a tall hedge. I stepped backwards; they moved with me. I clutched the parcel under my arm and slid my hand in the coat pocket with my phone in it. Overhead, dark clouds met to cast a cold shadow over us. Shit. Was I being mugged?

'How are you doing ... Radha?' The muscular young man in front said, seemingly taking pleasure in rolling my name over his tongue. I searched his features, partially hidden under a black baseball cap. Did I know him? Was he a patient? I didn't think so. He looked like a standard, white, working-class boy in his mid-twenties. Wide cheekbones, stubble. Puffer jacket. Tight-fitting jeans. I sensed his companion's threatening breath on me; snapped my head to his side.

He was scrawnier, had a younger face, pockmarked, nastier; a blue cap instead of black. Sinister, hunched shoulders, stomping feet in metal-toed boots, hands in pockets that could've held anything. A knife?

I spotted his overly white trainers. Was it the guys from the park? Had they seen me watching them the other day? But I hadn't done anything. Why were they after a random woman in the park? A sudden chill crept over my neck as it struck me: not random. They knew my name.

'What do you want?' I asked.

'We're customer service,' the smarter-looking one said, and nodded to my package.

The blue-capped mongrel at my side laughed. A nasty hyena shriek. 'Come to ask you a few questions about your satisfaction with your purchase,' he added. His nicotine breath invaded my nose as he shuffle-danced near me. I winced.

I looked around for help, but the streets were quiet, shops still closing up, people not yet returning home from work. 'Leave me alone,' I said, curling away from them.

The fidgety one picked a few of my hairs off my coat. I recoiled, sinking deeper into the prickly hedge. His creeping fingers returned; this time plucked hairs from my head. I flinched. My hand shot up to ease the pain. I stared at him, incredulous, as he wound the strands of hair around the middle three fingers of his left hand. His twisted pillage sickened me.

'Good stuff, innit?' Black Cap's voice hit me from the other side. He jutted his chin towards my parcel.

'How ...' Tears pressed against the back of my eyes. How could they know what was in there?

'Yeah, good stuff, that,' the scrawny one said. 'Wouldn't have thought a nice Indian lady like you would be a customer.' His eyes crawled up and down me as he rubbed his knuckle.

I shook my head. What was all this talk of 'customer'? 'Look, I have no money on me. Let me go, please.'

The broader one stepped back, his hand on his chest in mock shock. 'Are you accusing me of wanting to rob you?' He held his hands as if in prayer. 'No, we're just honest businessmen, aren't we, J?'

This J-person followed his mate's lead in giving me some space, though there remained a jumpy nervousness in his movement that I didn't trust. 'Absolutely. Here to strike a deal.'

I gauged my surroundings. I wouldn't be able to outrun them. 'What deal? What are you talking about? How do you know who I am?'

The one in charge flicked his finger against the box under my arm. Alarm shot through my body. I folded my arms over my breasts, skin crawling from the violation.

'You bought this from my website,' he said, proudly. 'I looked at the name on the order, the address, and a light went on.' He rubbed his chin in exaggerated pensiveness. 'Hmm ... Khanna ... in Pollokshields. And I got to thinking, I know a Khanna – the dentist. We got history. So I wanted to see who'd pick up.'

J spooked me by running his arm past me and pointing to the patch of green opposite the pharmacy behind us. 'We've been sitting on the bench all afternoon waiting for someone to come out of the shop with our orange box.'

'And would you believe it? It's the *new* dentist,' the older said, gesturing towards my uniform trousers. 'Which comes in very, very handy.'

The sky closed in. I was glued to the ground, my mind sparking in all directions. How was it possible they were behind the website? What about that doctor? What could they possibly want? What history could they have with Dad?

'But ... Doctor Jones ...' I stammered.

Both men laughed. Black Cap took a bow. 'In the flesh.' He must've noticed my shock, because he added, 'All right, I'm not the man in the stock photo.' He pointed to his face. 'Though I think there's a resemblance in the cheekbones, don't you?'

'Aye, and I look like a Hollywood movie star,' the other guffawed.

His mate snickered. 'Yeah, the spitting image of Adam Mooney.'

My eyes darted from left to right and back. Why was there nobody around to witness this? To intervene? My knees wobbled. I clenched my pelvis to not pee.

The leader pushed his cap away from his face and leaned in close, his nose thick like a boxer's. I shuddered. 'Here's the thing,' he said. 'We need your clinic as a ... um ... as an occasional place of business.'

'There's no way I can get you drugs,' I said. 'Why the hell do you think I ordered them online?' *So that nobody would know*, I whined inside. So that nobody would bloody know and now this! Who were these guys? What were they going to do to me?

He grinned. 'Calm down. We don't need you for drugs. We got plenty of drugs. Good ones too.'

'You should try the jellies next time.' J said excitedly, as if he was on them – whatever they were.

'We just need a space where we can drop things off and pick things up. Discrete-like,' Black Cap said. 'There's too much heat on us right now. Especially around here. So, what better than a dental clinic with people coming and going all the time?'

'That's insane,' I spat. 'You're criminals.'

'And you're not?'

I felt the blood drain from my face, panic rising within. 'No, I ...'

He gave his pal a bored look. 'Of course not. Nice professional people never do anything wrong. But you *will* do this for me.'

'Why would I?' I said, lifting my head in defiance while trying to control the tremble in my voice, the sensation I was falling into a deep gulf.

He sneered, squeezed his eyes into menacing slits. 'Because you're fucked.'

'What do you mean?' Still none of this made sense. I'd bought the pills online. These guys were real. And here. Knowing me, holding me captive.

J scuffled by my side. Jittery, like a cork ready to pop; his nervy chuckling in stark contrast with the icy calmness that came over his friend with each threatening word he spoke: 'If you don't do as I say, we'll destroy you. Get you struck off for being a pill-popper.'

I nearly collapsed to the ground; steadied myself against the hedge, its leaves spiky, scratching my flesh. They couldn't ... Could they?

Flashes of consequences filled my head: Arjun's clouded face, his shock, his anger, his back as he'd turn away, disgusted. Struck off – I'd have to leave the clinic. I imagined the whispers, my drug use for all to find on the GDC website. My Dad's shame, the dishonour. It would kill him. *I* would kill him.

I breathed in a staggered breath. 'You can't.'

'We can,' the vermin screeched in my ear. I raised my shoulder, cringing.

The other shrugged. 'Easy. A quick letter to the whatsit authority. Raise a bit of suspicion ... They come and investigate and, you know, maybe do a little test.' He looked over at his friend, his wide grin revealing plaque-lined canines. I followed his gaze. J held up his hand in a regal wave, dark strands of my hair wrapped around his sickly white fingers.

My hand shot to my mouth as it hit me. That's why the hairs: the drugs would linger. They'd come up in a test. Shit. They were smart. How could they be so smart? They looked like idiots.

'So,' Black Cap said. He placed his hand on my left shoulder. I shook him off. 'I think we can trust you to act in both our interests. Don't worry, it won't be for long.' He signalled to his mate it was time to go with a jerk of the head. As he and J took a few steps backwards, he said, 'Check your email. We'll be in touch.'

They turned away. The scraggy one clapped the other's back. I watched them until they passed the corner, paralysed by the possibility they might return. I stumbled backwards into the hedge, the held-in sobs given an escape at last. The orange box fell from my hands. Damned box. I counted slowly to ten to stabilise my troubled breaths. I got hot. My fingers tingled. A first flush of anxiety coursed through me.

This is how the attacks always started. I gulped in air. It hurt. I let out a wail.

'Lady, are you OK?' A child's voice. I cocked my head. A small boy held his green scooter, one leg parked on the ground. His mother was a few metres behind him, her pace quickening. I remembered how hard it was to keep up with Manesh. The child's curious eyes bore into me.

I wanted to shout for help. I needed help. But I didn't want to scare the boy. I bit the inside of my lips. What help could the mum offer? Call the police? I had a box of drugs.

I straightened up and did my best to smile. 'I'm OK. Thank you.' His mother reached us, frowning. She grabbed the T-bar on the scooter, clearly ready to drag the boy away from the strange lady.

I forced out an apologetic smile. 'Just a dizzy spell.'

'Come on, baby.' She coaxed the child forward. Doing what any mother would: protect him from the big bad world.

A bad world of my own making.

How was I going to get out of this?

What would happen to me?

To Manesh? Arjun? Dad?

To our life?

A whooshing sound filled my ears, mixing with the hard pounding from my chest. My temples burned. My lungs inflated; only thin air came out. I pulled at my collar. It was coming ... It was coming no matter what.

I scooped up the orange box and lifted the flap. Opened the smaller white package. The rush in my ears was overpowered by the soothing crackle of a breaking blister pack. I could already sense the release to come; that moment my body could start to relax, my mind could be still and no longer fear I would die.

I knew I'd have to stop medicating this way, but for now, I needed this. And with evidence entrenched in my hair for who knows how long, the damage had already been done. One more wouldn't matter.

The blue pill looked real. It all did. And if it was fake, and I died, so be it.

I probably deserved it.

CHAPTER EIGHTEEN

Gunbir

There were three cars in the driveway of the red sandstone house. None of them Radha's. There'd been two others on the street whose owners Gunbir easily identified after all these years. It was so hilly everyone always drove here, even if they all lived nearby. These streets in the exclusive 'Avenues' area changed incline with every intersection. They were too old for that.

Gunbir slid between the parked cars towards the house, running his hand over their bonnets. Two reliable Vauxhalls, one showy Audi. He climbed up the steps decorated with marigold garlands. The loose change from his taxi ride jangled in his pocket.

About to press the doorbell, he adjusted his tie and noticed a defiant muddy leaf stuck to his shoe. He pulled his finger back. He hadn't spent half an hour putting on his best suit to look shabby. The arched porch featured a small stone table with an empty flowerpot. He put his package down and latched on to the rim of the table as he doubled over, with a small groan, bending through his knees to reach the offending, squishy smear.

It took slightly less effort to get back up. He smoothed the hair on the sides of his head and triggered a satisfying *ding-dong* announcing his arrival. He picked up his parcel, gave it a gentle pat and grinned. They were going to be so impressed.

Shalini raised her arms up in delight before wrapping him in a warm embrace, the beaded decorations on her sari scratching against his suit. A blob of black hair was piled on top of her head, held in place with pink floral pins that matched her bright lipstick. Gunbir hoped he didn't have any on his cheek.

She stuck her head out the door. 'Alone?' she asked.

'They'll be on their way.' Gunbir wasn't certain that was accurate. He'd expected Radha to pick him up and give him a lift, but she didn't show and didn't answer her mobile when he called. He'd sat in front of the CCTV since returning from the clinic early afternoon; he knew she left around 5 p.m. One and a half hours ago. Watching Arjun lock up, he worked out what time he'd make it home and called their landline. Manesh picked up. No idea where his mother was. He was only just in from drama. Gunbir's chest swelled with pride at the thought of his grandson on stage. Could he hand the phone to his father? he'd asked.

Arjun had seemed most untroubled at his missing wife. 'She'll show up. Probably caught up somewhere. She wouldn't miss Diwali,' he said, and suggested Gunbir take a taxi. It wouldn't cost a lot.

Shalini led Gunbir to the living room. 'Look who's here!' she said to their assembled friends. Six familiar faces looked up in welcome, more wrinkled and weathered than when this merry band first assembled over forty years ago, but unchanged in terms of how they filled his spirits. Hindu castaways among a Southside ocean of whites, Sikhs and Muslims.

He'd been the only one to come from Africa, and they often teased him that he clung onto their customs a lot more than those who actually grew up in India. He rested his gaze on each of his friends, experiencing a fleeting sadness for the tragedy that turned their even number odd. The reason his was the only child that still came to this long-standing annual event: the unbearable absence of Meena.

'What did you bring?' Namrata asked, her arms reaching towards him. 'Give it here,' she insisted, in defiance of her husband's tiny smack on the thigh. She was too much, sometimes: ebullient, excitable, impatient. But great fun.

'Ah,' Gunbir said, winking. 'Let me show you.' He leaned over and motioned for the others to make space on the coffee table covered in drinks and small plates of nibbles. They smelled delicious. His stomach rumbled. If he hadn't waited to hear from Radha, he could have tucked in already. Where was she?

He pulled his three masterpieces from the box, each carefully wrapped in thin, blue tissue paper he'd found in Meena's gift-wrap drawer. He peeled the first layer away; frowned when two yellow grains of rice fell out.

The 'oohs' and 'ahs' as he presented his rangolis were music to his ears. The multi-coloured swirls of rice had taken an age to stick onto the cardboard templates, and he wanted them to get the attention they deserved. The ever-attentive Tamasi snatched a couple of tea lights from a brass plate adorning a side table and placed them in the centre of his decorations.

He was handed a yellow lassi. Peach. He pulled his trousers up at the knees and sank into a gap created for him in the deep, floral sofa.

Another one of Shalini's joyful exclamations sounded from the entrance hall. He heard the front door shutting, shoes being kicked off. He shifted in his seat to see. Arjun walked into the room holding hands with Radha, the top of Manesh's head visible behind her. The three other aunties jumped up, headed straight for the family, and swallowed them up like a silken tornado.

'We can finally eat,' he heard a deep voice grumble beside him.

Arjun went round the room shaking hands with the men, receiving the odd arm squeeze, while the women fussed over Radha's hair. She'd left it down and it was spun into a single curl that fell on her bare shoulder. Gunbir sighed. So like her mother.

His eyes met hers. He raised an eyebrow. She replied with a smile, furtive, narrow. She averted her sunken eyes and seemed to find succour in being called into the kitchen. Gunbir felt a growing foreboding. When Arjun reached him, Gunbir asked, 'Everything OK?'

'Yes, why?' Arjun searched his face, looking genuinely surprised.

Maybe Gunbir was seeing things. Maybe she was merely tired. It was a lot, working and being a mother. It's what Meena and he had wanted for her – the pinnacle of modernity – but now he wasn't sure. Should he have sold the clinic to someone else?

Sometimes, when he sat in reception and watched her race against the clock, hurry in and out taking care of patients, papers, staff – oh how he didn't miss having staff

– he wondered if he'd made the right decision to pass it on. All he wanted was to take care of her, to see her happy. She'd complained about Arjun working far away. And what better way to fix that than to take over the family business?

They never said – and he would never ask – but he suspected the alterations to the clinic put financial pressure on them. He'd be happy to help. He'd made enough money. Spent nothing. But there was no way to bring it up without the possibility of insult.

His hands rested at the top of his stomach. He knew he added to the stress, but it was Radha who insisted on feeding him lunch every day. He'd gladly give that up, if that made her life easier. Well, maybe not so gladly.

Sensing he was at risk of prying, Gunbir waved Arjun away and replied, 'It's nothing.' But his voice got lost in the female squawks coming from the two aunties surrounding Manesh.

Arjun sniggered as they watched Manesh squirm. He might have outgrown them all and become stick-thin from all the hockey, but there was clearly still enough fat on his cheeks to be pinched. Namrata locked her arm under his and pulled him deeper into the room.

'Isn't he the most handsome boy?' she said to everyone, squeezing his biceps. Manesh stared firmly at his feet. She bumped her shoulder into his arm. 'Stand up straight. Girls like a man who stands up straight.' She giggled. 'Not that I believe you'd have any trouble on that front.'

Radha walked in with a bare tray, presumably to clear the empties. Namrata stroked Manesh's shoulder, oblivious to the discomfort that any fool could sense. 'What are you going to do, Radha, when a young thing steals him away?' she asked.

Radha seemed taken aback for a second. Then she blinked, chuckled and said, 'If she's going to pick up the wet towels off the floor, she can have him.' The room erupted in laughter. Manesh rolled his eyes.

'I think we need to give the dear boy a break,' Gunbir said. 'Come sit by me.' Manesh freed himself from Namrata's grip and obliged instantly. He carved a space among the older men who bunched up without complaint; their oily fingers and crumb-covered lips confirming their number one priority was the food.

Gunbir gobbled up the last of his *gajar ka halwa*, finding the hints of cardamom irresistible. Some dishes he only ever ate on special occasions and this decadent, sweet dessert made with carrots, milk and sugar was one of them. A slice of roasted cashew squeaked between his teeth, releasing its nutty flavour. Heaven. He wondered why Meena hadn't cooked it more often. No shortage of carrots in Scotland.

He took another sip of water and asked Tamasi to refill his glass. How many had he drunk? Enough for his bladder to complain for the umpteenth time. He folded his napkin and excused himself again. When he got up, he was momentarily disoriented and grabbed hold of his chair. Radha's head shot up and she half-rose from her seat. He motioned for her to stay put.

In the toilet, he peed then ran his hands under the tap. The hand soap cast off an overpowering smell of coconut. The room felt too small. He pulled at his collar and cleared his throat. Looked in the mirror. The warm mood lighting made him look blurry. He pulled an eyelid down, revealing a snake's nest of tiny blood vessels through the white.

He knew he'd have to go. He was never comfortable taking his insulin at friends' houses. If nothing else, he wanted to avoid feeding the inexhaustible appetite among old people for talking about their medical problems. He was a diabetic. Big deal. Half of older Asian men lived with diabetes.

He pushed the handle and walked back into the warm hallway. The chatter in the dining room showed no signs of slowing down. As he walked in, he was met by the sight of Radha throwing her head back in laughter. He smiled. That was better. While she gesticulated animatedly at Namrata, a light shone in her eyes once again. Gunbir leaned over Arjun and whispered, 'Would you please take me home?'

Arjun looked at his watch, then turned to Gunbir, his eyebrows folding into a small frown. 'Are you sure?' It only took a mouthed 'please' to make him get up.

The other guests were deep in their conversations. Gunbir patted Arjun's sleeve to signal they should go quietly. The others would understand. It wasn't easy being sixty-seven.

They grabbed their coats and sneaked out, pulling the heavy wooden door silently into the lock behind them. Arjun took a deep breath of the cold outside air and smacked his belly. 'I'm stuffed,' he said, and pointed outwards. 'The car is right around the wall.'

In the confines of the comfy cabin, Arjun asked, 'Too much?'

Gunbir nodded. 'Yes, I need to rest. Please apologise to Shalini when you go back.'

'No worries,' said Arjun as he pressed the start button on his Lexus.

They rode down the hill in silence, Arjun deftly avoiding the ever-expanding craters in the neglected road. The council would patch them up again, at some point, but without a complete resurface, the plentiful rainwater that regularly rushed down would quickly prise the asphalt loose again.

The evening's conversations echoed in Gunbir's mind. News from the multiplicity of children and grandchildren. Promotions, sporting awards, grades. He hadn't heard from London lately so didn't have a lot to contribute.

He'd been shocked to learn of the three men who raided the gurdwara in balaclavas. Possibly attracted by the imposing, gold domes of the Sikh temple, they'd stolen artefacts worth thousands of pounds. Gunbir tisked. What was the world coming to? Crime everywhere.

'Did you hear about the post office?' he asked.

Arjun steered the wheel into Gunbir's street and slowed. 'No, what?'

'Bela got a letter today from Royal Mail. They've been accused of fraud.'

'What? That's ridiculous,' Gunbir said.

'Absolutely. They're the hardest-working couple I've ever met. Poor Bela is beside herself.'

Gunbir shrugged. 'It'll be a mistake. Nobody can possibly think they're guilty.'

The car stopped. Gunbir took off his seat belt. He positioned one hand on his seat and the other on the door handle, readying himself for the moment he'd have to hoist himself out of the vehicle.

'Apparently, they're sending a forensic accountant to go through their books, Arjun said. Can't imagine they'll find anything.'

CHAPTER NINETEEN

The heating in my car seat was on its highest setting, but had only just reached the kind of warmth you could feel through a coat, when we arrived home. It had been kind of Arjun to take Dad home first. I wonder if him being the only one not in a couple made these gatherings hard to bear.

I found the gate dongle in the cup holder and clicked. Arjun brought the car to a standstill at the top of our gravelled drive. I gathered the folds of my sari and stepped out of the car. Cold, wet stones nipped at my feet through my flat sandals.

I rushed inside, leaving Arjun and Manesh to unload the empty plates and pans from the dishes I prepared for the party. I was grateful Shalini washed them before handing them back. Saved me a job. I took off my coat and a shiver ran through me, made worse by an icy blast that blew in through the wide-open front door. The car bleeped as it locked.

Manesh stood in the hall, pots in hand, a dim look on his face – as though he'd forgotten where the kitchen was. The overhead chandelier's light hit him at an angle and reflected off his smooth skin. Something struck me as odd. I stepped closer.

'Did you shave?' I asked.

'Yeah,' Manesh replied, raising his shoulder against my inspection.

A hot, wet film covered my eyes. I missed it. His big milestone.

Arjun walked in, shedding his raincoat.

'Were you aware of this?' I asked.

His face was blank. 'What?'

'Manesh shaved. For the first time.'

'Mum, stop it.' Manesh turned towards the kitchen.

'Yes, I gave him my old electric shaver,' Arjun said.

'Were you there? Did you show him how to use it?'

Arjun slid a hanger into his coat and looked at me with a mocking smile. 'They're pretty self-explanatory, Babe.'

'But ...' I let my head fall.

But what? What would I say? That I would've wanted to go shopping with my son for shaving stuff? That I should've been there when he removed the dark fluff – forever to be replaced with the stubble of a grown man? I knew it was stupid, but I felt thoroughly cheated.

I pinched my lips together, not wanting to cry. This wouldn't have happened with a girl. I would've been there for her first period, teaching her what to do, how to stay clean. I would've been there when she wanted to shave her legs, explaining how careful you needed to be around the ankle. I would've been there when she wanted her ears pierced, helped her choose her first studs. The best gold, to avoid allergies – and because she'd deserve gold. But I never got the chance.

Arjun lifted my chin with his finger. 'What's wrong?' he asked, gazing into my eyes.

I leaned into him. 'My boy is all grown up.'

'Oh, honey,' he said, pulling me close. He kissed the top of my head and rocked me gently.

Manesh slid past us and began climbing the brown-carpeted stairs to his room silently.

'Goodnight to you too.' Arjun shouted sarcastically.

From a distance, Manesh replied, 'Goodnight.'

Arjun squeezed my shoulder and whispered, 'Why don't we go to bed? Tonight's been pretty full-on.' I nodded and he let go.

I took my mobile phone to the study to charge. There was a notification on the screen: a new email in that Gmail account. My heart stuttered. I picked up my phone, hovering my finger over the fingerprint reader at the back, new insight into how I'd head for my ruin only two taps away. What would happen if I ignored it? Deleted it? Pretended I never got it?

'Are you coming?' Arjun's impatient voice drifted in from the hall.

I left the mobile where it was and switched off the downstairs lights before ascending the stairs. While I brushed my teeth next to Arjun, I pondered what he'd say, if he knew what was happening. How he'd react.

He loved me. Would he understand? I imagined sitting him down in the lounge for a talk; pictured his face – curious, at first. His look of disappointment as I told him the truth, how I'd put everything at risk, everything we'd built together. And for what?

I shivered as I thought of him angry, standing up, throwing his hands in the air, pacing, shaking his head as

I confessed to my inadequacy, my deceit, the trap I'd fallen into. I could already feel his hot breath as he'd loom over me, closing me in by grabbing hold of the arms of my chair; his sneer enough to cut me. *'How could you?'* he'd shout. My elbow fell limply as I asked myself that same question.

He spat into the sink. I jumped, let out an awkward laugh.

'I've got that strange super-skinny woman from Giffnock coming in tomorrow,' he said. 'I wonder what she wants this time.' He dried his mouth on the towel. 'Still, it pays the rent, as they say.' He left for the bedroom.

I stared at myself in the mirror, a striped plastic handle sticking out of my frothy lips. A dribble of white ran down my chin. A rock formed in the pit of my stomach. I'd endangered the clinic. He'd never understand. Never forgive.

I spewed the toothpaste from my mouth, moisturised my face, and joined my husband – who could never know – in the bedroom.

Spent, I stood beside my wardrobe and undressed in automatic movements. I felt for the safety pin at my waist that held the blue lace border of my sari's fabric onto the part wound around my middle. I flipped the metal pin open and set it down onto the vanity unit. The safety pin at my shoulder was easier to find but required my arms at a difficult angle to remove. I draped the silk over my arm and twirled to pull free the panel that made up the skirt, then carefully positioned the six metres of pleats over the chair.

Arjun sat upright in bed, watching me take off my petticoat, sleeveless blouse and bra. His eyes glistened in the light from his bedside table and his appreciative smile reassured me that my increasingly rounded curves were still good enough for him. Just as well he couldn't see the decay inside. I covered it with a T-shirt as he slid under the covers.

I clicked off the overhead lamp and got into bed, goose bumps sprouting on my bare skin from the freezing sheets. I wriggled towards him. He instinctively turned to his side. I pressed my body against his back, my knees bent to fit inside the crook of his legs. I couldn't remember when I'd become the big spoon.

A lovely warmth spread across my belly. I wove my arm under his, and he held my hand against his chest. I snuggled against him, breathing in his comforting scent, desperately trying to bury myself in him, inside this duvet cocoon, and forget about the email downstairs. Forget what I'd done, and what I might have to do.

I closed my eyes, but they sprang open as images of the drug pushers haunted me, their fingers pointing in my face, taunting. I sighed. Stirred, tension in my neck. I'd never fall asleep.

A pill would help ...

But I was physically stuck.

And I'd already taken one today. When I'd vowed to reduce. Had to reduce.

Sensing my wakefulness, Arjun let go of my hand and lifted his arm over me, placing his hand on my bum. I felt a caress, a small nudge. I pushed my hips forward; a tingle spread through my groin. Arjun rotated to face me, and we kissed. He parted my legs with his knee and ran his hand over my breast. Softly. I sank back, inviting his touch.

His lips brushed my neck, my chest. He pushed up my T-shirt. He cupped my breasts and licked first one, then the other, his warm tongue hardening my nipples. I ran my fingers through his hair, caressed his shoulder. He slowly travelled down; each move pre-empted by a prickle of anticipatory excitement: my body knew the drill. He'd honed this routine over many years; a flowing dance of fingers and tongues choreographed for my satisfaction.

His breath moistened the skin above my navel. I let out a whimper as his fingers slid easily between my legs, a throbbing pulse beckoning him inside. I closed my eyes, tried to clear my head and give myself into the pleasure, but the menace shot back. I squirmed. Arjun fingered faster. I opened my eyes, he was looking up, grinning. I forced a smile, rubbed his upper arms.

I concentrated on his head between my raised thighs, illuminated only by a streetlamp filtered through our red curtains. I focused on his warm tongue triggering ripples inside me, the arousing pressure of his thumb slipping in and out of me, the pelvic twitches heralding the beginnings of my body's surging response. I moaned, closed my eyes. His arm reached up and squeezed my waist, pushing me into the mattress as his arousal grew. Feeling the weight of his limb, I was suddenly overcome by the sensation of imaginary arms grabbing me from inside the bed, clawing at me, pulling me down. Frightful faces contorted behind my eyelids. I panicked; breathed harder; wriggled. He groaned, encouraged; licked faster; pushed my body down further.

I bolted upright. 'Stop.'

He raised his head, eyebrows raised in surprise, a residual shine across his lips. 'No?'

'I ...' I stroked his face, his neck, his shoulder in one fluid caress. It was him, my Arjun. I should relax ... it was only him. A pang of guilt struck me. He'd done nothing wrong; I couldn't let him feel at fault, inadequate. I sighed softly. 'I want you to take me.'

His expression went from puzzled to gleeful in an instant. I lay back and he flipped to his knees. He entered me delicately and began sliding in and out; his head bent to watch his penetration – one of his favourite parts. As his thrusts grew, he covered me with his full body, his face buried in my neck. His smell grounded me, his familiar sounds a reminder I was safe.

And when, sunken under his weight, with limbs clutching at me, the demons pounced again, I kept my eyes on the ceiling, on the line of white where the light sneaked between the curtains. A sliver of escape.

CHAPTER TWENTY

I turned into the kitchen for breakfast and winced as the halogen spotlights bore into my foggy head. Twice during the night, I woke with a start; heart racing, my chest drenched with sweat. It had taken over an hour each time to fall back to sleep, thoughts of the men, my mistakes, my fate swirling through my head. Puzzling what to do next but finding no way out.

I pulled my cardigan tighter as the chill from the floor tiles travelled through my tights up my legs. I opened the fridge door. It hit against something with a thump. I pulled it back and realised I'd nearly smacked Manesh in the face as he'd simultaneously come in from the utility room.

'Sorry,' I said. He wore his school uniform; red-and-white-striped hockey socks and a small jumble of other clothes in his hands. 'Do you need me to wash that?' I asked.

'All done.' He smiled. 'I got up early.'

'Wow, well done,' I said, conflicting feelings of pride and guilt churning through me. I grabbed the large pot of Greek yoghurt from the top shelf and closed the door. 'Can I make you breakfast?'

He folded his kit on the butcher's block. 'No thanks.'

'But have you eaten?'

'Mum, I'm fine.'

I looked over at the fruit bowl: two kiwis and a bunch of black-speckled bananas that had seen better days. 'At least have some fruit.'

He groaned, grabbed his stuff and left.

My shoulders slumped. Why couldn't I just leave it? He'd even smiled before I went and blew it.

I sliced a banana to stir through my yoghurt. There were three left. I'd make banana bread later. He'd like that.

The clatter of hangers falling to the ground sounded from the hall. Another groan. I lowered my spoon and went to investigate.

A pair of shoes landed at my feet as I entered, seemingly thrown there by Manesh, who sat on the stairs. They were the blue suede ones we got him when he'd discovered Elvis. When was that? Two years ago? I remembered him *huh-huh-huh-ing* for weeks, his lip curled up. Our laughter at his hip spasms. Arjun learned *Jailhouse Rock* on the guitar, for fun.

'What's wrong?' I asked.

He pouted. 'They're too small.'

'That's a shame.' I stood silent for a while, waiting for him to volunteer what he needed them for. Now that he could make his own way to most places – school, hockey, friends' houses – I never knew what was in his social diary anymore. The silence was excruciating. 'Would you like us to go shopping and get new ones?'

Manesh rose; gave the banister a small punch. 'No, the dance is tomorrow. I'll have to wear my school shoes.'

'Is it the school dance?

'Uh-huh.'

I speculated whether he would take Beth but knew better than to ask.

He slipped on his black shoes and tossed his backpack over his shoulder. 'I'm off,' he said, and walked out the door.

I crouched down to pick up the traitorous shoes. I sighed as I held them, soles together, against my chest, and watched Manesh exit our drive through the gate.

Above me, the fire alarm gave a single beep. I looked up. A light flashed red next to the one that was normally green, now off. Must need a new battery. I was sure there'd be one of those square ones in the battery box. It flashed again. A grin crept across my face. Mr Winky. That's what Manesh and I called the fire alarm upstairs. He'd once pointed out the round white unit looked like a face; a curved slit for a smile, two lights for eyes and the test button for a nose.

I thought of how we used to lie on our backs on the landing, sinking into the wool carpet, looking up at the fire alarm. *'Wait for it ... wait for it ...'* Every forty seconds or so, the green light would wink. We'd squeal and wink back – though back then Manesh's winking was a clumsy double-eyed blink.

I scribbled a note for Arjun, whose shower singing echoed all the way here. I didn't have time to fetch the ladder and change the battery myself.

The thing beeped again. I hoped he wouldn't forget. I didn't think I could cope with much more of that. It reminded me of the burglar alarm, which we stopped using years ago. We'd managed to disable the sounds from the control panel but the mandatory, insistent beeping warning you there was only twenty seconds to close the door behind you completely stressed me out.

The image of the two men who accosted me the day before skipped through my mind. Maybe putting the alarm on again wasn't a bad idea. But it would have to be Arjun, since he tended to leave last. And how would I explain my change of mind? My sudden interest in greater security? I checked my watch. Either way, it would have to wait.

I fetched my phone from the study. My stomach twisted: the email notification was still there. I couldn't ignore it much longer. I didn't know what they'd do. But I also couldn't face it. Not yet.

I put on my work trainers, packed my bag and walked down the drive. The opening gates clunked against their posts as I reached the bottom.

Further up, I recognised my neighbour's swishy ponytail, the two young boys at her side. And their pretty grey dog – Blue, was it? He circled them, sniffing their feet. What a tragic story, their mum dying in a car crash. I watched the aunt walk briskly while the boys threw sticks for Blue to fetch. Probably a ruse to delay their journey to school. The smaller one laughed. Blue's tail wagged as he brought the stick back. The older boy shrieked and wiped what must have been a handful of slabber off his trousers.

A mournful sigh escaped me. Maybe I shouldn't have been so strict about not allowing pets. Manesh had been desperate for a dog. Years ago, not a week would pass without yet another of his friends getting a puppy. Almost as if it was an inalienable right, at age seven, to get a pet. Cockapoos and Labradors everywhere. But their mothers had more time than I did – and everyone knew that no matter how earnestly the eager children promised to take care of feeding and walking, it always came down to mum.

It got harder to refuse when his best friend got a pup. Manesh would come home from play dates with Arthur, stuffed full of dumplings and tales of how cute the tiny, fluffy Malteser was. Bursting with pleas: 'Please Mum, can I have one? Just a little one like Arthur's. It would be no bother at all. I could carry it everywhere.' And then the one that punched me in the gut. 'Please Mum, I'd really love one to play with.' Part of me didn't want a pet because I wasn't ready to give up on the idea of a sibling to keep him company. One I was ultimately unable to bear.

Walking behind those joyful boys, I wondered if protecting my feelings and putting my convenience over his wishes had impacted his happiness, made me a bad mum. I wondered if I could still fix it.

CHAPTER TWENTY-ONE

As I walked to work, a splash of blue coloured the sky in the distance, a promise of a brighter day. I crossed the road with a skip between two cars heading into the city centre. Other cars left their hard-conquered parking spots, only to have to pay to park elsewhere and face another tight squeeze when they returned. I sniffed in the cool air, delighted my commute was on foot.

I found myself a little out of breath and realised I must have subconsciously sped up when I'd neared Glencairn – where the men had ensnared me the day before. I banished the memory and focused on the trees, the railings, the cracks in the pavement. Anything.

Through the window of the clinic, I could see Pauline at the desk, speaking into the phone while frowning at the monitor. I was surprised she'd turned off the answer phone already. It was ten minutes to opening.

I stepped inside and mouthed a hello. She raised a finger and hung up.

'Got an emergency patient,' she said. 'Told him he'd have to wait, but he got quite agitated. Said he was in a lot of pain. So I slotted him in at ten twenty.'

'That's going to be a tight squeeze,' I said.

'Yeah, sorry.'

With the additional time pressure, I sailed through my first appointments. Cheryl and I tended to our tasks in a smooth choreography. The buzzer sounded, and we prepped for the next patient.

'Do we know the problem?' Cheryl asked.

'No,' I said. 'Let's hope it's an easy one.'

I leaned over the chair and rubbed the head rest with an antibacterial wipe.

'All right, ladies?' A male voice.

A shiver ran up by back. I spun round. It was him. He wasn't wearing his black cap this time, but it was unmistakably him.

And he was *here*.

I felt a bubble of air catch in my airways. I coughed. I turned to Cheryl, but what could I say?

She answered, 'Good morning,' with an unreasonably friendly smile.

Through the throbbing in my temples, I reminded myself I wouldn't be alone. There was a reason the regulations dictated there should always be a dental nurse in the room: a chaperone for the benefit of vulnerable patients, a witness to those that threatened abuse.

'I hope I'm not late,' the man said. 'I got caught up in my *emails*.' He gave me an insistent look, one eyebrow raised – the one sliced in two by a thick scar.

'On you come,' I said, gesturing towards the chair. 'We're on a schedule.'

'Yeah. I'm a busy man too,' he said, as he hopped on. 'Would have preferred not to have to come. But hey, needs must.'

I avoided his gaze. I pressed on the foot pump to bring him to the right height, intent on maintaining an outward semblance of calm, when my insides were screaming.

'What seems to be the problem?' I asked, as I secured my mask into place and snapped on my gloves. I gauged his movements. Kept an eye on his arms. Would he say something? Surely, he'd know that was stupid. Too many people. And any threats – verbal or otherwise – would be reported.

Cheryl clicked the mouse a few times and grumbled. 'I can't seem to get his file up,' she said. 'Probably not processed yet because he's a new patient.' She slid off her stool and crossed the room. 'Give me two ticks.'

Before I could say anything, do anything – scream – she was out the door. I was stuck to my seat, my limbs leaden.

The man swivelled round to my side, cornering me against the base of the lamp. I rolled my stool back, pulled down my mask. He took my hand. My stomach churned. He squeezed his eyes. 'Why haven't you replied?'

'I—'

He checked the open door. 'Never mind. This is what's going to happen. Tomorrow a friend will bring a package. Orange, but bigger than yours. You leave it at reception and another friend will pick it up a few hours later. Understood?'

'What will it say?' I asked.

'What?'

'On the box.'

He looked incredulous. 'Who cares?'

I pulled my hand loose. 'Well, I have to tell Pauline *something*. She's the one out front.'

'Fine. It'll say ... I dunno. Dave? Yeah. Dave.' He shook his head. 'Happy now?'

Bile burned in my throat. I struggled to keep my tears in. I quickly imagined the exchange, what to say to Pauline. She'd think it so weird, but what else could I do?

'Once,' I said, plucking up all my courage. 'You get to do this once only. Then we're done.'

'Sure, hen,' he chuckled.

Heat rose to my cheeks.

Cheryl walked in. 'All set.' She smiled at him. 'Sorry about that.'

I gave him a warning look. He took up his patient position. 'That's all right. Me and the doctor had a nice wee chat.'

My mask hung under my chin. I pulled it up. 'Open wide.'

'Ah.'

'Ah-ing is not necessary. Please place your hands, palms down, on your legs.' I imagined Cheryl wondering why. I kept my eyes firmly on his mouth as I blew air along his teeth. He flinched. As luck would have it, his second molar, bottom left, was decayed and needed a filling. How else would we have explained his so-called emergency? Cheryl took notes on the system.

I wondered whether he used his own name. Unlikely. Even if he did, what would I do with it? But there was the matter of billing. Did he qualify for free care? It's not like his kind of job was one you'd admit to on a form. Wouldn't put it past criminals to claim benefits while making their money on the side. I made a mental note to take him off the system. The last thing I needed on top of everything else was to be accused of defrauding the NHS.

I got to work on his filling. I didn't offer anything for the pain and began drilling before he knew to ask. His eyes bulged and his hands tugged at his trousers.

Served him right.

CHAPTER TWENTY-TWO

Gunbir

Gunbir sat in front of his screens, a sour taste in his mouth. He didn't like the way that chap grabbed hold of Radha's hand. Good thing the nurse came back when she did. He'd have to remind Radha never to be left alone. Too trusting, that girl. Gunbir, on the other hand, spotted there was something off about the man the second he saw him walk into reception. One of those slouchy walks. The way he loomed over Pauline, checking in. The sneer captured on camera as he stepped inside the surgery.

He switched off the monitor and pushed himself up off the chair. Time to go.

As Gunbir put on his suit jacket and found his shoes at the front door, images of the man's face danced in his consciousness. Not one of his patients, that he could recall. Yet there was something familiar ...

He bent over slowly to tie his laces and shrugged. They all looked alike, the scum of Glasgow. He faced Meena's portrait to say goodbye and it hit him with the ferocity of a heavyweight fighter: was the man one of *them*?

He grabbed hold of the top edge of the bookcase, winded. Were they back?

Why now?

He felt his way along furniture before sinking onto the stairs. He covered his mouth with a trembling hand, furtive fragments of remembrance shooting through his brain. Him and Meena laughing in the car driving home that night.

Like it was yesterday, he felt her hand on his thigh; his hand on hers. Her lingering, loving look as they neared home. He remembered the rain lashing on the windscreen, the wipers distorting streetlights into flickering smears.

Then the thump.

His stomach twisted. Would he ever forget that sickening thump? It was grafted inside him, resurfacing like a reproachful spectre whenever his car jerked to a halt too hard.

Brake – thump. Muscle memory conjuring sound.

Gunbir looked up from the stairs at Meena's portrait. He could still hear her too. The panic in her voice. 'Was that a man?'

He rubbed his thigh, remembering the cold spot on his leg as her hand had shot up to her mouth. His mind was transported into the evening that changed everything.

He heard himself say, 'Stay here.' Felt the upholstery, as he stepped out of the car, in a daze. Where had the man come from? He must've jumped out between parked cars. What now?

A dark shape lay on the ground. Shards of rain cut through the glare of the car's headlights, ascribing movement to where there was none. Gunbir stepped forward, a tense squeeze in his chest.

The man moved. 'Fucking hell. Ow, fuck.'

What a relief. 'I'm so sorry. I'm so sorry. I didn't see you. You're wearing black.' The man flinched and groaned as Gunbir took his arm. 'Here, let me help you.'

Another groan and he was upright. He wobbled on his feet, Gunbir quite unsure if he was injured or drunk – or both.

Meena reversed and parked the car. She got out.

Three more men barrelled down the hill from Titwood park onto the street. They were shouting, but Gunbir's attention was focused on bringing the man to safety on the pavement. Meena stood by with a blanket. Gunbir sat the man down, kneeling into the wet stone to make sure the man's back was balanced against the park railings. 'Tell me where it hurts,' Gunbir said.

'What did you do to my mate, you Paki bastard?' a newcomer shouted.

Meena cowered behind the man they'd struck. He pushed her and the blanket aside. Gunbir gave her a warning look. Stay.

Gunbir got up and wiped the dirt from his wet knees. He put his hands up. 'Now look. Your friend here is fine.'

'Skinny? Oi, Skin, are you all right?' one of the other men asked. Taller. Older, with a white lightning bolt on the side of his head, shaved into his dark hair. The two younger ones sniffed and twitched by his side, eyes darting between Gunbir and this man he figured was the leader.

'Fucking Paki hit me,' Skinny said, hugging himself. 'My fucking arm hurts. I think it's broken!'

The leader stepped forward. 'Seems you hurt my friend,' he said.

'I'm very sorry. He came out of nowhere.' Gunbir noticed one of the human attack dogs was holding his mobile phone. Was he calling the police? Gunbir's insides twisted. What if they tested his eyes? He'd been meaning to have them looked at ... The doctor had warned him the diabetes could affect his vision, but he'd put the optician off.

'I think you owe him an apology,' the leader said, his shoulders seeming broader by the second.

Meena had slipped to safety in the car, an orange flash confirming the doors were locked.

'I ... I have apologised,' Gunbir said. 'We can get him to a doc—'

'Give me your wallet,' the injured man shouted.

'What?'

The leader jutted his chin at his friend. 'You heard him.'

Gunbir took his wallet from the inside pocket of his blue blazer. He opened it and flicked his thumb through the bills. 'I have about two hundred pounds.'

'Throw it over.' The leader pointed at Skinny. Gunbir spotted a tattoo of a spider on the hand.

The injured man fished the notes out and chucked the wallet into a puddle. Gunbir swooped it up in silence, his breathing measured. He wasn't in a position to complain. One bad move and these thugs could do anything, unlikely to care that he and Meena were old – and not actually Pakistani.

One of the younger ones went to help Skinny up. The other approached the leader, his phone still in hand, the flashlight on. He elbowed the main guy, snorted and laughed, sounding like an atonal idiot.

'Right,' Lightning-bolt said. 'That takes care of him. Now what about us?'

Gunbir's felt his heart plummet. What did he mean? They weren't hurt. 'I don't underst—'

'Well.' The leader stepped forward, opening his arms theatrically. 'We've been severely traumatised by this incident, haven't we chaps?'

The three others laughed. 'Yeah, never going to be able to work again, me,' the one without the phone said.

'But I've just given you everything I had.' Gunbir held up his sodden wallet.

The big guy flicked drizzle off his forehead. 'Everything you had *on you*.'

Gunbir's face flushed with anger. What the hell were they up to? 'That's all you'll get from me,' he said, walking slowly towards the car, increasingly convinced these men would never call the police – whatever the circumstances.

'We'll be in touch,' the leader growled.

The donkey held up his phone to face Gunbir and brayed 'Aye, might give you an Oscar for this.'

Adrenaline flew through Gunbir's body: the screen showed the guy had been filming it all. But from when? Gunbir shook. What would it reveal? What had he admitted to? What would they even do with it? Surely there wasn't much to see on such a dark, rainy night? No, it had to be an idle threat. How would they even know who he was?

Sitting on the carpeted steps in the safety of his home, Gunbir trembled with residual adrenaline. The experience still hit him hard today.

He thought back to how he'd joined Meena in the car and driven off, reassuring her that everything would be fine. They'd be OK.

What a fool.

In the days that followed, he was jumpy, felt a presence at every turn. He tortured himself with thoughts of losing his GDC registration for having hit a man – and left. In agitated moments, he calmed himself with the knowledge that the man had been quite happy with the cash. He wasn't even that badly hurt. Probably lied about it all. But was he sure? Perhaps he'd gone to hospital. Perhaps they'd asked how he broke his arm.

After a week or so, he lovingly stroked Meena's shoulder as they sat watching TV on the sofa, confident it had all blown over.

And then they found him.

Gunbir remembered that evening. He'd locked up the clinic and stepped outside. A group of men passed him as he turned into the pavement. He paid them no attention – they were nondescript: tight dark jeans, jackets, baseball caps. Then one of them squawked, 'Hey, it's you. How's the driving old man?' Gunbir's blood had run cold. The scum had walked away backwards, pointing at Gunbir, laughing, making the universal charade gesture for film. 'I've got you,' he shouted.

As he pulled himself up on the banister of his staircase, Gunbir sighed. He dusted the back of his trousers with his hand. If he didn't go to the clinic soon, they'd start wondering where he was.

He scoffed. If he was honest, he'd have to admit it was more likely Pauline and Radha wondered why he was there at all. He knew they put it down to loneliness, an inability to let go of his status, his past. And there was a certain truth to that. But if one of those men was now back …

A shiver ran across his shoulders. A reminder of the horror he and Meena endured three years ago.

At first, someone had merely stood outside the clinic at various points during the day. Unmistakably one of them, a constant reminder he'd been found. Then they stood outside the house, sometimes stepping into the garden through the back gate, intentionally leaving conspicuous footsteps in the mud, so they'd know how close the intruders had come. He instructed Meena to stay inside unless accompanied. He even considered a dog.

The men only stood there, silently taunting them. He and Meena agreed to ignore them. They'd have to go away eventually. Meena suggested the police but what would they complain about: men minding their own business? And in the pit of his stomach, he worried about the video – it could prove he hit a man and bought his silence.

He'd subtly asked Manesh what could happen to a video on the Internet. Some went 'viral', he'd said. Viewed and shared by millions. And all it took was one click to 'upload'.

It was almost a comfort when the lightning-bolt-shaved leader came to see him at last. He'd demanded more money, or else.

'Or else what?' Gunbir had asked.

The man's mouth curled into a wily grin. 'Just, or else.'

'I won't pay you a penny. Because I've seen your type. You'll merely come back for more.'

Gunbir's refusal was met with a deep sigh. Nothing else.

It got unnervingly quiet, after. And then the vandalism began. Small things, really: rubbish tipped into the front yard, a punctured tyre, a scrawl on the wall in marker pen. The worst was the green paint splashed across the clinic window.

The bastards were cunning. They remained perpetually out of sight of the newly installed CCTV cameras, baseball caps obscuring their faces when filmed.

And dear, tenacious Meena cleaned up, having grown to accept the police wouldn't be the answer. 'But what is the answer?' she'd asked, wringing out a stained mop.

'I wish I knew,' he'd said. 'But when you stand up to bullies, they eventually leave you alone.' Wasn't that what they'd taught the kids? The thugs never asked for money again, seemingly enjoying this game of taunting and punishment much more. Gunbir had never understood what they got out of it.

He checked his pockets: keys, wallet, medication. As he stepped out of the house, a freezing wind snaked through his hair and chilled the area under his eye where he'd wiped away a tear. Had he known then what he knew now, he would have given them everything he owned.

'Forgive me,' he mentally whispered to Meena, as he did most days, regret a permanent stain on his heart.

He'd been right; they stopped eventually.

But only after they killed Meena.

His foam-lined shoes cushioned his feet as he strode towards the clinic, convinced more than ever that was where he needed to be. He'd always kept a niggling sense this story wasn't over. He jangled the change in his pocket nervously.

What could the bastards want with Radha?

CHAPTER TWENTY-THREE

A. B. C. D. E. F. G.

I hoped I'd complete the song's twenty seconds of hand washing before the automatic air freshener above the clinic's toilet door squirted its suffocating spray of floral essence into the tiny room. I'd been caught out before; scented particles of sickly sweetness clinging to my hair for hours, making me smell of loo.

I stuck my hands under the insufferably hot hand-dryer, reciting today's growing to-do list in my mind. And there was the drop tomorrow ... I breathed deeply. I'd prepped Pauline with a nonsense story about the parcel. I had done my bit. I could try to forget about it now.

I struggled to draw in air, like sucking a fat milkshake through a straw. Who was I kidding? I'd taken a pill already that morning; I'd been hyperventilating so much. How would I cope tomorrow?

I stepped out into the corridor.

Opposite me, Dad reversed out of the cleaning closet.

'Why are you in there?' I asked.

'You're meant to keep the green mop and the blue mop separate,' he said. 'Someone's put them in the same bucket.' He shook his head with the same disapproving look he'd given me for any grade less than eighty per cent. I instantly felt like that young girl again. He lifted his index finger. 'Completely defies the point of preventing cross-contamination of zones.'

'I'll have a word with the cleaner,' I said.

Dad pursed his lips. 'You do realise the Health Board inspector would've spotted that instantly?'

In my head I shouted, *I do, Dad. I frigging do, because I'm not an idiot. I'm doing the best I can.* But I bit my tongue, grinned meekly. 'You're right. Thank you for pointing it out.'

He clasped his hands behind his back. 'Good, good. How's business?' he asked.

I began walking towards my surgery, hoping he'd get the hint this was not a good time for these kind of questions – not that I invited them at any time. The finances were none of his business. I wished he'd stop worrying about his damned legacy. 'It's fine,' I replied.

He slipped in front of me, slowing my progress. 'Any new patients?'

'One or two.'

'What are they like?' His eyes bore into me. 'Are they ... nice?'

'Nice? Does that matter?' I kept walking. He followed. What on earth did he want? I didn't have time for small talk. Had he run out of sudokus?

At the door to my surgery, I held onto the frame, barring his entry. 'If you want to help, Dad, I'd really appreciate it if you refilled the fishbowl at reception with sample tubes of Colgate. People keep taking more than they should.' He nodded, no doubt recognising the petty theft from his own days. 'In fact, it would be lovely if you generally kept that topped up. The box is in the break room,' I added.

He wavered at my door. What was up with him?

'Everything else OK?' he asked, shuffling one foot.

A flutter crossed my chest. If only he knew. But I couldn't tell him what was going on. I couldn't bear his disapproval, that frown and deep sigh that could hurt more than a punch ever could.

The buzzer sounded; a patient would be along soon. 'Pauline could probably do with some help on the policies,' I offered.

His sombre nod triggered a pang of guilt. He turned to reception.

It was tedious work; beneath him. But what else did he think he could contribute, sitting here every day, watching, confusing patients? Needing to be fed. I clenched and unclenched my fists, trying to temper my irritation.

As I inspected the tools Cheryl laid out for me, I tried to think of ways to occupy him – somewhere else. Maybe Shalini could help? She often joked about how she trained her husband to stay out from under her feet after retirement. And they were all friends ... God, they'd been so close. The four inseparable couples who'd bound their friendship with vivacious soirees and boundless, boisterous fun – making up for each of their tough beginnings.

My hand twitched, thrusting a silver scaler off the tray, as my mind shot to the night of the party. The night I found Mum. The night the laughter died.

CHAPTER TWENTY-FOUR

After the last patient left, I changed into my jeans and stuffed my uniform into a plastic bag to be washed. Arjun would lock up later.

I walked home, opened the front door enough to throw my laundry inside and stepped into the car.

Commuter traffic slowed my drive to the supermarket. I idled behind what must've been at least seven cars at the Helen Street roundabout, most of them looking to access the M8. The red-bricked police station stood on my right, its blue-and-white-checked sign grimy with pollution. I'd never gone inside. And hoped I'd never have to.

They'd come to Dad's house, though, along with the ambulance. Not adding much value, as far as I could see; making a big deal of 'checking the perimeter' and saying there was nothing suspicious. They'd deemed Mum's death an unfortunate fall. Well, duh. Who'd want to murder a sweet, Indian old lady in her own garden?

I remembered my parents' friends at the party jumping to action, despite their shock. Arjun had swiftly taken Manesh as soon as it became clear what had happened.

Shalini quietly cleaned the kitchen as they took Mum away. Tamasi had fussed over Dad, had offered to stay, but he sent her home. He'd sent all of them home. Including me. I could've sworn the uncles held onto their wives just a little more closely than usual as I watched them leave through my tears.

Arjun had waited up for my return. His broken wife.

The next day the aunties had rallied, phoned around to set up a schedule. Dad needed feeding. The house needed cleaning. Flowers needed cutting. Grief needed dealing with.

I was struggling to deal with mine. Left them to it. Felt guilty. Wasn't ready to be helpful, yet wasn't willing to be a burden. It took Namrata phoning me after a few days, saying she was worried about Dad, to get me to find purpose again. And that purpose was to stop Dad watching Mum die on their CCTV.

He was convinced he'd seen something, a hand, a person. Someone who'd pushed Mum. There was nothing there, nothing identifiable. Could've been anything, but he wouldn't be told. He wouldn't accept Mum had merely tripped on the steps. Saw ghosts in every shadow.

I'd been embarrassed when he'd called the police back in. They'd been kind and humoured him; even spent time watching the files, listening to him as he pointed at flecks and flutters on screen.

Privately, the officers and I agreed it was a heartbroken man's quest for a reason. People didn't cope well with senseless accidents, they'd said. They dared say that to me. Me! Who'd just lost her mother. Like I didn't bloody know. I saw her figure everywhere. She shouldn't have died.

To his face they'd been less honest, dismissed his evidence but still left the door open – caused his obsession to continue when they could have set him straight. Idiots.

What did it take to become an officer anyway? They clearly didn't have the damned drugs under control on their patch! And they'd probably look at me and think what a nice lady I was ...

A lead weight pressed on my chest.

I stepped on the accelerator and veered right at the roundabout, arriving at ASDA seemingly along with everybody else in Glasgow.

The only trolley I could get my hands on had a wonky wheel. The refrigerated air stung my cheeks as I entered the supermarket. I gathered my supplies, weaving in and out of the paths of others. There was a scramble at the top of the aisle, while a staffer brought the discounted goods with today's sell-by date.

As I passed the commotion, a man pushed aside a tiny, ancient woman in a trench coat. She stumbled backwards and clung onto my arm. Her wispy white hair brushed my chin. I abandoned my trolley; caught her before she fell. She looked up at me, crinkly skin and watery terror in her eyes. I gasped, nearly let go. My heart raced, my mind a jumble of frightened elderly ladies – dying.

I was overcome by a clinical smell, transported to the old woman on the chair of my practice, persistent beeps, shouts in my ears. A flash of green, the paramedic.

Cold, now. Outside. The paramedic trying to get me to let go as I prop up Mum's lolling head. Her mouth falls open; thick blood oozes down her cheek. Drips. Drips. Onto my hand.

My hand bloody.

The sink pink.

My baby, gone.

'Thank you,' I heard. Whose voice?

I was startled by a grip on my arm. Looked down; adjusted the focus in my eyes. I was in the supermarket, where dropped window cleaner pooled on the floor. Nobody died. The woman was fine. Thank goodness. I balanced her upright and spun round. The man was long gone.

The shock took a while to subside and I wandered along, stressed and befuddled, the lights too bright for my eyes. The front of my trolley scraped against the toilet rolls and three packs flopped to the floor.

'Watch what you're doing,' a stout woman with black hair and terrible roots yelled at me. She shook her head, lips turned down in disgust. I crouched to pick up my mess and heard her mumble, 'Fucking immigrants.'

I gripped the trolley's handle, my eyes fixed on the small assortment of items inside. I probably needed more rice. I probably needed more ketchup, biscuits, peas. Deodorant. But I swerved towards the check-out. I had to get out of there.

I honked at the top of the drive and pressed the button to open the boot. I turned the car off and lifted my handbag onto my lap. I exhaled.

Home.

Manesh came running out the front door. He headed straight for the rear of the car, pulling out the bags of shopping. We brought them in, and he helped me put everything away, conditioned over years into accepting this as a non-negotiable job.

'No biscuits?' he asked.

'I ... I got distracted, Sorry.'

He slipped away as quickly as he'd come.

Arjun was out at a business networking event. I was invited too, but I'd rather have poked my eye with a fork than endure people asking me what it was like to work with my spouse and how I managed my life-work balance again, when this was never asked of Arjun.

Later, as we shared an omelette, I asked Manesh, 'What's tomorrow looking like?'

'It's Friday. Band practice in the morning.' I thought it was as much as I was going to get. Then he asked, 'What about you?'

'Huh?'

'Tomorrow. What are you doing tomorrow?'

The word landed in my stomach like a brick. *Tomorrow.* Handover day. He looked at me expectantly, those beautiful cheekbones, those trusting eyes. That innocence. Innocence I'd lost.

'Oh, the usual,' I said, diverting from the fact it would be anything but. I lifted my fork. 'Do you like the peppers I put in?'

'Yeah. It's nice.'

He helped me clear the dishes. 'Wanna do something?' I asked hopefully.

'I've got a Business test.' He shrugged.

I followed the sound of his footsteps as he climbed the creaky steps to the attic. I put my hands on my hips and looked around the kitchen. I straightened the tea towel on the oven handle. Everything else was fine. I walked to the living room; grabbed a book. The letters were like dots dancing on a page, failing to form words I could absorb. I picked up another. No better. Maybe some TV? I surfed the channels. Didn't laugh at Jimmy Carr – unusual. And I'd lost track of EastEnders years ago. I switched the device off; tapped my fingers on my knees. Looked at my watch. A bad time to call Bela.

It felt as though time was crawling forward, forcing me through a slowed confrontation with what I'd agreed to do. Tomorrow.

I remembered my eyebrow pencil needed sharpening. That was something I could do.

The smell of sweaty feet coming out of Manesh's bedroom had reached an unacceptable level. I stepped inside and opened the window. The airlessness was bad enough, but why did he also insist on keeping his depressing black blinds down?

A few balled-up tissues surrounded the bin, with more inside. I frowned. I didn't remember him having a cold. I hunched over and pulled up the plastic bin liner. I tisked. He shouldn't be harbouring germs in there. I walked over to his bedside table and saw his box of tissues was empty. As I picked it up, I caught sight of something I immediately realised I shouldn't have: pink and lacy and sticking out from under his pillow.

Startled, I dropped the bag. It fell onto my foot, which I promptly lifted up – now realising quite what kind of germs were in there. I laughed at my silly reaction, the spontaneous 'ew' I'd uttered. I laughed even more when I saw the box in my hand had *Mansize* printed all over it.

Of course, he was wanking! He was a healthy fifteen-year-old boy.

I leaned over, holding the box with only two fingers, figuring the best thing I could do was put it back. I was reminded of a time when Arjun and I were still engaged, lying in bed, naked limbs intertwined, sweaty. We'd joked about what we'd do if we ever found porn under our future son's bed. Little did we foresee it would all be on screens nowadays. Arjun's horribly evil answer was to leave it, but to move it just enough that our boy would know we'd seen it.

I shook my head. Mansize. Still funny.

'Mum?' My body stiffened, speared into place by Manesh's voice. 'What are you doing?' he asked.

I turned and held the box behind my back. 'Nothing, darling, I was taking out the rubbish.' I kicked the bag to the door and while his eyes were set on this white lumpy mass rolling along the floor, I threw the incriminating box back.

'Please don't come in here,' he said.

'I understand. You need privacy. But what about—'

'I'll do my own cleaning, Mum.'

I nodded, biting my lip as chuckles still rippled inside.

It didn't feel so funny anymore when he slammed the door in my face.

CHAPTER TWENTY-FIVE

A bounce of the bed shook me awake the next day. A kiss on my cheek. I opened one eye. Arjun lay sideways in his pants, on top of the duvet, smelling of shampoo. 'Hello, gorgeous.'

'Time's it?' I asked, trying to un-scrunch my face against the bright light entering the room from the hallway.

'Seven.'

'Oh.' My mouth was dry.

'Come on, sleepy.' He jumped up, causing another bounce of the mattress that shook my brain.

When did he come in? It must have been late; I'd lain awake for hours. How was he so chipper when I felt like I'd been hit by a truck?

'I brought you these,' he said, plonking his bum back on the bed. In his hand were two treats wrapped in a shiny lilac foil – chocolates, I supposed. 'We each got one at the dinner, but I nicked another one as I thought you'd like it.'

I rose onto my elbows. 'Thank you.'

'Bad night? You were tossing about a lot.'

If only he knew.

If only he knew how I hadn't been able to keep my eyes shut last night, going through all the permutations of what could go wrong today. If only he knew the guilt and disgust I felt at being complicit in the transfer of drugs – my only comfort being that if their pills hadn't killed me, they were probably safe for others. I'd justified to myself that those drugs would make it out onto the street some way, with or without me. I wasn't *adding* to them. I wasn't forcing anyone to take them.

If only he knew how deeply I'd sunk. How little it would take for our whole lives to come crashing down. But he would never know. I would do this one thing and that would be that.

Dread filled my chest. This *one* thing. It would be more than that, no doubt. I'd wracked my brain half the night trying to remember what the man said. *'Until the heat blows over.'*

But after that. After that, we'd be fine. And I would quit the pills because then it would be all over and we could go back to how it was before. I'd only taken a pill last night to sleep better so that I could get through today; today was going to be extra tough. After, I'd come out the other end. I was certain of it. Only harm could come from telling Arjun at this point. Let sleeping dogs lie.

I stroked his wet hair, taking in his handsome face, and smiled. 'Sorry about the tossing.'

He pecked me on the head and got back up. 'No worries. You know me, I sleep through everything.'

It was late morning in the clinic, and there was no sign of them yet. I stuck my head around the corner and checked reception again. Three patients waited, absorbed in their screens. Dad was sitting beside Pauline at the desk, poring over some documentation. At least he was making himself useful.

'Radha, great,' Pauline said, spotting me. 'You've got a few minutes. Do you mind if I take five?'

'That's fine.' I remained standing, my hand resting on the back of the chair Dad was occupying. 'All good?' I asked.

'Seems adequate,' he said. I bit my tongue, recognising this demoralising statement was in fact high up on his praise scale. Any grades under eighty per cent at school had been met with deep-furrowed brows and the question, 'What went wrong?' Never mind that many of my girlfriends consistently got Bs. Those kinds of grades were not adequate. They weren't an option for his children. His children weren't permitted to fail.

I sighed. All that meant, of course, was that when we did fail, we hid it. Like now. I looked at the top of his head – the hair on its sides thinner again; the brown stains on his skin. *You'll never survive knowing what I hid from you*, I thought.

'I think the steriliser maintenance is due,' Dad said, bringing me back to the stresses of every day.

I figured it would explain why the damned machine was making so much noise. 'I'll check the stickers on its side later.'

The frosted glass door opened. A capped man entered with an O-legged swagger and a bright-orange box under his arm. When he looked up, I recognised him as the nervy sidekick of the blackmailer, the man whose dirty business I was now forced to support. He lifted the box towards me with his wiry arms. A small white label on the side. 'Delivery, hen.'

Dad rose from his chair, glowering. What was up with him? He seemed to have purposely positioned his heft between the man and me. I slid my arm past Dad and pointed at the empty side of the desk. 'Just leave it there, please.' There was no way I was touching it.

The thug did as instructed and ambled away again, all the while being stared down by Dad. Why? What did he know? It didn't look like they'd met before: the man completely ignored Dad. I felt my heartbeat speed up. Hadn't the other guy said something about history?

But this wasn't him. And Dad wasn't here when the drug dealer showed up as an emergency, to talk to me. Even if he had been, he wouldn't have heard anything. I searched my brain but no, there was no reason to be suspicious. I was just being paranoid.

'What's up with you?' I asked, as I nudged him back to sitting.

'Don't like the look of that man,' he said. 'What's in the box?'

I hoped the heat in my face didn't show. 'Oh that? It's not for us. I agreed with someone he could have his parcel delivered here.' I leaned over him to check the appointments list and called out the next name.

'Why?' Dad asked as I turned towards the corridor.

'He needed a place. No biggie. It's getting picked up later,' I said. Out of sight, I rolled my eyes. This shit was stressful enough without Dad getting all weird on me.

CHAPTER TWENTY-SIX

The child's crying was excruciating. His shrieks pierced through me like a cold, serrated knife. I pressed my lips together; this was the hardest part of the job.

Two tiny, brownish-cream stumps, with only a spot of remnant enamel, lay blood-rimmed on the tray. The poor little boy's face was flushed, fat tears rolling down his cheeks. I shushed and pulled my mask down to smile and say, 'Only one more. You're doing fantastically well.' His mother held down his flailing legs with all her might. I needed all of mine not to punch her.

No matter how much we sent out letters, no matter how much we educated and encouraged, gave out free stuff, there was always one. Always one neglectful horror of a mother who put fizzy drinks in the baby's bottle, condemning their offspring to a childhood without teeth. 'He doesn't like milk,' they'd argue, and, 'he won't let me brush.' I seethed with fury. There was no excuse.

Cheryl kept the boy's head still, stroking his forehead with her thumbs. I gently held his mouth open with my gloved hand. I closed my eyes, breathed in deeply and pulled the last ravaged tooth out.

I escorted the neglecter out with yet another lecture on how to prevent decay. I caught sight of Arjun's sleek, blue-glazed door and sneered. Easy for him: he didn't need to deal with rotten baby teeth, festering abscesses. He merely had to make people pretty. But then I realised in many ways, the private patients were the most difficult of all: sky-high expectations and the belief that money can trump basic physiology.

Reaching the reception area, I walked in on an Asian man rudely pointing his finger at Pauline, saying, 'I don't believe you.'

Dad reached them before I did and placed his hand on the man's shoulder, who promptly lifted his upper arm and elbowed him aside. 'Stay out of it, old man.'

Propelled by my residual anger at the irresponsible mother, I shouted, 'Stop.' The waiting patients looked up from their devices. I flinched and lowered my voice. 'What is going on?'

Pauline shrunk into her chair. Her chin wobbled. 'He's after a parcel. But it's not here.'

My stomach dropped. Shit. I scanned the desk, the shelves, the windowsill ... Where was it?

'I handed it over,' Dad said.

The man and I simultaneously said, 'What?'

'Pauline was away for a minute. He came in. I asked if I could help and he said he came for the orange box.'

I frowned. Looked at Pauline. What the hell?

The man straightened up, stretched his neck to one side and tugged at the collar of his puffer jacket. He faced Dad square-on. 'So who d'you give it to, old man?'

Blasts of stress ignited inside me, but Dad just smiled benignly and said, 'It was a young man. He looked a lot like you.'

'Like me? Asian?' the guy asked, running his hand over his razor-sculpted hair.

'Yes,' Dad said, a picture of calm.

'Are you sure? Asian?'

'I'd like to think I know my kind,' Dad said, nodding.

The man paced. 'You said young. How young?'

Dad grimaced. 'I'm sorry. When you're my age ...'

'Goddammit!' The man punched the air.

Pauline recoiled. A row of heads by the window popped up again. I stepped in, heart racing. 'You need to go. Now.'

He swayed side-to-side for a moment; his brow furrowed. He dropped his shoulders, appearing to relent. I ushered him to the door, keeping my arms wide around him to ensure he wouldn't veer off course, as he continued to utter a string of curse words under his breath.

I stepped outside with him, and sensing he was already on the back foot, I released my pent-up rage. 'I cannot have this in the clinic. Tell your boss, or whoever, that this is not on. I did my bit. You people obviously screwed up. Sort yourselves out.'

'Whatever, bitch,' he said, and left.

I waited for the shaking in my knees to stop before going back in. Dad stood by the door.

'Are you all right?' he asked.

I squeezed his hand and said, 'Yes. Sorry about all that.'

'I've seen worse.' He breathed deeply, pensive. 'Maybe a good idea not to take in parcels anymore.'

CHAPTER TWENTY-SEVEN

Later, I pressed the top of the dispenser pump on the reception desk and slathered a thick blob of sweet-smelling lotion onto my dry hands. What a day.

'Goodnight, then,' Cheryl said as she and Pauline left. All that remained was to leave a note for Arjun and his nurse that I'd gone. His 5 p.m. was a woman whose veneer had snapped; that would take a while. It didn't matter. I had somewhere to be anyway.

As I slid my left arm through my coat sleeve, the door opened. It was the drug guy. Not a face I'd forget but the pulled-low black cap gave it away first. I froze. My coat dangled off one shoulder and, with the other women gone, I felt exposed in more ways than one. 'What do you want?'

He raised his hands in appeasement. 'Look. Things didn't go well today. That's not good – for either of us.'

I slipped on my other sleeve and stepped forward. 'Stop. You and your ilk have caused enough problems. My husband's at the back.'

'I only need a minute,' he said. He fished his phone from his pocket and turned his cap to face backwards. 'We've got

a problem. No one is admitting to fetching the box. So, the
... the recipient ... thinks we're lying. But here's the thing...'
He swiped his finger across multiple screens. 'I have fucking
proof we dropped it off.' He flipped the phone to show me
a photo taken through the window from outside the clinic,
the bright box clearly visible on Pauline's desk. He lowered
his hand and gave me a sinister look. 'Who took it?'

I wrapped my arms around myself, wondering what
would make him go away, make everything go away. How
did this all go horribly wrong? 'I don't know,' I said. 'An
Asian man.'

He stroked his neck. 'Yeah, so I heard. And that's good.'
He lifted his phone up again. 'Because that means it's
someone on the other side. Have a look at these.' He took a
step forward; I took one back. 'OK, fine,' he said, and flung
the phone towards me. It nearly slipped from my lotioned
hands as I caught it.

The screen was full of thumbnails of Asian men. 'What
is this?' I asked.

'You need to tell me who's the guy that took the parcel.'

'I wasn't here. My fa—' My heart skipped. No. 'My
receptionist was away for a minute and an older gentleman
in the waiting room helped your man who came in.'

The drug dealer frowned. 'Why the hell ...?'

'Who knows?' I said, as casually as I could. 'Retired
people. They meddle. I'm sure he was only trying to help.
But he was adamant the man asked specifically for the box
and gave the name on the label.' I felt a flutter in my chest.
I had no idea if this was true or what was on the label, but
I needed him gone. This was their problem, not mine. I'd
bloody done my bit.

He seemed to mull this over. 'That's new information. Means they're definitely lying, if they knew the code name,' he said. I didn't like the way he was speaking to me, like I was one of the team. He snatched the phone from my hands and tapped it against his chin, thinking. 'The old man. Can you show him these pictures and ask him who it was?'

'Are you crazy? He's got nothing to do with this.'

'You're right. Shit.' He paced, looked around. 'What about the CCTV?' He pointed up.

'What?' I followed his finger to the camera. 'Oh.' Fragments of conflicting thoughts collided in my mind: I could help, but would that help me? It would make him go away, but they'd see Dad handing over the box, maybe figure out who he was, and I wasn't about to put him at risk of anything. Yet if they found who from their gang had lied, they'd leave me alone. What would they do to that person? On top of everything else I'd done, I didn't want blood on my hands.

'That's only there as a deterrent, sorry.' I felt a lump in my stomach. Was suggesting our CCTV was fake a good idea? What if they broke in?

'Fuck's sake.' He spun towards the door. Holding onto the handle, he said, 'There's another drop off next week. I'll tell you what day. I have to deal with these lying cunts first.'

I took three steps forward, ready to lock the door behind him, eager to erase him from my life – to whatever extent I could.

Halfway out, he turned to me again. 'Find a fucking better place to put the box next time.'

The radio blared inside the car. I was alone, safe. I needed this: 80s anthems that banished the searing self-recriminations that infected my mind; provided an escape from the constant worry, the exhausting search for a solution that simply wasn't there. Today had been a shit show. I'd messed up. Badly. And I wished I could keep on driving forever.

On the M74, I passed the large sign for Flip Out, the trampoline hall where we held Manesh's thirteenth birthday party. As I thought of his flushed and sweaty head when he ran up to tell me this was 'the best party ever', *Sweet Child of Mine* came on and it took an effort to not break down and cry. I'd make mistakes with him too. I shifted in my seat and steered purposefully towards the left lane. At least I could make up for one thing.

The sat nav instructed me to take the Cambuslang exit and turn right at the bottom. I recognised the area from playdates; plenty of families from school lived here. A few streets further along I turned right again into a narrow residential road. A tile with *29* on it told me I had reached my destination. I took my handbag from the footwell onto my lap.

The property looked like a perfectly ordinary family home: a bay-windowed, two-storey semi. I rang the bell. A meaty smell hit my nose as the door opened. Shoes cluttered the entrance. The rug had been disturbed. I looked up; the rug's folds mirrored in the creases on the owner's harassed face.

'Hi,' I said

'You made it.' She wrapped her house coat tighter against the cold. 'Come in, come in.'

I followed her into the narrow corridor. 'I'm glad you accepted my offer,' I said.

'Are you kidding?' she replied. 'I don't know what got into me. What was I thinking? You're seriously saving my life.'

CHAPTER TWENTY-EIGHT

I was buzzing with anticipation the whole way home. The best feeling I'd had in months. I bounded up the steps to our front door. The outdoor spots on the garage sprang on. I slid my key into the lock and shoved the sticky door open.

'Manesh!' I shouted. I couldn't wait to see his face.

Arjun stepped out of the study. 'Ah, there you are.'

'Where's Manesh?'

He shrugged. 'Not sure. Out.'

'Oh. I was hoping he'd be home.' I tried not to look too disappointed. I reminded myself the surprise would keep. 'Come give me a hand. You'll never guess what I got.'

Arjun's steps crunched on the drive. I pressed the lower button on the car fob. The grey metallic boot opened automatically.

'Oh my G—' Arjun laughed so hard he bent over.

The puppy yapped excitedly.

I joined in the laughter.

Then Arjun shook his head and raised his eyebrows. He sported that expression he always used when I did something silly, like buying the completely wrong size of clothing online or accidentally using salt in a dish instead of sugar: an unsettling mix of mirth and judgement. 'What's got into you, Babe?'

The stout brown-and-white spaniel licked my motionless hand through the bars on his crate. I picked up the box overflowing with bedding, bowls, and who knows what else. The previous owner passed on everything I might need – probably more.

'I got a puppy,' I said, as though that was a perfectly normal thing to do.

He carried the dog inside, then crouched down to let the little thing sniff his hands. 'He's cute, but this is incredibly irresponsible. It's really something you should have discussed with me.' His knees creaked as he rose. 'What is this about? This isn't like you. You've been really out of sorts.'

There was so much I couldn't tell him, so much I needed to keep hidden because I couldn't imagine him ever forgiving me for what I'd done. But this I could explain; this didn't make me a bad person or stupid or crazy – merely human. 'I miss Manesh.'

A look of concern crossed his face. 'What do you mean?'

I bit my lip. 'I just ... I feel I'm losing him. Like I'm not needed anymore.'

'Oh, honey.' He placed an arm around my shoulders and squeezed me tight. 'And you thought a puppy would help?'

I sensed his smirk; buried my face in my hands. 'Maybe it was stupid.'

He sighed. 'OK. Well. It's here now.' He unbolted the cage and tucked his hand under the dog's bum as he fished him out. 'Who's this, then?'

'He's a King Charles spaniel. His name is Sparky.'

'Sparky, huh? Where did you get him?'

'Another mum at school. I helped her out. She ... she couldn't take care of him well enough.'

'I'm not surprised.' Arjun handed him over. 'I mean, never mind the feeding – who's going to walk him?'

'I was hoping Manesh would.'

Arjun humphed. 'Good luck with that.' He shook his head. 'Seriously, Radha. What the hell? We're too busy.'

'But we're home at night and in the mornings. He doesn't need much walking. She said ten minutes for every month of his life. So only sixty minutes a day – and split into two.' A chill fell over the room as Arjun seemed to make the mental calculation I was trying not to highlight: at one year old he'd need two hours. 'And he's not a puppy-puppy anymore, he's had some training. Surely it can't be too hard? We could always get help, a walker.'

Arjun rolled his eyes. 'Oh great, more staff.'

He must've seen my face fall and added, 'Listen, we've both been very preoccupied lately. Why don't we go out and have a nice dinner?'

I nuzzled Sparky. 'I'd like that.'

'Great, I'll book it.'

'OK,' I said, somewhat surprised. This kind of thing usually fell to me to arrange. Sparky wriggled. I had enough on my plate. Maybe I should give Arjun the benefit of the doubt?

As he headed towards his study, he turned and asked, 'By the way, did you check the CCTV in reception? See if Pauline was abusing the prescription pads?'

I felt a rumbling panic. I steadied myself by holding the puppy close to my chest, our heartbeats thumping against each other. 'Yes. I did. Nothing to see, thankfully.'

'Hmm.'

'I bet it was nothing more than an NHS error. Must happen all the time,' I said with my best attempt at nonchalance.

'Speaking of horrible mistakes ... have you heard anything from Bela?'

'What do you mean?'

'About the fraud thing,' he said.

'What fraud thing?' Alarm shot through me.

He scratched his head. 'Did I not tell you after Diwali? Sorry. It seems they've been accused of fraud by Royal Mail.'

Every muscle in my body jumped, primed to save my friend. 'What? That's insane! What are they saying?'

'That's all I picked up. Sorry.'

Sorry? That's it? That's all he had to say? 'I have to speak to her.'

I placed Sparky on the floor. He sniffed at my shoes. My phone was in my handbag. I composed a new text three times, settling on something simple.

I've only just heard the news. I'll come see you tomorrow. Radha X

Poor Bela.

I glanced at my SMS history and noticed there was still no reply from Arthur's mother. Typical. Then again, we were all busy, caring for others. And now I owned a dog too. I hoped I'd done the right thing, as I watched Sparky slipping on the marbled floor tiles.

The front door opened. Manesh, earphones in, head bopping, oblivious.

I grabbed the dog and hid him inside my cardigan.

Manesh nearly stumbled over the cage. He looked up, saw me and removed the white gadget from his right ear. 'What's this?'

'I've got a surprise,' I said, my grin as wide as could be. I uncovered Sparky, who blinked, his black eyes adjusting to the light once more.

Manesh laughed. 'Mum, what ...?'

I offered him the puppy. 'He's for you.'

His smile fell. 'For me?' He seemed reluctant when he took Sparky from me. Why wasn't he happier?

'You always wanted a puppy,' I said. 'You used to go on and on about it.'

He let his two bags slide off his shoulder onto the ground. 'That was years ago, in primary school.'

'So he's a little late,' I quipped, uneasily.

He stroked the red-brown fur on Sparky's ears. I hoped the white fluffy snout would capture Manesh's heart, but he said, 'I also wanted a Monster Truck lunchbox, but I wouldn't want one now.' He handed him back. 'He's lovely, Mum, but you can't make him my responsibility. I haven't got time.' He shook his head as he took off his coat and headed for the cloakroom with all his stuff, leaving me standing alone, unheeded, full of dread.

If this hadn't worked, would anything?

CHAPTER TWENTY-NINE

The next morning, I walked down the stairs, the spongy carpet absorbing my languid steps. Thank goodness it was Saturday. I'd woken twice to Sparky's whining, and spent half the night helping him settle in the utility room. The previous owner had given me a big folder with training instructions the breeder had given her, but I'd been too wiped out to look it over beyond the first three sections scored with red exclamation points.

I'd learned through practice that it helped when I left the crate door open and, after a lack of activity on the potty pad, I reassured myself he'd stay put, snuggled in his brand-new, round, tartan bed.

The downstairs light was already on. Clattering came from the cloakroom. Manesh rushed out and I was met by a cloud of Lynx. He wore his orange hockey shirt and white shorts. What time was it?

He spotted me. 'Have you seen my shin pads?'

'What?'

'My shin pads. I've got a game,' he said, practically walking in circles, hands in his wet hair.

'Not in your bag?' I asked.

'I've looked in my bag.'

'What about your room?'

'I've checked my room.' He rolled his eyes.

At me.

This had nothing to do with me. But, oh, it's always the mum's fault.

'Maybe if you kept them in the utility room where they belong—' I started.

'Argh.' He struck the wall in frustration.

I felt a tug of guilt. Snapping wouldn't help. And if they were at the rear of the house, then at least – for once – he would've done the right thing. I took a deep breath. 'Fine, I'll help you look.'

He followed me to the kitchen. Sparky's crate formed an odd dark shape through the glazed door to the utility room. I gently pressed the door handle. The dog's little head sprung up from his bed. Bless him. He'd slept.

Manesh stormed past me towards the shelving unit, and rummaged through the sports equipment, a shower of trainers falling from above.

I knelt and patted the floor, coaxing the pup to come out. As he rose, I saw a glint of something yellow.

Manesh shouted, 'I've found *one*.'

No sooner had I said, 'Then the other should be there too,' that I knew I was wrong. Behind Sparky's hind legs and wagging tail lay a damp-looking shin guard, pockmarked by puppy teeth.

'Oh God,' I heard Manesh say beside me. I reached inside and retrieved the shin guard with two fingers, avoiding the drool marks.

'Sorry,' I said. I got up with the dog under one arm and walked to the utility sink. As I turned on the tap to rinse the saliva off, I felt Sparky shiver and a warm trickle run down my hips.

I closed my eyes and sighed. What the hell had I done?

CHAPTER THIRTY

Gunbir

Gunbir placed his coffee cup in the sink to wash later. He never bothered with the dishwasher anymore. When you used as little crockery as he did, the machine merely became a vehicle for the cultivation of germs, whose yeasty stench hit you in the face every time you opened the door.

He checked his watch. Radha would be here any minute to examine his feet. He walked back to his desk and turned off his CCTV monitor. She'd long stopped asking why he felt compelled to always watch what was going on outside. 'Just because' wasn't really a satisfying answer, but it was the only answer he ever gave. What good would it do to tell her what went on all those years ago? Why they were targeted by the vandals at the clinic. She believed they'd been junkies looking for drugs. He let her.

After a while, he chose to pretend he wasn't watching anymore. It was easier. Particularly now, with the clinic online again for some obscure reason. He'd seen enough to feel unsettled and supposed she wouldn't want him to ask, let alone watch – and that was without her knowing about the hidden camera in the surgery!

He heard the key turn in the lock and rose to greet her at the door. As he walked, he adjusted his belt, slipping the thin, metal bar into a fresh hole. He stuck his tongue out as he struggled with pushing what was by now a very short end of brown leather through the rest of the buckle.

A brown-and-white ball of fur pounced on his feet, surprising him. He jumped back; heard Radha say, 'Sparky, come here.'

It took Gunbir a split second to realise she was talking to a dog. A puppy! An absolutely adorable little round-headed creature that sniffed his slippers, tail wagging as though it had discovered the world's biggest treasure.

'You got a puppy?' he asked.

'Last night,' she replied.

Sparky raced between stacks of boxes in the hallway, his long lead like a golden thread through a labyrinth. Radha pulled him back. The tautened lead sliced through a pile of books, the top half cascading to the floor. 'Sparky, stop it,' she said.

'Ach, it's OK,' Gunbir said. 'Let him loose.' He bent his stiff knees enough to pick the beastie up. It fit perfectly in the crook of his arm, sitting atop his stomach as if on a display shelf.

'And have him make even more of a mess? Honestly, Dad. When are you going to let me sort all this out?'

Sparky buried his nose in the fold of Gunbir's armpit. It tickled. 'Leave it, Radha. This isn't your job.'

'But I don't mind. I could—'

'You have enough to do.' Gunbir shook his head as he scratched behind Sparky's ear and sighed. Did they really need to go through this every time?

'Well, you can't—'

'I can do what I want. I'm a grown man. This is my house.'

Radha's face fell into a sulk. Her protruding lower lip reminded him of when she was a teenager, forever having strops when he offered her solutions to her problems. She'd complain about something; he'd suggest an approach to take. It seemed like the right thing to do. But she'd reject it and moan about a new thing. It made no sense, and his attempts to highlight the lack of consistency or logic in her protestations only seemed to upset her more. Meena would take her away, stroking her long, dark hair. Next thing he knew, Radha would be bounding up the stairs again.

Meena had once explained Radha wasn't looking for solutions; she merely wanted sympathy. A twitch of sadness tugged inside. If only Meena were here ... Maybe Radha would open up to her. There was clearly something up, something unarguably not right. But experience had shown there was nothing to gain from him probing – quite the opposite. Gunbir offered her the puppy instead.

She smiled. 'You're right, Dad. I'm sorry.'

He nodded then turned to the lounge. His comfy chair beckoned. 'All right, let's get these feet done, shall we?'

Radha put the dog down. 'I'll fetch the bowl and a fresh towel,' she said, and headed for the kitchen.

As soon as he sat down, Sparky's little white paws scratched at Gunbir's trousers as he hopped on his hind legs, trying to climb up. Gunbir moved to pick him up but found he couldn't fold that way anymore. He chuckled. 'It's the floor for you, little one.'

Radha returned with a green chequered towel thrown over her shoulder, and the grey, oval bowl held in her hands, walking carefully as Sparky danced around her legs. 'Your milk is out of date.'

'Why are you looking in my fridge?'

'For exactly that reason,' she said, sternly, and he had to concede on that point. 'And what's with all the insulin?' she asked.

'I'm getting as much as they'll give me. I don't want to run out.'

'You know it goes off, right?'

Gunbir frowned. 'I am aware of that. I was a medical professional for many more years than you, lest you forget. But I've seen enough political upheaval and disease to believe you can never be too prepared.'

Radha sighed. 'Fair enough.'

He leaned back into his chair, satisfied with the point he'd scored.

CHAPTER THIRTY-ONE

After seeing Dad, I walked home to drop Sparky off, forced to stop at what seemed like every tree and streetlamp for a sniff and a few legs up with little to show for it.

Dad had offered to walk him but with his middle toe still numb, we couldn't risk putting excessive pressure on it. Seeing the disappointment on his face made my heart sink. But it was the right thing to do – and he knew it, however much he wanted to believe he was still a fit man.

Bela had picked Ollie's for our coffee, and I found her sitting on the yellow, rounded bench at the window when I entered. She looked haggard; old for the first time. A scattering of frizzy, grey strands of hair sprouted untamed from her head.

I took her into my arms, and judging from the duration of our hug, it was one she desperately needed.

'Hey, thanks for coming,' she said.

'Of course.'

The waitress was at the coffee machine, her back to us. Other patrons swayed and craned their necks to catch her attention. I figured our order might be a while. At least the moreish cube of fudge that came with the hot drinks was worth the wait.

'What's going on?' I asked.

Bela rubbed her forehead with her hand, as though ironing out the folds of worry. 'I thought something wasn't right with the new software Royal Mail gave us for the post office side of the shop. Remember, I even told you? I contacted them but I kept getting put on hold. And then they'd say to try a million things, but we could never replicate the problem. So they argued there wasn't one.'

'How frustrating,' I said. I looked around for the waitress. Bela deserved a coffee; she kept rearranging the artificial flower in its vase.

'They sent emails saying how they were struggling to cope with the volume of queries and to please be patient. So I am sure it wasn't only us. It has to be their fault but—'

'What can I get you?' the waitress interrupted.

Bela gave a thin smile. 'Cappuccino.'

'Me too.' I squeezed her hand. 'But what?'

'They're accusing us of fraud.'

'Oh, Bela, that's horrible.'

'I know, right? Actual fraud!' She shook her head. 'Like we're criminals. I mean, come on. People like you and me? We spend our lives being the bloody good girls and this is what you get.'

I diverted my eyes, turned to face a ray of sun to have an excuse for the flush that was spreading across my cheeks. Good girls ... If only she knew. I shuddered, thinking how little it took to ruin a life: one misunderstanding, one mistake, one misstep. One person watching – and someone was always watching. I could still hear the bastard's voice when he caught me in his trap: *Easy. A quick letter to the whatsit authority.'* He'd have worked out by now it was called the GDC.

'It's outrageous,' I said, and meant it, fully trusting that she would never commit a crime. It had to be an error. A pinch in my chest reminded me she'd probably swear the same about me. The coffees arrived. 'I'm terribly sorry this is happening. How are you two coping?'

'Well, you know what men are like ...' She smirked. 'Means I'm dealing with it while he rationalises – thinks it will somehow go away by itself.'

I raised my cup in a toast. 'I hear you.'

Bela smirked. 'Well, thank heavens I started keeping paper records of all the transactions. I'm getting them copied and shipped over ASAP so that every auditor, detective or whoever they're putting on it can see that we are not thieves. And ...' She wagged her finger. 'And if they think I've forged those then they are welcome to check the bloody CCTV and rewind past every person buying something from us in the last two months.'

My neck tingled. That footage contained me buying the prepaid credit card. What if the amounts didn't match up? Would they need to come speak with me? Verify the purchase? Would they ask what it was for? Check the online purchase I subsequently made with the card?

'Radha?' Bela waved her hand in front of my face. 'Yoo-hoo. Is my impending demise boring you?'

'Oh, no. Of course not. Sorry. I'm just incredibly angry for you.' I held up my hands and curved my fingers as if to strangle someone. 'I was fantasising what I'll do if I ever lay my hands on them.'

'Ha. Like you could ever hurt someone.'

CHAPTER THIRTY-TWO

Sparky lunged out of the front door when I came home with the afternoon's shopping. I dumped the four bags on the stone steps and sprinted after him, his wagging white tail leading the way like a tour guide's flag.

My ankles buckled as I ran across the lumpy, mossy lawn and I fell flat on my bum. Sparky raced back and jumped in my arms. I tried to keep my face out of reach but eventually relented to his over-enthusiastic tongue. Who knew it could tickle so? I burst into a big, freeing laugh. A laugh that made my stomach rise and drop like I hadn't a care in the world, as I lay on the grass being attacked by a fluffy drool-monster.

The surprise on Manesh's face when he found me made me laugh even more, triggering him as well. Soon, Manesh and I were both howling – accompanied by Sparky's excited yaps – wiping tears from our eyes and grass from my back. I wanted time to stop, right then. Forever.

'You're all dirty, Mum.'

I shrugged. 'What's more laundry?' I got up. 'Come help me get the bags in.'

The puppy followed us, more sluggish now. I picked him up and placed him in his bed in the utility room. 'Time for a little rest.' His big black eyes shut almost instantly. It was easy to forget he was only a baby.

'I'm glad you're home,' Manesh said as he unpacked.

'Oh?'

'I need a lift to the Citz. We have rehearsals all afternoon, and my props are too big to carry on my bike.' He pointed to a collection of items in the corner: ancient gardening equipment from the shed, an old-style, black telephone seemingly made of duct tape, and a papier-mâché globe.

'Did you make those?' I asked.

'Yes. What do you think?' His face beamed in anticipation.

My heart swelled. He wanted my opinion! 'I think it's wonderful. I love your commitment to drama both at school and at the Citizen's theatre. I'm forever amazed that you have the confidence to be on stage like that. I can't imagine how—'

'OK, OK, Mum. I get it: you're proud.'

This was already the longest conversation we'd had in ages and I hoped I hadn't blown it. 'I am. If that's all right?'

'Yeah,' he said, shuffling his feet. 'Just, you know ... maybe not *that* much.'

'Fine. I will be averagely proud.' I put away the few groceries I'd bought. 'When will we be able to buy tickets? I'm sure Grandad would love to come.'

'They'll be telling us that today, I think.'

I folded the plastic bags into squares and tucked them into a bigger bag in the larder. 'What time do I need to take you?'

He grimaced apologetically. 'Um ... now?'

There was something eerie about how silent the cabin of this car was. I noticed it when Arjun had first brought the upgrade home. Maybe it was the quietness of its electric engine or because the thick leather seats absorbed any sound. In a possible case of silence begetting silence, we all seemed to have stopped talking while driving places. I watched Manesh look out the window from the corner of my eye; cursed the muting car for ruining our earlier moment.

Cathcart Road was busier than expected for a Saturday afternoon, but all was explained when I spotted the beer-lugging Celtic supporters milling around the green-and-white fronted Brazen Head pub. They were all in T-shirts; their loosely wrapped club scarves the only nod to it being November.

I signalled to turn right. Manesh sat up. 'No, keep going straight, Mum.'

'But the parking's at—'

'Please drop me out front.' When he saw me hesitate, he added, 'The parking at the back is tight. There will be a lot of people.'

'Fine.'

We drove the last hundred metres down Gorbals Street, and I slowed down as the squat, brick theatre came into view. I checked the rear-view mirror and swerved into the bus lane.

'Bye,' Manesh said, as he jumped out without a second glance. I opened the boot with the push of a button so he could retrieve his props.

The traffic light turned red just as the boot door shut. Manesh bounded across the street in front of me, his attention captured by Beth who'd stepped out of the theatre. I saw her lean in and him recoil, nudging his head towards me.

Of course: no kissing in front of Mum.

I'd been relegated back to invisibility. I hated to admit it hurt.

Beth took the globe from his hand and led him inside, holding the other. My boy. My boy she'd get to spend time with all afternoon. My boy she'd no doubt escort to their friend's party that night, do God-knows-what with ... while I'd be stirring in bed, unable to sleep until I heard the comforting click of the front door. Until my boy was home again.

A loud honking shook me upright. The bus driver behind me pointed angrily at the now green light. Frazzled, I missed the accelerator pedal and hurt my already sore ankle. Anxiety coursed through me. 'Bear with me,' I mumbled as I pressed the start button, tears beginning to well in my eyes. 'Just frigging bear with me.'

CHAPTER THIRTY-THREE

The next morning, Arjun's cycling boots click-clacked in the hallway. When I joined him, he was zipping up his backpack.

'You off, then?' I asked.

'Should be back at two,' he replied, as he put on his helmet.

'Have fun.'

He leaned in for a kiss, but his helmet bumped against my face. He laughed and stroked my shoulder instead. 'Remind me next time to put the damn thing on *after* a goodbye kiss.'

It was still fairly dark out, even if it was 8 a.m. I watched him guide his bike down the drive, his bum looking oddly round in his padded shorts, his chiselled calf muscles visibly flexing with every step.

The hallway tiles were cold beneath my bare feet. My bathrobe hung limply around my body, a cup of tea my only source of warmth. If I wasn't forced to walk Sparky, I'd still be in bed.

I climbed the stairs; strained my ears as I passed Manesh's room. Not a peep. No surprise: he only came in at midnight

– a curfew I was delighted he kept to as I'd predictably lain awake until then. He was likely to fester in his bed until noon. I imagined him moaning *It's Sunday*, if I dared to knock on his door.

As I put on my clothes in the bedroom, I saw a trickle of dog walkers on the street, heading for the park. That would be me, now. I remembered when I ran into Heather and some of the other mums with their pets and cringed. Imagine having to see them every day. All the more reason to get Manesh to do it, though that would be easier said than done.

Did his friend Arthur not walk their dog? I seemed to remember Manesh joining him in the past. He lived nearby. Maybe I could arrange something for the two of them? Maybe his mum and I could finally have that coffee too?

Feeling like I'd hit on a win-win, I picked up my phone and found her in my contacts. The log showed me she'd still not answered my text. I swallowed my resentment and chose to see it as an opportunity for a fresh start.

'Hello?' A male voice. How odd.

'Hello, it's Radha.' Assuming it was Arthur's dad I added, 'Manesh's mum.'

'This is not a good time, Radha,' he said.

'Oh, I'm very sorry. Is everything all right?'

'We're only just back from hospital. Arthur died.'

I sank through my knees, landing on the edge of my bed. 'Oh my God. I'm so sorry. How? How horrible. How are you? What a shock. Is there anything I can do?' My heartbeat pounded harder with every babbled question. This couldn't be happening.

'I need to go,' he replied wearily.

'Yes, yes, of course. I'm awfully sorry. I can't imagine how—'

'Damned drugs,' he said, and the line went dead.

The sun was peeking out from under the clouds, its wintry rays not quite strong enough to warm me as they hit my face. How long had I sat here, numbed by the news? The incomplete news ... What about drugs? What did Arthur do?

I pressed my fingers against my lips and took a deep breath. I wrung my hands and rose. Manesh should hear it from me.

Leaning my forehead against his white, wooden door, I clutched onto the brass knob, building up courage. A faint snore rose from inside. I knocked; he groaned.

'I'm sorry darling, but we need to talk,' I said.

'Time's it?' He squinted against the intruding light, his black venetian blinds normally maintaining an adequate darkness.

I swiped the towel from the floor and threw it on the chair, on top of a pile of jumbled clothes – some I recognised as only recently ironed. He sat up, holding his duvet against his bare chest. 'Jeez, Mum. It's Sunday.'

I sat next to him and rested my hand on his thigh. 'Baby, I have some bad news.'

His eyes widened. 'Is it Grandad?'

'No, no. Grandad's fine. It's ...' I blew out a long breath. 'I wanted you to hear it from me. It's Arthur. He's dead.'

'What? No. How?' He reached for his phone, the one he wasn't meant to have in his room at night. He angled it away from me but even I could see his screen had blown up with notifications. 'Shit.' He bit his lip. It didn't stop the tears flooding out.

I leaned forward to catch his eye, itching to hold him, but he hadn't let me touch him naked for years. I scooped a T-shirt off the floor and handed it to him. He wiped his nose with it. I grabbed another, its smell suggesting it had been worn more than once. 'Here.' As Manesh stuck his arms through the holes, I asked, 'Do you know what happened? His Dad said something about drugs.'

He turned to me, his red-rimmed eyes searching my face. Was he afraid? 'It's OK, sweetheart, you can tell me. I promise.'

He slunk into a heap and flopped across my lap, sobbing. My maternal heart ached as if it had been struck by a stone. I stroked his hair, and when his sobs reduced to mere hiccoughs, I ran a line with my thumb from his forehead to the tip of his nose. That had always soothed him as a baby. He cleared his throat. I reached for the glass on his bedside table, but the dribble of water within was coated with dust. 'It's OK ... it's OK ...' I murmured whenever he took a breath.

He ran the back of his hand under his nose and sniffed. Sat up. 'It's why we fought.'

'What is?'

'The drugs. Arthur was taking pills. Started out as a laugh but then he got hooked, I think.'

'What kind of pills?'

He shrugged. 'I dunno. MDMA to party, jellies to relax. Different coloured ones. Some blue.' He faced me with puffy, pleading eyes. 'I tried to stop him. When I got suspended it was because I was telling him to quit, trying to take the drugs off him. But he wouldn't have it. You have to believe me.'

'Shh ... I believe you,' I said as I wrapped my arm around his shoulder. I rocked him gently. 'So, what happened to him?'

Manesh picked up his phone and waved it in the air. 'They're saying he OD'd last night after the party.'

My body tensed. A thousand questions about the party swirled in my mind. I had to tread carefully lest Manesh clammed up again. I sighed. Why was Arjun not here when I needed him most? As calmly as I could, I asked, 'Were there drugs at your party?'

'Yes. And alcohol. But he was fine when I left. And the party was wrapping up.' He curled into me again, crying. 'A few of them took an Uber to another party. I should've made him come home with me. Us ... I wanted to walk Beth home.'

'Hey. Nobody is blaming you, darling. Nobody.'

We sat in silence for a while, him hopefully accepting he was blameless, me pondering the horror of losing one's child. Those poor parents. I squeezed Manesh closer. I knew it wasn't the time to ask, but I longed to hear the truth. The hypocrisy of what I was about to ask made my stomach churn. 'Are you doing drugs?'

He shook his head. 'No. I drank a beer.' He looked straight at me. 'Only the one. Honest. I didn't even like it,' he said, flashing his handsome smile. I cupped his cheek with my hand, feeling unending relief, and drank in his oh-so-familiar face.

A face I would do anything to keep safe.

CHAPTER THIRTY-FOUR

We all went to bed early that night.

Arjun had come home and, on hearing the heart-wrenching news, sat silently at Manesh's side for what must have been three hours. I'd paced outside the room; suggested to Arjun he should shower given his sweaty top must feel cold, but he merely shook his head. I left snacks at the door. Later on, soup and chunky bread. They were left uneaten.

Sparky got a life-draining walk out of me.

I lay with my head rested on my usual two pillows in a futile attempt at sleep. Every time I shut my eyes, they sprung back open, visions of those awful dealers filling my mind. Did they sell Arthur his pills? A cold shiver ran over me. What if they were from that orange box at the clinic? The one that went missing. The one I'd let into the world somewhere.

I imagined the scrawny, merry Arthur I knew. Memories of him aged three, nine, fourteen. A boy who instantly took his shoes off as he entered, who uttered the most pleases and thank yous of any child I met, who covered his mouth when he laughed. He loved strawberries. I'd fed him a giant bowlful when his braces finally came off and the seeds were no longer a threat.

And now he was dead. What went wrong?

I scoffed. I knew what: drugs.

More than anyone, I understood how easy it was to slip into dependency. One little pill. What's the harm? And then one little pill leads to another, and another until it becomes habit you can't imagine ever having been without.

I'd been kidding myself that it was fine – that *I* was fine. But I wasn't. And it had to stop. A flush of anxiety rushed up my spine; the prospect of coping with work, stress, family – everything – all by myself was terrifying. But I knew what I needed to do. Now was the time.

Before I could change my mind, I stepped out of bed and into the bathroom. I removed my two remaining strips of pills from their hiding place inside a box of tampons – as repellent a thing as could be found in a house of men.

One by one, I popped my little blue lifelines from their safe confines of the blister pack into the toilet bowl. Some sank faster than previous ones as they hit the water. Others caused air bubbles to rise to the surface. All caused my throat to constrict ever so slightly more, until I could hardly breathe, cold sweat on my brow. Could I do this?

There was only one way to find out.

I pressed the lever down to flush. I washed my hands, not sure why. Habit. The water flowed between my fingers in a reassuring caress. As I rinsed off the soapy lather and watched the suds drain away, I felt cleansed.

Arjun stirred when I slid back under the duvet. I snuggled up and he turned onto his right. 'Evthing OK?' he murmured.

'Shh ...' I replied and curled in as the big spoon, his welcome warmth on my stomach.

His black hair was peppered with the occasional white. How many thousands of times had we lain here like this? So normal, loving, trusting. But things were far from normal and the guilt of keeping him in the dark all this time felt so wrong; like all the promises we'd made each other were broken at once. Maybe I should tell him. But how would that improve things? Would he be any better at getting rid of the dealers? Or would he be considered complicit if I got found out?

My mind ran through scenario after scenario and there was no easy answer. But one decision was clear. There was one irrefutable way forward: I could not let them deal through the clinic again. Not after Arthur. This I vowed. I wouldn't be able to live with myself if I caused someone – a child – to die.

So now what? How could I get out of this terrible mess I'd made?

I thought of Arjun's side of the wardrobe, where we kept the safe. Would they accept money? Could I pay them off to not report me to the GDC? I tried to remember how much cash we held there. About a thousand, just in case. In case of what, we'd never really discussed.

Would it be enough? I imagined the handover, the dealers walking away satisfied, never having to see them again. How I might then slowly replenish the cash I'd taken to ensure Arjun wouldn't find out. I had time; the envelope with money had lain there for years, untouched.

My shoulders relaxed. I grew more confident as I puzzled through this seemingly workable solution. But I couldn't shake one niggle: there was nothing to stop them coming back for more. Once they had you, they had you. Might as well offer no money at all and take whatever punishment came my way.

All I could do was hope the GDC didn't act on random tip-offs. And if they did, that the video and photos of orange boxes in my possession would mean nothing without seeing what was inside. And even if there was an investigation, my drugs would have left my hair by the time they'd want a sample. The more I thought of the holes in the dealer's threats, the more empowered I felt.

I stroked Arjun's thigh. Strong. That's what I needed to be now.

Deny them what they want. Face the consequences.

But what if I was wrong? What if the GDC did investigate and found that I took drugs? What if they somehow even managed to discover the fraudulent prescriptions? My hope deflated. I would end up struck from the registry. If I was truly honest with myself, I deserved it. I knew that, now. Not only for what I did to myself, but what I'd possibly done to others. I was forever tainted, guilty.

Arjun's hand reached behind me and cupped my bottom.

We'd be fine even if I were de-registered. Wouldn't we?

I fantasised he'd find another partner for the practice. I'd welcome them on board. We'd survive the shame – eventually – more than if I dragged him into it. Better to have the blame fall squarely on me; for me to be the punished one. He'd be squeaky clean.

I sighed and pushed the comforting dream further. I'd still have a husband and son to care for, whose love would be dented, but unwavering. Was that too much to ask?

A tear travelled over my nose onto my pillow as my lip trembled and reality came crashing in: this would destroy us.

CHAPTER THIRTY-FIVE

I poured my breakfast cereal into my favourite yellow bowl while I waited for the kettle to boil. A splash of milk landed on my hip. I wiped it away with a wet sponge, the growing damp patch cold against my skin.

I fished my phone from my trousers. No notifications. Why hadn't they answered yet? Arjun appeared in the doorway, still in his bathrobe; I slipped the phone back.

'How's your lover doing this morning? he asked.

'What?'

He chuckled. 'You're always sneakily checking your phone lately. I figured it must be a new man.' I feigned a giggle. He walked over and gave me a peck on the cheek. 'I'd better improve my wooing game. How about dinner at Rogano on Friday?'

'That sounds lovely.' I smiled. I hadn't expected him to remember the promised date night.

Sparky scuttled around our legs, his nails tip-tapping on the stone tiles. Arjun bent down to pet him. 'Hello, wee man. How was your walk?'

'It was fine,' I said, perhaps too tersely. Arjun frowned. I added, 'Just, you know, a walk ... It's cold.'

He went into the utility. I snuck a peek at my phone. Nothing. I'd emailed the dealer while walking Sparky. With it being Monday morning, there was no time to lose. I still couldn't believe I did it: told them in no uncertain terms we were done – that *I* was done. I'd been buoyed with confidence after last night's deliberations. I was calling their bluff.

But in the hour since, my dread grew, my heart beating faster with every imagined vibration in my pocket. What would they say? The uncertainty was killing me. Whatever they decided to do, at this moment, it felt like the wait was worse. I longed for the pills I'd flushed away; the sense of calm they gave me. The ability to focus and see things for what they really were, not the frenzied thoughts that could tip me over.

I picked at my cereal, the hard granola like flavourless rocks on my tongue.

Arjun returned carrying his ironed shirts over his shoulder by the hanger. 'Is Manesh off school?'

'Yes, his year are being given a day of mourning. The school's been quite good, actually. They've offered counselling to Arthur's friends.'

'Any news on the funeral?'

'None as yet.' I held my tea close to my chest. Moist swirls of Earl Grey filled my nose. 'His poor parents.'

Arjun caressed my cheek. 'It's awful.' He breathed in deeply. 'Still, he's got exams this year. I'll go and wake him.'

I thought Manesh deserved a break, but it didn't sound like Arjun was asking for my opinion. Perhaps it was something they'd discussed while they excluded me from their huddling yesterday. I shrugged; I had to go anyway.

I tidied the kitchen, grumbling at the jumble of misplaced crockery in the dishwasher. I gave Sparky a snuggle, threw his banana toy at him and set out the door.

The weather had cleared up a bit since I was out with the dog. Dew glistened in the neighbours' yards. On every corner, I stopped and checked my phone, my mind darting between panic that they'd already be on the phone to the GDC and reassuring myself that not only was the GDC not open yet, but drug dealers were unlikely be up this early.

Around the last corner, I was proved wrong: the black-capped man stood opposite the clinic. He leaned against the cabin of an SUV, his legs crossed at the ankle. On his phone. My pulse pounded in my ears; my chest tightened. I walked on, my pace somewhere between purposeful and cautious. Would he hurt me?

When I was only a few metres from the start of the clinic wall, he looked up. My stomach lurched. He locked his eyes on me, a wry grin on his face. How close would I need to come before he said something? I pressed my lips together, held my head high and continued to put one step in front of the other, despite the violent nausea growing inside. I paused briefly before turning into our yard, hesitant, confused. I glanced at him one last time before I'd have my back to him. He winked and nearly stunned me to a stop.

He'd winked. That was it. Nothing else.

I struggled to breathe through my palpitations as I rushed to unlock the door, feeling his eyes crawling all over me, my insides screaming: WHAT DOES HE WANT?

CHAPTER THIRTY-SIX

The day's first consultation was routine. A check-up, nothing special. The usual advice to floss, knowing full well it wouldn't be followed. Cheryl didn't notice the super-human effort it took to keep my voice steady, my hand steady. As the patient left, thoughts of the man outside flittered through my head. My stomach churned. Was he still there? Could I send Cheryl to check?

The buzzer announced the next patient. Shit.

I concentrated on regulating my breath as the gentleman climbed into the chair. Slow ... deep ... you can do this. I began my exam; tried to ignore the small bubbles of air gathering at the back of my throat making me feel like a balloon was inflating inside. I coughed gently into the crook of my elbow.

It was hot.

I inhaled silently as I scraped the patient's teeth with my probe. 'Relax,' I said, more to me than to him.

I wiped my heated brow with the back of my hand; subtly waved the air from the 3-in-1 nozzle past my face.

Almost done.

Breathe.

My fingers tingled as I held the drill against his decayed tooth. Like a warning: don't slip up. And the more I thought of not slipping up, the more I trembled. I maintained a wide smile as I swallowed back tears, struck by the realisation I could no longer function without my pills – not when faced with that bastard outside and no idea what he'd do to me.

The consultation nearly over, the fresh smell of the blue rinse being spat into the small sink brought some relief. I survived another patient. But could I do it again?

'I'll be right back,' I said to Cheryl.

'Sure,' she replied, clearing the tray of instruments.

Reaching reception, I looked through the window. I had to take a few steps forward and sideways to spot him, still there, on the pavement, just out of regular sight. Forty minutes. He didn't seem to have moved at all – if nothing else, I would've expected the neighbour to complain about this strange man leaning against his car.

'I'm going outside for a moment,' I said to Pauline. 'I need fresh air.'

'But it's freezing.'

I smiled. 'Some day you'll be a forty-something woman and you'll understand.'

I breathed in courage as I walked through the door; the cold air battered my face.

He was tapping on his phone. His lips curled into a smile. A funny video, perhaps. But when I caught him glancing at me from the corner of his eye, I knew that grin was meant for me. Why didn't he look up? He continued to tap and swipe while I approached. A great wave of trepidation crashed over me. How far would he make me come?

When only four feet away, he licked his lips, making me feel even more like I was walking straight into a wolf's lair.

'Hello,' I said firmly, though the blood rushing in my ears and his lack of response left me unsure of my volume.

After a few more strokes on the screen, he finally looked up. 'Fancy seeing you here, Doctor,' he said, feigning surprise.

I crossed my arms. 'I sent you an email. I won't be participating in any more of your activities.'

'I saw,' he said.

Confused by his apparent disinterest, I doubled down. 'Good. Then we're clear. No more boxes changing hands through the clinic.'

He nodded slowly. 'Message received.' He raised an eyebrow. 'Anything else?'

What game was he playing? Where was the trap? There had to be a trap.

Anger bubbled inside. His presence had made me a wreck all morning, risking my patients' safety. And I wasn't having it. 'Do it already,' I said.

'Do what?' He placed his hand on his chest in mock offence.

'Whatever the fuck you came here to do.'

His eyes flashed in surprise. He tutted. 'That's no language for a lady.'

I roared in frustration. 'Fuck fuck fuck. Fuck you. Just tell me what you're going to do, you ... fucker.'

He threw his head back and let out a loud belly laugh.

I was shaking. Energy soared through my body, my fear like spikes on my skin. 'I'm glad you think this is funny, but it is most definitely not,' I pointed my finger in his face.

'Mum?'

My blood ran cold on hearing Manesh's voice.

The man and I both looked to the side. Manesh stood on the pavement, not five metres away, holding a paper bag. 'Is everything OK, Mum?' he asked, tentatively.

'Yes, darling. This man and I are merely having a little disagreement about the steriliser repair cost ... Aren't we?' I signalled with a widening of my eyes.

'Aye,' the man said, crossing his arms. 'That's it.'

I turned to Manesh. 'What are you doing here?'

'You forgot Grandad's lunch on the kitchen counter, so I thought I'd bring it.'

I forced a smile. 'That was kind. Put it inside, will you? I'll be right there.'

Manesh walked the path to the door, turning twice, his eyes searching. We waited. Once he was inside, the man uncrossed his ankles and placed his phone in his pocket. He adjusted his cap and, as he unexpectedly walked away, he said, 'Nice kid. Hope he doesn't get into trouble.'

CHAPTER THIRTY-SEVEN

'I'm done for the day,' I said as I popped my head into Arjun's surgery later that day. 'Will you be late?'

'I've got a seven-ten coming for fillers and that'll be me,' he replied. He opened one of his drawers and frowned. Opened another one. 'Where did she put it?' he mumbled.

'I'll wait with dinner, then,' I said. 'Pasta OK?'

He looked up, puzzled, as though he'd forgotten I was there. 'Sounds great.'

I left him to his rummaging.

I'd normally help him look for whatever it was he'd lost – they called me 'the great finder of things' at home – but I was dying to get out there. My feet were killing me, and the emotional aftermath of that morning's confrontation had really floored me. Even though the dealer had left, I remained cloaked in dread while treating each patient, expecting him to barge through my door and grab me at any time. My instincts hadn't been completely wrong: I noticed he'd returned to his stalking place after lunch. My nerves prickled all afternoon, my forehead warm, my hands clammy. I concentrated on my job, blanking out his mocking voice from my mind as I reassured patients with, 'Everything's going to be fine.'

A peek through the main window in reception confirmed what I already knew: the threat was gone. He'd left around 3 p.m. I figured it wouldn't be the last I saw of him, but for now, I seemed safe.

I grabbed my coat and bag, and headed outside. The reddish light of the streetlamp flickered, as if in warning. I squinted into the obscure streets. Nobody. For now.

As I walked along the houses, I drew comfort from seeing people going about their business through their front windows. Most stood far from the street, behind extensive driveways and front lawns, but I was in no doubt that, in this quiet neighbourhood, a scream would have them with their noses to the glass in an instant.

A squirrel raced across my path. I yelped. My pulse raced as it scrambled up a tree; my shoulders tensed as I anticipated it flying into my neck with his rabid claws. But it quickly disappeared into the dry, spiky branches. Get a grip, Radha.

I walked on, manoeuvring between the many wheelie bins that had been set out early for the next morning's collection. As they hobbled in the wind, I imagined their dark bodies rolling towards me as if on command, toppling over and catching me in a trap. Too heavy for me to escape. Dizzy and with faltering breath, I rushed to my house. I needed water, calm, home.

When I approached, I noticed our gate was open. I sped up. Who was there? I turned at the end of our hedge, into the drive. Light shone from my open front door, mingling with the yellower shade of the porch lantern to illuminate a dark shape, a grown man, standing on our steps ... speaking to Manesh ... handing him something. I craned to see but I was too far away.

I drew closer. The man turned. The light reflected off his baseball cap. He tugged at his puffer jacket.

Manesh held an orange box.

No!

I sprinted up the drive, my inner mama-bear awakened. 'Go away,' I spat at the man as I shoved him aside. He stumbled slightly and shouted, 'Fuck you.' I didn't care. I saw red.

And orange.

The box in Manesh's hands. The fuckers. They went after my boy. A red veil of rage clouded my vision.

'Mum, what are you doing?' Manesh asked, his eyes as big as the moon.

'Give me that box.' I extended my arm as I rushed up the steps.

'What? Why?'

'What did he say?' I asked.

'Who?' Manesh took two step backs into our vestibule.

I cornered him against the large houseplant, grabbed the box from him. I couldn't let him anywhere near what was inside. 'That man. What did he say?'

'Nothing. I don't know. "Good evening?" Mum, you're scaring me. What's going on? It's just my shoes.'

The furious rushing in my ears stopped dead. 'Shoes?' I focused my vision on the box; a knot formed in my stomach. The label had his name on it. Beside it, a pink logo. *Very*, the online store. My knees buckled; I rested my back against the wall. 'This came from a store?'

'Yes ... I-I got new shoes.' He gently tugged at the box, keeping his concerned eyes on me. I let go. 'Here, let me show you,' he said, prying open the lid.

I looked on, too stunned – too embarrassed – to speak. What the hell had I done? He must've thought me mad.

'They're blue suede,' he said carefully. He slowly tore apart the folds of white wrapping paper. 'Like before.'

'The Elvis *huh-huh-huh* shoes?' I asked, through a sob.

He took my hand and smiled. 'Yes, the *huh-huh-huh* shoes.'

CHAPTER THIRTY-EIGHT

That night, Arjun and I turned on a new BBC Scotland drama one of his patients featured in.

'She only plays a waitress in the background, but she'll be expecting compliments when she next comes in,' he explained. He sunk into the sofa next to me with the remote, the increasing volume adding to my throbbing headache. I'd had some wine to soothe my jitters after the incident with the shoes, but it had made matters worse: edgy and groggy was not a pleasant combination.

I'd had to make up a story for Manesh, he'd been so worried. Fuelled by residual adrenaline, my mind had sparked with a credible tale. Well, credible enough for Manesh to at least think me not entirely cuckoo. I said I'd read in the newspaper that they'd discovered a box of anthrax at a doctor's office in Govan. (Why my brain came up with Govan, I'd never know.) And the box had been orange. So, when I'd seen his box ...

'God, Mum, talk about overreacting,' he'd said. As he'd been witness to my 'women's issues', I blamed the hormones. I didn't think he believed me, but it was an unsavoury enough topic that he let it lie. Besides, a phone call with Beth had beckoned.

Sparky ambled into the lounge and lay down at our feet, placing his chin and a single white paw on Arjun's shoe. He let out a satisfied sigh. I smiled at Arjun and rested my head on his shoulder, a faint whiff of clinic still tainting him this late.

The show contained its requisite share of eerie music, visuals in darkened alleys, and men popping out from nowhere. It was doing my nerves no good at all. 'I'm going to take Sparky out,' I said.

'Stay. Have Manesh do it.'

With the dealer's threat hovering in my mind, there was no way I was letting my boy out in the dark. But should I be going out? What if the bastard was standing outside again, looking to clear up unfinished business?

I stood and pulled a gap between the heavy red curtains. Drizzle flickered in front of our streetlamp. The trees' bare branches all stretched sideways in the wind, like a gym class. I scanned the street for further movement. Nothi—

My heart skipped as the neighbour's cat jumped up on our side wall.

'Would you mind going?' I asked Arjun.

'Now?'

I shrugged. 'She's a waitress. We've seen her. What more can happen to her?'

'I'll call Manesh.'

'No, please. You go. He's done all the dishes. And he's mourning.'

Arjun frowned and pushed himself up. 'Fine. But you keep watching this, then, and report back.'

Sparky danced around Arjun, his fluffy tail wagging hopefully. 'Yes, yes, we're going walkies,' Arjun said, to which Sparky responded with a twirl on his hind legs.

I turned the sound off; the actors were mumbling anyway. It seemed to have worsened over the years: the better the sound quality in recordings, the more the background noises drowned out the speech. Besides, I only needed to keep an eye out for when the couple – where I predicted the lawyer husband was most definitely cheating on his wife – returned to the bright and cheery café.

I grabbed the soft, brown blanket from the arm rest and threw it over my lap. The house felt empty, cold. I strained my ears to pick up any noises from upstairs, but all was quiet. A chill ran over my shoulders and I pulled the blanket up. If anything happened to Manesh ...

On the screen, a policeman handcuffed a long-haired woman. For a split second, she looked just like me. I'd missed what she'd done – but I knew my crimes. How could I have ever thought it was OK to prescribe myself Diazepam? I'd been a mess, though, when the old woman died. And taking that first, blessed pill someone gave me, was like treading on a slippery slope. I knew that now, not then.

I looked at my fingers, my short nails – dentist nails. How close I'd come to losing it all; to no longer knowing who I was, if not a dentist. To letting everyone down. I picked at the wool bobbles on my lap, small, rounded tufts that evidenced the blanket's age: it was my mother's. I sighed. Maybe if she'd still been there to give me comfort, hold me, stroke me, forgive me, I wouldn't have reached for the drugs.

But she wasn't.

And I'd gone on after the first, second and third pills. Way after it was excusable. Way into illegal territory. Straight into the dealers' trap.

I was hooked and it was time to admit it. It wasn't a physical addition; I knew I could cope with that, difficult though it may be. I was hooked on prevention. I lived with a perpetual rumble of dread, attuned to any sensation – a tingle in the finger, a flutter of the heart – that could indicate a panic attack was on its way. Without my pills, taken at the right time, any hint of worry would snowball into full-blown anxiety. And I wouldn't be able to function.

I grabbed the iPad off the side table and pressed my thumb to unlock it. Where to start? I searched for Help with drugs. But the results weren't suitable. They were for hard drugs, real addicts. There was a drug crisis centre in town, but I couldn't risk being seen. Not among those people. I imagined the meeting: *'Hello, my name is Radha and I'm a drug addict'*, like in the movies. I scoffed. I only needed a little help. It was diazepam, for heaven's sake – not bloody heroin.

I found Stop the Score, a helpline. I checked my watch. 9 .54 p.m. They were still taking calls. As I dialled the number on my phone and waited for it to connect, I scrolled down their web page and their many info leaflets: cannabis, ecstasy, cocaine.

Call handler Paul introduced himself with a warm, soothing voice. I figured that would've helped him in getting the job. He reassured me everything we talked about would be confidential. But there wasn't much to say in the end. After I explained my predicament, using a false name, it was clear that all he wanted me to do was to get professional help.

As if. I'd have to disclose that to the GDC. What would they do then?

'Surely you give advice yourselves?' I pressed.

'Not really, but with the kind of anxiety you're describing, many people report success with calming visualisations. Imagining themselves in a happy place at the first sign that you're getting anxious. Do you have a happy place?'

'I'm not sure.'

'Some people visualise a loved one, to ground them.' An image of my mother flashed before me. 'Or,' he continued, 'I remember one person saying it felt like a balloon was inflating inside her—'

'Yes! I get that.'

'Good. What worked for her was imagining she pricked the balloon with a needle before it grew too big.'

The front door slammed shut. I heard Sparky's pitter-patter and Arjun dropping his keys in the bowl.

I quickly hung up on Paul.

It was up to me now.

CHAPTER THIRTY-NINE

Four whole days and nothing. Nothing but torture.

Since Monday, a man had stood there, opposite, though a smidge to the side of the clinic, leaning against the (still not incensed) neighbour's car, on and off, every day. Presumably no longer worthy of the head Honcho's time, I'd been handed over to ever-scrawnier, ever-spottier youths. The one today looked restless; scratched at his upper arms; chewed gum. And did nothing. Like the others.

I never acknowledged their presence. Not when passing in the morning, back straight, head held high. Not when darting to the reception window in between patients to check if anyone was there, occasionally catching their eye and jumping back again, heart pounding. But even when they weren't outside, they were tormenting me inside. I couldn't concentrate; my patient care suffered. I'd had to hide in the cleaning closet while panic attacks ravaged my confidence. I was jumpy, always wondering: is someone there right now? Is it him? Will today be the day they act? How long can they keep this up? Why?

Mostly why.

And what could I do? It was harassment, that was clear to me, but I couldn't report it. I couldn't go anywhere near the police. Besides, I bet they wouldn't see it that way: the men were just standing there.

I followed my latest patient back into the waiting area. Dad sat in his chair, a sudoku booklet in hand, his back to the street, thankfully. Nosy as he was, he was bound to have noticed people hovering outside. But if he had, he hadn't mentioned it. I joined his side, an excuse to peek out the window again. 'Hi, Dad, how's the puzzle?'

He looked up in surprise. 'Fine.'

'Would you like another cushion?' I offered, leaning across him to check the length of the street. No one.

'Don't fuss, dear, you have patients to see,' he whispered, signalling the others with his eyes.

'You're right.'

Pauline handed me an envelope. 'A GDC one came today.'

My throat constricted. I took the letter and spun on my heels towards my surgery. I breathed in but couldn't breathe out; the air forced itself into my lungs as though through a one-way valve, inflating, inflating ... Nerves tingled at the back of my neck. Was this it? Did the dealers report me? Were they waiting outside until the letter came, wanting to see my reaction? Is that why they were there: a sadistic desire to witness my destruction first-hand?

Tears pricked in the corners of my eyes. I rushed to the toilet and leaned my face against the cool wall, letting freezing water run over my wrists.

Keep it together.

I closed my eyes and stepped into my new calming ritual. I pictured myself holding a red balloon by a golden ribbon. When I struggled to breathe, the balloon increased in size; the tension on its surface grew, the latex thinning until it was see-through. Inside the balloon, I saw my mother sitting at her sewing table. Her long black hair ran down her back. Rendered inside the balloon, everything looked pink. Her head was bent forward. Her elbow moved rhythmically as she stitched. '*Mum*,' I called. She turned around; her smile beamed like sunlight. '*Help.*' She got up and extended her arm upward, the needle in her hand glinting. She blew me a kiss and pricked.

Pop.

I doubled over and exhaled. I breathed in and out a few times until I felt stable; ran my clammy hand over my forehead.

I nearly cried as relief washed over me. It worked, again. Over the last few days, I'd practised the visualisation; and while the panic blinded me in some cases, obscuring my imaginary haven, I seemed to have turned a corner. And if this kept working, it would keep me sane.

I checked my watch. Shit. Late. But I had to know what the GDC would do. I put down the toilet seat cover, sat and pulled the letter from its white-and-blue envelope.

It was nothing: a routine reminder of the requirements for my Continual Professional Development. I laughed out loud, a near hysterical squeal. I shook my head thinking I needed to stop overreacting like this, as I walked back to my surgery.

But as I entered, my insides churned. If the GDC wasn't their plan. What was?

In the break room at lunch time, Dad and I ate last night's leftover curry. There was a dribble on his chin he didn't seem to feel. I would've offered a tissue had he not looked so contented, chewing appreciatively, eyes near shut under bushy salt-and-pepper eyebrows that would soon need a trim.

I smiled. He was a nuisance, but he was my nuisance. How lucky I'd been with two wonderful parents. My cheeks slackened as I thought how disappointed he'd be – they'd both be – if they knew how I'd failed. I remembered my graduation, how they'd clutched my arms, one hand on each shoulder for the photo, proudly laying claim to this successful woman they'd made. I'd been thrilled about my degree, of course, and the promise of my future; but that day, I was mostly joyous for them. Mum had prepared a feast, smiled and boasted so much to the aunties she could hardly aim any food into her mouth. I wanted to cling onto the memory, but the picture in my mind turned grey. Mum dropped her fork. Her smile disappeared, her daughter a disgrace.

My phone pinged. A text from Bela.

Can you talk?

'Excuse me,' I said to Dad and moved to the window to get a better signal. I pressed Bela's profile in my contacts. 'Hey, what's up?'

'Radha, hi. You're not going to believe this, but it's over. There was no fraud. I told them there was no fraud. And I was right. Turns out it was a software glitch. Can you believe it?'

'My God, that's wonderful news.'

'Dozens of postmasters were affected by this – all accused. It's an outrage.'

'That's shocking.'

'I tell you what, Radha, the way they treated us ... The stress! We were going crazy. I mean, if we hadn't been a strong couple, facing this together, I'm certain I would've turned to drink. What a waste of space I'd be then, eh?'

A bitter taste filled my mouth. 'I'm glad.'

'Anyway,' Bela continued. 'On the plus side, they have to pay us oodles in compensation. Serves them right for branding us criminals. So, I wanted to take you out tonight to celebrate. My treat.'

'That's very kind. I would've loved to. But Arjun made reservations at Rogano.'

'Ooh, special occasion?'

'No, actually,' I replied. 'It's just been a while. Rain check?'

'Of course. How about tomorrow? If you can still walk after your hot date tonight.' She cackled.

'Oh, shut up, you.' I smiled, delighted she seemed to have become herself again. 'You're on.'

'Yay. Saturday night on the tiles!'

I laughed, our idea of being *on the tiles* so very meek compared to a typical night out in Glasgow.

The last patient for the day was new; a teenage girl. Tall. Her disproportionately long legs were level with the bosom of the older woman by her side, whose jet-black hair made a heroic effort to deny her wrinkled face. I ushered them into the surgery.

'So, welcome, Samantha. And you are ...?'

'Her granny,' the woman replied.

'I'm Radha and this is Cheryl. Please have a seat here,' I gestured to the plastic chaperone seat. 'And you, Sam, hop on the big chair.'

'Samantha,' the girl said sternly.

I nodded. 'My apologies.'

She climbed on. She twisted her long brown hair into a tail and threw it over her shoulder before leaning back; a bleached streak dangled across her forehead. 'It's all right. Just don't like people thinking I'm a boy.'

'Pretty girl like you? There's no risk of that.'

'Why thank you,' she said coyly, and batted her mascaraed lashes cartoon-style. 'But these need whitening if I'm going to be an actress.' She bared her teeth at me.

'How old are you?'

Granny replied, 'Fourteen. And don't you be getting any ideas.'

'I'm afraid I have to agree with your grandmother, Samantha. You're too young for teeth whitening.'

She sulked.

'Let's have a look, shall we?' I adjusted the light as Samantha opened wide. 'And your teeth are perfectly fine as they are.' She relaxed into the chair, seemingly unafraid despite the previous fillings. It made a nice change from the majority of folk who were instantly terrified, no matter what you did. She smelled of Daisy, a perfume I'd worn before. I probed along her gum line and between her molars. 'I'm afraid you have a small cavity. Cheryl can you prep please?'

As I pressed the drill on, I heard a groan. I stopped. It wasn't the girl. I turned to Cheryl, who jumped off her stool, a worried expression on her face. Next to her, the old woman groaned again, pulling at the collar of her polo neck jumper.

'Are you unwell?' Cheryl asked.

Samantha closed her mouth and looked over. 'Granny? Are you all right?'

'Aye, well no.' The granny puffed. 'I think I need some air.'

'Here, I'll take you.' Cheryl lifted her by the arm.

'You go on,' the woman said, waving at me. 'I'll be fine, hen.'

I waited until they reached the door, anxious she might collapse. 'You OK to continue?' I asked Samantha. She nodded and settled back again.

It wasn't long before Cheryl returned. 'She's in reception. I made her comfortable in your dad's chair.' She placed her hand on Samantha's shoulder. 'Your granny's fine.'

'And we're almost done,' I said, smiling.

Samantha blinked her understanding.

'You'll be numb for a few hours yet,' I said as she got up.

'Good thing you haven't got a screen test lined up,' Cheryl joked.

The girl laughed, and promptly caught a dribble of drool that escaped from her mouth.

We escorted her to reception where her granny sat, quite happily, dunking a biscuit in her cup of tea. We didn't have biscuits in the practice – for obvious reasons – and I chuckled internally at the thought of her carrying around a roll of ginger snaps in her handbag.

'Do you need help getting home?' I asked.

'My dad's picking us up,' Samantha said. A man's close-trimmed head popped around the front door as if summoned. He tapped on the inside of the door with his flat hand. 'Can we go now?' he said to the two – not bothering to acknowledge me.

After they left, Cheryl went back to tidy up.

'How are things looking for Monday?' I asked Pauline.

'Good, I think. I'll be amazed if the Health Board inspectors find anything wrong. Your dad and I have combed through the Health and Safety files twice. He's been a great help.'

'Brilliant,' I said. I was about to dismiss her for the weekend when I realised that would mean being left alone. Arjun had gone to Dundee to give a guest lecture. I walked to the window and peered out. The flickering streetlamp cast a strong enough light on the road to verify there was nobody waiting for me. In fact, I hadn't seen anyone since first thing that morning.

Had the thugs grown bored? I hoped so. Maybe they'd realised it would be too difficult to report me to the GDC without exposing themselves and had come up with this silent torture instead. I'd survived four days of this; I could survive more. And I'd now get some reprieve: no point them standing here over the weekend. I'd be home with my feet up for a well-deserved rest.

After a nice dinner, that is.

CHAPTER FORTY

Gunbir

Gunbir burped. The taste of ginger languished in his mouth. Lunch had been delicious, but it wasn't fully agreeing with him. Radha must have put okra in the curry. Okra was not his friend.

He rubbed his stomach and resumed his viewing. The monitors on his desk showed the surrounds of his house and two clinic feeds in six neat, black-and-white squares.

The young patient must be new, he observed. He didn't recognise her or the old woman she was with. Funny how many new clients had joined the practice recently. NHS waiting lists must be reducing. In his day, you'd be hard-pressed to register with a practice quickly – unless you benefited from special contacts. He'd seen people jump the queue inexplicably more than once. He'd chosen never to ask how.

What was Cheryl doing? Oh. The old woman wasn't well.

He watched Cheryl take the woman away and waited for them to appear on the reception feed, but there was a delay. Maybe the woman needed a breath? He took a sip of his coffee and was reassured to see the woman walking unaided into the waiting area. Cheryl propped one of the cushions on his chair. Good, she'd be comfortable there.

Pauline ducked out of view and when she returned with a cup of tea, she bent under the desk. She picked up her handbag and while seemingly chatting to the woman, pulled out a roll of biscuits. Gunbir tutted. Pauline knew better. Still, the sugar would probably do the old bird good right now.

His eyes went to the surgery: Cheryl once again perched on her stool, Radha seemingly finishing off a filling. He tracked them as they returned to reception. Cute girl. Chatty. Roughly Manesh's age.

Then the man's head popped in through the door, two stripes shaved into the side – like *him*. Gunbir leaned in for a better look but the angle was wrong, the video too grainy. Damn this crappy system. He squeezed his eyes. The man's hand reached round the door to hit it. Gunbir gasped. There. The spider tattoo. That unmistakable black rounded body on a fragment of web, its thick, hairy legs crawling over the knuckles onto the fingers. The same one.

'It's him,' Gunbir sputtered. 'Meena ... It's him.'

Hot blood rushed to Gunbir's temples.

Rage bubbled inside.

Him.

CHAPTER FORTY-ONE

'How was Dundee?' I asked as Arjun took off his coat.

'Dundee's about as attractive as it's always been,' his voice sounded from the cloakroom.

I giggled. 'That's not fair. They've got that beautiful V&A museum now.'

'True. But thank goodness you and I have dinner plans, because the others wanted to drag me to the Tally Ho.'

'No way, is that still open?'

He shrugged. 'No idea. I ran, lest we'd end up at Fat Sam's!'

I laughed. He came close and nuzzled my neck. 'I already picked up the one chick I wanted to pick up in that dive. No reason to go back.'

I shoved him away playfully.

'Manesh here?' he asked.

'No, he's hanging out with Dad tonight.'

'That's nice.' Arjun pulled at his shirt and sniffed. 'I'm going to need a shower before we go. Actually, if you don't mind, I'd like to go for a quick run. The drive was murder. I could take Sparky?'

'No, I'll take him. He can't go very fast yet.'

'I know that. I'll take it easy.'

'OK.'

Arjun bounded upstairs to change. 'Sparky!' I shouted.

I heard his steps before I saw him appear from the dining room. 'Good boy,' I said, and hunched down for a pat. I stroked his back, ran my fingers around the edges of his brown and black patches. Sparky turned a half circle and looked up at me with those big black puppy eyes. 'Do I need to scratch this side too?' I rubbed his body down vigorously with both hands, his happy tail tickling my nose.

'Right,' I said, getting back up. 'Let's get your lead and then I'll put a nice dress on.'

Sparky cocked his head; his little pink tongue stuck out from his rounded snout.

'Yes, I know. It's not often I get to dress up.'

Arjun ran down the stairs in skin-tight leggings I instantly looked forward to peeling off him later. I fetched the lead while he put on his running shoes. Sparky sniffed at their soles. There would be more of those smells in the park.

As they left, my phone cast a distinctive tone in my pocket. My stomach jolted. I quickly swiped to the hidden app where I kept the email account I'd set up for my online order – since hijacked by the dealers to send me their threats. Yet it didn't appear to be from them.

It was from Dropbox, which I knew to be a file sharing platform, telling me in the subject that [blank] had shared a file with me. Could it be spam? It seemed very unlikely. I'd only ever used the email for one purpose. I clicked to open.

Hey, doctor, watch this, the email read, with a link. Had it not referred to me as doctor, I would have binned it, but this was clearly for me, and it could only be from them. I hesitated before clicking through.

A download started immediately, and I worried it might be a virus. Would it harm my phone? Weren't viruses only bad for PCs? Why would they send me a virus? In the download status I noticed the file extension: MP4 – a video.

I wracked my brain as to what this could be while the grey status bar moved interminably slowly to the right. The only video I knew they had, was of me picking up the parcel. Were they showing me what they'd send to the GDC? What if they'd edited it to make it look worse? As my breathing quickened, I felt my ribs press on my lungs. Were they filming me at other times, when I wasn't watching?

I shook my phone and groaned. They grey bar blipped near ninety per cent.

Come on.

Ninety-eight.

The white screen turned dark. I heard a murmur, turned up the sound. The camera faced a chair, standing alone in front of a black curtain. A metal chair, like in a trendy bistro. A woman walked in and sat; her features hazy in the scattered light. The camera adjusted its focus onto someone's face. It was a girl. Wait, it was Samantha, that girl from earlier, with the granny.

What was this?

She flung her hair over her shoulder and tucked her blonde streak behind her ear. She pulled at the collar of her red blouse – she'd changed outfits since earlier. She settled onto the chair, her back straight, and held onto the seat with both hands, arms outstretched by her side, looking very uncomfortable. Just as I began to think the worst – that she'd been abducted – she nodded as though in response to a signal, and spoke.

'I was never nervous about the dentist. I've always been good, you know? Brushing and even flossing.' She flashed a smile. 'But after today, I don't think I can ever return.' She cast her eyes down and sighed.

I grimaced. What was she on about?

'You never think about how vulnerable you are, lying back in that chair. You lie there with your mouth open, exposed. And you trust. Because why wouldn't you?' Her lips trembled. 'I closed my eyes: the light was shining too bright. That's when it happened.' She brought both hands to her mouth to contain a sob. 'At first I was confused. Why was the dentist holding my arm? And then I felt it. My zip being pulled down, fingers slipping into my ...' A large sob this time. 'I should've screamed. I should've run away,' she said, shaking her head. 'But I was paralysed. I just wanted it over. I wanted the fingers out of me.' The girl's knuckles were white from gripping the chair.

Bile rose in my throat. How horrible. What kind of animal could have done this to her? Was it the dentist before me? Because I'd be able to find him ...

Samantha ran the back of her hand past her nose and sniffed. 'Then it stopped. The dentist stroked my arm and told me I'd been a good girl. Then leaned in close and said that if I ever told anyone what had happened, my family would get hurt.'

Her cries pulled at my heart. I had to help her. Find who did this.

She looked into the lens with a new intensity, a flash of anger crossed her eyes. 'But I will not be quiet. I will not let this happen to another girl. I will shout from the rooftops: my dentist abused me! And I will name.'

The screen turned black again. I was stunned. So many questions swirled in my mind. Why was I sent this? Did they want my help? Then the letters began: fat, white lower-case letters dropped from the top of the screen, one by one. I watched the letters slowly form words.

the
dentist
is

My stomach twisted into a knot. She was naming!

radha

What? A chill ran down my cheeks.

ba

No. I choked. No, this couldn't be ... My head spun. I leaned against the console table for balance as my knees buckled when the last few letters dropped and completed my name.

I chucked the phone away. I blew out a deep breath, but it was no use. I ran to the toilet and threw up.

My plait hung limply beside my face; its bristly tip dangerously close to the bowl. I folded a few squares of toilet paper, coughed and wiped my mouth. A spittle of stinking vomit clung to the porcelain wall, resisting the flush. I sat on the tiles, staying close to the bowl in case I wasn't done, my head resting against the cold enamel.

That girl, that friendly girl. She was with *them*. But the sick granny ...? My eyes widened as I realised the significance of the granny's funny turn. It was a ploy. Dammit, that's why we had dental nurses. But Cheryl had taken her out of the room leaving the girl – and me – alone, unchaperoned. It would be her word against mine.

And I could lose.

I clambered up, washed my hands and rinsed my mouth with fresh water. All week I'd thought they were engaging in some sort of mental torture by standing outside – which was bad enough – but all the while they'd been scheming, setting this up. And this was infinitely worse.

I picked up my phone. There was a new email. This time from them. The reckoning.

Did you enjoy our wee film? Another box is coming to the clinic on Monday for you to pass on. Do it or else the video gets shared.

I imagined this video landing in the lap of the po-faced committee of the GDC. The shock. The immediate striking off; my name forever tarnished on their public web page, where my peers would greedily read the professional conduct rulings after hearing the gossip. Like I'd done, more than once.

Shame burned my cheeks. Then it hit me. It wasn't the GDC I had to worry about. It was the police! God, what if they shared it with the police?

But would they? Surely, as criminals, they wouldn't want to get anywhere close to the police. They'd have to interview the girl again. They'd talk to Cheryl. They'd figure out there wasn't enough time for me to do these things. I gave the girl a filling. That takes time.

No, it was a bluff. It must be. Another one of their mind games. No way these guys would go to the authorities – any authority. They were messing with me.

I'd made my decision not to help them again days ago. Whatever the risk to me, I had to stand firm; couldn't be pulled back towards criminality. My thumbs jumped around the keyboard as I formed my reply, fuelled by an odd mix of certitude and anxiety. I re-read it twice before sending.

No. And good luck with the police.

The answer came almost instantaneously.

Ha. Not the police, you cunt. THIS.
https://youtu.be/q0zkPHdRxsg

I frowned. YouTube? I clicked through to a dark screen above the title *Girl accuses paedophile dentist.* I swallowed a lump in my throat. They wouldn't ... The video played automatically. Shit. It was her.

No, no, no. It was on YouTube, for all to see! How could they do this? I pressed my finger on the screen and dragged the time counter all the way to the right, to the end, to the black screen and the first of the letters falling.

the
dentist
is

I screamed. How could I take this down? There was no coming back from this, ever. Everyone would see this.

Arjun.

Dad.

Oh God, Manesh.

The mums at school.

All the other dentists.

Everyone.

And it wouldn't matter that I was innocent. It wouldn't matter that this would never stand up under scrutiny. The mere accusation of being a paedophile was enough to put a bad smell on you that would never, ever wash out.

They had me.

I was ruined.

But as the letters continued to appear, I saw the text had changed. They weren't naming me – not yet. I felt a wave of relief, despite the inescapable threat of the last word.

the

dentist

is

warned

Arjun crashed through the front door, the water-logged wood making it stick in its frame again. His hair and face were wet; his soaked shirt clung to his chest. Water sprayed across the vestibule as Sparky shook himself dry. Arjun jumped back. 'Sparky, no!' He looked at me and narrowed his eyes. 'You OK, sweetheart?'

How could I explain I was about as far from OK as I'd ever been?

'Come,' he said, taking me by the elbow. 'Let's pick a nice dress for you.' He wrestled the phone from my hand. 'And put that damned thing down. There is nothing urgent or important enough to come between us and a lovely meal.'

CHAPTER FORTY-TWO

We didn't speak much on the way to town, both choosing to watch the dark streets pass through the windows of the black cab. I held my satin clutch on my lap and wondered why I'd brought it; Arjun made me leave my phone at home. I hadn't been able to reply to the email and could only hope the YouTube video was nothing more than a warning shot. That they would leave my name off until I had time to ... to what? To do what they wanted?

The taxi turned into Queen Street and dropped us at Royal Exchange Square, an imposing presentation of Georgian architecture denoting the city centre. I looked up. The traffic cone sitting atop the Duke of Wellington's head gleamed in the low-hanging moon. The horse-backed commander's sculpture with its orange cone had become the unofficial symbol for the city – nobody ever bothering to look at the slaughter of South Asians depicted in its frieze. And judging by the proliferation of merchandise bearing its image, the icon cast a large shadow over the city's preferred emblem of a pink square with *People Make Glasgow*.

Arjun held the door open for me as I swivelled out of the cab, careful to avoid sinking my high-heeled sandal into a deep puddle. The uneven cobblestones forged a tricky terrain as we walked arm in arm under the canopy of twinkly lights, a celestial ceiling for the open square.

A homeless man sat at the foot of the stone arch leading to the restaurant, a Starbucks cup in his hand. The blue fabric of my long dress brushed his weathered sleeping bag as Arjun pulled me past; a powerful illustration, if one were needed, of the country's screeching inequality. I gave the weary man an uneasy smile. The drizzle grew into droplets and I worried where he might sleep tonight; wondered how easy it might be to fall that far.

We ducked into the restaurant, its yellow frontage no doubt unchanged in its seventy-five years: a giant lobster sitting on two tins of caviar, perched over the green letters *Rogano*.

Inside was like a time warp. A maître d' took our damp coats in an anteroom with a sunken wooden stall, the kind a hat-check girl might have sat behind. We were led past the rounded booths of the art deco bar, bustling with guests dressed to the nines, enjoying the champagne and oysters the place was renowned for.

In the restaurant section at the back, the decor took a turn to the boring, in contrast to the beautifully presented seafood on gold-rimmed white plates I spotted on the tables.

The waiter was so keen to describe their many splendid cocktails it was difficult to stop him. 'We don't drink,' Arjun said.

'Of course,' the waiter said, nodding respectfully. 'How about a Shirley Temple for Madame then?'

'I'll have a sparkling water, thank you,' I said. Not drinking alcohol didn't automatically make you a child.

The menu gave us something to talk about and, as we ate, so did the other diners. Like different specimens placed in separate enclosures, one side of the room consisted of middle-aged couples like us; in pleasant but strained conversation after years of marriage, no doubt clinging to the notion that an expensive meal was automatically romantic.

The other side held larger tables with boisterous men in suits. On one, a greying executive-type had loosened his tie, raised his hand high to summon the waiter and made a big song and dance about the chosen wine.

'Wanker,' Arjun said. I nearly spat out my drink.

Many of us came to Rogano for the fish; others came to show off. It was a place to flash the cash and, looking at some of the more muscular patrons with gelled hair whose pretty, young consorts laughed loudly at their jokes, I wondered where that cash might have come from. It reminded me: 'We got a renewal letter from the home insurance.'

Arjun finished chewing his bite. 'OK. I'll take care of it.'

'No, it's fine, I was merely making you aware. We shouldn't rush to accept their price.'

He sighed. 'Yeah, and going on *CompareTheMarket.com* falls outside my skill set.'

'What's that supposed to mean?'

He took the napkin from his lap and wiped his mouth. 'It means I'm tired of you acting like I'm incompetent.'

A flash of tension crept up my neck. 'What? You're not incompetent.'

'Well, I know that. But whenever I offer to do something you say no. Because I wouldn't do it properly – not *your* way.'

'That's unfair. What? No.'

'Oh, come off it. You're doing it more and more lately. I see you moving things around in the dishwasher after I've loaded it.'

'But that's so ... unimportant.'

'Maybe to you. But when you get smacked down every time you want to help – like you're some kind of idiot – it's insulting.'

Tears welled in my eyes. 'Is that what you think? No. I do things so you don't have to. Because they're boring or dirty or tedious or involve people you don't like. Things that aren't worth your time.'

'That's not how it comes across,' he said, raising one eyebrow.

I shook my head, incredulous. 'I offer to do everything so you can have fun and aren't saddled with this kind of stuff. I can't believe ... How long have you thought this?'

'Always.' He shrugged. 'It's part of who you are – just not your finest side.'

A giant lump formed in my throat. I tried to swallow it but it stuck there, solid, acrid. 'All these years? All these years I was making your life nicer, giving you the gift of time and you thought I was criticising you?' The room swirled; the others guests' faces contorted into menacing caricatures, their laughter denigrating, directed at me. Me, the bad one – when I'd only ever meant well. I clung onto the edge of the table, felt the blood drain from my face. This couldn't be happening. 'Why didn't you say anything?'

All this time ...

'I didn't want to rock the boat.' He looked at me and reached for my hand. 'Sweetheart, it's OK.'

I felt panicky, pushed my chair back. 'No, it's not OK. I ... I just ...' It hurt. This hurt a lot. Like my throat had been sliced open, life pouring out of me.

'I need to go.' I ran off as he tried to grab my arm.

'Radha, wait.'

The gale nearly toppled me as I stepped outside. Dazed, I'd left without my coat. I wrapped my arms around myself and walked head down, tears flowing, in the opposite direction from where we'd come, cutting through Buchanan Street towards Central Station. I needed to get away. To escape. To go back in time. To change ... everything.

I wove through the onslaught of Friday-night revellers. I sobbed. Two drunken men bumped into me. I felt watched. As I neared the station, the rancid smell of chip shop made me gag. The queue for taxis was a mile long; the diesel fumes turned my stomach. If I didn't hurry, I would be sick. I walked on. Fresh air. Walked south, over the bridge. South, all I needed was to walk south. I shivered. I strode on, slowed only by the wet bottom of my dress becoming entangled between my ankles as it swished with each step.

'You all right, hen?' ... 'Can I help?' ... 'Aren't you cold?' The voices of concerned passers-by were drowned by my distressed hiccoughs. My tears and snot merged into the rain.

I deserved this. I deserved for it all to fall apart. This life that wasn't even real. Everything was wrong. Who even was I anymore?

My mind drifted to the YouTube video, the drug dealer's face, the orange box.

What had I done?

What would I do?

I floated aimlessly along the streets, yet somehow found myself outside my house. What time was it? The driveway lights were on, as was the tall lantern by the front door, but inside was darkness. My heart sank. I reached into my clutch for the keys.

The coat I'd worn to the restaurant hung like an accusation over the banister. Arjun was home. I took off my sandals and tiptoed up the stairs, aided by the neighbour's security light shining through our stained-glass window.

I went into the bathroom, took off my water-logged dress, its blue fabric now jet black, the sequins dull. I pulled my bath sheet from the towel warmer and wrapped myself inside, its heat suppressing my shivers. I wiped my face with a corner, transferring streaks of mascara. I dropped onto the stool, numb; looked at the reflection in the tall mirrored cabinet: me and not me.

Me only because of my hair, these long dark locks everyone admired. It was almost all they saw. Inside my cotton pod, a drop of water fell from the tip of my hair onto my breast. This hair that seduced my husband – though that too, could be a lie. These black silken strands that comforted my son, as my mother's had comforted me.

But he didn't need me anymore. Nobody did.

If anything, with all I'd done, I was a liability. Failing to protect my family when that was my job, my one true job.

I walked over to the cabinet and opened Arjun's side. I took his nails scissors, pulled a thick clutch of hair from out of the towel and cut.

And cut.

And cut.

CHAPTER FORTY-THREE

I was awakened by a mauve light filtering through the purple curtains of the guest room. My head jerked up. Did I oversleep? But it quickly dawned on me it was Saturday.

It took a second to make sense of where I was; to remember why I was there. I was naked except for my pants. An uneasy feeling took hold of me. Had Arjun come home? Had he known I was here? Had he even cared that I'd returned?

A strand of hair fell across my nose. It only reached my lips. I recalled the snipping sound of the tiny scissors, the mound of hair on the bathroom floor. I'd swept it with my hands, gathered it as best I could, and pressed it down into the small bin. I shook the towel out in the shower cubicle and watched as the quivering black lines were washed away. I balled up the towel and stuffed it in the laundry basket. Naked but for my damp underwear, I'd looked in the mirror at the new me.

But it was still me.

Nothing had changed. Nothing had been solved.

Still me, but choppy.

Stupid me.

The sound of pans clattering rose from the kitchen. Then laughter. I sprinted across the landing to fetch my robe from the back of my bedroom door. While there, I pulled a scarf from my wardrobe and wrapped it around my head.

The door to Manesh's room was ajar; his blinds still drawn. Discarded clothes carpeted the floor. Between them some sweetie wrappers, plates and an upturned glass. That was dangerous. I picked it all up to carry down then changed my mind. He'd asked for his privacy. I placed the glass and plates back exactly where I'd found them and headed down the stairs.

Sparky must have sensed me coming as he was pacing at the bottom. He hadn't mastered stairs yet and it was probably best to keep it that way. I gave him a tickle behind the ears and proceeded to the kitchen.

Arjun stood in front of his bean-to-cup coffee machine. The sound of frothy milk spurting into his mug drowned out his words. Manesh wiped down the counter and seemed to have heard him. 'No, I think the Balloch Castle loop is a steeper climb,' he replied.

'Time will tell,' Arjun said. He turned, spotted me. A barely perceptible frown crossed his forehead. His eyes paused on my head scarf. 'Good morning,' he said, and lifted the coffee to his lips.

Manesh looked up and grinned. 'Hi Mum. Are you feeling better?'

'Umm ...'

'Dad said you took a funny turn at the restaurant. Food poisoning.' He stepped towards me and placed his arm on my shoulder. 'How's your stomach? Did you manage to sleep?'

I nodded, felt the makeshift turban wobble on my head. I pressed my hand against its side. 'I'm OK. Thanks. Might ... eh ... have a nap later. What are you two up to?'

'We took the dog out,' Manesh said. 'So you wouldn't have to.'

'Not because you don't do it properly,' Arjun added dryly, while Manesh was distracted by Sparky licking his bare feet.

I bit my lip. Arjun was angry. Of course he was angry. I made a scene in the restaurant and he would've had to deal with the consequences, the stares, the curtailed bill. But I was angry too – and hurt. And I didn't know how to make it better.

'We're going for a cycle ride after Dad has his coffee,' Manesh said.

'That's great, darling.' I looked at my husband, this lovely dad, and smiled. Was it fair to be mad when he'd never complained? When all the while he'd taken my perceived slights and criticisms and never grumbled? I wasn't sure. But one thing I did know: we were fragile. I needed to tread carefully, sort out my problems myself.

'Nice turban,' Arjun said sarcastically. 'Going Sikh, are we?'

'I'm going to get my hair cut,' I said. 'I fancy a change. A fresh start.' I stared straight into his eyes.

'Hmm.'

You'd normally need an appointment at Namrata-aunty's salon, but I phoned as I got dressed, hoping she'd make an exception. There had to be some advantages to being regarded as family. I wondered whether it was smart to see her – she'd want an explanation – but I'd never get a slot anywhere else on a Saturday morning.

'Ai, Radha.' She tutted on the other end of the line. 'It's busy. Can it not wait?'

'No, Aunty, it's an emergency.' It wasn't a lie: I had dinner with Bela that night. I could not leave it like this. How would I explain it to Arjun? Manesh? To Dad when I saw him tomorrow?

She sighed. 'I'll fit you in, but I can't promise what time. You'll need to come here and wait.'

'Be right there.'

I jumped in the car, my feet still sore from the long walk home on heels. Two minutes later, I drove down her road, grabbing a rare parking space as someone exited Bela's shop.

The smell of hair dye and warm wax hung in the salon's air. Namrata acknowledged me with a curt nod as she used tongs to create perfect angel curls on a woman's head. In the next chair, a younger woman, white, sat with a crown of metallic folds on her head, flicking through a magazine. I presumed Namrata would have to finish her first.

I patted my bum and thighs. Shit. I'd left my phone behind. I'd still not checked back in, after the video, and now I was stuck here. Nothing I could do about it now; I had to get myself seen to.

I picked up *No1!* magazine, the layout of the front suggesting this was Scotland's answer to *Hello!* Except I soon saw it was filled with lesser celebrities and generally shorter people in sparklier outfits, at the legion charity events they reported on. I flipped through the pages and came across the photo of a woman I vaguely recognised.

Scanning the first few lines, I placed her: Cheryl went on about her, a contestant on a reality TV show on an island somewhere. She'd been sent home for punching one of the guys.

Her teeth were decidedly straighter than when Cheryl showed me photos in the gossip rags, and I couldn't help but notice a tell-tale man-made plumpness to her lips and cheeks. It seemed all it took was a scandal and a make-over to stay in the limelight. In one photo, she was promoting a new line of skin care, in another, she stood next to a politician, somehow having become a campaigner for the ***MeToo movement.

'Nobody should go unpunished,' a quote read. 'Where there's smoke there's fire.'

The words made me freeze in my chair, as if strapped in, an interrogation lamp turned on me. But what if you were innocent?

I thought of the girl, Samantha; her disgusting accusations. It was all lies. But she was a child. Who would believe me? We'd all seen how ruthless 'trial by public' could be when a man abused a grown woman. But a child! A child would truly bring the pitchforks out. I pictured myself on the news, holding my hand in front of my face to shield from the cameras, claiming it was all a mistake. Hung by a social media lynch mob before I'd even get a say, before I'd have to face the police.

People would swarm the clinic, our house – oh God, Manesh's school. My reputation, all that I worked for – Arjun, Dad – would be ruined. The story all the more newsworthy because I was a woman.

A perverted woman who preyed on kids.

I swallowed back tears. Why had the girl done this? Who could possibly have put her up to it? Even if she was one of them, somehow; maybe merely doing what her criminal family was asking her to. Surely, she must understand the harm she'd cause?

Namrata snapped her fingers in front of my face. 'I've been calling you. Chop chop. I haven't got all day.'

'I'm sorry. Yes. Ready.' I glanced at my watch. Hours had passed in a fog.

I sat in the chair. 'Don't freak out,' I said as I removed the scarf.

She blew out a long breath of air. 'Radha, my girl, what have you done?' She pulled at strands of my hair and looked at me wide-eyed from the mirror, her hands heavy on my shoulders.

'It's a long story.' Out of all the aunties she was the one I trusted the most. Maybe because she was a hairdresser. Didn't they hear everyone's secrets? I remembered telling Namrata about a boy I liked when I was thirteen. I swore her to silence because I didn't want Mum prying. Mum would have been way too invested. Who was this boy? Who was his family? Should we meet them? Namrata had kept her word, and the youthful relationship fizzled out. But this secret was too big to share. Too big for anyone to carry. I placed my right hand on hers. 'Don't ask, OK?'

She frowned and sucked her tongue. 'And you want me to turn this botch job into something?'

I winced. 'Yes, please.'

She walked back and forth around me in a semi-circle, eyeing the damage. 'All right.' She wiped her hands on her apron, picked up her comb and scissors and went to work. 'What a waste. But don't worry, I won't ask.' I felt her curious eyes bore into me as I gave her the expected appreciative smile in the mirror. 'You have your hair from your mother. So beautiful, she was.' She shook her head with pursed lips. 'What would she make of this?'

'It's only hair, Aunty. I just fancied something new.'

She shrugged. 'Speaking of fancying. My friend came in here the other day talking about a nice man she'd chatted to. I asked her where she'd met this seemingly polite and jovial man. And guess what?'

'What?'

'It was in your waiting room!' She chuckled. 'It was Gunbir.'

'Dad?'

'Yes. I'm going to set them up. You'll see. She's very nice.'

The idea of my father dating threw me. Dad with another woman? How did that even work at that age? Where would they go?

'She's a great cook,' Namrata added. 'I've already warned her he's a diabetic, to lay off the sweets.'

I pictured another woman at my mother's stove, touching her pans, her cutlery. It felt wrong. But then I imagined Dad sitting alone at the kitchen table, eating in silence. He deserved more. The empty chair could be filled again; there could be laughter. In my mind, I heard Dad's belly laugh. I smiled. It was a strange idea, but if Namrata said she was nice ... Plus, Dad would be out of my hair – whatever was left of it.

CHAPTER FORTY-FOUR

I stood at my door; the back of my neck chilly. I ran my fingers over its shaved area. Rough. I took a deep breath before opening.

'Hellooo,' I sang.

'In here,' Arjun shouted from the back.

I found the two of them in the utility room: Manesh rinsing one of his cycling boots, muddy clumps falling from the cleat, Arjun hanging the helmets on their pegs on the wall, both wearing the same striped, tight-fitting top.

'Did you have fun?' I asked.

Manesh turned; his eyes widened. 'Wow.'

I patted my head, followed the curve of my bob. 'Do you like it?'

'It's ... different. Bit of a shock. But yeah, sure,' he said. 'If you like it.'

My right side prickled; I sensed Arjun looking at me. I turned my head slowly, searched his face.

'You're beautiful.' He came close and swept my fringe slightly to the side. He pressed his lips together into a tight smile, small dimples forming in his chin. 'As always.'

I leaned into him with my shoulder.

'Oh, Mum, I need to show you something.' Manesh raced to the kitchen, leaving us alone.

'Are you all right?' Arjun asked. 'Is this because of last night? Because if it is, I'm sorry. I shouldn't have mentioned it.'

'No, it's OK. You were right to. I wish I'd known earlier.'

'So, the hair? Midlife crisis?'

I pulled at his jersey. 'Look who's talking, Lance Armstrong.'

'Might need to start taking drugs too, with the abysmal time I rode today.' He laughed.

My cheeks tingled. I laughed along, but it came out awkward. His eyes narrowed. I averted my gaze; spotted Manesh's shape through the glazed door to the kitchen.

'Wonder what he wants to show me,' I said cheerfully, and spun away.

Manesh had laid out a set of papers on the kitchen counter. I joined him, moving the tall salt and pepper shakers to the side to see. 'What's this?'

'It's the flyer for our show. And the order form. We can order up to four tickets, but we'll only need three, with Grandad.'

'Great.' I picked up the shiny, full-colour advert for the play. It looked professionally designed. A cast of about a dozen teens posed in 1940s outfits on the set, in front of the façade of a green, two-storey home that immediately conjured up small-town America. Like any mother, I zoomed in on my child.

'I love the hair, and the braces on your trousers.' I pointed my finger at a girl in a floral, calf-skimming dress towards the back. 'Is this Beth?'

'Yes.'

'Who does she play?'

'The neighbour's daughter. The lead role – the mother – went to Sam ... eh ... Samantha.' My head jerked up. He rolled his eyes. 'Samantha sounds more sophisticated, apparently,' he said.

I held the sheet a little further away; her face came into clearer focus. It was *The Girl*. And that was her name. Through the patio door, a warm beam of sun hit me, as though I were being drawn out of a dark cave. If that was her real name, I'd have her details on the clinic's system. Her address. I could find her, reason with her. If she was a friend of Manesh, maybe she'd retract ... Maybe ... My heart quickened, freedom within grasp. Her last name had an A. A-something. 'Samantha Andrews?' I asked.

Manesh frowned. 'No, Samantha Scott.'

I sank onto the breakfast stool, hope pulled from me like a magician's tablecloth. It was no use. Her address would be fake too. Then it dawned on me: I still knew where to find her. And I didn't have a moment to lose.

'I can't wait for the show. It looks amazing. What time's rehearsal?' I asked.

He glanced at the clock on the microwave. 'In half an hour.'

'Come, I'll give you a lift.'

Manesh looked puzzled. 'Weren't you going to take a nap?'

'You know, I feel a lot better now. Energised.'

CHAPTER FORTY-FIVE

Delayed by Manesh's last-minute grooming needs, we drove down Cathcart Road. We passed that odd, derelict, building at the Y-junction, bushes sprouting from the stonework at the base of what always seemed to me like a mini-Parthenon.

Further on, I turned right, towards the theatre's car park. Manesh put his hand on the dashboard, as if to slow me. 'You can leave me out front.'

'We're almost late, though. Besides, I fancy going in with you today.'

'To show off your new hair to the other mums?' he teased.

I cursed inside. In my haste to catch the girl, I'd forgotten the reason I stopped dropping Manesh off for his classes as soon as he'd been able to make his own way. It was near impossible to enter without a mummy-interrogation.

We stepped through the glass revolving door into the bustling lobby. A small queue waited as the seemingly harassed young chap at the box office table struggled with the credit card reader. I made a mental note to check when registrations opened to pay for the next session of classes. Spaces went lightning fast.

'I'm gonna go, Mum,' Manesh said. I watched him join Beth and some other kids as they streamed into the rehearsal room on the right. The teacher or director or whatever stood at the door, her hand clasping it high, so that the ample sleeve of her twinkly, peach kaftan fell over the entrance like a welcoming curtain. She scanned the foyer for stragglers.

Another woman bellowed from the back, urging the '-eleven to fourteen' class to hurry.

With most of the kids gone, the parents congregated by the coffee bar, chatting, while the two baristas danced around each other in the tiny space, serving the pricey cappuccinos and fruit scones that helped support the perpetually underfunded venue.

I craned my neck. Perhaps she hadn't gone in yet? But by now it was almost entirely grown-ups hugging their mugs and joining friends on tables at the rear. I sighed.

As I turned around to leave, a person bumped my arm, rushing inside.

'Samantha?' I said.

She stopped, looked back and smiled. 'Oh, it's you. Hello.'

Why was she being nice? Why wasn't she more shocked?

'Why are you here?' she asked.

'I'm Manesh's mum,' I said.

'Ah, my doting husband.' She smiled. 'Who knew?' She caught sight of the closed rehearsal door. 'I've got to go.'

'I need to speak to you about the video.'

She frowned. 'What video?'

The curtain woman re-emerged from the room on the right. 'Samantha, for crying out loud,' she shouted.

'Sorry,' she said, and ran off.

My hands hung limply by my side; my feet welded to the ground. I chewed my lip, bewildered. How could she not know what video I meant? She was in it. She named me.

There was movement in my eye line. A wave.

Shit.

'Yoo-hoo, Radha. Over here.' Heather was waving from a table to the side of the coffee bar. Two other mums' heads popped up like meerkats. I beamed my best smile and raised my hand in reply. I walked towards them, reckoning that if I stayed for coffee, I might catch Samantha on the way back out.

'I nearly didn't recognise you,' Heather said. 'Very like Twiggy.' Her eyes cast down to my thighs, which were anything but.

I curled the only strand of hair that could reach behind my ear. 'Oh this? I've been planning it for a while. It's easier, for work.'

I smiled at Kathryn, the mum I'd met at the gala, who'd brought the laundry. I'd remembered her name eventually. She'd seemingly infiltrated the in-crowd despite her relative newness. 'Hi,' I said.

She licked cocoa-flecked milk froth from her teaspoon. 'Don't you want a coffee?'

'I'm fine, thanks,' I sat down, shoving aside a newspaper. 'How is everyone?'

'We were talking about poor Arthur,' Lucy said, pulling her lips into a frown.

Heather shook her head. 'A tragedy. Those poor parents.'

'It's hard to imagine they never noticed he was taking drugs. I mean, you'd know, right?' Lucy asked, seeking validation.

She wouldn't get it from me. I kept my hands folded on the table; my ankles crossed under my chair.

Kathryn stirred her drink. 'I've never met them.'

'He was a nice boy. In Emerald's year,' Heather said. 'Manesh's too. The funeral is a week on Tuesday. The whole class is meant to go.'

Lucy's eyes widened. 'On a school day?'

Heather pulled a face. 'Indeed.'

'I heard they've stepped up surveillance around the school,' Lucy said.

Heather sat up, the mention of official school business being her domain. 'Yes, the parent association held a very good meeting with the police, who—'

'Anyone else think these scones are dry?' Kathryn said. She smacked her lips and ran her tongue along her teeth.

I wanted to shove the pastry down Kathryn's throat. Here was my chance at vital information and she'd changed the subject. As though Arthur's death meant nothing. Like what the police were doing wasn't important. But it was. My fingers throbbed; my pulse quickened. I picked at my nails, concentrating on the fine cuticles to stay calm. If they stepped up policing around the school, the dealers would be forced to keep finding other places to deal – they'd never let me stop.

The black screen with accusatory white letters spelling out my name flashed through my mind. I imagined the news spreading through school. Some child would see it and the mothers would pounce. What choice did I have but to do what the dealer asked?

But Arthur ... Where had his pills come from? What if I caused another Arthur? What if Manesh ...?

'Radha, you OK, honey?' Heather asked.

'Huh?' Everyone's eyes were on me. Could I go back to talking about the police thing or would that be weird? Suspicious even. I figured the moment had passed. I'd get the low-down elsewhere. 'Yes, the scones at Olly's are nicer.'

Kathryn put her plate, with partially eaten scone, on top of the papers on the edge of the table.

Heather took in a deep breath. 'You can't cover Adam Mooney up like that!' She laughed and pulled the newspaper's cultural supplement from under the plate. She pretended to brush crumbs off the movie star's close-up photo on the cover, the dark lighting amplifying the blue of his eyes, the sharpness of his profile. 'He's such a hunk.'

Lucy licked her upper lip. 'I would.' The two laughed.

'Even after the thing with that woman and her blog?' Kathryn asked.

Heather shrugged. 'I think that was completely overblown. And what? Should I not let Emerald near him because some floozy threw herself at him and then changed her mind? This could be her big break.'

'Emerald?' I said. Weren't we talking about some Hollywood actor? How did Heather always manage to bring everything back to herself?

'Yes, the audition,' she stated matter-of-factly. 'Did Manesh not tell you?'

'Tell me what?'

Heather leaned back in her chair. 'And this, ladies, is why I love having a girl. She tells me *everything*.'

A flush of anger rose inside. How flipping insensitive. But I pressed my nails into my palms and breathed in deeply. She wasn't to know I could've had a girl too.

Heather pointed at Adam's portrait. 'He's filming his new movie here in Glasgow. They need two Scottish teens, a boy and a girl. Speaking parts! They've approached the Citizens – because it's the best class in town – to offer auditions to the pupils here. Bit strange of Manesh not to say ...'

'Oh, *that* audition.' I hit my forehead with the base of my palm. 'Duh.' I made a dopey face. 'It slipped my mind. Manesh's up to so much lately, with having the lead here, the school show *and* playing in the Scottish cup for hockey and all.'

'And your new dog,' Lucy said. 'I hear you took in that poor neglected pup.'

'I did.'

Heather bared her Hollywood-white teeth. 'Aren't you a saint.'

Kids tumbled like an avalanche from the rehearsal rooms, prompting the grown-ups to rise as one to catch theirs.

I spotted Samantha and rushed towards her. I reached my arm out to tap her shoulder, but I was shaken by a man's shout.

'Samantha, come!' Like a dog.

The girl jumped and spun to where it came from. Her ponytail swished as she skipped towards him: a broad man in cargo pants and black T-shirt standing by the exit with his fists on his hips. He leered at me and snarled.

Did I know him? I stepped back, observing him from the corner of my eye. I vaguely remembered a man picking Samantha from the clinic, but I'd paid more attention to her granny. The stripes shaved on the side of his head didn't ring a bell and he was older than the creeps I'd had to deal with. Yet he was involved; he had to be.

'Creepy, huh?' Heather appeared by my side and whispered, 'That whole family gives me the heebie-jeebies. There's just something about them.'

'Do you know them?' I asked.

'God, no. And I'm not being a snob or anything. There's plenty of nice families here also from the state schools. But they're pushy, hugely. It's all about making Samantha a star.' She flashed jazz hands then patted a finger against her nose. 'There's something fishy about how Samantha got the lead in the play and not my Em.' She shook her highlighted hair and jutted out her chin. 'But Em's going to wipe the floor with that girl at the audition.'

'Well, good luck to her,' I said, having lost sight of Samantha and the man.

'Ah, there is my angel!' She threw her hands in the air as though there weren't fifty people standing huddled inside a small space.

As she fussed over Em, I searched for Manesh and caught him walking through the revolving door with Beth. I quickly followed.

'Wait,' I shouted.

They turned. 'Mum, you're still here?'

'Yes, I, well ...' A drop fell on my cheek. 'It's raining. I thought you'd like a lift.'

Manesh stared at his feet; shuffled. 'I'm walking Beth home.'

'But it's raining! I'm sure Beth would like a lift. Wouldn't you?'

Manesh threw his head back, shoulders slumped. Beth's gaze darted between us. 'Thank you, Mrs Bakshi. It would be nice to not get wet.'

'Let's go,' I said. 'You can give me directions.'

Once in the car park, Manesh opened the passenger door. Beth took the navigator seat. He slunk into the back, behind me. I snatched a view of only his partial face in the rear-view mirror, but it was enough evidence I'd get the silent treatment back home.

I started the car and Beth told me where to go.

'I heard about the auditions,' I said. 'That's exciting.' No movement in the back seat. 'Are you auditioning, Beth?'

'I'm not, Mrs Bakshi, I'm—'

'Please, call me Radha.' A tiny groan sounded from the rear.

'They won't have me because I have braces.'

'What's wrong with braces?'

Beth raised her shoulders. 'They were very specific: no braces or glasses.' She gestured where to turn the car left.

'So, Manesh. What about you?' I asked.

'They'll never pick me. I'm Asian.'

'Were they specific about that too?'

'No,' he replied. 'But the audition is during school hours, so you'd probably not let me go anyway.'

I couldn't deny we'd always valued schoolwork above everything, but this was a real chance at something great, something he loved. A memory popped into my head: Manesh, aged around six, my black kitchen apron around his neck like a cape, sitting on his knees on one of the breakfast stools, pointing in the distance. 'Thar she blows!' Arthur behind him, straddling a stool and pretending to row their makeshift boat with a long wooden spoon. 'I'm giving it all she's got, captain,' he'd cried. They'd laughed so hard at the misplaced Star Trek reference, that Arthur fell off the stool and hurt his wrist. His mum was not best pleased. I remembered his disappointed face when she picked him up immediately after I'd phoned her, berating him for risking his violin exam with a stupid, preventable injury.

A weight pressed on my chest. Poor Arthur. So much promise. Where did it go wrong? What was the point of life if it wasn't for living?

'I'm sure we can make an exception for something this big, sweetheart,' I said. 'Assuming that's what you want ...?'

He leaned forward between the front seats, his face glowing like on Christmas morning. 'For real? That would be awesome.'

'Told you she'd let you go,' Beth said.

I was really starting to like this girl.

CHAPTER FORTY-SIX

I pulled up outside Beth's home. The kids got out. Without needing to be asked, I drove on about thirty metres so Manesh could say goodbye unseen.

He jogged back to the car and stepped into the passenger seat. 'Thanks.'

'No problem.'

Rather than turn on the radio, he put his ear buds in and selected a song from his phone. So much for conversation.

When we got home, he dropped his coat on the console table in the hall. 'I'm going to have a lie down,' he said.

I watched as he climbed the stairs, his gangly limbs longer and thinner by the day; growing at such a pace it was no wonder his busy days drained him of energy. Was he eating enough?

I hung both our coats up in the cloakroom and decided to bake a cake. There should be enough time before my dinner with Bela. I popped into the study to let Arjun choose between banana and vanilla. He sat reclined in his comfy seat, his feet on the stool. He looked like a cartoon robot with his giant headphones on. I stepped forward quietly, careful to avoid his many audio cables. As expected, his eyes were closed. Sparky lay on his lap, dozing soundly in the silence of his master's voice.

I raised my hands to my chest and smiled.

In the kitchen, I put the kettle on. I pulled the eggs and butter from the fridge and fetched the flour from the cupboard. The bananas in the fruit bowl by the window weren't blackened or squishy enough, so I reached up into the spice cabinet for my little bottle of Madagascan luxury. It was rarer for me to bake this one and I fished my phone from my pocket to remind myself of the recipe.

My jaws clenched automatically, making me bite my cheek, as I spotted an email notification.

WHAT THE FUCK? screamed the title. I clicked through.

Stay the fuck away from the girl.

Or else.

https://youtu.be/q0zkPHdRxsg

My legs felt as though all their bones had been removed, and I clung onto the worktop to stop myself from flopping to the floor. Another video?

The same darkened room came on screen, Samantha sat on the chair. My pulse was thumping so hard in my ears I didn't hear her words, but she wore the same outfit, had the same mannerisms. This was the same video. Why was he sending it again? I gasped. Unless ... I tapped on the screen, an interminable sequence of ten-second jumps until the black screen at the end; the white text.

the
dentist
is

Where it had stopped before, new letters fell like the blade of a guillotine.

ra

That was it. The screen turned black. My hand shot to my neck; an air bubble was growing in my throat. Soon, my lungs would inflate, and I wouldn't be able to stop the air from coming in ... but not out. I massaged my throat to try to break it, push it down. My temples glowed with heat. Pop. Pop already. Please. What if it won't stop?

I squeezed my eyes shut, tears wetting my lashes. I conjured the image of the red balloon, my mother, her back to me, the pink sheen on her hair. *'Mum ... Help ...'* But she didn't hear me, and continued sewing as I suffocated. I scrambled towards the sink for cold water, arms flapping. I hit the stainless-steel kettle with the back of my hand. Yelped, as the scalded skin stung. I rushed my hand under the cold tap, then my lips and as my breath began to return, my whole head.

I sobbed and buried my face in a tea towel, drops of water sliding down my neck into my top. The bastards had me. They could destroy me with only a few more letters – only three would be enough.

They were waiting for an answer: my submission, agreement that I would accept another parcel at the clinic.

My answer could now only be *'Yes.'*

CHAPTER FORTY-SEVEN

I managed to recover, chat to Arjun, change clothes and cement my fate by emailing the dealers back, all before Bela arrived to take me to dinner. The planned cake had fallen by the wayside.

Under her open raincoat Bela wore a taupe shift dress, against which her subtly made-up face looked luminous. What a difference good news could make. A striking necklace hung low across her chest; two chains of silver loops interspersed with brightly coloured enamel butterflies.

'You ready?' she asked at my door.

I peeked out at the dark sky with its ominously fat, black clouds hanging low. 'Are we walking?'

'Don't be daft,' she said, holding up her car key. As she brought her hand down, her sleeve button caught on her necklace and broke one of the links. 'Oh no!'

I helped her scoop the chain as she unwound it from her neck. 'What a shame,' I said. 'But maybe we can fix it. Come in.' We inspected the damage. Two small silver loops had broken open. A short strand of connecting circles had fallen to the floor, the outstretched wings of the blue butterfly thankfully unharmed.

She succeeded in putting the bits back in order; but closing the broken loops by pressing with her fingers proved trickier. She raised the whole to her open mouth and positioned the chain between her molars. I smacked her hand away. 'Are you nuts? You'll break a tooth!' I wagged my finger at her. 'Don't you ever do that again.'

I took her to the utility room and opened the cupboard with the toolbox. I pushed the lid aside and searched for the pliers. I spotted a plastic bag deeper in the cupboard with Manesh's soldering kit, from his short-lived ambition to become an electrical engineer. Could we use that? I reckoned pliers would do the trick, even if they were too bulky for the job. Would've been better if we'd been in the clinic. Plenty of utensils for dainty work there.

With a few well-placed squeezes the chain was intact again, the butterfly safely returned to its habitat. 'Ta-da,' I said as I held it out.

'Nice to see those nimble fingers could tide you over as a jeweller if things went to pot with dentistry.'

I laughed along, though my innards squirmed at how close to home she'd hit. If my crimes came out, chances were rather than shaping cuffs out of gold, I'd be wielding hand cuffs in prison.

'Did your mother not make jewellery?' she asked.

'Yes, now you mention it. Only for friends, though.' I smiled as I recalled the carved, wooden box she kept her bits and bobs in; spare beads, metal wiring, tiny picks and pliers.

'I think my mum asked her to fix the metal embroidery on a sari once.' Bela wound the necklace in place again. 'Thanks for that. Shall we go?'

We passed Arjun on the way out. I raised an instructive finger, 'Tonight's dinner is the chicken with—' I pulled my hand back. 'You know what. You'll figure it out.' I locked arms with my friend. 'We're off.'

***

Malaga Tapas, the Spanish restaurant only a few streets away, bore a new sign outside, The *T* of Tapas creatively shaped like a bull's face.

The small room was bursting at the seams, and it took a little while to get our drinks order in. I didn't mind; the low lighting, red walls and thick, wooden pews made me feel safely enclosed. No scary men here – only greying couples, a group of foreign-sounding students and us. It was warm too, and the spiced cooking smells were comforting.

Bela and I fought about our order. She was paying, so I naturally ventured to the cheaper choices; but, greatly encouraged by the descriptive waiter, she insisted on picking something nice from the specials board. I relented.

She chatted away and I was relieved to see her usual spark. I couldn't imagine the stress she must have gone through, yet here she was, freshly rebounded. I admired her resilience. I picked at my *pescado andaluz*, fried fish nuggets that sounded more glamorous on the menu.

'Are you going to tell me?' she asked.

'What?'

'Don't you pull that innocent act on me, Radha. Something's up. Nobody goes and gets a radical haircut randomly.'

I smiled. 'I'm fine.'

'Bollocks. I've known you all your life.'

I couldn't tell the truth. She'd judge me like she judged heavy drinkers – worse. Would she even still be my friend? But I had to give her something or I was certain to face one of her giant sulks. 'Arjun and I had a fight last night, at Rogano. Well, not a fight-fight.'

'What do you mean?'

'He said something. And it shocked me to the core. Truly hurt.'

Bela's eyes widened. Her hand reached for mine. 'If the bastard—'

'No, it's nothing like that. It's stupid really. But after nearly twenty years, you think you know someone. You think your relationship is working ...'

'OK, now you're killing me. What the hell happened?'

'Turns out, every time I took it upon myself to do something, so that he wouldn't have to – all the domestic crap, the administrations, small tasks around the house – he thought it was because I didn't think he could do it properly. But it wasn't that! I wanted to be a nice wife; one that didn't nag, didn't complain. I did these things as a gift, in order for him to have fun with his music and bikes. No matter the cost to me.' I slumped forward. 'And it's been this enormous misunderstanding. Rather than recognising my sacrifice, being grateful for all my efforts, he felt insulted. It's like we've been living in different worlds all these years.'

Bela blew out a long breath. 'Oh, sweetie, that's awful.' She took a sip of her red grape juice. 'It does sound like you're not understanding each other's love languages.'

I frowned. 'Huh?'

'Love languages. I read about them a few years ago. People have different ways of expressing their love and then that's the way they want to receive love too. Let me think ... There's five.' She held up her fingers and bent one down for each one on the list. 'You've got time – which is the one where people long to spend quality time with you; touch; gifts; acts of service and ...' She held up her last finger and twirled it in the air. 'Dammit. Oh yeah, words of affirmation. Saying nice things, basically.' She clasped her hands together like a teacher ending class. 'So, yours is acts of service.'

'And time, I think. I want to spend time with Arjun, with Manesh – with you.'

'Then what are his?'

I thought of all the taps on my bum as he walked by, all the inconvenient little neck-snuggles in the kitchen, all the times he'd stroke my hair. And I'd gone and cut it off ... 'Touch, it's gotta be touch.'

I fiddled with my bracelet, a cheap bangle with a shaped lump of yellow and brown I only wore because it went with this dress. Arjun had brought it home one day, saying the golden flecks in the amber reminded him of my eyes. I didn't have the heart to tell him the amber was in fact plastic.

'Shit,' I said. 'Gifts. He's always giving me silly trinkets. Random key chains. The chocolates from conferences. Don't get me wrong. He buys nice stuff as well, and he gets thanked as he should ... except for the knick-knacks.' I raised my hand to my mouth. 'He must think I'm an ungrateful cow.'

'Hey, don't get upset. You didn't know. And the good news is now you do, and you can stop this accidental emasculation.'

'This what?'

'It's like you've been chipping away at his ego without realising it, making him feel less of a man. But you can turn it around. Recognise his gifts for what they are. The best thing you can do is make him feel needed. Ask him for help.'

As I plopped a green olive in my mouth, I wondered if I could. Could I tell him about the drugs, or would it break everything?

CHAPTER FORTY-EIGHT

The next morning, Arjun and Manesh were tying their bikes to the back of the car. I stood on the porch, wrapped inside a chunky cardigan. The wind blew my hair in front of my face and nipped at my ears.

'Make sure you don't tire him out. It's showtime tonight.' I flinched as I said it. Time to stop micromanaging. I waved my hand as if erasing what I said, and started over: 'Have fun, guys. See you later.'

I spotted a damp patch on the ceiling of the vestibule as I closed the door. I decided I'd ask Arjun to take care of it. I took out the recycling. Ran a cloth – again – around the fridge door handle. What was it with men and sticky fingers? I opened it, took stock of our supplies. They'd lasted well, given the supermarket shop was over a week ago. I'd avoided going after my panic attack last time, but I couldn't put it off much longer. Maybe try online? A twinge in my temple reminded me that online shopping hadn't turned out so well last time.

I shuffled in my slippers, alone in the house. I yawned. The broken nights were wearing me down, a heaviness pounding at the back of my head. How Arjun managed to sleep through my restlessness I didn't know. If I wasn't throwing the duvet off me, sweating from a sudden spike in temperature, I was snuggling up to him feeling an extreme cold – or fear, as red, threatening shapes formed inside my closed eyelids. Hands, faces, claws ... The dealers hooked into me like blood-sucking parasites. Never letting go.

Could I tell him? How would he react? He loved me ... Whenever I convinced myself this was the right way forward, I imagined him caring and understanding; whenever I imagined him making it all go away somehow, slumber would take me, but I'd wake again, heart racing. What if I was wrong? What if this would destroy us?

I'd almost confessed this morning, as I took him a cup of tea. But he was in a good mood, looking forward to his bike ride with Manesh. So, I bit my tongue. Later would be no good either: we needed to be a united front for Manesh's performance. Tomorrow?

I swallowed a lump. Tomorrow would be too late. They were expecting me to push ahead with a handover. I couldn't risk an angry confrontation in the clinic again. I had to let it happen.

And then I'd tell Arjun.

Afterwards.

Maybe.

With the transaction inevitable, I needed to figure out how it would work. It was a disaster last time. *'Find a fucking better place to put it.'* The bastard's voice had swirled in my mind as I fretted in between moments of sleep. I visualised every location at the practice but kept bumping against downsides and risks for each of them. Dad would see. Pauline would grow suspicious – and I didn't want to implicate her. Strangers weren't allowed at the back. Someone might steal it if left outside.

I called Sparky, picked up my keys and headed to the clinic. Perhaps if I rearranged some furniture ahead of time ...

The grass was patchy in the small front yard of the clinic, the low wall shielding the greener edges from the wind. We'd added plant pots to make the place more welcoming; but these stood empty in winter, their blue ceramic flecked with soil splashed up by rain. Sparky determined the one on the right to be the most attractive place for a wee.

As I entered, I took off my gloves. My hands remained rigid; the radiators weren't programmed to run at weekends. I tied Sparky's lead through the armrest of a chair. Couldn't have him sniffing around everywhere. Keeping my coat fastened, I performed a circuit of the place, leaving a trail of exhaled vapour behind.

I stopped by the steriliser. Cheryl had stuck a large Post-It on it recording the noise levels it made with every batch on a scale of one to five. She must've become fed up reminding me. Then it hit me. There was one way to get strangers to the rear: repairs. If the first guy came in with the box and said they were parts, then the second guy could pick it up again claiming the supplier contacted them to say they'd sent the wrong thing and to collect it. I tapped my fingers to my lips. It could work ...

The phone rang in reception. Who'd call on a Sunday? I was tempted to let it ring until voicemail picked up, but if it was an emergency, it might make them feel better to speak to a real person. No harm giving a little extra customer service.

'Dental practice,' I said.

'Good morning.' An American accent. 'I'm looking for Arjoon Bakchee?' the woman asked. Given her butchering of his name, she couldn't be an existing client. Probably a random sales call.

'I'm afraid we're closed.'

'But it's an emergency.'

I stifled a sigh. 'The Glasgow Dental Hospital have 24/7 care and can accommodate you. Or you can make an appointment for later?'

'Look, we were told to call here because he was the best. We need the best, and now. And complete privacy. Money is no issue.'

Trust Americans to throw money at everything. All the same, that steriliser wasn't going to fix itself. 'What's this about?' I asked.

'Can you guarantee your absolute discretion?'

I nearly laughed; this was getting more ridiculous by the minute. 'Yes.'

'It's for Adam Mooney. He needs urgent care. His cheek is swollen.'

Now that was a name I hadn't expected! I blinked a few times and used my most professional voice to ask, 'Swollen how?'

Her annoyance shone through in her voice. 'He's got a growth on his gum. I don't know, like a big blister.'

'Sounds like an abscess. I could take care of that. But it's not classed as an emergency.'

'It's an emergency when it costs thousands of dollars to stop filming for even an hour. Can you get mister Bakchee for me?'

'It's Bakshi. I'm his wife, also a dentist. And unless Adam Mooney wants some new veneers, I'm the one you want for this. I deal with abscesses every day.'

'OK, fine. But can you see him immediately?'

I looked at my watch. It would be quite something to treat a huge Hollywood actor; bring Arjun down a peg or two when he teased me about my patients. If only I could tell Heather. I pictured her expression: wide-eyed wonder with a shade of green.

'Why not?' I said. 'Where are you?'

'Blythswood hotel.'

No surprise. It was one of the few five-star hotels in town. 'It will only take you fifteen or twenty minutes by taxi,' I said, and gave our address.

I quickly popped on the heating. Pulled my mobile from my pocket. I found Cheryl in my contacts but stopped short of calling. She would absolutely freak out. Cheryl was a good, conscientious girl but there was no way she'd be able to stay quiet about something this big. My thumb hovered over the green call icon. I didn't technically need her; it was merely for protocol.

A shiver ran through me remembering the last time I'd been left without her. When the bastards set me up. The image of Samantha's video flashed through my mind. The nerves in my neck prickled.

But this was different.

I'd get this woman – presumably his assistant – to stay with us. I placed the phone back in my coat pocket and went to ready the instruments.

While waiting, I chuckled at the thought of charging them an extortionate fee. What could I get away with? Thousands? Given his status – hell, given prices in the USA – he'd pay it without blinking. But I consulted Arjun's price list and settled on a defensible two hundred.

A black cab parked outside. A head of long blond hair ducked out first. She held open an umbrella – more for privacy, it seemed, than actual rain – and a man stepped out wearing a grey hoodie. Butterflies filled my stomach. I opened the door.

'Hi, I'm Debra. We spoke,' she said folding the umbrella down. Adam kept his head down and followed her inside.

'I'm sorry it's so cold,' I said. 'The heating's not had enough time.'

'No worries,' Adam said, pulling down his hood. 'My face feels like it's on fire anyway.' He gave a lopsided smile that didn't detract from his good looks. 'Who's this?' he asked, bending through his knees.

'His name's Sparky,' I answered as Adam stroked his snout.

'I love dogs. Hate coming to the UK because I can't bring them with me.' He shrugged. 'Quarantine sounds horrible, don't you think?'

His assistant interrupted. 'Where do we go?' She eyed the back of the room.

'This way,' I said. 'I'll need you to chaper—'

'—need Debra to chaperone.'

We'd spoken at the same time. We laughed awkwardly, me unsure who the predator was meant to be. Women must throw themselves at him all the time. But hadn't there been rumours of sexual assault? I remembered Heather mentioning it the other day – overblown was the word she'd used. Either way, a witness seemed to suit us both.

'Come with me,' I said, waving them through to my surgery.

Debra sat in the corner, keeping an unnerving eye on me. Adam was a good patient – smelled nice – with possibly the best cosmetic dentistry I'd ever seen. His teeth gleamed as white as a new sink in the overhead lamp. It didn't take long to drain the abscess. 'The swelling will go down quickly. You should be good to film again tomorrow.'

'I can't thank you enough,' he said, his cheek visibly tighter. He jumped out of the chair and reached out to shake my hand. I pulled my gloves off first. 'I feel better already,' he said, cupping my hand in both of his. 'You're amazing,' he added, his blue eyes boring into mine.

I wished I'd kept my mask on because I was sure I was blushing. 'It was nothing.'

'Nonsense. You saved me. I won't forget this. Anything you need, you ask. Debra?'

She was by his side in a flash. She tucked into her handbag and took out a silver case from which she handed me a thick business card with gold lettering. 'This number comes straight to me. Do not ever share it.'

Back at home, I sat with Sparky in the living room, trying to read a book but finding myself distracted, my ears pricking with every sound. When I finally heard the car's tyres on our drive, I shot up.

I stood in the hallway, dancing in place like I needed a wee. Arjun looked surprised – and sweaty.

'Hi Mum,' Manesh said. 'I'm going for a shower. Not much time before the show.'

I waited for him to be out of earshot. 'You'll never guess what?' I said, practically pirouetting.

Arjun laughed. 'What's going on?'

I spread my arms wide and said, 'I treated Adam Mooney today!'

'The movie star? How come?'

'He had an abscess. Someone recommended you. I happened to be sorting some stuff at the clinic when the phone rang.'

'That's crazy.' he said, walking to the rear to hang up the helmets.

I skipped beside him. 'Crazy!'

'I hope you put in a good word for Manesh for the audition.'

I slapped my forehead. 'Oh crap. I never thought of that. But it wouldn't be fair anyway.'

He shrugged. 'Hollywood doesn't strike me as the most meritocratic of places. It's all about who you know.'

An idea bubbled in my head, one that could change everything.

When Arjun was safely in the bathroom, I patted my coat pockets until I found what I needed: Debra's business card.

I dialled the number, listened to a foreign ring tone go on and on. I was about to give up when I heard a curt, 'This is Debra.'

'Hi, it's Radha Bakshi. The dentist. From today.'

'Uh-huh.'

'Listen, when Adam said I could ask a favour. Do you think he meant it?'

'Yes. He's a man of his word. What is it you need?' she asked, in a tone that suggested I should consider it done.

So I told her.

CHAPTER FORTY-NINE

Gunbir

The posh car's seat belt was digging into Gunbir's shoulder. He ran his thumb under the wide, red-stitched strap to pull it looser, ensuring the lapel of his suit jacket was in the right place before he let it snap back. The pressure from the strap around his waist made him want to wee, but that sensation was nothing new.

Over time, he'd learned to recognise when it meant his bladder was truly full – in which case he had little time to lose – or when it merely led to his squeezing out a disappointing dribble in keeping with his age. Either way, the Citizen's theatre was reassuringly nearby. He stretched his legs in the roomy foot well and rotated his ankles.

As the streetlights flickered past, he looked at Radha in the passenger seat. Her profile was partially obscured by a curtain of her new hair. She kept trying to curl it behind her ear, but it would slip out again within seconds. She'd called it a bob which seemed a strange name for a woman's hairdo. He'd been so shocked, at first, when she came to his door to pick him up. He hadn't given it a good look before.

Mostly he worried what was behind this sudden decision. Was it stress? With what he'd seen, he wouldn't be surprised. He'd have to pay extra attention in future. See where he could help.

He examined the choppy cut, the way the lower part at the neck seemed to have been shaved, revealing dark spots on a strip of pale skin. It was miles away from what he was used to. All the women he knew kept it long, even as they aged, and it became streaked with coarse, springy greys. His stomach stirred with a memory of running his hands through Meena's long, silky locks, cupping her face and staring into her deep brown eyes.

He had to admit, the cut suited Radha. It was as if it framed her face, drawing attention to her rounded cheeks, putting her lovely button nose – Meena's nose – on display. He liked the green dress she was wearing too. And with Arjun in a nice blue blazer in the driver's seat, he'd be proud to walk into the theatre with them to support his grandson. He ran his hand over his freshly shaved chin. He tugged at the creases in his trousers and swiped away a white dog hair. He smiled. That wee beastie got into everything.

Maybe he'd need to tidy up the house a bit, make sure it was safe, now that Radha had asked him to watch Sparky in the afternoons. It had taken her only two days to realise the pup would be too lonely otherwise. *Well, he's not going to be lonely with me*, Gunbir thought. It was easy enough to pick the dog up from their house after having his lunch at the clinic.

He'd already started teaching Sparky to roll over. It was mostly a drop sideways onto the floor at this point, but Gunbir was confident they'd get there, even if it did cover his elephant rug in fur. Gunbir remembered how well Sparky had managed getting to 'legs in the air' on Friday.

He might have even gone all the way had they not been interrupted by the doorbell.

As though having the dog's company wasn't delightful enough, he got to see Manesh more often too, who'd been tasked with collecting him after his school activities. He never stayed very long – quite the busy schedule – but it was enough to have seen his excitement about the show tonight.

He wondered how Manesh would be feeling. Such a big audience! A warmth filled his chest. Proud didn't begin to describe it.

Arjun slowed in front of the theatre. 'Why don't you two get out here?' he offered. 'I'll park out the back.' Gunbir didn't think it would make much of a difference: they'd get just as rained on crossing the road as coming from the car park; but he appreciated Arjun's concern.

A damp, muggy air hit him as they entered, the result of too many people breathing and milling about a small space in wet coats. A man spoke too loudly near Gunbir's ear; a woman's hair swiped his cheek as she threw back her head and laughed.

'Can we go to our seats?' he asked.

'Why?' Radha said, absentmindedly. She appeared to be scanning the room. For whom? Surely Manesh would be backstage?

'I'm uncomfortable,' he said.

'Right. OK.' She sighed. She took the tickets from her handbag and handed him his. 'Go in and I'll ... get some sweets.'

Sweets? She hadn't let him have sweets for years. What was going on? He followed her gaze but saw only what you'd expect: a room full of anxious parents. Maybe that's all it was. Nerves for Manesh.

The curtain fell and the room was left in darkness for a moment. On what seemed to be the final note of the morose piano music that accompanied the last, heart-wrenching scene, the audience erupted into applause.

'Which one is his girlfriend?' Gunbir asked Radha as the curtain was yanked up again and the kids flooded the stage to take their bows.

Radha pointed slightly to the left of centre. 'That one, with the floral dress.'

'Ah! She did a good job too. Very convincing. They all did,' he said while his hands began to burn from clapping.

The curtain fell once more, and Radha jumped up and turned to leave. But everybody knows the curtain goes up and down twice. Actors always came back for more.

'Where are you going?' Arjun asked, leaning across him.

'I'm desperate for the loo,' she explained. *That makes two of us*, thought Gunbir.

Radha smiled reassuringly. 'I'll find you in the lobby.' She slipped in front of the man to her left, who looked annoyed when he had to retract his legs.

Across the stalls, audience members sprung up in small pockets. Gunbir frowned. Why this modern-day obsession with standing ovations? They used to have them only for truly outstanding performances. Now, whenever he went to the theatre with his friends – admittedly an increasingly rare occurrence since Meena's death – he was struck by the level of whooping and hollering. As though they were at a common football match. Nevertheless, Gunbir decided to join in. His grandson had been excellent in his role, and it did no harm to boost the young people's morale.

As he stood up, he became light-headed, and held onto the back of his seat. He shouldn't have eaten all those Minstrels, but their smell had been irresistible as Radha and Arjun had passed the bag between them, and they'd been too engrossed in the play to notice him sneaking quite a few out as they travelled in front of him.

Arjun took his elbow. 'You OK?' He helped him out of the row.

Gunbir patted his arm. 'I can take it from here. Thank you.'

As they reached the lobby, they each craned their necks around the many heads and shoulders surrounding them. 'Why don't you go sit, Gunbir, and I'll find her,' Arjun said while indicating a cordoned-off section by the coffee bar. 'We need to wait for Manesh to come out anyway.'

Gunbir eyed the entrance to the toilets. Two queues stretched into the lobby. He'd missed his chance. He unfastened the bronze clip that held the red velvet rope in place. The ushers would be cleaning the stalls and if anyone asked what he was doing there, he'd just play the old man card. Usually worked.

He stuck his hand up when a woman with long black hair exited the toilet area, but he quickly retracted it. Not Radha. Keeping a check on that general area, he glanced across the rest of the lobby. Wait. There she was.

Radha had her back to him. She was talking. Her bob shook; she gestured animatedly. She took a step sideways, enough to see she was speaking to a man in a dark T-shirt. Gunbir tutted. A T-shirt at the theatre ... His sleeves were rolled up; he obviously liked showing off his muscles.

Radha held her hands together, as if in prayer. She looked ... she looked as though she was pleading. Who was this man?

Gunbir didn't like this one little bit. Staying low, he slid to the adjacent table, where he could see the lower part of the man's face. He was talking, seemed insistent. He scratched his cheek, then nodded. He shifted his weight to the side and his full head came into view, sending a jolt through Gunbir's body. Stripes were shaved into the side of his hair. Was it him?

Gunbir peered around for Arjun; spotted him holding court with other parents, paying his wife no attention at all. He flipped his gaze back to Radha. She and the man were shaking hands, both nodding. What was this about? Gunbir's mouth was dry. He ducked a little as Radha turned, but managed to catch the man speaking again. Angry, pointing at her. With that hand! Gunbir's heart jumped. The spider tattoo was unmistakable.

Why, oh why, had Radha got herself embroiled with *him*?

He was shaken by a tap on the shoulder. 'Boo!' He spun round. Manesh was laughing. Gunbir exhaled and shook his head. 'You got me.'

Manesh's face was flushed with excitement. Remnant smears of stage makeup speckled his hairline. 'So? What did you think?' he said, letting himself into the enclosure.

'Wonderful. Truly wonderful,' Gunbir replied. 'Let's go find your parents. I need to go home.'

'Mum's right here,' Manesh said as Radha appeared at the cordon out of nowhere.

'Out, you two,' she said, unclipping the rope. 'You're not meant to be there.'

Gunbir pinched his lips. Who was she to lecture him on what you're meant or not meant to be doing? 'Who was that man you were talking to?'

'Me?' she said.

'Yes, you.'

'Oh, that was Samantha's dad. You know, the lead girl.' She put her arm around Manesh and squeezed. 'I was congratulating him on her stellar acting.'

'She *was* great, wasn't she?' Manesh asked. 'Where did she go?' he said. 'I didn't get to say goodbye.'

Gunbir followed his grandson's line of sight until he heard him say, 'Oh.'

The young girl was walking through the glazed revolving door. Followed by that man, his puffer jacket held over his shoulder – despite it being freezing out. A younger man, also in a puffer jacket, rotated out of the building and joined them on the pavement. He lit a cigarette; threw the empty packet on the road. Scum. They were all the same. Yet, there was something familiar about the young one. Gunbir's jaw slackened as he recognised his cocky walk ... It was the chap who'd walked into his clinic like he owned the place, leaving behind that cursed orange box.

CHAPTER FIFTY

Gunbir

The whole ride home, Gunbir stewed but didn't show it. It would be unfair on Manesh. He couldn't interrupt the boy basking in his parents' enthusiasm and praise. Who wouldn't love that? Gunbir also doled out compliments, though more measured. Couldn't have the boy getting big-headed.

As soon as they dropped him off, Gunbir wasted no time in settling at his desk. He woke his computer, which did its thing, whirring and scratching into action at a snail's pace. He was loath to replace it. Didn't want to risk losing any files – least of all these two.

His dappled beige mouse wore a layer of black at the buttons, where he touched it most. He moved the pointer across the screen, navigating through a series of folders hardly paying attention. He didn't need to. He'd been down this road a hundred times – though not for a while.

He shuffled in his seat, finding his familiar indent in the orthopaedic cushion. He cleared his throat; took a sip of water. Was he ready to see it again?

The directory window held file names that were a jumble of letters and numbers, except for two he'd renamed for easy reference. He clicked on Evidence_01.mp4.

Knowing what would come, he pulled his crumpled handkerchief from his suit's inside pocket. It had been years since he'd had an ironed hankie. Three years, four months and seventeen days.

The screen filled with grainy black-and-whiteness. The garden was illuminated only by a distant streetlight. You could just make out the small greenhouse at the rear, the glass glowing with reflected beams. Nothing much else yet. Gunbir checked the timer on the left upper corner of the screen. Only a few seconds to go.

A spotlight came on, bringing into clearer view part of the back door and the stone steps leading to the grass. Gunbir twisted a corner of his hankie. His beautiful Meena stepped out; turned back to the house and laughed. Who'd made a joke? Gunbir tried many times to remember what they'd talked about at the party before this moment, but it was no use. How could he have known then how important that funny comment would be? He hoped it came from him.

He watched her duck and sweep something off the steps with her hand, a slug perhaps. He lost her after two steps into the garden as she turned left towards the vegetable boxes. His heart raced; he wiped a bead of sweat from his upper lip, the soft cotton of the hankie comforting against his face.

His eyes locked onto the clock and when it was time, he concentrated on the whole screen again.

3 ... 2 ... 1...

Meena took a backward step into view, her right hand reaching behind her for the wrought iron stair rail. She missed, lost her balance. And there ... There was the unnatural movement of her hair, her curled ends lifting up and forward in a jolt, her fall accelerated.

To Gunbir, it was unmistakable evidence she was pushed. To others, it was evidence only of a gust of wind hitting her as she tripped – no matter how often he'd argued his case. There was something else, a white flutter, an odd shape that flashed in and out of view. It could be a hand, he'd pressed. But it could be a dozen other things, a trick of the light, even, the others had said. It was merely a bit of white and black. A hand would've been more white, bigger, Radha sensibly explained. And in the end, there was only so many times she wanted to listen, only so many times she'd agree to watch the tape.

Understandably.

Feeling the tears well in his eyes already, he clicked on the red X to close the video before the last part, where her head hit the step; where open eyes stared straight into the camera as though asking for help, blood pooling around her head, her one hand clutched across her chest, holding three courgettes she'd gone to fetch.

It would be eleven minutes and twenty-three seconds before Radha would step out.

Evidence_02.mp4 came next: the footage from the other outdoor camera, the one that was meant to capture the side of the garden she'd been in and the back gate. Gunbir shook his head. If only he'd fixed that camera as soon as the storm had blown it off course. But the ladder was in the garage and the wallpaper table was still there, folded out. How little would it have taken to move it out of the way? But no, he'd gone in, taken one look at the heavy pot of glue and five rolls of premium paisley paper for the bathroom sitting on top of the table and figured he'd do it tomorrow. Then tomorrow passed, and the day after tomorrow. And though it was always there at the back of his mind, there was also a deep pit of excuses: fatigue, full stomach, no other place to put the wallpaper things, rain, Meena wasn't around to hold the ladder, can't find the garage key. And with the vandals seemingly slowing down and concentrating on the clinic, it mattered most that those cameras worked. Or so it seemed at the time. How wrong he'd been. And in his sloth, he'd failed her.

He clicked the yellow triangle on the bottom row. The white numbers at the top began changing. With the help of some Googling, he'd saved his CCTV files in such a way that they both spanned the exact same timeline, give or take a few tenths of a second which his system did not record. It would have been better if he'd worked out how to run the two videos side by side on the screen – like when they ran live on his monitor – but after trying to make sense of search results, and downloading a huge, complicated piece of software with innumerable options and technical terms that confounded him, he'd given up.

This second camera was focused on the hedge, the wooden gate frustratingly out of view by only the tiniest nudge. Nothing but dark ground leading up to further darkness, but vertical and bushier. He checked the seconds, held his breath. A white-and-black flash passed along the edge of the screen, so quickly that it took him many attempts to train his reflexes to pause at the precise moment the hand came into view. Because that is what the white fleck was: a hand covered in a spider tattoo. Dismissed by others as *'could be anything; a bird'*. Admittedly you couldn't fully make it out, but Gunbir could feel it in his bones. Meena had to have been pushed. The universe wouldn't take his marvel away for no good reason. An accident seemed ... disrespectful.

He remembered the snot-nosed policeman on the night Meena fell – couldn't have been more than twenty, a child – flipping his notebook closed after performing only the most cursory tour of the garden. His interview, if he could call it that, was peppered with sorry-for-your-losses but little insight. The paramedics deemed it an unfortunate accident. Unfortunate!

And that was that.

Why would they have thought anything different at the time; him, Radha, the couples? They'd been inside, having fun – the guilt of which made his throat constrict, still. They'd been enjoying a grand old laugh while the love of his life lay there, conscious for how long? She hadn't called out, not with her mouth. But how long did she wordlessly seek help; had she wondered where they were? Pined for him to rescue her? How long had her life been salvable, if only they'd paid attention?

It was only in bed, later, in the loneliness of a half-warmed sheet, that suspicion stirred.

As Gunbir sat in front of his screen, his limbs heavy from his theatre outing, he recalled the eerie stillness of when he'd walked downstairs that first night, guided by the moonlight streaming through the window on the landing. He'd rewound the CCTV tape; made sure to back it up so it wouldn't be recorded over as the system normally did. He didn't find anything then, sitting in silence, poring over the muted picture. If only he hadn't been too cheap to buy the CCTV with audio. He might have heard something – a threat? – that would have told him things were amiss straight away. He couldn't see anything, but he felt it in his gut: she did not trip.

He and Meena had been suffering torment for weeks and never gave in. Was this the ultimate retribution? But why her? Why kill?

In the days that followed Meena's death, his friends fussed over him, cajoled, force-fed foods that went down like mud. Then Radha came and they grieved together. He still searched but she'd shouted at one point, in tears, '*Stop watching Mum die.*'

He did, but only when she was there. At night, he would tap the space bar for hours on end, moving the action forward frame by frame. With every viewing, after every contemplation of the laws of physics and their possible impact on Meena's hair, his mistrust grew. And then he saw what had been there all along.

When he'd called the police with his find, they sent that same hopeless juvenile with his excess of aftershave. Gunbir showed him the recordings from both cameras. The hand. But like Radha and his friends before, Gunbir was dismissed, branded – with the most well-meaning terms – an unsurprisingly muddled, heartbroken fool. He knew his case was weak, with no leads to a perpetrator – no evidence there even was a perpetrator – and no motive that he could share. After politely hearing him out, the officer left Gunbir with the scant comfort of more sorry-for-your-losses.

Like so often in these solitary years, Gunbir now wondered: what if he'd told them? Should he have come clean to the officer about the harassment he and Meena endured? Would they have investigated properly then? Found the bastards?

Going through the varied scenarios in his mind again, he settled on his usual answer. If he'd told them, they would've wanted to know why they'd been targeted. He would've been forced to confess to hitting the man with his car, leaving him injured, paying for his silence. Gunbir could offer little in the way of description beyond *'white man, muscular, shaved head, puffer jacket, tattoos.'* He hadn't paid any attention to possible discernible attributes in his terrified state. There would've been nothing of substance to go on. And if the authorities somehow did find the culprits, his shameful crime would come to light: the video in which he'd paid off the victim of the accident.

Gunbir sighed and wriggled his toes to get some circulation going. No, he'd been right not to bare it all. His world was irreparably broken, and confessing would only have caused trouble for him – with no justice for Meena.

He leaned back, blinked a few times to relieve his tired eyes. Homing in on the screen once more, he squinted. There was no denying it. An overwhelming feeling of anger washed over him. Yes, it was only a split-second flash but Gunbir believed with a feverish certainty that it was *him*, *his* hand. The tattooed hand that had pointed at Gunbir to fork out the cash back then; the hand he'd seen pointing at Radha tonight. The hand of the bastard he would never let hurt his family again.

CHAPTER FIFTY-ONE

'Can I have a Coke?' Manesh asked as we got home from the theatre.

I poked him in the belly. 'Fat chance. It's late and a school night.'

Arjun took off his coat. 'Plus, I think you'll have trouble enough sleeping as it is.' He cocked his head in the direction of the stairs. 'On you go,' he said to Manesh.

'But I want to read the audition scene they gave us,' Manesh whined. 'I would've done it in the car, but you always give me grief if I turn the light on.'

'Fair enough,' Arjun said. I disagreed, but let it slide.

We followed him to the kitchen. He flipped on the lights and climbed onto a bar stool. I served up three glasses of filtered water from the fridge door. Arjun and I leaned against the worktop. Manesh's lips moved soundlessly as he read, eyes brimming with excitement.

'Oh,' he said, dropping the hand holding the script into his lap.

'What's wrong?' I asked.

He pulled a disgusted face. 'They kiss.'

Arjun laughed. I shot him a look.

'The boy and the girl they're auditioning for?' I asked.

Manesh sighed. 'Uh-huh.'

I smiled reassuringly. 'Well maybe this is only the audition piece and you don't actually need to do it.'

'No,' he said. 'They told us this was the actual script.'

Arjun took the papers from his hand. 'Well, kissing scenes are part and parcel of being an actor. And I wouldn't have minded some smoochy action when I was fifteen.'

'Dad! Gross,' Manesh said, punching his father on the arm.

'Shame Beth isn't auditioning,' I snickered.

'Stop it you two,' he wailed. 'Can you imagine if Emerald gets the part? She's a pain in the ass.'

I frowned. 'Now, now. Em's all right.'

'You don't know her, Mum. She's a nightmare.' He batted his eyelashes and pursed his lips. 'I'm the star, I'm the best,' he mimicked in a high-pitched voice.

'Maybe she's the best kisser too.' Arjun roared at his own joke.

'Stop it,' Manesh and I shouted together.

The hairs on the back of my neck prickled. Here was an opportunity. 'What's Samantha like then?'

'She's not too bad,' Manesh said, shrugging. 'Though she scares me sometimes.'

My stomach lurched. What had she done to my boy? 'How so?'

'She's so driven, can get very intense in her scenes,' he replied. The tension in my shoulders dissipated. Manesh looked at his scene again. 'Oh, what's the point?' he moaned, jumping off his stool. 'I'll never get that part anyway.'

'Hey,' Arjun said. 'What kind of attitude is that?'

'Sweetheart, you've got this in the bag. I promise,' I said.

'You're my mum. You have to say that.'

Arjun grabbed him by the shoulders. 'Come on. Where's that killer spirit?'

'What? Like Samantha? Once, she threatened to cut Emerald if she stood in her way.' He scrunched his nose and shrugged. 'She didn't mean it.'

My knees wobbled. Didn't she? With that family?

'Like your mother says: you're talented. I believe in you. You've got this.'

Manesh's face lit up, eyes shining with the promise of tomorrow.

More than ever, I knew I'd made the right decision to call Adam Mooney's assistant.

CHAPTER FIFTY-TWO

Thick beams from the rising sun funnelled through the red sky and the kitchen's patio doors, drawing a fiery halo around Manesh's head. He held my chin and looked at me with grave concern, his forehead furrowed, his voice little more than a whisper. 'I understand you're scared. But trust me. No matter what the world throws at us, we can face it – together.'

I banged my spatula on the cast iron pan. 'That's a wrap!'

Manesh stepped back. 'Ugh,' he groaned, shaking his arms loose as if ridding himself of the melodramatic awkwardness of the audition piece.

I flipped the three pancakes in the pan, the smell of browned goodness making my mouth water. Judging by Sparky's wet-nosed nudges at my bare ankles, I wasn't the only one whose hunger was awakened by the scent. I smiled at the air bubbles slowly escaping the dough, leaving a cratered surface, like flattened moons. If we were going to bunk off school and work, we might as well have the best possible breakfast.

'I can't believe you've got all those lines memorised, Mum.' Manesh said, licking his fingers to pull spikes in his hair, which he checked in his reflection in the oven door.

'What do you expect? We've been practising for ...' I counted in my head, '... three days.' How was it Thursday already? I felt I'd achieved nothing all week. And now a morning off again.

Thank goodness the Health Board's inspection of the clinic went marvellously on Monday. I'd pre-emptively reserved some slots to deal with the possible aftermath, should they find fault. But incredibly, they had little comment and it seemed we were in line to pass with flying colours – in many parts thanks to Dad. The sudden availability of patientless slots meant I was able to take Manesh to his audition. Butterflies filled my stomach. This movie mattered more to me than he would ever know.

Manesh's phone pinged. A wide smile filled his face as he examined the screen.

'Good news?' I asked.

He angled the phone away from me. 'It's a text from Beth.'

'Oh?' I eyed him eagerly.

'Just wishing me luck for later.'

I'd spotted many more lines than that in the text, in the millisecond I'd caught a glimpse, but if that was all he wanted to share, I needed to respect that. Whatever teenage sweet nothings might look like in this day and age, I was confident they were nowhere near as corny as the pseudo-romantic rubbish from the film script. It was no wonder he hadn't wanted to rehearse with his girlfriend. She was only new. Not that declaring his unwavering devotion to his mother was any more comfortable.

I watched my man-boy as he typed his reply, his long brown lashes, his smooth cheeks with a hint of peach fuzz that stopped abruptly at his bare upper lip. An increasingly square jaw invading his gentle, rounded features. I suspected he'd also chosen not to rehearse with Beth so as to not rub her nose in the fact she hadn't been able to apply. I hoped his kindness would stay.

'Get the plates, will you?' I slid the last three pancakes onto a wobbling pile. 'Do you think I've made enough?' I asked jokingly.

'I don't know, Mum, I'm a growing boy, remember?' he replied, patting his stomach. He laid out two place mats on the breakfast bar, and the plates. 'What do we do about Grandad's lunch if you're not at work?'

'Did I not tell you? Grandad is coming too.'

His eyes widened. 'You know you're not allowed inside, right?'

'Don't worry. I told him we'll have to wait outside the hotel. But he's incredibly keen to come. He's been asking lots of questions about how it will all work. I think he just really wants to be there to support you.'

Manesh grinned. 'That's sweet. I think he was genuinely surprised about how good the play was on Sunday night. He's been talking about it every time I've collected Sparky. Wanting to learn everything about the cast.' He chuckled. 'I think it's his not-very-subtle way of finding out about Beth.'

'Ha.' I chose not to tell Manesh I'd found Dad to be in a funny mood all week. And Pauline had reported he'd been sitting in reception looking intensely at everyone who came in, rather than doing his usual puzzles. I'd put it down to nervousness about the inspection on Monday, but it continued after. I took a deep breath, guilt pressing down on me like a weighted blanket. I'd have to have a word. Hanging around being the sympathetic patriarch was one thing, but I couldn't have him creeping out the patients.

I took a bite of my pancake, the springy dough squeaking between my teeth as I mentally practised what I'd say. Poor Dad. It must be hard to grow old all alone, to not have a purpose in life anymore – not really. Work had meant so much to him. He'd built his clinic from scratch, making it thrive to be able to achieve the epitome of success: sending his two children to private school. And for that privilege, I was going to kick him out.

Sparky whined at my feet, eager for some of what I was having. He'd become quite the little beggar; had quickly mastered how to angle his snout and widen his eyes to make you melt. I bet it was Dad's fault, feeding him bad habits. I smiled at the image: Dad in his armchair, tray of snacks on his lap. Sparky scratching his shin, maybe performing a trick or two for which he'd get ample reward. Then it hit me. I knew how I could make it up to Dad.

'These are delicious,' Manesh said, chewing. He placed his hand on mine, causing my heart to skip. 'And whatever happens today, Mum. Thank you.'

'It's my job.'

I walked to the fridge for some orange juice. A sheet of paper fell to the ground, one of the many school letters, take-out leaflets, bin collection calendars and assorted reminders adorning the fridge door, held in place by a multi-coloured tour of the world in garish tourist magnets that I'd come to realise were tokens of Arjun's love. I bent over to pick the sheet up and felt punched in the gut. It was Arthur's memorial invitation.

I thought about Tuesday's ceremony; the image of the children walking into the crematorium in single file, heads bowed, uniforms on. A chain of golden school crests on blue blazers parading by the other mourners and filling in the three rows behind Arthur's grieving family. I remembered sitting with the other parents further back, watching our babies' shoulders shake from afar, hearts breaking as we recognised our child's sob among the many, with no opportunity to comfort them. Lumped together, helpless, we shared our shock and commiserations – but not what we were all thinking: thank God it's not my child.

It was the school's idea to have the pupils in uniform and all together, to reinforce their motto of *One Community*. What good would that do Arthur's parents? He was their only child. The school could get stuffed.

I recalled wondering if they blamed the school for not picking up on his habit earlier, not calling in the police at the first complaint about suspicious men roaming the alley.

A wave of nausea hit me now, as it did then. Would they have cause to blame me? Did I contribute to Arthur's death by letting those awful men trap me, use me, deal through the clinic? I wiped my brow. Warm.

Would there be more children harmed?

Not if everything went to plan.

The cacophony of the Citizens Theatre sounded in my ear again, a vivid memory of it mixed with my thumping pulse as I'd approached Samantha's dad – clearly the leader of this gang, his otherwise threatening son merely hobbling behind him that evening. I rubbed my jaw, remembering the tension. I could still picture his eyes narrowing when I asked for a delay. Doing a drop off on the day of a Health Board inspection was bound to draw unwanted attention to them, I'd argued. His eyebrows jumped in surprise and a sly grin formed as I'd suggested another arrangement. An arrangement for which it was make or break today.

No, I would have no hand in other deaths.

Not if this man was to be trusted. This was ultimately what it came down to. So far, there was no reason to doubt it. I'd been left alone all week.

He'd nodded; smiled, even. Shaken hands on it. Surely, even amongst criminals that counted for something?

I closed my eyes and inhaled slowly. Was I being a fool?

Even if he got what he wanted, there was no guarantee he wouldn't be back with more demands, stringing me along forever.

I balled my fists. All I had was his word. And if he broke that, I'd kill him.

CHAPTER FIFTY-THREE

'I think it might be time to head back,' Dad said, covering his watch up with his shirt sleeve and resting his arm on the fragile-looking glass table of the trendy, city-centre café.

I glanced at the clock on the wall which consisted of nothing more than thin, black stripes in four directions with two red pointers indicating the time. If I hadn't expected it to be nearing eleven o'clock, I wouldn't have been able to read it.

'You're right.' I tipped the dregs of my coffee in my mouth. 'Let's go.'

Dad put on his coat and patted his pockets. We headed to the exit. My cheeks burned as I was hit by a waft of hot air from the heater, positioned above the door as though intended as a parting gift to those about to brace the cold.

We walked back the four blocks where we had dropped off Manesh, two excruciating, nerve-racking hours ago. Though I did my best to not let my excitement influence my speed, I noticed Dad kept up surprisingly well. Perhaps my nagging about massaging his feet daily was starting to pay off.

'I've got something to confess,' I said, figuring this was as good a time as any.

Dad stopped in his tracks. He cleared his throat; inhaled deeply with a quick shake of the head. He clasped his hands together and placed them on his stomach. Nodded solemnly.

I smirked. 'Don't look so serious. What on earth do you think I'm going to say?'

A confused frown furrowed his brow. 'I don't know.'

'Listen, you've been awesome at taking care of Sparky in the afternoons. And I know you've been frustrated that I didn't want you to walk him because of your feet. But I can see you're doing a lot better,' I said gesturing towards his chunky brown shoes. 'I hate to admit it, but you were right. We are too busy to properly care for a dog. It's not fair on him. What I wanted to ask was: would you take him in?'

He stared at me, blinking. 'You mean adopt him?'

'Yes. He's a lovely little fluffball. We'd miss him, but it's the right thing to do. And it just means we'd have to visit you more often.'

He raised his hand to his face, scratching at his nose; seemingly taking a moment, not catching my eye. 'I would love that,' he said.

I threw my arms around him and gave him a big squeeze. Feeling a slight shake, I held on a little longer than necessary. No point embarrassing a proud man. 'Thank you,' I whispered.

We slowly walked up the final steep climb and arrived in front of the Blythswood hotel. Its width never failed to impress me. I gauged the imposing Georgian building to be three times wider than its four storeys in height, spanning a whole block. It looked out onto a meticulously groomed garden at the centre of the square.

I could still taste the frothy mocktail I'd been served one night in the first-floor bar. Rhubarb and rosemary. I'd been seven months pregnant with Manesh, feeling like a bloated cow in the glitzy room. I remembered struggling to get out of the oversized red, velvet statement chairs and Arjun laughing as he pulled me up and nearly fell backwards into the large window.

We wouldn't be getting inside today. Two security guards stood on top of the short flight of stairs, standing stiff and upright, as though they'd been hired as the fifth and sixth stone columns to grace the porch.

Three reporters with cameras leaned against the wrought iron fencing, fiddling with their phones. Other people filled the pavement in little groups, wrapped up in thick, hooded coats, fighting the shifty winds like wobbling bowling pins.

Dad and I positioned ourselves slightly to the side of the entrance. Just as well we hadn't left it too late. More people arrived on foot from the square's radial streets, becoming quite a crowd leaking into the street. They couldn't all be concerned with the auditions.

Young people took selfies with the hotel in the background, checked their phone screens and gushed excitedly to their friends about what they'd learned. I overheard that not only had everyone apparently found out Adam Mooney was in town and where he was staying, but they also seemed to believe he'd be coming out soon.

My breathing quickened. Not long now.

At my side, I felt Dad patting his pockets again. 'Have you lost something?'

His hands snapped to his side. 'No.' A pause, then he grinned. 'Force of habit.'

'You're not getting all old-man-forgetful on me, are you?' I joked.

He tapped a finger against his temple. 'Memory like an elephant.'

I smiled as my heart warmed. Him and his elephants.

A frisson of excitement spread through the crowd. Had somebody heard something? I craned my neck to catch a glimpse of the entrance. The reporters jumped to attention; long black lenses pointed at the steps.

Debra, Adam Mooney's assistant, stepped outside, her long blonde hair blown into the sky like a fanned flame. She cast her eye over those assembled, her clipboard held firmly against her chest. She grimaced slightly before returning inside.

She reappeared seconds later, to a giant murmur. She stood by the side of the enormous black door. A boy exited, looked around glumly, descended the steps and turned towards what must have been his family. Another boy came, equally morose, then a girl, and another. This one concentrated on her feet and turned in our direction as she hit the pavement.

Behind us, I heard a maternal, 'Oh darling, I'm sorry' and a sob.

I rubbed my gloved fingers together, fighting the cold. I sensed Dad rocking back and forth.

Another girl came out. Emerald! I peered around. Was Heather here? I hadn't seen her arrive. Emerald hesitated on the top step, wiped her nose on her sleeve. Her shoulders slumped as she ran down. She shoved aside a few onlookers then buried her face in her mother's bosom. Heather kissed the top of her head, while giving Debra a death stare.

Relief washed over me, though a niggle persisted in the pit of my stomach. No matter how abhorrent her mother, I hated seeing pain inflicted on the girl. *Little would she ever know I might have saved her from more*, I thought, Manesh recounting Samantha's threat if she lost ringing in my ear.

Dad knocked my shoulder with his elbow. He was waving at Manesh at the top of the steps. Manesh waved back, holding an A4 folder in the air and displaying the most magnificent smile. He turned to Debra, who pointed to the ground while shouting an instruction. He bounded down the stairs.

I wiped away a nascent tear, the rough wool of my glove scratchy against the delicate skin under my eye. He ran to us, weaving through the spectators, and stopped with a final, gleeful skip. 'I got the part!'

I held his face with both hands, rubbed my thumbs along his cheeks. 'Of course you did, my fabulous boy. I never doubted it,' I lied.

'Well done, Manesh,' Dad said, wrapping an arm around his shoulder.

'We need to stay here for a moment,' Manesh said, breathless with excitement. 'Adam's coming out.'

I pressed my hands against my tummy to soothe the knot inside.

Moment of truth.

There she was! I shuffled for a better look. Was she happy? A folder. She held a folder too. Thank God. I stepped forward, couldn't lose her. I felt something underfoot; a woman gave me a dirty look. I didn't bother with an apology. I stood on my toes and watched as Samantha ran to the far side of the crowd and jumped into the arms of her father, the stripes in his hair easily recognisable. He twirled her around, not caring who he hit. He put her back down and searched over people's heads as he held her near.

I rocked further onto my toes, pretended to scratch my head to subtly give him a wave. At last, his eyes met mine. He smiled.

He smiled!

And nodded.

It was over.

A beam of sunlight pierced through the dark clouds. I leaned into my son, my head fitting perfectly in his chest, and nearly wept as he put his arms around me. I was finally safe.

I spotted Dad looking intently in that same direction, with the angry face that always made me cower as a girl. What happened? Then Manesh was knocked sideways, stumbled, had to let go. Something was up. I turned to face the hotel again.

Debra descended and used her clipboard to encourage people to step back. The reporters took advantage of the extra room to settle into prime position. Displaced fans objected and a little kerfuffle broke out.

A voice at the rear began chanting 'Adam, Adam.' Soon everyone joined in. The security men pulled at their vests and checked their belts. Debra retreated to the safety of the first step and held on to an ornate spike on the fence.

Adam Mooney exited the hotel. Screams erupted. I thrust my hands onto my ears. Elbows and shoulders pushed us forward, squashed tighter, suffocating. I held onto Manesh. I caught sight of Dad's profile as he was swallowed by the masses. Was he frightened? I shouted, 'Dad!' But he couldn't hear me. I couldn't even hear myself.

My fingers tingled, the first sign of a panic brewing. I closed my eyes and swayed with the throng to stem the disquiet inside. He'd be fine, I told myself. People will make room for an old man. He'll find a way out.

When the movement subsided, Adam gestured for silence. An array of phones on selfies sticks shot up, obstructing my view. Manesh pulled at my sleeve just as I thought I saw Dad.

'Mum, get your phone out,' he said. 'Adam's going to call me up.'

The actor took a moment to rest his gaze on each section of his audience, as if he were on stage. 'Hello, everybody. Thank you for coming out, particularly in this weather. I'd been warned November might not be the best of times to visit Scotland,' he said, tugging at the light-blue scarf wrapped around his neck. 'But where else could we get the guaranteed rain we needed for a movie about a giant flood?' He flashed his wide Hollywood smile, inviting laughter that came on cue. I noticed that the swelling in his left cheek was most definitely gone. 'Only kidding,' he said. 'This is a beautiful country with lovely people.' A cheer erupted. He grinned; clearly knew how to play to the gallery. 'I look forward to visiting when the sun is shining and—'

'Don't hold your breath!' someone shouted.

'Aye, and ye'll be food for the midges then,' another quipped, rewarded by knowing titters.

'OK, OK. As you're all aware, we are filming in this city for the next few weeks. Many of you have been standing out here patiently for days. So ...' He acted out a small drum roll. 'I think it's time to let you in on a little secret. Our cast will be joined by two young people from your very own city, Glasgow. And I am delighted to introduce them to you.' He checked in with Debra, who raised her hand and snapped her fingers.

Adam snuck a peek at what must have been scribbled notes in the palm of his hand. 'Manesh Bakshi, where are you?'

'I've got to go,' Manesh said.

'Hang on.' I put my hand on his shoulders and conga-lined through the gap forming between the applauding fans.

'And Samantha?' Adam asked, scanning the block. A shriek from the far side. He clapped. 'Samantha Scott everyone.'

I joined Debra on the pavement as Manesh and Samantha bounced up the steps and posed with Adam for the dozens of cameras. Adam held both their hands up like boxers in a ring. The money shot for the tabloids.

'You got lucky,' Debra said. 'It was a very close call between three girls, so it was easier to give you what you wanted.'

'I can't tell you how grateful I am. You have no idea what this means to me,' I said. 'And Manesh ...' I shook my head in disbelief. 'It's amazing.'

'Yeah, I saw the name on the list this morning and wondered. Then I saw you with him.' She cocked her head towards the trio in the limelight. 'He's quite a talent.' She picked at her clip board. 'It's none of my business, but if he's your son, why did you ask me to give this Samantha a part?'

I wanted to tell her I had every confidence in his acting, that I didn't think he needed the help. But that would be a lie. Knowing I'd only been granted one wish, I'd opted for survival.

A cluster of angry shouts sounded from the right. Debra seemed to curse and trotted up the stairs. I looked up for Manesh. Adam's California-tanned face became pale. He let the kids go and sprinted inside. The security guards blocked the entrance.

Around me, bodies were moving like crashing waves. I grabbed hold of Manesh's hand when he came down, wound it around a bar in the fence. 'Stay here, I need to find Grandad.'

'Mum—' he pleaded.

'Stay.'

I skimmed the edge of the fence, careful not to let the horde consume me. People scampered from the square; space opened up. The familiar round shape of my father appeared towards the front, as though expelled by the herd. I ran to his side. 'Dad!'

His head swivelled to find me.

'Where were you?' I asked.

He clutched my arm, dazed, as though he'd seen a ghost.

'It's all right Dad, I'll get you out of here.'

CHAPTER FIFTY-FOUR

The doorbell rang. I opened our gate with the dongle and stood by the glazed front door, watching our postie traipse up the gravel. I smiled through the glass pane and pulled the door open, waiting for the last minute, to avoid letting in the cold. 'Good morning,' I said. 'Apologies for the robe and slippers.'

'No worries. You'd be surprised what I see on a Saturday.' She handed me a couple of large white envelopes, a stack of junk mail and a small cardboard box. 'Hang on.' She took the scanner off her belt and bleeped it at the parcel.

'Thanks again,' I said as I stepped back inside.

I set the boring post down onto the console table and used my nail to loosen the tape on the box addressed to me. Inside, I found an order confirmation sheet and counted twelve small zip-lock bags full of colourful beads. I replaced the cardboard flaps neatly, contented. They'd got it right. You never knew with eBay sellers.

I passed the door to the study, threw one of the envelopes and a catalogue from a music store on Arjun's desk, next to him. 'If you get another guitar, I will divorce you.'

'Oh yeah?' he said, grinning. 'What's that you've got?'

'I bought some beads. I thought I'd have a go at making jewellery. Like my mum used to.'

'That's a good idea. You probably need a nice relaxing hobby.'

I brought my parcel to the kitchen and stuck the kettle on. While waiting, I began emptying the dishwasher, but stopped after a few plates. Manesh had been getting an easy ride since winning the part two days ago. It was time our movie star landed back on Earth.

I headed to his room, holding the handrail as it curled up to the first floor. A female voice came from behind his door. I frowned. It was way too early for screens. I knocked gently.

'Come in.'

I sniffed. Only a faint hint of sweat today.

Manesh was lying on his stomach, his elbows digging into his duvet, his chin resting in his hands. The iPad cover was folded into a triangle. The colours from a video danced across his face. The woman spoke again. A freezing sensation filled my veins. Could it be? I leapt to his side.

On the screen, that same black curtain-like background, Samantha sitting on the chair, her hands clutching the seat. My forehead felt instantly hot. A rushing sound filled my ears. But wait ... She had a blouse on, green, not red like before. What was this?

Why was there another video?

We had a deal.

Rage roared inside. They'd sent it to my son. The bastards. After I'd given him what he wanted. We had a deal ... and they broke it. I'd make the fuckers pay.

'What are you watching?' I asked tersely.

'Samantha's YouTube channel.'

'Her what?'

He hit the screen. The sound stopped. 'Come see.' He flipped onto his bum, scooched aside and gestured for me to sit. 'You know Samantha? She got the girl part in the movie? She is such a good actress. I'm studying her videos for tips.'

I leaned forward. The text below Samantha's face read Prom Night. My finger trembled as I pressed play.

Samantha twirled her long hair, her blond streak catching the light, and rolled her eyes. 'Well, I was never going to go with Robbie. He's a loser. He picks his nose in class.' Her accent sounded American. I paused the video again.

'I don't understand,' I muttered, more to myself than to Manesh.

'That's her channel,' Manesh said. 'It means a place where someone with a YouTube account posts their content. And others can subscribe to their videos.'

He pressed a key that made us jump to a page with multiple videos. 'Samantha's got over twelve hundred subscribers. Means she's even making money from ads.'

'But ...' I swiped my finger up. Small rectangles, all with her face, paraded by. 'How many are there? What are they about?'

'Oh, there's tonnes. She's been at it for a while, hoping to get discovered by an agent or something. She calls them her show reels. Her big brother helps her out with them. He's even in them, sometimes. Let's see ...' He took over the scrolling. 'Here.'

The younger drug dealer's face leered at me from the screen. I clutched the duvet with both hands, the shock throwing me against the wall, winded. I quickly pressed the white X in the top corner, returning us to the mosaic of her other films.

Then I saw it. The one with her in red. It was titled *Sexual Assault Accusation*. Underneath: 5041 views. 4 months ago.

I felt the room close in on me. What was going on? Four months? That made no sense – I only just met her. So many views. My throat narrowed. Did it have my name? I couldn't check here. I couldn't let Manesh see.

'That's nice,' I said, forcing a cheerful tone. I took his iPad and hoped off the bed. 'But it's not screen time yet. So can you please empty the dishwasher?'

'Now?' Manesh whined.

I breathed out, steadied myself by clutching his doorknob. 'Yes, now.'

I spun towards my bedroom, changed my mind. Where was my phone? I remembered having it the night before. I checked the weather, chatted to Bela. Where? The news. I'd been watching the news. I raced downstairs and fetched my mobile from the lounge table. Arjun stepped out of the office. Crap. Why was there never any privacy?

I escaped unseen to the utility room. I trod on a squeaky toy. Jumped. Dammit. We must've forgotten it when we packed Sparky's things up to give to Dad. I picked up the pink rubber bone and stuffed it in my robe's pocket. Later.

The door to the boiler room stood ajar. Manesh would be down any second; could see me from the kitchen. I hid inside, turned on the light. The uncovered bulb blinded me for a split second. I leaned my back against the metal shelf unit that held our towels and spare bedding.

The iPad had stayed on the same page. My finger trembled as I hit play, then dragged the white line all the way to the end as her face and body jerked in triple time. My fat finger obscured how much was left. I let go, hoping to have reached the end.

Samantha held her arms wrapped around herself. 'The dentist stroked my arm and told me I'd been a good girl.'

Not it.

I couldn't push the white line further precisely and ended up tapping a series of ten second jumps.

Samantha's eyes projected a fiery intensity. This was it. 'I will shout from the rooftops: my dentist abused me! And I will name.'

I held my breath as it faded to the black screen, the white text. But instead of a name – my name – it merely said:

Thank you for watching. Please subscribe. Samantha X.

But I'd seen it, my name. I couldn't have imagined it, could I? The first video they'd sent me had been an attachment. But the second, the third, they were YouTube. They were public ...

I grabbed my phone from my robe. Found the email with the last video link; clicked through. The title was different, as was the account. No subscribers here. I fast forwarded, watched the same scene play out. I skipped to near the end to see the text again.

'I will shout from the rooftops: my dentist abused me! And I will name.'

A dizzying thought flashed into my mind. *'And I will name,'* she'd said. Not *'name him'*, not *'name her'*. I rewound all the way back; listened to snippets, looking for a clue.

The dentist. She kept saying *'the dentist.'* Not *'he'*, not *'she'*. I sank to my knees, my back scratching against the shelves as I dropped. This was never about me. No wonder Samantha had been so friendly at the theatre; she wasn't any part of it. This was nothing more than an audition tape and they'd used it. Used her. Used *me*.

Played me.

My head dropped forward and I started to laugh, chuckling hiccoughs that quickly turned into sobs, saliva slipping down the side of my mouth.

The boiler rumbled into action for hot water, reminding me I wasn't alone. I turned and buried my head in the linen, the pillowcases absorbing my scream.

CHAPTER FIFTY-FIVE

Late that night, I shivered in bed.

I snuggled closer to Arjun, who lay wrapped in what must have been three-quarters of the duvet, judging by the pathetic sliver of cotton I managed to pull halfway over my shoulder.

He snored. I tugged at the covers, freeing up another scrap – just enough for the fullness of my hips. The snoring stopped. It was only a matter of time before it started up again: he'd battled a cold all week.

Not that it mattered. Sleep was a stranger to me, insomnia a regular affliction since ... when? A curse to be endured like the horrendous periods and cramps, the haemorrhoids and IBS that snuck in little by little as the years progressed. New feminine scourges replacing the endometriosis that robbed me of a second child. Treasonous bodies.

I remembered Dad complaining about not being able to sleep more than five hours a night. Where was that skill when he was still working, juggling family and professional responsibilities? he'd grumbled. What was the point of having swathes of time in the day when his beloved Meena was no longer there to enjoy it with?

My head rested in a comfortable well in my pillow as I gazed into nothingness. I'd learned to stop fretting over whether I would fall asleep or not; it only seemed to make matters worse. And deep inside was a voice that said it was only fair for me to suffer. After all, my sleeplessness was self-inflicted.

It had been so easy with the pills: slipping into oblivion with a simple swallow. But they were also what started it. I peered at my alarm clock, the digital numbers a bloody red, like the frightful images that had taunted me whenever I closed my eyes. Those men, silent howls, distorted faces and limbs attacking me, grabbing. But they weren't there tonight, not after our last encounter, not after today's discovery. Proof the menacing video was a fabrication.

I flipped over and spooned Arjun, throwing a limp arm over his side. He stirred, sleepily grabbed my hand and held it to his chest. The coarse hairs tickled my pinkie.

It was hard to believe I'd risked everything; made everything worse with my secrets, my weakness before I finally built the courage to act. No more pills – a real struggle – but I overcame it. No more watching over my shoulder all the time, dreading every email. No more danger.

With my nose against his neck, I took in his musky smell, and was filled by a deep sensation of love. I'd been right not to tell him. Things would never have been the same. There would have been no more trust, no more lustful, admiring glances, no more perfect wife to boast about – only shame ... and possibly disdain?

I closed my eyes and felt my weight sink gently, guiltlessly into the mattress for the first in the longest time. Whatever I might have done, whoever I might have hurt, however I might have been played for a fool, the one good thing to come out of this ordeal is that I was no longer a slave to my anxiety. I would never touch the pills again.

An echo of Manesh and Arthur's laughter floated into my consciousness. I pressed my eyelids together more firmly. No. His death was not my fault. This, I needed to believe for my sanity. He would've gotten hold of the drugs with or without me. I needed to move on. I'd done what I could – what I had to do: succeeded in extricating myself from an untenable situation.

My lips curled into a small, satisfied smile. I'd found the bastard dealer's weakness and pounced. And after today, they were no longer a threat. I sighed, falling deeper into slumber. Yes, it was truly over now.

CHAPTER FIFTY-SIX

My upper body was halfway inside the boot of the car as I slid Manesh two chock-full carrier bags to take inside. I'd been able to face the supermarket again after – finally – a good night's rest. It hadn't been too bad for a Sunday afternoon and I'd stocked up.

I hooked my hands through the handles of the two last, crumpled bags-for-life, and stepped backwards while ducking my head, having learned the hard way to avoid the boot door's protruding catch.

'Excuse me,' a voice sounded from the street. I turned around; the heavy cargo tugged painfully at my arms. Two people in black uniforms stood at the gate.

'Mum, police,' Manesh said, stepping out of the house for the last load.

'Let them in, will you?' I dropped the bags and spun round. Needing to close the rear of the car gave me a chance to recover from the shock. I stared at the black rubber mat lining the boot, counting the ribbed stripes as I focused on my breath. What did they know?

After a swift inhalation, I faced the visitors and walked a few steps down the drive to greet them. 'Hello,' I said, extending my right hand.

The man, tall and wide, took it first. 'Ma'am.' The woman shook my hand with only a nod and a movement of the eye that made the lines around them deepen. It made her seem older than the freckled twenty-something by her side, but perhaps she was more the serious type.

'How can I help you?' I said. I jutted my chin to the pavilion across the street. 'Is it the bowling club again? The alarm does go off an awful lot.' I smiled, projecting my best air of innocence. *Innocent until proven guilty*, I thought.

'No, Ma'am. It's something else. May we come inside?' the male asked, tipping his hat.

'Of course.' I led them to my door. Their boots crunched in the stones. A tent-like swishing sound followed me, which I eventually realised was her thighs rubbing in her canvas trousers.

They wiped their feet. 'Can I hang your jackets up?' I offered.

'No thank you,' the woman said, nonetheless taking the liberty of dropping her rounded hat onto the console table. His was still under his arm.

She looked around the hall like a decorator calculating how much to overcharge. 'Mrs Bakshi. My name is PC Cox and this is PC Strang. We are from Police Scotland. Is there somewhere we can sit?'

Strang took a notebook from his inside jacket pocket. His stiff white shirt looked new; folds still visible. Two pens stuck out from his shirt pocket. If he was going to write, I thought it best to give him a table. 'Yes of course. Follow me.'

The dining room was open plan with the kitchen, where Manesh was packing away the groceries. Thank goodness Arjun was out cycling.

I pulled out two dining chairs using only the tips of my fingers, worried my sweaty palms would darken the fabric. I circled to the other side of the table. 'Manesh, sweetheart. Deal with that later, OK, and leave us?'

The man held up a finger. 'If you don't mind, Mrs Bakshi, we'd like to speak to your son also.'

Manesh and I exchanged surprised glances. 'All right,' he said, and joined my side.

As he sat, I jumped up. 'Where are my manners. Would you like a coffee or a tea?'

'No thank you.' The woman primmed her lips, her stark features not helped by an overly tight ponytail. 'This shouldn't take long.'

I returned to my seat and clasped my hands on the table. 'What is this about? And why do you need my son?'

The woman brought a thin briefcase to her lap and pulled out a green folder. 'We are investigating the death of Jamie Scott.' She fingered through the inside of the folder and took out a single photo.

I flipped my right thumb to the inside of my domed hands and pressed its nail into my flesh to keep calm. It was him.

Manesh's mouth fell open; he blinked. I placed my arm over his back.

'Do you know him?' she asked.

'Yes. I mean, vaguely. He's the father of a girl in Manesh's acting class. At the Citizens Theatre on a Saturday.'

'Samantha,' Manesh added as though she'd appeared in front of him. Tears pooled in his eyes. 'We're going to be in a movie together. She was so happy and ... This is horrible.'

I squeezed him to me.

I stared at the photo. A close-up, like a mug shot. But it wasn't. His gaze went past the camera and if you looked past the sneer, there was a snippet of a Rangers scarf behind him. Was he in a pub? Were the police watching him?

Questions sparked in my mind like a swarm of fireflies spooked from their nest. Had they seen him with me? Is that why they were here? How much did they know? Was the clinic in trouble? Did they come to arrest me? Why was Manesh here? Did he do drugs?

Wait. My mental flutters stopped abruptly. Dead? How was he dead?

I wetted my thick tongue on the roof of my mouth. 'What happened?'

'Mr Scott died on Thursday,' the woman said. 'We believe he was murdered. Therefore, we are interviewing anyone who was at the Blythswood hotel between nine and eleven a.m.'

'There is quite a long list of people to see,' the chap said. I noticed he'd scribbled something down already, his spidery handwriting unintelligible. What did he write? We'd not said anything yet.

'There were eighteen of us at the auditions,' Manesh confirmed. 'And their families.'

'Yes,' the chap said, flipping back some pages. 'The production assistants were very helpful in providing us with the names and addresses of those they knew were there.'

The flap of the folder slapped the table as the policewoman opened it. 'Sadly, there are many we haven't got names for.' She drew out a stack of photos and laid them out onto the wooden table side by side. Six CCTV shots of crowds huddled together; parts of the manicured Blythswood Square garden recognisable in the background.

'Why are you interested in the people in the crowd?' I asked, relaxing into the idea they weren't here for me.

The woman's mouth twitched. 'The pathologist determined the homicide would've been committed around ten, eleven a.m. His family confirmed his whereabouts as being at the hotel, with his daughter.' She pointed at one of the photos, his unmistakable striped hairdo one of many heads, closer to the entrance than I remembered him being. 'Here.'

The word *'homicide'* lingered in my brain. The man was a criminal. He would've had plenty of enemies. Turf wars, gang wars – whatever they were called. I remembered him cursing about the lying cunts who'd picked up the box of drugs at the office, showing me photos of those he suspected of the theft. Betrayal. Surely, those were the kind of folk the police ought to be looking for?

I briefly wondered if I could help. If I thought really hard, I could remember the date the box was taken. We could check my CCTV, the one I'd told that Scott prick didn't work. I could give the authorities a real lead, an opportunity to clean up the streets ...

My excitement withered as I realised I couldn't possibly explain any of this without implicating myself.

I gently shook my hair loose. No matter. Not my job. I only cared that he was gone. I reckoned the police would be aware of all these gangs anyway. They'd taken his photo in a pub; maybe they were watching others, maintained a file. They wouldn't need me. Hell, being a Rangers fan was already enough to get you cut in some parts of town.

'Was he stabbed?' I asked. Would make sense. Knives were nothing new to Glasgow.

The man seemed to seek his partner's approval before replying. 'We believe he was given an overdose of insulin.'

I grimaced. 'He was a diabetic?' Didn't look the type. Too fit.

'No,' the woman said firmly. A vein in her temple moved like an unearthed worm. 'Which is why this is a murder investigation. You seem very interested in the details of the crime, Mrs Bakshi. Is there anything you want to tell us?'

An anxious prickle spread across my chest. I hoped it wouldn't rise to flush my face. 'No, no. Umm. I'm a dentist.' I flashed a smile. 'Occupational hazard to be interested in medical things.'

Neither officer appeared amused. I cleared my throat, vowed to say nothing unless asked.

Strang picked up the photo of the crowd that featured the murdered man. 'Do you remember seeing Mr Scott at the hotel?'

My mind's eye replayed the scene of Samantha jumping into his arms; the happy daddy-daughter twirl; his smile to me. I'd kept my side of the deal in guaranteeing his precious daughter would get the movie part. And his nod in the distance reassured me he'd keep his side of the bargain: to leave me alone.

He certainly would now. And nobody in that awful family of his could ever get at me again, with their fake video.

The policeman tapped his pen on his notepad. I looked up. How long had I dithered?

'I'm not sure,' I said. 'I did see some other parents, but I don't know them very well. They didn't really register. Manesh what about you?'

'I don't think so, Mum. It was all such a buzz.'

'How so?' the woman asked, kindness returning to her eyes.

'Well, I'd just been given extremely good news and all I wanted was to tell Mum and Grandad. And Adam Mooney came out and everyone went nuts. And—'

'Grandad?' she asked.

'Yes, my father was with us.'

She slid a new photo towards us. 'Is that you two, here?'

The crowd was dense. I recognised my coat, my hair. Manesh, half a head taller than me at that angle. 'Yes, that's us.'

'And where is your father?' She fanned the photos out like a winning hand of poker.

'I don't ... I couldn't find him. We became separated. It was busy. There were a lot of fans.'

'After the screaming, it all got crazy,' Manesh said.

She frowned. 'Tell me about the screaming.'

Manesh gave me a questioning look. 'Go on,' I said.

'When I was on the steps with Adam Mooney – and Samantha – there was a lot of noise. Some people were even yelling my name. But then I heard a scream. I remember because that same voice cursed very loudly. I mean ... bad cursing. The C-word. It came from somewhere around here ...' He brought his finger to one of the photos, having found his bearings among them quicker than I had, but pointed at the table, just to the side of the image. 'And then all these people, right here ...' He pointed on the photo itself. '...were stepping back and bumping into each other, like a wave. I think someone even fell.'

'I can see how that might be memorable. Do either of you remember Mr Scott being in that location at that moment?' she asked.

'Isn't he here?' I said, lifting the first photo up again.

The policewoman took it from my hands and laid it back down. 'Not the whole time. He seems to have moved out of view after a while, to towards where your son is pointing.'

Her colleague added, 'Sadly, the CCTV doesn't cover the whole width of the block. And the council's cameras only capture further along.'

'And then what?' she gestured for Manesh to continue.

'I think Adam got spooked. He shoved me away and ran inside,' Manesh said, unable to hide his disappointment.

'Is this what you remember, Mrs Bakshi?' she asked.

I shrugged. 'It was all a big commotion. Lots of noise. I don't remember a scream, specifically, or hearing swearing. But I was on the other side. Frankly, all I cared about at that point was to get Manesh back and find my father who'd been swept away.'

She sighed and nodded at her partner. He closed his notebook and reached over the table to collect the photos.

'All right,' she said. 'Thank you very much for your assistance in this matter. That is all we need from you for the moment. Could you please give us your father's details?'

I imagined the not-so-warm welcome Dad might give to police officers randomly appearing on his doorstep. He'd been funny about them since Mum died. I remembered him calling them *'imbeciles'*. It stuck in my mind only because his newfound aversion to authority seemed so odd.

And because it was a funny word. 'I have some things to bring over. Why don't I take you to his house? It's nearby.'

'Is there any reason why he would need you there?' she said, in a disturbingly suspicious tone.

'No. I just … He lives alone. He's quite old.'

I turned to Manesh for support, but he seemed shaken, impassive eyes in sunken sockets. Maybe I should stay.

Cox rose. 'If you think that's necessary, please take us.'

Strang picked up the folder and handed it to her.

'Will you be OK, Manesh?' I asked. 'Your dad should be home soon.'

He shrugged. 'I'll be fine. Say hi.'

I followed the officers to our door and grabbed my coat. As I opened the front door, she said, 'Weren't you bringing something?'

'Yes, yes of course. Thank you.' I searched my brain for something useful, struggled. I then darted upstairs, saying, 'I'll meet you on the pavement.' In the bedroom, I unhooked my robe from the door and pulled out the pink squeaky toy I'd stepped on before.

I met Manesh on the stairs. 'Please call Grandad. Tell him I'm coming over with the police. But make sure to explain why.'

CHAPTER FIFTY-SEVEN

The police drove me to my father's house.

As we entered his drive, I could see his silhouette growing in the stained-glass door. He opened even before I rang. Sparky wagged a warm welcome at his side. Dad wore the cashmere striped cardigan I got him last Christmas. He'd swapped his usual slippers for shoes.

'Good afternoon,' he said, stepping back.

I entered first and pecked his cheek. I gave Sparky the toy from my pocket. He seemed delighted and ran off, bone squeaking. 'Dad, these people from Police Scotland are here to talk about the day at the Blythswood hotel. Someone died.'

'Yes, Manesh called,' he said. I saw an exasperated look pass between the two officers.

'This is my father, Gunbir Khanna,' I said. 'A retired dentist,' I added with a respectful tone, mightily fed up with their accusatory airs.

They stuck their hats under their arms and shook Dad's hand. 'This way,' he said, and took them in the direction of the kitchen.

As I followed, it struck me that there were fewer boxes lining the hallway. Had he tidied for them? No, there wasn't enough time. The dining table off the kitchen, normally covered in clutter, held only two stacks of papers and a ceramic bowl of bits and bobs. Not the usual shambles.

'Please sit,' Dad said.

I pulled out a chair. 'Maybe we could have that coffee now, Mrs Bakshi?' the woman asked, all subtleties out the window. The message to make myself scarce well and truly received, I made my way to the kettle.

Clean mugs lined the drying rack. Finding the coffee was never a difficult task; there were jumbo-sized jars of instant all along one corner of the work surface, standing on a beach of spilt brown granules.

I strained to listen to their conversation as the boiling water rumbled. I caught snippets.

'... suspected murder.'

'... your whereabouts ...'

'... to the victim.'

I stepped back into their meeting. They fell silent. 'Milk and sugar?' I asked.

'Yes please,' the man said enthusiastically, as though the decision to reject a drink at my place hadn't been a shared one.

'Milk for me,' said Cox.

'Dad?'

'No, darling.'

The white fridge gleamed in the overhead spotlights. Its handle felt surprisingly un-sticky. There were two green-topped jugs of milk in the door. Above them, almost a dozen eggs, out of the carton, each inserted upright in a hole of the dedicated plastic holder that would normally have been covered in crinkled butter wrappers and half-cut onions. I looked inside the main cavity. There wasn't much food there, but what there was seemed sensibly distributed. A variety of jars stood label-forward on the top shelf. Even his insulin vials were arranged in two orderly lines. I picked one up. It was in date. There were fewer than last time. I hoped this meant he'd listened to me and binned the out-of-date ones. I opened the vegetable drawer. A cauliflower and a red pepper. No shrivelled carrots. No bag of salad swimming in a lake of brown juice. I even sniffed, not quite believing my eyes. It smelled of ... nothing.

I pulled my head from the appliance and peeked at Dad. What was going on? He sat leaning back in his chair, his arms crossed. Spoke with few words.

I brought the two steaming mugs to the table. The photos were sprawled across the table. The policewoman went quiet again. Why so secretive? They'd merely be asking the same thing they'd asked me. I sighed. I didn't need to be told twice I wasn't welcome and scampered back to the kitchen. I began inspecting the closest cupboards behind them – to my father's annoyance, judging by his frequent sideways glances. My eavesdropping bore fruit.

Her voice: 'Can you tell us about the commotion?'

'There was a scrum when the actor came out. People were excited. They all pushed forward.' Dad replied.

'And this led to you being separated from your family.'

'That's right.'

I heard something sliding over the table. 'Can you show me on one of these where you went?'

'I'm not sure. I tried to elbow my way out of the crowd, but it was very difficult. There was a lot of noise at one point and everybody moved – in all directions. I got out eventually on the far end, found a bench.'

'Do you remember any screaming from that end in particular? We believe this may be where Mr Scott was when he was assaulted.'

'No. It's hard to remember. It all happened so fast.'

'Can you point to your bench?'

'I'm not sure it's on here.' Dad sighed. He sounded tired. I walked in, ready to call time.

She spotted me. 'Mr Khanna, is there anything at all that you can remember as being unusual when you were separated from your daughter?'

'No, all I wanted was to get back to her. Make sure she and Manesh were safe.'

———

After letting the officers out, I flapped the woman's business card in my hand, which she'd given should any one of us suddenly remember anything of interest. As if.

If I never thought about that horrid man again it would be too soon. As far as I was concerned, his death was nothing but karma.

Manesh's shocked expression shot though my head. What would happen to the girl? Her dad might have been asking for it, but she didn't deserve this.

Mum's portrait smiled at me from the wall. I ran my finger over the bottom of the frame. I didn't dare to caress the canvas, though I spotted a faint smudge by her lips. A memory flashed by: me kissing her still-warm forehead on the garden steps. *'Wake up, wake up.'*

I remembered how different that was to the very last, cold one. I'd pressed my lips hard on her powdered face, wanting to imprint the memory on my mind. Pulling back from the open casket, I noticed I'd left an imprint on her too, a blot of lipstick on her temple. As she was lowered into the bowels of the crematorium, and grief consumed me, I comforted myself with the idea that somewhere among those grey ashes would be a fleck with a hint of pink. I wore the same lipstick all through the thirteen days of mourning, marking all the aunties and uncles and everyone who'd loved her, as though that meant she was still with us. Then I never wore that shade again.

My thoughts returned to Samantha. If losing a parent could hurt this much as an adult, how traumatising would it be for a child?

I heard movement from the lounge. I made my way there through the uncluttered corridor that seemed to have doubled in width, the vivid colours on the edges of carpet an embarrassing contrast with the sun-bleached strip down the middle.

Dad sank into his favourite armchair as I entered. I watched Sparky jump onto his lap, nudging his head under Dad's hand for some stroking. I felt a rush of warmth. I'd done the right thing with those two.

He ran his thumb over the pup's snout. 'I feel bad for his daughter.'

'Yes, awful.' I sat down on the sofa, facing him. 'I wonder what happened.'

'They're going to have some job talking to all the people who were at that hotel,' he said.

'If they can even work out who they are. They've only got the CCTV to go on and they can't even find the man himself on that.' His desk in the open study caught my eye. 'Speaking of CCTV, Dad. Where's yours?'

He picked at his arm rest. 'I've packed it away. I no longer have a need for it.'

'Is that part of the big clean up? I noticed the place is much tidier. Well done.'

'Slowly but surely,' he said.

'What brought on this sudden urge?'

'Time to move on.'

'Yes, I feel that too.'

He chewed his lip. 'And Namrata is coming to visit with a lady friend tomorrow afternoon.'

'Ah. I see.' I grinned. 'That's great, Dad.'

'Namrata says she's a very accomplished cook,' he said, eagerly. 'She's bringing a meal.'

'Well, I will not be offended if at any time you want me to stop making your lunch. I've got enough feeding to do with a big teenage boy.' I peeked around the room. Still a mess, but maybe he'd get enough done before she came. He'd need to hoover, at minimum. The elephant rug was speckled with coloured rice.

'By the way,' I said. 'I've decided to have a go at jewellery making, like Mum. Any idea where that wooden box she kept her beads and tools in is? Not that I'm expecting you to know.'

'Let me dispel these low expectations you have of me. I know exactly where that box is,' he said, rubbing Sparky's ear. 'It's on the table, next to the sewing machine in her craft nook.'

'More fool me,' I joked. I heaved myself off the sofa. 'I'll fetch that and get out of your hair.'

I walked towards the hall, heading for a box room my parents had nibbled from an oversized dining room using a flimsy partition. I remembered getting annoyed at Mum's sewing machine rattling when I used the big table for homework, after my brother monopolised the kitchen.

'Wait,' I heard him shout. 'I'll get it for you.'

'No need. I'm up.' I ignored his further mumbled protestations.

I opened the door; an overwhelming sensation of calm overtook me. This little space was in my vision, the one I'd been using when I got anxious. Minus Mum. I sighed. She'd never know how much she was helping, still.

The space had been left untouched: the sewing machine without cover, multiple lengths of yellow silk hanging off a mannequin. I stepped over and ran my hand through the soft fabric. As it moved, something orange flashed at my feet. A box. My heart quickened. A big orange box exactly like the one...

'Radha, no.'

I spun round. Dad stood in the doorway, his mouth agape. I lifted the box, keeping my eyes on him. 'What is this?'

He grimaced. 'Don't.'

The sticker on the side of the package was the same shape as when I'd seen it in the clinic. The crumpled tape hung loose; a dark shadow between the cardboard flaps showed they'd been separated at some point. 'What ... where ... why ...?' I hyperventilated these questions out, my brain a fuddle. 'You took this? Why would you take this?'

And if the box was here that meant I didn't ... Arthur. Not my drugs. I trembled. Thank God.

He stepped forward, slowly, his arm outstretched like a zookeeper approaching an escaped animal. I clutched the drugs to my chest, felt my heart pounding against it.

'Now, Radha, you need to understand. I took it to protect you.'

'Protect me?' I shrieked. 'Do you realise how much trouble you caused?'

He grabbed hold of the box, tried to tug it from my hands. His deep stare unnerved me. 'But it's over now, isn't it?'

I frowned. 'What do you mean?'

'He can't hurt you now.'

I let him take the box and put it down. My hands fell limply to my side. 'Who's *he*? How do you know ...? What did you ...?'

He put his hand in his pocket and raised the policewoman's card up. I gasped. I stumbled backwards, landing with my bum on the edge of the craft table. I heard shouts rising from the back of my mind. The horde at the hotel. I felt Manesh's hand, squeezing hard, not letting go. Saw a flash of Dad looking angrily in the distance. In *his* direction. I had a vision of Dad disappearing, engulfed by the crowd. A snippet of his profile. Not scared – I'd worried he'd be scared but now I saw his expression again, in a new light. He was purposeful.

I wrapped my arms around me, shook my head. 'Your insulin. I was just in the fridge. There are only a few vials left. Where's the rest of it? WHAT DID YOU DO?'

'I did what I had to do,' he said, standing proudly upright.

'You killed that man?'

He wrestled my hand free, held it to his chest with both of his. 'I don't know what you were up to or how you got mixed up with these people. And I don't need to know. But you're the only one I have left.'

The shock paralysed me. That's why he insisted on coming to the audition. He'd killed him.

'The last in the herd.' He smiled awkwardly. Then his eyes took on a fiery intensity. 'And I was damned if I was going to let him hurt my family. Not again.'

'Again?'

His chin dropped over our intertwined hands, as if in prayer. 'Your mother.'

I frowned. 'What are you saying? That this man, Jamie Scott, who I've only just met, killed Mum three years ago?'

'Yes.'

I blinked, dazed, as it dawned on me his delusions about her murder were no longer so far-fetched. What I had classed – what we'd *all* classed – as the unfounded obsession of a mourning man, might in fact have been grounded in truth. Could it be? Gangsters wanting to murder my mother made no sense at all. No, he'd only seen what he needed to see on those grainy tapes.

But look what Dad had done. Surely, there had to have been a reason for him to think she'd been a target? A secret he hadn't shared. I only needed to look at what *I*'d done to know it was conceivable ... There was a dark, murky world full of things we didn't talk about.

'Why?' I asked.

He pulled me into the hallway, where there was space, light. I followed meekly, like the child I was, blind to the machinations of his mind.

'It doesn't matter. What's done is done,' he said.

Injustice roared inside. But it did matter. It did to me. I watched him, standing there so unreasonably calm. Was he truly expecting me to just leave it? Let him keep all these secrets from me? Saddle me with the knowledge *my father was a killer* and to not let me know why?

My hackles lowered as I realised he'd let me keep my secrets, shielded me quietly, from a distance. Never asked; didn't judge. Did I not owe him the same?

I leaned against the bookcase. I ran my fingers over the leather book spines behind me, contouring every ridge, and trailed my hand over the edges of the shelves, feeling the wood, its solidity. Because this all didn't seem real.

Mum murdered? It was still so improbable. Whatever motive could they have had? What on earth had my parents done to deserve the wrath of drug dealers? I knew first-hand it didn't take much. And did I really want to know?

An awful thought surfaced in my mind. What if Dad was wrong and Mum had only tripped. We'd never know the truth but more importantly, I could never suggest it. Because then, he would've killed an innocent man. I shook my head. No, not innocent. A criminal. A destroyer of lives, even if he was no longer a threat to me – I'd made sure of that.

It occurred to me that was something Dad couldn't have known. He did what you'd expect any parent to do: he protected me. Like I would, if Manesh got into trouble. A primary instinct that bound us. Just like our unspoken – unspeakable – acts.

My mind raced. Did *he* need protecting now? Could it ever get back to him? I couldn't see how. I rubbed my lips. The police were clueless, literally. There was no CCTV. Only a scream to go on. Would it have been pain from the rapid injection? Nobody would've seen what happened, with all eyes on Adam Mooney.

No, as far as the police were concerned, Dad was a kindly old man, a useless witness to tick off their list. Not the kind of person to arouse suspicion. Neither of us were, that much I'd learned.

I began to feel he could actually get away with this. Had he planned it this well?

Dad gazed at me serenely. The flutters in my brain began to settle.

'Now what?' I asked.

'Now nothing.'

Acknowledgements

My midlife crisis shows no sign of abating. When I wrote 'In Servitude' on an existential whim, I never expected I would get to three books.

I have my editor Sara Cox to thank and/or blame for that. She's not only made me a better writer over the years, but she also won't let me stop. Ever.

My thanks to my Pollokshields breakfast posse, primarily dentists, whose stories of shocking misconduct (other people's, obvs) inspired this book.

I'm indebted to those who helped me research dentistry, anxiety and other medical matters, to my generous beta readers, and to those who performed sensitivity reads so that I could feel confident in doing my South Asian characters justice: Karen F, Kiren P, Shalini G, Laura McC, Aileen T, Laura S, Jules S, Linda WB, Meggy R, Ally O'C, Sarah S, Mauricio A. Kudos to proofreader Nic Perrins for calling out my Americanisms and many other bad habits.

I'm grateful to my agent, Annette Crossland, for all the work she puts into championing me. This industry is a tough one, and I would've given up a hundred times had it not been for the encouragement of my author friends —

special shout out to Rob Parker, Awais Khan, Claire Duffy, Sarah Moorhead and Marion Todd who are only ever one despairing DM away.

The bloggers, librarians and readers who have read, reviewed and shouted about my books are the best, and I hope I'll continue to deserve your support.

Apologies to real-life doctor Radha for stealing her name for someone whose actions she'd disapprove of wholly.

Lastly, to the first reader of every manuscript, my husband Grant, for putting up with my neediness and for giving me the freedom to explore this strange side of me.

Thank You.

About the Author

Heleen Kist is a Dutch, formerly globetrotting career woman who fell in love with a Scotsman and his country, and now writes about its (sometimes scary) people from her garden office in Glasgow.

She was chosen as an up-and-coming new author at Bloody Scotland 2018. Her debut, 'In Servitude', won the silver medal for Best European Fiction at the Independent Publishers Book Awards in the USA and was shortlisted for The Selfies awarded at London Book Fair. Her feminist thriller 'Stay Mad, Sweetheart' was a finalist in the Next Generation Indie Book Awards and won third place in the inaugural Book Bloggers' Novel of the Year award 2020.

As if she needed another excuse to spend time on social media, she invites all readers to connect on Twitter (@hkist), Instagram or Facebook.

Did you enjoy reading about Radha?
Find out what happened next door...

Do you owe your family your life?

PAPERBACK - EBOOK - AUDIOBOOK

Or delve into the murky history of Adam Mooney
in this contemporary feminist thriller:

There's a fine line between justice and revenge.

HARD COVER - PAPERBACK - EBOOK

Made in the USA
Middletown, DE
23 June 2022

67573062R10217